CROWN
OF FIRE

CROWN OF FIRE

CRAIG & JANET PARSHALL

HARVEST HOUSE PUBLISHERS
EUGENE, OREGON

All Scripture quotations have been taken from the 1535 Bible translation of Miles Coverdale (1488–1569). The spelling has been modernized for inclusion in this book. An electronic transcription of the Coverdale translation was used, courtesy of Jeff Garrison of StudyLight.org. Their online Bible resource site, which can be found at www.studylight.org, "is packed with the most Bibles and study resources found on the net—everything needed to help you in your study of God's Word."

The Scripture passages whose references are not noted in the text are as follows: page 15, John 3:8; page 105–106, Psalm 136:3-9; page 247, Psalm 119:161 and 119:105; page 255, Acts 8:1; pages 270–271, Psalm 16:8-11; page 318, 1 Corinthians 10:21; page 339, Matthew 21:13.

Cover by Left Coast Design, Portland, Oregon

Cover images © Steve Cole/Photodisc Blue/Getty Images; Digital Vision/Getty Images

CROWN OF FIRE
The Thistle and the Cross series
Copyright © 2005 by Craig and Janet Parshall
Published by Harvest House Publishers
Eugene, Oregon 97402
www.harvesthousepublishers.com

Library of Congress Cataloging-in-Publication Data

Parshall, Craig, 1950-
    Crown of fire / Craig and Janet Parshall.
        p. cm. — (The thistle and the cross ; bk. 1)
    ISBN-10: 0-7369-1278-9 (pbk.)
    ISBN-13: 978-0-7369-1278-5
    1. Scotland—History—16th century—Fiction. 2. Knox, John, ca. 1514-1572—Fiction.
3. Scots—England—Fiction. 4. London (England)—Fiction. 5. Reformation—Fiction.
I. Parshall, Janet, 1950- II. Title. III. Series.
    PS3616.A77C76 2005
    813'.54—dc22   2005001908

Printed in the United States of America

05 06 07 08 09 10 11 12 13 / BC-MS / 10 9 8 7 6 5 4 3 2 1

To all of those who have suffered for the cause of Christ.
For the rest of us, may our lives show how their sacrifices
were well-spent.

Acknowledgments

Our editor, Paul Gossard, and Steve Miller, with whom he consulted, not only did a yeoman's job in the traditional editorial process of this book, but also brought to it a true passion for the subject and creative input as well. For that we are very grateful.

The inspiration for this book has been lingering long with us. It was fueled by our ancestral connections—Craig's to England and Janet's to Scotland—and by our interest in those great lands' common histories, their kings and queens, the courage of the early gospel preachers there during the Reformation, the poetic influence of Shakespeare, and the cultural and political whirlwind that engulfed that time.

We owe a debt of gratitude to both our family lines: to William Gunning Campbell Paul, Janet's grandfather, who was born and raised in Campbelltown, Scotland, and whose spiritual legacy bore fruit through multiple generations, all the way down to ourselves and our family. And to those members of the Parshall line who produced the Parshall family book and the genealogies contained in it. It proved to be a helpful guide across the ages and the oceans, including in the naming of our hero, Ransom.

And lastly, we thank all of those lovely people of Scotland whom we have met in our many travels there, enjoying your lilting brogues, your kind hearts, your keen sense of humor. Search these pages and you will find something of yourselves tenderly preserved there.

Chapter 1

1608–St. Andrews, Scotland

It was a blustery day. The tall windows had been opened, and now the lace curtains were gently fluttering. From his canopied bed within the bedchamber of his apartments on the second story, propped up in his infirmity by several pillows, the old man could see the peak of the remains of the castle at the end of the street. But he could see no farther.

The castle lay in ruins, its walls blasted to rubble back when the old man was a boy. And the gray stone cathedral not far from it now was home to moss and weeds. It too had been blown apart...so many years before. Its high arches were now only vacant and empty eyes. Staring out blankly onto the North Sea.

Ransom Mackenzie, who had just turned seventy-six, was dying. He had been told that by his personal physician, who had stepped out for a moment after examining him. But the good doctor Oliver said he intended to return as soon as he could to keep the vigil with his old friend.

Ransom heard some noise from downstairs and vaguely recognized its source. Jean Macleod, a widow and a friend of Ransom's family, had been his housekeeper for the many years after his return to St. Andrews to teach, and write, and live out his last days. He suspected she knew of his impending demise, as she had often busied herself with knowing all of the personal news concerning Ransom Mackenzie.

"The second-greatest man of all Scotland," is how Jean would describe him.

Ransom's thoughts wandered to the man who occupied the first place.

John Knox, his friend and mentor, had been at once the most loved and most hated man throughout Scotland. But Knox had been dead these last thirty-six years. How it seemed just a few days before that Ransom had been studying under the tutelage of the demanding master. And there, just down the street in the barricaded, besieged castle, was where Ransom, Knox, Knox's other students, and the group of reformist rebels had faced a terrible onslaught. The cannons exploded, the thrones of Scotland shook, the fires burned.

Now, dying as an old man who had lived to see the birth of a new century, Ransom felt as if time had rushed by him at a dizzying pace, like a boy clattering down the steep heather hills in a wooden cart, gathering speed as he went.

"I was there..." Ransom murmured as he gazed at the ruins, speaking to himself only, as he was now alone.

His son Philip would not attend his passing. Nor could he. Philip had, the year before, shipped out from London, an adventurer yet again, and this time he had taken Ransom's grandson with him. He was bound for the other side of the ocean, to the Virginia colonies. To a place called Jamestown.

Andrew, the other son, had been summoned to his father's side. He had left his offices in Edinburgh, riding hard. But he too would not be at his father's side when the time came.

Ransom could now hear Jean's footsteps coming up from below. She was carrying a fresh bundle of pillows for him.

Reaching toward his side, Ransom effortfully grasped for something...groping for an object most precious. For the most fleeting instant, he thought he saw it lying next to him on the bed. A clear crystal box, sealed by wax, soldered at the edges.

Inside the box lay a circle of dried heather, carefully twined together into a kind of wreath…by a young girl's hands. The glass had been tightly sealed—closed up against the air, the damp climate of the Highlands, and the changing seasons.

He grasped for the box…but it was not there. He wondered if it had been a dream, a wisp of an image from the wellspring of what his soul had both mourned and exulted in. With his last fading thought, he realized why the glass box was no longer his to keep. In his weakness, he managed a slight smile.

"I was there…" he whispered. "And *she was with me…*"

With the image of his beautiful beloved before him, like a voice in a dream that calls one to a great awakening, he leaned back against the pillow and breathed his last.

When Jean reached the room, she knew in an instant that Ransom had passed. Crying out and dropping the pillows, she rushed to his side. And through the beginning of her tears, she noticed the merest beginning of a smile on his lips—and that his hands were framed as if to grasp something not there, a thing real but invisible to the passing world.

Chapter 2

1546—Sixty-Two Years Earlier

As far back as Ransom Mackenzie could remember, there had always been an air of dark mystery and simmering turmoil permeating the city of St. Andrews, his hometown. That atmosphere, with its vague sense of foreboding, would sweep into his mind like the cold mist coming off the North Sea, when it would shroud the narrow streets and the row houses lined along them in a fog bank.

Ransom would be particularly attuned to those feelings when the clouds would weep with a slow, soaking rain, and the skies were iron gray. Or when the waves of the ocean would crash up against the rock seawalls of the harbor in a cold and foamy rush.

But on that particular day, it was different. Ransom was fourteen years old at the time. Although it was only late February, a time of year that would often display a singular dreariness, that day was bright, and the skies were blue. Huge white billowy clouds were sailing overhead. There was even a hint in the air, from the scent of thawed and spawning field and garden, that spring might come earlier than usual.

Ransom had been wandering down along the thin band of sandy shoreline. In truth, he had taken a detour. And he felt a bit guilty about it...but not so guilty as to stop him from running along the ocean and admiring the host of ships anchored in the harbor. He would usually see an abundance of the smaller merchant ships, and an occasional three-masted vessel. On one occasion, Ransom had even spotted a French galley ship, with its single sweeping sail shaped like the wing of a sea bird, sprouting dozens of oars from its sides, which were manned in a frightful manner—or so he had been told—by the toil of captives, slaves, and vagabonds who were chained to their stations in its belly.

Just thinking of the plight of such unfortunate souls would shoot a quick shiver over Ransom's skin.

His father, Hugh Mackenzie, a printer and bookbinder by trade, had given him a package of Latin prayer books for delivery to St. Salvators College, which was only a few blocks away from Mackenzie's printing shop down North Street, which ran parallel to the sea, one street away. After the delivery, Ransom had scurried down to the shore and run along its edge, in the very shadow of the high, jutting walls of the castle.

Ransom did not tarry under the shadow of the castle. His father had warned him clearly enough. So he ran headlong down the shoreline, daring only to throw a glance or two up at the dark, stone walls and parapets only a hundred feet away.

He picked up the pace and ran even faster, now along the harbor and up the cliffs. Then he took a shortcut across the corner of the grounds of the great cathedral and priory, yet another site his father had forbidden him from visiting.

"Take this package of books to the front room of the university, where we have delivered before," Hugh had told his son, looking him straight in the eye. "And be quick about it. I need you back in the shop. There's a bit of work still left for the day.

"And make sure you get the name of the person in whose hand you deliver it," he added. "And give 'em the bill of lading as well. We're not in the business of givin' away our services…particularly to the likes of those that run that particular institution. Now get on with you!"

Hugh had handed his son the books, wrapped in a brown cloth and tied with string. Slipped under the tightly wrapped string was the paper that listed the amount due for the binding.

As Ransom was returning to his father's small establishment, which was tucked in among the shoulder-to-shoulder shops and narrow row houses of Market Street, he knew he did have one argument to be weighed against his tardiness.

At least, he rationalized to himself, he had made good on the delivery of the books to the right office at the college. Even more importantly, Ransom had presented the bill for services rendered. So how could his father be too stern with him if he was a bit late?

Not even late, really, Ransom thought. After all, who is to say what is truly late and what is not—when a specific time was not given for his return? And even if he were tardy, it was a small matter really. It was, at the worst, but a minor lateness...as small as a lamb's tail.

When Ransom sprinted into the shop, Hugh was cleaning the ink off the platen—the large square plate connected horizontally to the worm screw that ran up and down through the center of the press.

His father was wiping his hands off with a rag. But his fingertips and fingernails were stained indelibly with the permanence of a printer's trade—stained beyond the ability to clean or restore.

As Ransom stood panting, his father did not turn around. That was not a good sign.

"I told you to come back straightaway—that I needed your help. Did I not?" The voice was firm, the back still turned.

"Aye," Ransom muttered quietly.

"And did you?"

"I ran..." Ransom said, hedging a bit.

"Aye. I am certain you did indeed," Hugh answered, now turning slowly to face his son. "But the question is, *where* were you running, boy? Running home to help your father with chores—with the trade that pays for your food and for the clothes on your back?"

Ransom couldn't look his father in the eye. So he stared at the wooden planks of the floor.

"Or did you, perchance, choose to do your running down at the harbor?" his father continued. "Lollygagging about—daydreaming and admiring the ships?"

Before Ransom could answer, his father got to the real business.

"Did you make the delivery as I asked?"

"Yes, father. And I gave the bill to the man. I placed it in his hand just as you told me."

Hugh took a step toward his son, studying him more closely.

"And the name of the man into whose hand you delivered the books and the bill?"

"The name?" Ransom asked weakly.

"The name," came the stern reply.

Ransom struggled to recall. Did he get the man's name? Who was it?

"And when I am not paid for all my labors in binding those books— and I call on the good clerk of the office of St. Salvators College and request payment, and he replies there is no proof of delivery of the goods—then who, my son, shall I say was the recipient of those goods... seeing that you have no such recollection?"

Ransom was squirming. He silently ordered his young mind to respond—to counter the seemingly flawless logic of his father's argument.

"Is it...not true..." Ransom began slowly, "that there is only one clerk of the college?"

Hugh eyed his son closely.

"Aye. But what of it?"

"And is it not true that the name of the clerk of the college is a thing...that many know of? And that...somewhere it is listed for everyone to see?"

"And?"

"Well," Ransom concluded with a small measure of triumph, "the man who received my package was in the office that had a sign over the door. It read 'Clerk of the College.' So that is your proof—he must have been the clerk. No one else was around—and he had the air of a man who looked like he was in charge of the place."

Now Hugh was right in front of his son. He bent down eye-to-eye with him.

"I can now see that all of the tutoring from Master John Knox—all the learning in logic and rhetoric—has now come back to be used as a sword against your own father."

But Ransom could see his father struggling against a smile.

"Well...after all," Hugh continued, "it was the wish of your dear mother, God rest her soul, that your quick little mind be trained in such disciplines."

And then he said, "But I had better be on my guard. If your mind gets any quicker, your poor father will be hard pressed to catch up with it!"

Hugh stood up. "You do love a match of wits, lad. May the Lord preserve us—if you end up becoming a lawyer."

Ransom now risked a small smile of his own. He felt that the worst of it had now passed. Punishment would probably be moderate. Perhaps only a few extra errands in the shop.

"Now take that broom and sweep the floor," Hugh said, proving Ransom's surmise. "We have customers who frequent this place, you know."

Ransom stepped lively to the corner of the shop where the broom lay against the wall. On his way he passed the large, rectangular printing case lying on the table, and a cloth was over it. But a corner was slightly uncovered, revealing some of the iron type carefully arranged.

Usually his father would leave the box of typeset letters out on his typesetting rack, which looked like an angled weaver's stand, in the other corner of the shop. That way he could keep working steadily till he was done. Then the box containing the arranged type would be slid into the housing at the bottom of the press so the printing could begin.

But this box was on a table near the cellar door.

Ransom slowly lifted the cloth off the case and began reading:

> *The wind bloweth where he will, and thou hearest his sound: but thou canst not tell whence he cometh, and whither he goeth. So is every one, that is born of the spirit.*

It had a familiar ring. Had he read this before?

"Ransom Mackenzie!"

His father's voice startled him and he jumped.

Rushing to the table, his father quickly covered up the case. Then he wrapped his big, leathery hand around his son's chin.

"Did you read what was in that case?" he asked sternly.

"I did."

"Now—you will listen to me. You will do as I tell you." There was a passion and desperation in his father's voice that Ransom had not heard since the day, now only vaguely recalled, when his father had told him his mother had died.

"You are to forget what you have just seen. Do you understand me, lad?"

"I do, father."

"You will never tell anyone about what you have just read in that case—is that clear to you, boy?"

"It is," Ransom replied meekly, confused about the urgency of his father's command.

"There are words in this land…words that kill. If certain words are printed in the common tongue—and the wrong people find out—it'll be the end of your father. Do you know that? The end of me, I can assure you of that. And a bitter, terrible end it'll be."

Hugh Mackenzie gave a deep sigh. Then he placed his hand on the sandy hair of his son in a kind of paternal blessing and whispered, "May the Lord protect us and keep us, in His providence and mercy."

Then he told Ransom to leave the sweeping to him and hurry upstairs, stoke the fire, and start peeling the potatoes for the stew.

Ransom obeyed. But as he trudged up the narrow stairway to their apartment, he saw, out of the corner of his eye, his father carrying the heavy printer's case through the door to the cellar below.

As he stoked the fire and saw the flames begin to lick up the blackened flue, he thought of his father's dire warning.

How can words be so dangerous, he thought to himself as he watched the crimson and amber of the flickering flames, *that they make even a grown-up man fear he might die?*

Chapter 3

John Knox, the master tutor, removed his black, padded cap and swept the sweat from his brow. Then, he smoothed his hair down, replaced the cap, and ran his hand across his dark beard, which, well-trimmed, reached down to the middle of his neck.

Knox was only thirty-three years old, but his face, though handsome, had an older, weathered look. His eyes, by contrast, seemed paradoxically youthful, lively, and occasionally even playful.

Yet as Ransom sat across the plain wooden table from his tutor, he did not sense anything playful or even remotely casual about John Knox. How could he? His teacher always seemed unyieldingly strict and uncompromising in his academic expectations. It would not be until much later that Ransom would learn the sensitive, even frail side of John Knox. But for now, the boy knew only that Knox's face often took on the look of cold, impervious stone, like the great blocks from which St. Andrew's Castle was constructed.

"My question is still unanswered," Knox said. "Where did we leave off on our last lesson?"

"Canto V."

"Of..."

"Of the *Commedia*..."

"Authored by..."

"Authored by Dante."

"Full name?"

"Authored by Dante Alighieri."

"Very well," Knox replied, but then he caught his student casting a longing look out the window of the small apartment. Out in the street, Ransom's friend Philip was talking with his pretty, red-haired cousin, Catherine. Ransom's glance at Catherine was caught by his tutor.

"Remind both of us," Knox said in a voice suddenly louder and more precise, "why it is that I am tutoring you, master Ransom."

"To prepare me for entrance examinations."

"At..."

"At the University of St. Andrews, the College of St. Salvators," Ransom replied dutifully.

"Which, judging by our progress thus far," Knox continued, "will be a full year from now at least. So, please discontinue your errant gazes out the window and concentrate. Now, please continue reading where we left off. You will recall, in this Canto, Dante speaks of what he finds in the second circle of Hell, where he encounters a most unfortunate lass named Francesca. She suffers the punishments of the next life because, as Dante describes it, she has been seduced by the carnal desires of a man. Now proceed."

Ransom nodded, trying to hide his embarrassment at the passage he was required to read. After locating his place in the book, he began reading out loud:

> One day, for our delight we read of Lancelot
> How him love thrall'd. Alone we were, and no
> Suspicion near us. Oft-times by that reading
> Our eyes were drawn together, and the hue
> Fled from our alter'd cheek...

Ransom, encountering the more fleshly part of Dante's verse, hesitated.

"Continue reading," his tutor said firmly.

Ransom complied.

> *By one so deep in love, then he, who ne'er*
> *From me shall separate, at once my lips*
> *All trembling kiss'd. The book and writer both*
> *Were love's purveyors. In its leaves that day*
> *We read no more—*

"Now," Knox interrupted him, "the story of Lancelot—let us digress. Was this lad, the knight Lancelot—was he a courageous fellow?"

"I do think so."

"Well-trained in the use of horse and sword?"

"Oh yes," Ransom said enthusiastically.

"But of his passions—was he master of those as well?"

Ransom blushed slightly and looked down.

"No, Mister Knox…"

"Indeed not!" Ransom's teacher thundered. "In that story, he broke trust with his friend King Arthur and seduced Queen Guinevere, committing adultery. Succumbing to carnal lusts and temptations."

Ransom looked frantically around the small room as if hoping to find some place of escape from the embarrassing lesson, but finding none.

"And so," Knox plowed onward, "young Francesca is reading this lurid tale of Lancelot's lust—reading this carnal text in the close company of a man who is using it as means of breaking down her will and her chaste character…"

He studied his student's face for some glimmer of understanding.

Not finding any, he added in a slow and deliberate explanation, "And so, that is why Dante says that 'the book and writer both were love's purveyors.' The book and writer of that story were sowing seeds of sin in the hearts of the girl Francesca and her man companion."

Ransom nodded, then glanced quickly out the window again to catch a last, fleeting glimpse of the lovely young Catherine walking out of sight.

Then the student looked at his tutor. Knox could recognize, in Ransom's face, the look of some unresolved issue reaching for expression.

"And your question?"

"Just that…Dante speaks of love, Mister Knox."

"Yes?"

"And you have said that God is love, and the source of it."

"Indeed I have. The Holy Scriptures teach it clearly."

"Then, how can love be sin?"

Knox paused, cloaking the temptation to smile at his student's question. Ransom's query showed that, at last, he was beginning to cast the searing light of God's Word onto the dreary stuff of his studies.

"Love," his tutor replied, "and by that I mean *true* love, is that which obeys the commands of God and emulates His design for our affections. Carnal love—the pursuit of the pleasures of the body in violation of God's holy plan—is the devil's substitute…always inviting, tempting all of us, but never able to satisfy, never able to reflect God's perfect design, which is that of marital affection and fidelity."

Ransom sat dumbfounded. John Knox, his stone-faced tutor, had dared to speak as if he…even he, could be afflicted with the temptations of the flesh. As unthinkable as that seemed, the young man simply could not deny what he had just heard.

Another thought struck Ransom, and before thinking, he blurted it out.

"And the second circle of the infernal regions of Hell, which Dante describes—where is that?"

"You will find such a place *only* in the imaginings of Dante Alighieri, and nowhere else, I assure you," Knox said confidently. Then the teacher, after some reflection, added, "And some of the doctors of metaphysics, such as Tycho Brahe and his disciples, have also suggested rings of ether surrounding the heavenlies…so perhaps Dante postulated such rings within the burning fires of perdition. But know this—Holy Scripture provides us with no such doctrine of inner circles of the regions of eternal damnation. Hell is real, be certain of that. But the sections and divisions of hell you read of here are purely products of the fleshly speculations of Dante."

"Then why are we studying them?"

"Because the entrance examinations of the university, which I know well—having been both a student and an instructor there—will inquire of you on those subjects. Even though such teachings are entirely at odds with the holy and perfect Word of God—"

Knox caught himself. He leaned close across the table and looked his student in the eye.

"And what I have just said—it must not be repeated by you…ever…"

Ransom's eyes widened. But he nodded obediently.

"In matters of church doctrine and the things of the Spirit, you must address your questions to your father. When, in his wisdom as your caretaker, he decides it is time to confide certain matters to your understanding, then *he* will be the one to do so."

Knox's vague but adamant warning was unmistakable. For some reason, questions about God and church were as highly dangerous as the kegs of black gunpowder he had seen being cautiously unloaded at the docks in the harbor of St. Andrews.

Now the instruction from Knox cast a spell of mystery. Coupled with the clandestine behavior of Ransom's father concerning the typeset box in the printing shop, John Knox's words had fueled the fourteen-year-old's curiosity about those things that dared not be spoken.

Chapter 4

It was late at night. Ransom had been in bed fast asleep. But the voices, hushed and murmuring in the next room, had awakened him.

He recognized his father among them. And it sounded as if his tutor, Master John Knox, was there also. A third voice belonged, perhaps, to Mr. Angus Atcheson, a friend of his father's…although he could not be sure.

In the past, Ransom's father had often met with these men late at night. The boy would usually open a sleepy eye, then go right back to sleep.

But that night it was different. He had wakened with a start. No longer sleepy, he was fixed on the voices in the next room. And his mind began to race.

What caused these men to speak in whispers? Did this have something to do with his father's admonitions? About the typeset case and the forbidden message spelled out there? Or perhaps the warnings from John Knox about those church matters that could not be spoken aloud?

Ransom slipped out of the feather bed. He took several cautious, tiptoe steps, hoping not to land on a creaking board. Kneeling down, he peered through the space between the door and the jamb.

None of the men were in sight. They must be up closer to the fireplace, out of his range of vision. He could see the flickering reflections of the fire playing against the wall and on the ceiling between the dark oak rafters.

Ransom strained to hear. Now he could discern the men's voices clearly.

Angus Atcheson was talking.

"And I'm telling you there was a trial. My man inside the castle—you know who I'm talking about—he tells me he saw the proceedings with his very own eyes."

"And it was George Wishart himself as the accused?" Hugh Mackenzie asked.

"Indeed it was," Atcheson replied solemnly. "I wish to God Himself it were not so. My man tells me that a gang of Marie de Guise's own jackmen rousted him out of the Sea Tower and led him in chains to the privy chamber."

"And who were his judges?" Knox asked. "As if we did not already know…"

"Cardinal Beaton," Atcheson replied. "And with him, the Archbishop of Glasgow, who had just arrived for the occasion."

"Of course," Knox said with a tinge of disgust. "And what of his defense, man? What defense did Wishart plead?"

"The authority of Holy Scripture," Atcheson replied in a voice almost inaudible. "Then Cardinal Beaton calls him a 'corrupt and indurate heretic.' Those were his very words. The Cardinal calls him an 'abuser of the Mother Church.' To which Wishart cried out that if he were to be condemned for heresy, then it must be on the basis of the Word of God alone—and not on the doctrines and fancies of either the Pope or any of his bishops."

"Did they make allegations," Knox asked, pressing further, "regarding the absurd pretensions that Wishart would actually plot a murder attempt against Beaton?"

"Yes, indeed they did. Wishart denied it most vehemently. And he cried out for one single iota of proof…calling them lies from the devil's own making. Beaton and his prosecutors could make no proof—"

"That would be their devious cloak for a sentence of death against him," Knox said bitterly. "They will pretend he was guilty of treason to lessen the gall of their real motivations—that they detest he is a preacher of the gospel of Christ. And that the trumpet blasts of his preaching would topple their castles and cathedrals of power..."

After a lingering silence had fallen over the room full of shadows and voices and dancing reflections from the fire, Knox spoke again.

"He will burn for sure. In our hearing is fulfilled the saying of the Gospel of John in the sixteenth chapter—'The time cometh, that whosoever putteth you to death, shall think that he doth service unto God.' If only I had prevailed upon my good friend to be on guard against the evil designs of the queen mother in Edinburgh and Cardinal Beaton in St. Andrews."

"No, John," Ransom's father said with passion in his voice. "George Wishart knew the path he was choosing. Did he not tell you to your face that you must not impede his path—even if it led to his own fiery death at the stake? Do you not remember? 'One is sufficient for sacrifice,' he told you—he seemed to know he would soon be arrested. And that his end might follow."

"Aye, these words are burned like fire into my soul," Knox replied, "but I fear it will not be just one for sacrifice...It will be many..."

"They did not return him to the Sea Tower," Atcheson added.

"Where did they take him?" Hugh asked.

"To the Bottle Dungeon."

"Then it will be soon...very soon," Knox intoned, his voice thick.

"The point is this. We must now chart our course. The present situation is clear—and most troubling. Mary Tudor, an ardent papist, has powerful designs to sit on the throne of England occupied by her late father, Henry VIII. Her power to achieve exactly that seems to be unassailable. In our own Scotland, Marie de Guise, the queen mother, also a disciple of the church of Rome, occupies the throne room in Edinburgh until her infant daughter, Mary, the so-called Queen of the Scots, now in France, is old enough to rule."

"It appears there are more dangerous Marys abroad in the land," Knox remarked sardonically, "than bad pennies."

"So, with an eye to Cardinal Beaton's false charges against Wishart," Atcheson continued, "perhaps a conspiracy of arms against St. Andrew's Castle, and against Beaton, and against the whole lot of those vipers is exactly what we need. How can we afford to wait?"

Another silence fell on the room.

"I recall Jesus' admonitions against the use of the sword," Ransom's father said softly. "If George Wishart is willing to die for Holy Scripture... shouldn't we be willing also to live by it?"

"Yes, yes," Knox said impatiently, "but the apostle Paul, in the Epistle to the Romans, also instructs us that the lawful use of the sword rightly belongs to those authorities assigned by the providence of God—"

"Exactly. So what if," Atcheson interjected, "the people of Scotland— and God's Christian army—are the agents of God to overthrow those that have so abused their lawful authority?"

"Do you know what you are saying?" Hugh Mackenzie whispered, stunned.

"Aye. I do," Atcheson replied. "And you, Master John Knox, have raised the same question. I've heard you speak it with my own ears."

"Raised the issue. But not decided," Knox replied slowly. "My sole guide is the Word of God...and His Spirit, which instructs our understanding of it."

"One thing is clear," Atcheson said curtly. "Hugh—your plan for printing of the Gospel of St. John must cease for the time being. We cannot afford to be exposed."

"Yet I would think," Hugh said, countering his friend, "as the days become darker, the need for the light of the gospel would be even greater."

"Our first task," Knox said with a note of both solemnity and finality, "is to pray for our dear friend George Wishart. That the Lord would strengthen him for his ordeal."

Knox paused.

"Do you realize what day it is today?"

No one could answer.

"Today—the very day of Wishart's conviction for heresy and sentence to death," Knox continued, "is exactly eighteen years—to the day—from the death of Patrick Hamilton. Burned to death at the stake not a long stone's throw from where we sit at this very moment...martyred for the cause of Christ for daring to preach the reformed gospel."

"Let us also pray for courage," Hugh Mackenzie added. "For ourselves. To be there with George Wishart when the end comes—as the end also came for Patrick Hamilton."

By the time the meeting ended, Ransom had fallen asleep on the floor next to the door of the bedroom. After his father had stoked the fire one last time and prepared for bed, he found his son on the floor.

Gently picking him up, Hugh carried him into his bed. He smiled at the effort it took. Gone were days when he could swoop up the boy with one arm. As he stroked his sleeping son's head, he knew that Ransom must have heard their conversation.

He also knew that the time had come, whether he liked it or not, for his son to begin receiving full and proper instruction about the great struggle that was sweeping the land.

He did not want that time to come. It would, he was certain, require the sacrifice of some measure of his son's innocence.

On the other hand, he hearkened to the lesson from the apostle Paul. When boys become men, they must put away childish things.

As he looked upon the still boyish face of his only child, he longed for his wife to be there with him. But no matter how his heart ached for his dead wife, it could not be so.

And Hugh Mackenzie also wondered at something. *Why is it,* he asked himself, *that when strife breaks out and evil takes up arms, boys must be conscripted into manhood before their time?*

Chapter 5

"You're taken with her!"

"Am not."

"Are so!" Philip answered his friend, laughing. "You're taken with my cousin Catherine. You are all the fool whenever she comes around."

Philip, slightly taller than the stockier and more muscular Ransom, had a gangly gait as he walked. "You, my lad, are following her around like a street dog hungry for a bone!" he added.

That called for retribution, so Ransom shoved Philip, who almost lost his balance.

"Don't make war with me, little laddie," Philip retorted with a laugh. "You'll be the worse for it!" Then he shoved Ransom back hard. But Ransom had anticipated the attack and braced himself.

"Well, well—what have we here," Philip remarked, "and just waiting for us. It's my cousin Catherine…You approach your true love, master Ransom!"

Ransom gave Philip another quick shove, and the other boy staggered forward several steps before he caught himself.

Down the narrow, crowded lane, standing before a little fabric shop next to another girl, was Catherine Fawlsley. The two were admiring a display of colorful silks—so much more luxurious than the rough, hand-woven cloth that was the customary shield against Scotland's harsh winters.

Catherine's hair was a fiery red, and it cascaded down from underneath her stylish cap. Her pale blue eyes shone out from fine, delicate features, set off by white unblemished skin. When she spotted Ransom approaching, she suddenly raised her voice and laughed, flirtatiously glancing over to him and then back to her girlfriend.

As Philip and Ransom got up to the pair, the two girls were giggling quietly and whispering to one another.

"So, are you two little hens talking about us?" Philip said loudly.

"Of course not!" Catherine answered briskly. "Whatever makes you think such a thing?"

"Perhaps because we are the bravest and the strongest lads in St. Andrews!" Philip was eyeing Catherine's friend.

"This is Joanna Robertson," Catherine said. Then she continued coolly, "And who is your friend, cousin?"

Before Philip could answer, Ransom blurted out, "My name is Ransom Mackenzie."

"What does your father do?"

"He runs the printing and binding shop."

"Oh, yes," Catherine answered with a wicked little smile, "I think I've seen him going in and out—he is the one with the terrible black fingers and stained fingernails!"

"It's from the ink," Ransom shot back, slightly wounded.

"Yes, I know that," she retorted. "I am not ignorant. Do you mean to say that I am?"

"Of course not."

Catherine had moved slightly toward Ransom, and her face was close to his. He had never been so close to her—or, for that matter, quite so close to any girl who wasn't related to him. He was suddenly lost in the pretty face just inches away from his.

"What are you staring at?" Catherine smiled, cocking her head to the side slightly. But she did not wait for an answer, and she quickly turned with a flourish and began walking away, giggling with her girl-friend.

"She has driven us all mad," Philip sighed.

"Yes. I can see…" Ransom threw a glance at the departing Catherine.

"I mean our family, you *cullurune!*" Philip said, laughing at his lovesick friend. "She is totally selfish and vain. She won't do chores."

"Why do your parents allow it?"

"We have to take care of her. Her parents have gone to the palace—"

"At Court? In Edinburgh?"

"Nay—aren't you well-taught?" Philip jibed. "They're at the Court in London. She wanted to join them, but they said she was too young. And because…well, there is some danger in the English Court…at least I've heard my father and mother speak of it."

"What kind of danger?"

"I don't know. Perhaps because no one knows yet who will rule England—and because of those dangerous, terrible reformers, the Protestants."

Ransom grew quiet.

"Do you know about them…the reforming rebels?" Philip asked.

"I'm not sure…"

"Is your father for Cardinal Beaton…or against him?"

"I have never heard him speak about it…much."

"My father says we must be for the Cardinal—and we must be on our guard," Philip said. "Everywhere now there are those who preach dangerous doctrines—against the Roman Church—against the Holy Father."

"Doctrines—like what?" Ransom asked, trying to be nonchalant.

"I am not sure," Philip said with a puzzled look on his face.

Then he stopped in his tracks and turned to face Ransom.

"Who is that strange fellow who is your tutor?"

"He is…" Ransom was struggling now to speak as little of it as possible "…he is a friend of my father…"

"You should get proper tutoring like me—at the cathedral. The bishop's teaching assistants teach me—Latin, Greek, the writings of the ancients…"

"I heard," Ransom said, changing the subject, "that a French man-o'-war put in down at the harbor. It's sporting huge cannons all over it."

"Let's go!" Philip said, punching his friend in the shoulder.

Their walk turned into a race. Philip's longer legs gave him a quick lead, but Ransom's strength and stamina served him well. By the time the harbor was in view down below them, with a scattering of large ships moored in it, Ransom had nosed out his friend.

They both stopped on the hillside overlooking the docks and the gray blue of the sea, panting and catching their breath.

After a few moments Philip spoke up.

"We shall always be friends," he declared, "against everything else in the world if need be!"

"Even against the cannons of the French fleet!" Ransom cried out in response, with a laugh.

Philip nodded and smiled, still breathing heavily. He patted the back of his friend, and the two friends shook hands over it.

Ransom had no way of knowing how their whimsical pledge, there on the wind-swept hills of St. Andrews overlooking the harbor, would someday be put to the ultimate test.

Chapter 6

The next day, Hugh Mackenzie sat at his tall, wooden desk, scratching entries in his ledger with a quill pen. The afternoon was waning. It was almost closing time. Ransom appeared in the front room of the printing shop, broom in hand. He sauntered up to his father's desk and leaned his chin on the broom handle with theatrical fatigue.

"Father, I'm finally all done. Can I go now? Please?"

"Go where?" Hugh took a cloth to his ink-stained fingers and tried to rub them clean.

"I'd like to go down to the beach—to look at the ships."

"So, you have finished all your jobs now, have you?"

Ransom nodded enthusiastically.

"*All* of them?"

Ransom nodded even more energetically.

"So then," Hugh continued, "does that mean you have arranged all of the type in its proper order?"

Ransom looked down at the ground sheepishly and, sighing a great sigh, let his head fall backward dramatically.

"I take it, lad, that you have not. Please attend to it—*now*."

Ransom was trudging toward the back room when he stopped in his tracks, still holding the broom.

"Father, I must ask you a question."

Hugh turned, at first taken aback by Ranson's emphatic tone. But the older man was wise enough to recognize this, not as impudence, but as the budding of boyhood into manhood. He had been expecting that, any day, Ransom would share how he was beginning to grapple with troubling issues he could no longer ignore.

Having a good idea what his son's questions were, he nodded, inviting Ransom to continue.

"Why do you have those racks of type stored in the cellar?" his son asked. "And why are they always covered?"

Hugh silently eyed his son with a look Ransom had only seen a few times before—a solemn look, tempered by caution, born of adversity.

As Hugh was choosing his words carefully, Ransom continued.

"And why do you keep the cellar locked? And why have you told me I may never talk to anyone about what is down there? And what about the message I saw in the rack yesterday?"

Hugh stepped down from his stool, put his hands on Ransom's shoulders, and looked deep into his son's eyes.

"Ransom, I have spoken to you from time to time about the way things are here in Scotland. And the need for loyalty and trust—between you and me. And I have told you that as you grow older, more things will be told to you—matters that may seem to be mysteries now. Do you remember that?"

Ransom, wide-eyed, nodded.

"I have told you that printing is a most noble and honorable profession. We printers take the words of the few, and we give them to the many. But there are those who rule this land with an iron fist. They fear that the words of the Lord Jesus may be printed in the common language…while *they* revere and honor them when they are printed in Latin, a language the people cannot understand. Those who print the Bible in the common tongue are arrested—and many of them are strapped to the post and burned for their faith. I've spoken to you about this. It is a fearful thing—but such is the way of things now, like it or not. Do you understand what I am telling you, son?"

Again, Ransom nodded, but a slight grimace showed on his face.

"You know well that I am a friend of Master John Knox, who is your tutor," Hugh went on. "He loves God's Word. And I am also a follower of George Wishart, a great preacher of God, who has been arrested and lies in the Bottle Dungeon, not a mile from here. My lad, if you were to tell the chancellor of this city the things I just shared with you—I would be in danger of death myself."

"Is it because of the queen? Queen Mary?" Ransom asked.

"Marie de Guise, the queen mother, who exercises power in place of her daughter—yes, she has sent out the edict. But others, like Cardinal Beaton here in St. Andrews, seem to take particular pleasure in enforcing her dastardly orders."

"Are you afraid, Father?" Ransom was looking up into his father's face with an intensity Hugh had not seen before.

He paused and thought.

"What have I told you about the three essentials of the printing press?" he asked. "Name them for me."

Surprised by a question that did not match his query, Ransom searched his memory for a moment.

"Well, sir," Ransom began, glancing at Hugh's stained fingers, "ink. Printing needs ink."

Hugh smiled. "That was an easy one. Now what are the other two?"

Ransom thought for a few seconds.

"Letters. Raised letters set down properly."

"Very good. But there's a third—what else?"

Ransom pondered the one element of printing he had forgotten. He shook his head and shrugged.

Hugh walked over to the press on the other side of the shop. He put his hand on the wheel and spun it slowly. As he did, the main vertical turnscrew at the center of the press began rotating, and the large plate lowered down toward the type that had been arranged within the base of the press.

Hugh turned and raised an eyebrow, waiting for the answer. But Ransom was silent.

"Pressure, my lad, *pressure,*" Hugh said. "The handle turns the screw, the screw lowers the plate, and the plate presses down upon the paper, which forces the paper down upon the inked type. You've seen that a thousand times…"

As he removed his apron and hung it next to the press, he beckoned Ransom to his side.

"There is much in life that is like this printing press. When the turn of the great screw brings pressure down upon you—when you are threatened with being crushed, pressed down—all because you know the right and the true of it, then that is where you take your stand. When such pressure is brought down upon you—that is the true test of the man."

Hugh stroked his son's hair and then gave him a gentle push toward the back room.

"Now, finish your work, and then you may go down by the harbor. But stay clear of Cardinal Beaton's castle when you do."

But a noise outside the shop caught the attention of father and son.

Several people ran past the front window, heading toward the hill at the end of the street, up toward the castle and the great cathedral that adjoined it.

Then a man thrust his head in the doorway. It was Angus Atcheson. He was nearly out of breath, and his eyes had a wild look about them.

"Hugh—step lively—they're bringing him out today!"

"Wishart?" Hugh asked.

Angus nodded vigorously.

"Aye—it's his day for burning. God help him!"

In an instant, he was gone.

"What—what is it, Father?" Ransom cried anxiously.

Hugh whirled and grasped his son's arms, squeezing them tightly.

"Listen to me, boy," he said. "You must go upstairs to the apartment. And then you bolt the door. Do not open it for anyone, except for me. Do you understand me?"

Ransom nodded soberly.

Hugh ran out the doorway and turned up the street in the direction of the dark castle from which Cardinal David Beaton meted out the authority of Marie de Guise—and where George Wishart had been imprisoned within the depths of its dungeon.

The tall, massive stone edifice faced the North Sea, on a prominent hill at the end of High Street. Beyond the barred front gate and within the castle's inner court, there was an anteroom secured by a heavy oak door. Within the floor of the room was set a large round hole, skirted by inlaid stones.

Three guards were pulling a rope through the bottleneck opening, lifting up their human cargo from the dungeon below.

George Wishart was slowly being pulled from the darkness of the prison below, its lightless confines putrid with the stench of standing water and human waste.

Grimacing, he closed his eyes tight against the light from the blazing torches in their brackets on the walls. His gray hair flew about his head wildly—his face was grimy, and hollow from hunger and deprivation.

"One big pull now," one of the guards shouted.

As the three pulled simultaneously, Wishart's frail body, with its filthy, tattered clothes, was yanked through the bottleneck hole, and he flopped onto the stone floor like some great, vanquished fish.

While Wishart struggled up onto hands and knees, and tried to behold his captors through squinted eyes, the biggest guard pulled a long chain from a corner of the room and tossed it to his assistant.

"When we tie him to the stake, you make sure his shirt is pulled from him and the chain is wrapped about his chest. Then we'll see his flesh seared like a pig on a spit!" The head guard laughed loudly.

His assistant winced slightly as he looked at the chain and the broken man lying on the floor before him.

"And who did this poor devil murder?"

The big guard smiled and shook his head.

"Murder? Oh, no—this man is guilty of crimes far worse than murder," he chortled mockingly. "He didn't just kill the body. Why, he poisoned the soul!" Laughing again, he grabbed Wishart by the arm and jerked him to his feet.

As the three guards dragged Wishart outside the castle grounds to the stake that had already been set in the middle of the street some two hundred feet away, an observer high above the town was looking down.

On the top floor of the castle, within the shadows of a great arched window, Cardinal David Beaton stood resolute, eyeing the proceedings below. He approached the window to get a better look, his red satin and silk clerical robes rustling quietly, and clasped his two gloved hands in front of him in a posture of contemplation.

A crowd gathered on the street below, encircling Wishart as he was lashed and then chained to the post, and as wood and hay was heaped at his feet.

As Cardinal Beaton stood calmly, his chief counselor stepped next to him discreetly.

"Your Eminence, let me repeat again my strong protest at your decision."

Beaton did not respond—his gaze was riveted to the street, where torches were now being set to the kindling and wood.

"I most vehemently protest—" The cardinal swung his head around quickly, and fixed his aide with his gaze.

"*Protest?*" he intoned with controlled intensity. "You dare *protest* my decision regarding this heretic? This is the work of God, sir, to destroy the devil's army. And you lodge a protest?"

"Let me say then, that I strongly...*advise* against this course. I find this exercise inconsistent with the missive of Christ's Holy Church."

Beaton was unmoved.

"George Wishart has preached lies—damnable lies, heresy, and vile deception," he said sternly. "He uses—indeed, even publishes abroad—God's Holy Word in the common, filthy tongue of the peasants. He preaches rebellion against the righteous rule of the Mother Church. He denounces the Mass. And he denies—yea, sir—he even *denies* the Real Presence of the Lord Jesus Christ in the Host of Holy Communion. This profane babbler encourages the commoners to actually believe that heaven can be obtained through simple little prayers of 'faith'—in disregard of the Rule of Faith and the teachings and the authority of the one true Church of Christ. Do you care so little about men's souls—so little that you would permit them to be led astray by this son of darkness?"

The counselor did not respond. As the flames reached Wishart's torso and he began writhing in pain, the counselor spoke again.

"Then, Your Eminence, I have one final suggestion."

"And what, pray tell, is that?" Beaton asked.

"That if you have any more heretics to burn—you do it in the basement of the castle, where the stench of their burning flesh cannot be smelled and their cries of salvation by faith cannot be heard by the masses. For it is eighteen years to this day—on this very day, sir—that Patrick Hamilton was set afire for his reformist beliefs, not one half mile from where we stand. And his death sparked a rebellion that plagues us to this day."

The counselor bowed and quickly left. Beaton turned back to the window to study the blackened, tormented figure of Wishart below, noting how his gaze seemed fixed on some invisible point above him.

The cardinal shifted his attention to the crowd, which was gathering in greater numbers around the pyre.

In the middle of the people, John Knox fingered the grip of his long, two-handled sword. He was ready to make his move.

He pushed forward to the front of the crowd, his sword grasped firmly, holding it in front of him.

Within the flames, shuddering with agony, Wishart caught a glimpse of his friend with his sword.

His body charred by flame, his flesh bubbled and peeled and oozing, Wishart prayed that God would forgive his persecutors. He cried out to his followers in the crowd: "Love the Word of God for your salvation, and suffer patiently!"

And then he called out to his friend and protector, John Knox.

"Stay your sword, John—remember, one is sufficient for sacrifice!"

Knox lowered his sword, and his shoulders began to heave with sobs. The big guard swept over to his position, eyeing the sword.

He stared at Knox with an icy glare. "You will be putting that sword away now—or I will have you put on the same stake as your friend," he growled.

Hugh Mackenzie pushed forward, grabbed Knox by the shoulder, and turned him away from the flames, which were now up to Wishart's charred face. As the preacher fell into unconsciousness, Hugh calmly addressed the guard. "Never mind about Mr. Knox. He means no harm, I'll vouch for that."

His eyes flooded with tears, he put his arm around Knox and moved him gently through the crowd. "This is not the time, John. You heard what George said—your death now would do us no good. We need you among us—to carry on the work."

"Aye, but what work would that be?" Knox replied, gasping with sobs. "To run and hide? Or proclaim the truth of Christ like a trumpet? I am tired of seeing my brethren led to the flames—when will this stop? This is madness! Surely God's nostrils have smelled the sacrifice of His children long enough!"

As Hugh reached the back of the crowd with his friend, he noticed a figure off in the distance, staring in horror. A young boy. His face was frozen, his eyes fixed on the burning corpse of George Wishart at the stake.

Hugh rushed over to his son, who did not take his gaze off the fire, even as his father grabbed him and shook him.

"Ransom—I told you not to come—I told you to stay home! This is not for you to see!"

Hugh covered his son's eyes with his large right hand and pushed him away from the sight.

He turned to Knox and whispered.

"I will bring Ransom to you for his tutoring lesson. Day after tomorrow, as usual. But you and I, John, must talk."

As Hugh walked his son home, he turned slowly for one last glance at the shape now engulfed entirely by the flames.

Eventually, night cloaked the streets of St. Andrews. Those who had flocked to witness the horror finally dispersed, shops closed for the day, and men and women scurried back to their homes.

But the flames at the stake at the end of High Street were still flickering. Thick smoke continued to spiral up to the night sky, and the smoldering, crimson coals cast an eerie light on the surrounding buildings…and on the face of the castle at the end of the street.

The glow of the fiery pyre of George Wishart could be seen beyond the castle street, all the way down at the harbor, and out to the merchant ships that were anchored in the shallows of the North Sea.

Chapter 7

Three Months Later

It had been a quiet night in the castle of Cardinal Beaton. Before retiring for bed, he and Marion Ogilvie, his mistress, had been working late on his financial accounts.

"Marion," Beaton called out to her as she prepared to leave the bed-chambers well after midnight, "take care not to be detected. Prudence and propriety are the watchword..."

She nodded and sighed. She had heard that warning before. Then she slipped out quietly, down to the shadowy streets of St. Andrews, and left Beaton alone in his room.

The cardinal settled into bed. He could hear the crash of the waves of the North Sea a hundred feet below his apartments. His eyes were heavy, and he floated into a peaceful slumber beneath the massive oaken rails of the canopy bed. He melted into the ease of his goose-feather quilt, not fearing the night.

Why should he fear? Though the Protestant rabble had noisily lamented the execution of Wishart, their itinerant spiritual leader, the ensuing months had seen only words, no actions. The cardinal believed he was secure. The castle was well-fortified against direct attack. He had ordered additional masonry work at any areas vulnerable to marauders who might attempt to scale the walls.

By five in the morning, the cardinal was dreaming fitfully in his luxurious bedchambers. He could not have known that the first of the Protestant conspirators bent on vengeance for Wishart's death had already arrived at the kirkyard not far from the castle walls. As the men gathered there, they were cloaked from view by the moonless night.

Several had arrived the day before. All of them had entered the town limits of St. Andrews separately, and from different directions, so as to avoid suspicion. Will Kircaldy of Grange, along with six of his men well armed with swords, was there. He had been joined by the trio of Leslies—John, William, and Norman—as well as Peter Carmichael of Balmeadow. James Melville was also with them. But he was different from the fiery Leslies, who had come from their family stronghold in Ballinbreich to see Beaton's blood spilled on the castle floor—and spilled freely. Melville was there, he said, to see to it that the work of God was done. "Everything in order," he intoned solemnly.

Their plan was simple, confirmed in hushed whispers. Melville asked that each man voice his participation. Each man nodded and added his "aye" when asked by Melville if what they were about to do was the product of prayful deliberation, accompanied by both certainty of soul as well as mind. Then, as the gray dawn began to break over the city, the men separated into two groups and quickly disappeared to their appointed places.

It was not long before the first of the workmen began to arrive, as usual, at the front gate of the castle. Most were stonemasons, along with a few carpenters. The castle porter, flanked by two guards, had lowered the drawbridge to let them in. In all, there were more than a hundred workmen who, with their rumbling wagons and hand tools, slowly made their way across and into the castle grounds. A few of them joked coarsely and loudly with each other. But it was early, and the day's work, if it were like that of every other day, would be long and hard. So, most of the workers filed through the arched opening of the castle quietly, pondering drearily the fact that it would be nightfall before they could cross over the drawbridge again and trudge home.

But this day would not be like any other day. Among the mass of laborers, Kircaldy and his six swordsmen, dressed like stonemasons, were bringing up the rear. They kept their heads down as they walked, fixing their gaze on the paving stones of the castle grounds.

The guards left the gate and disappeared to their watch. But Kircaldy and his men lingered by the door. Before the porter could raise the drawbridge, they surrounded him, blocking his view, and started to ask him about the day's construction assignments. The three Leslies, armed and thirsty for retribution, slipped over the drawbridge and onto the grounds and, undetected, scurried into the entrance of the northern wing of the castle—that led toward Beaton's bedchambers.

By the front gate, the porter was growing suspicious.

"Say, I don't remember you fellows working here before…" He eyed Kircaldy's group more closely. He caught sight of a sword under the one of the men's work clothes.

The porter dashed to the drawbridge, trying to yell out to the guards posted up on the walls.

Before he could sound the alert, Kircaldy's men grabbed him, and one of them smashed his skull with his sword's handle. The porter fell lifeless to the ground. Snatching his keys, they threw his corpse into the fosse underneath the drawbridge opening and ran to the inner entrance to join the other group, which by now had traversed the long hallway that led to the door of the cardinal's bedchambers.

Beaton, having heard a noise, had quickly jumped from his bed and run to the window. Workmen down below yelled dreadful news.

"The castle's been taken!"

Beaton sprinted to the door of his bedchambers and bolted it shut just as his attackers were arriving.

"Open the door, Cardinal!" John Leslie cried out.

"Swear first," Beaton pleaded, "swear that by God's wounds you will not slay me!"

Leslie, sneering, turned to his men.

"Burn him out."

The men gathered torches and a brazier filled with burning coals from the hallway and laid them at the foot of the oak door, setting fire to straw and rags they stuffed below its edge.

In a few minutes smoke was billowing into the bedchambers, and the wooden door was beginning to smolder. The cardinal ran to his window in hopes of summoning help. But what he saw there sent his heart sinking. The drawbridge had been lowered, and the workmen, rather than coming to his aid, were scurrying into the town for safety by the dozen. The guards had fled the castle to round up additional troops. Beaton was helpless and alone.

He knew his only chance was to strike a bargain with the rebels, relying on his cunning and skills at negotiation.

"Is Norman Leslie there?" he called out.

"I am John Leslie," the reply came, for Norman was on the level below, acting as a lookout.

"I will talk to Norman Leslie...I once counted him as friend of the queen mother..."

"Nay, you will have to be content to address those who are out here, Cardinal."

The cleric hesitated for a moment, poised in front of the burning door and covering his face from the billowing smoke. Then he reached out and slid the heavy metal bolt back.

Instantly the door was thrown open. The men stamped out the fire on the floor and waved their capes to disperse the smoke. Standing before them was Cardinal David Beaton in his nightcap and nightgown, with a look of barely controlled panic.

The group of rebels eyed their opponent. No one moved for a few seconds. Beaton's hands were clasped together in front of him—he was unconsciously rubbing them together, as if he were Pontius Pilate attempting to wash his hands of the dark deeds that had been done at his direction.

Then the band of men flipped open their capes and pulled out their swords in a simultaneous deadly choreography.

The cardinal stumbled backward as the men rushed him. Falling back into a plush chair, he began begging for his life.

"I am a priest! A priest! You will not slay me—"

As he held his hands over his face, cowering, John Leslie stepped up to him, took his sword, and thrust it violently into the clecric's chest. Peter Carmichael followed, sticking his sword into Beaton once, and then again as the man shrieked and moaned.

That is when James Melville pushed his way to the front and ordered his fellows to stay their swords.

"Men!" he shouted. "This is the work and judgment of God that we are about…It must be done with greater gravity."

He pointed his sword directly at Beaton.

"Cardinal," Melville began, addressing the profusely bleeding cleric with an official and somber tone, "repent thee of thy former wicked life, and especially of the shedding of the blood of that notable instrument of God, George Wishart—repent ye, sir! And acknowledge that ye are an obstinate enemy against Jesus Christ and His holy gospel!"

But the cardinal simply sat there, his hands pressed on his wounds and blood running through his fingers. He shook his head and muttered.

"I am a priest…a priest…fie…fie…all is gone…"

Convinced of the cardinal's unrepentant heart, Melville himself thrust his sword in several times. At the final jab Beaton slumped forward and, as Melville pulled his sword out, the cardinal fell to the floor dead.

There were shouts from the courtyard below.

"There are troops approaching!" came the yell of the Protestant rebels.

Leslie and the others could see that their comrades had managed to pull up the drawbridge. Outside the castle, a contingent of Marie de Guise's army were demanding to know the condition of Cardinal Beaton.

"They will know soon enough," Leslie said. He instructed his men to carry the body of the cardinal through the castle to the window nearest to the front gate, where the troops were gathered.

"What have you done with the cardinal?" one of the sergeants outside the wall yelled up.

At Leslie's word, the corpse of Cardinal David Beaton, tied by the ankle with a rope, was dangled out of the window.

"Behold your pagan god!" Leslie yelled down.

A maddened roar rose up from the soldiers outside the castle.

"What if they attack?" one of the rebels asked Leslie as they peered down from the wall.

"Several weeks ago we requested that English troops join us in the battle here," Leslie replied. "The English throne has no love for the queen mother or her papist sympathizers. This is the beginning of our revolution—against the queen and against the Roman Church's rule over Scotland!"

"But what if the English troops don't arrive?"

Leslie glanced down at the queen's soldiers, and then he looked back over the small band of rebels gathered around him.

The look on his face gave away the answer. He was certain beyond any doubt that if the English did not come to their rescue, the castle could not be held—that the queen's army would mount an attack, and the rebels would be slaughtered. And all would be lost.

Chapter 8

The news of the slaying of Cardinal Beaton and the capture of his castle had spread through St. Andrews—and far beyond—like a fire put to dry kindling.

In the weeks that followed, the castle continued to be held by the Protestants, but barely. The tense standoff would ebb and flow—days of quiet would then be punctuated by a series of skirmishes between the queen's men on the outside and the band of rebels within.

One night, Ransom was in bed. The evening air was filled with the sounds of men yelling, their voices echoing down the streets and narrow closes of the city. The occasional distant explosion or the single shot from a blunderbuss would be followed by a pall of silence falling like a heavy curtain. Ransom would count the seconds of quiet, wondering how long the tense absence of sound would last. Ten seconds. Twenty. And then suddenly the eerie noiselessness would erupt into more shouting, gunfire, and explosions.

His father was downstairs in the shop—doing what, Ransom did not know.

Another brief silence. Then, from out in the dark, a sound of footsteps approaching their house. Then they stopped—though Ransom wished it were not so—at their front door.

Ransom's tense immobility was broken by his father's heavy tread coming up the stairwell, coming fast.

"Ransom—boy!" Hugh said in a guttural whisper as he burst into the bedroom.

"Get up! Grab your clothes and out with you—down into the cellar—and go out by the little window hatch—"

The house shook with a thunderous banging at the front door. And then an angry call from outside: "Hugh Mackenzie—show yourself and be quick about it!"

"Up!" Hugh whispered in a strained voice, pulling Ransom out of bed. "Run to the house of John Knox. Stay there until I fetch you—now go!"

Ransom threw his vest, pants, and jacket on, jammed his boots on his feet, and scurried down the stairs.

Once downstairs he paused for a moment, casting a final look at his father. Hugh was poised at the front door, which was still bolted shut. But the angry voices on the other side, and the banging, were getting louder.

Hugh motioned with both hands for his son to flee. Ransom hurried down the cramped stairs to the cellar. He felt his way along the dirt floor in the dark through boxes and crates and spare equipment. More yelling and banging at the front door. Someone was threatening to burn the house down.

He was now directly under the small hatch window with its wooden chute that led up from the cellar floor.

Ransom scampered up the chute to the hatch door and unlocked it. Above, he could hear his father, who had waited to give Ransom a clear chance to escape, sliding the heavy metal door bolt back.

Pulling himself through to the ground outside and closing the hatch behind him, Ransom was up on his feet in a flash.

He was running faster than he had ever run before. His lungs were burning as he sucked in the cool night air, his heart thundering in his chest.

Would his father be safe? "God help him, please!" he gasped out. What if they arrested him...perhaps taking him down to be chained to the oars in the dreaded bowels of a galley ship...never to be seen again.

The others who were dear to him also sprang to mind. What about his friend Philip—was he safe at home? And what about the pretty, taunting Catherine—where was she?

When Hugh opened the door of his shop, a long wooden staff struck him in the chest, wielded by the high sheriff, an ally of the late cardinal.

As Hugh staggered back, doubled over with pain, the sheriff, surrounded by three of his deputies armed with long swords, strode inside.

"That was for your tardiness in opening," the sheriff said evenly. "If you delay in supplying answers to my inquiries, you shall find me even more disagreeable."

As he told two of his men to search the shop and apartment, he stepped closer to Hugh.

"Mackenzie, it is time you and the other printers of this town be flushed out of hiding. What do you know of this insurrection? The hellish conspiracy against Cardinal Beaton—the seizing of the castle—this dastardly insult to the authority of the Scottish Crown?"

"Nothing," Hugh, still bent over in pain, was clutching his chest.

"Oh?" the sheriff asked incredulously. "I find that hard to believe. It is common knowledge you printers always hear the latest murmurings—and moreover, on my part I do believe that these so-called Reformist pamphlets and writings are coming from the likes of you..."

"Hard to believe or no," Hugh replied more firmly, having gotten his wind back, "you will have to be satisfied with my answer...for it is the truth."

"Satisfied? I will be satisfied," the sheriff said through clenched teeth, "when every Protestant rebel who has given aid and comfort to this conspiracy is stretched on the rack, and then cut into pieces with a dull blade. And I think they ought to start with the printers first!"

The deputies returned and reported that no one else was in the house.

"Take him," the sheriff snapped. "We will discover soon enough what he knows…"

Ransom had reached Knox's house and had tapped several times at the front door. Through the wavy glass of the front window he saw a light enter the room. The small slide in the upper door panel snapped open, and he could see his tutor's eyes.

"Who is it?"

"Ransom Mackenzie."

The door swung open.

"By God's grace," Knox muttered as he pulled Ransom inside and quickly closed the door.

"Where's your father?"

"Dunno…men came to the front door…"

"Men? What manner of men?"

"Dunno…couldn't see them. But they sounded angry."

"Beaton's gang," Knox said with disgust. "The sheriff and his men, most likely. Scouring the city in revenge for the cardinal's death."

"My da says I should stay with you…till he comes for me."

Knox could hear the strain in the lad's voice. He placed a large hand on Ransom's shoulder and mustered a quick smile.

"Then stay with me you shall, lad. You will be my constant shadow… until your good father shall come to fetch you home."

Chapter 9

When Ransom appeared at the door of John Knox, he thought, in his boyish naivete, that in a matter of hours he would see his father again. But hours turned into days, then weeks—and would eventually run into months. His anguish was inconsolable at first. He had never experienced such a loss before.

True, there was his mother, but she had died when he was very young. Whatever his mind recalled of her now was not clear; and all else consisted of vaguely warm feelings based on stories told him by his father. The only other trace was the little portrait of her in the bedroom—a pretty but somewhat plain woman with a gentle smile and kind eyes.

But Ransom was surprised, even shocked to the point of feeling guilty, when after a while the pain in his empty heart started to subside. As if it were starting to callus over. The hurt was slowly being replaced by a fierce commitment that he would not forget his father—and would not rest until he learned where he was…and what had been done with him.

He asked Knox daily on that score. After the first week, his mentor and teacher had managed to learn that Hugh Mackenzie had been arrested by the high sheriff and taken to the castle of the archbishop for interrogation. The archbishop's castle—at Monimail, about twelve miles inland to the west of St. Andrews—had also become the temporary site for operations of the university of St. Andrews. The ongoing battle against the Protestant "Castilians," as they were now called, was being prosecuted by Catholic forces who were using the university grounds, and many of the buildings there had been seriously damaged by return fire from the reformers in the castle.

While the castle had been hit repeatedly, it had not been destroyed, and the Protestant rebels—reinforced by a larger number who had managed to slip inside in the first few days of the siege—were still holding it, though by the slimmest of margins.

But in the following weeks Knox could learn nothing further about the fate of Ransom's father—though he made numerous inquiries as he gradually became more actively involved within the conflict. Most recently he had even been permitted, during the lull in the fighting, to parley with the rebels. The commanders of the Catholic armies had thought he might be useful as a mediator who could convince the reformers to give themselves up.

What they did not know was that the learned scholar's heart and soul were steadily migrating in the opposite direction. Knox had become all but convinced that, at this time and in this very place—within the battered stone walls of the castle of St. Andrews and amid the hungry and war-ravaged band of reformers—was where the revolution for the Protestant gospel would truly begin in Scotland. The only question remaining for him was simple, but excruciating in what it would exact.

What role was God calling him to play in that revolution?

One morning Ransom rose from his straw-stuffed bed and walked into the main room, where Knox was bent over his table murmuring his prayers. On the table was a large Bible, a quill pen, and several sheaves of paper.

Ransom stood quietly until his tutor was finished praying.

"So, ye're up?"

"Aye. Have you heard anything about my Da?"

"No," Knox answered matter-of-factly.

"How much longer will they keep him?"

"Dunno. I've tried my best to find out. Only God knows."

Ransom turned to leave with a dejected look on his face, but Knox stopped him.

"I have taken pity on you...for the absence of your father. But time passes, and I do not know that he will return—or if he does, when that will be. So now we must press forward, you and I. Did your father have the custom of morning prayer and Scripture reading with you?"

"Aye."

"Good. Then you shall join me at this table every morning for the very same."

Ransom nodded.

"And therefore you will rise when I do—which is a mite earlier than you have been demonstrating..."

Ransom nodded to that also.

Knox continued to study his young guest, his eyes penetrating him as if he were standing there naked and shivering just out of the bath— as if the older man were trying to see all the way down into his soul.

"Shall I tell you the place where I am going today? And the thing I shall soon do?" he said in a voice that was hushed and breathy, and full of mystery.

Ransom had no response to this strange comment except to stare back with wide-eyed expectation.

"You are called to be a man now, not a boy. You are no child, Ransom...those days are gone forever. And so I tell you the things I would tell a man."

Ransom waited without breathing for the revelation.

"Cardinal Beaton has been executed for his sins. I did not help that act of retribution—but neither did I prevent it. Beaton's castle has been captured by the reformers who wish to banish the Catholic tyranny and create a Scotland free for the preaching of the gospel. This much you already know. But I tell you this, young Ransom—that I will today meet within the castle with the reformist rebels…and will make provision to join them soon. They have asked me to provide spiritual comfort for their ordeal, and when I join them, then my fate shall be joined to theirs—whether for blessing and success…or for destruction."

Then he pointed a bony finger at Ransom.

"Do you understand what I am telling you?"

"I think so…yes, sir."

"Good. Then know this—if I join those inside the castle in the battle against the forces of the queen mother, I must decide what becomes of you…"

For a few seconds Ransom took the question as one of those decisions that grown-ups must make, and that young men must simply acknowledge and obey.

But Knox continued to gaze into Ransom's eyes. As if he were asking a question only his young student could answer. Ransom was beginning to get the feeling that his tutor was actually asking him to decide something—to make a decision that belonged solely to him—to decide, though he still felt himself to be only a boy, something fearful, and manly, and even brave.

Then Knox rose, collected his Bible and notes, and disappeared into his bedchambers. After a moment he returned, with his black skullcap and black cape.

"Don't leave the house. I shall return by nightfall, Lord willing…"

Then he was gone.

Ransom complied at first, but he could not forget Knox's announcement. If he was going into the castle to join the rebels, what would happen to the young man he had pledged to protect?

It seemed to be an insoluble problem, until Ransom thought back to his initial sense of their conversation. He had felt that Knox was inviting him to make a decision. Now it was becoming clear what question he was facing.

If he voluntarily joined Knox in the castle, then his teacher and mentor could fulfill both duties—to follow his conscience by uniting with the rebels, and to satisfy his promise to look after Ransom until the fate of his father was known.

But the thought of joining the ranks of the rebels sent a shudder through him. How could he be asked to do such a thing? He was only a boy.

Then he remembered Knox's words. Like it or not, he had been cast into the role of a man. But before he could make a man's decision, he felt he needed to see his own home with his own eyes. Somehow he might find there a clue about his father's fate, and counsel on the decision that now weighed heavy on his heart.

Ransom slipped out and scurried through sideyards and back alleys, keeping an eye out for the queen's soldiers. Here and there he saw sentries posted at street corners.

Then he rounded North Street. Looking down the street, he saw no one near, and he ran pell-mell toward the front of the printing shop. He stopped at the door and caught his breath.

And there it was. A large bill with the sheriff's seal had been posted on the door. It announced the seizure of Hugh Mackenzie "on suspicion of treacherous acts and high treason against the peace of the Queen Mother, Her Majesty, Marie de Guise, being suspect of conspiracy with various and sundry assailants who have committed wanton murder against the person of Cardinal David Beaton, the lawful agent of the Queen Mother…"

The notice further warned all citizens to refrain from entering the printing shop or home of Hugh Mackenzie.

Ransom's worst fears were posted there on the front door for all of St. Andrews to read.

He slipped around the side of the shop and leaned against the stone wall, his eyes welling with tears, choking back the bitterness of helpless grief. He closed his eyes as the tears ran down his cheeks.

A hand, with surprising tenderness, touched his shoulder.

Ransom turned and wiped his eyes, which were still bleary with crying.

A girl stood before him, smiling a strange little smile.

It was Catherine Fawlsley, Philip's cousin.

"Aren't you afraid of being seen with me?" Ransom asked, trying hurriedly to compose himself.

"You mean that old thing?" She motioned to the notice on the front door. "Not at all. My parents are at Court. They are very important people. They wouldn't let anything happen to me. Besides," she added, "they were acquaintances of that Cardinal Beaton fellow. So I would never be suspected of being a rebel…"

Then Catherine surprised Ransom by approaching him and, gently placing her lips on his, she kissed him, lingering there in a youthful embrace for just a moment. She stepped back and laughed.

"Why did you do that?" Ransom asked, bewildered.

"Because…" she said with a mysterious smile.

"Because why?"

"Because you and I have something in common…"

"What?"

"Both of our parents are away from us—and we are like little children alone in the woods…both of us, all by ourselves…fending for ourselves…"

Ransom didn't understand, but before he could ask another question she darted forward, gave him another quick kiss, and ran down the street.

"And don't worry—I shall not tell anyone you were here!"

As Ransom watched her disappear, he felt as if he were nearly drowning in a swirl of conflicting emotions. Exhilaration, confusion, fear, passion—all of them flooding over him, in a torrent he could not control, and certainly not comprehend.

In his dazed state, all he could do was wonder, as he scurried away from his father's shop, whether such feelings were also part of the manhood that John Knox had forced upon him.

Chapter 10

"Are you sure, lad?"

"Aye. I am." Ransom tried to sound brave, but Knox detected a quiver in his voice.

"Absolutely sure?" Knox said, pressing in.

"Aye. On my…on my father's life I am."

"And you have prayed to the Lord God—asking for His divine wisdom?"

"I have."

"And how has His Spirit borne witness to your spirit on the matter?"

"I have peace in my heart," Ransom said, now with boldness, "that I should go with you and your other students…into the castle…and there to be counted with you—and taught by you there."

"You'll be the youngest there…"

"I don't care. If you will have me, I will be a willing student."

"Though you are the youngest, you are still one of the brightest." Knox smiled. "It will be my privilege to continue your studies within the castle walls."

Knox laid his hand on his pupil's shoulder and brought them down on their knees together on the hard wood floor.

Bowed low, he implored God to protect them. To guide their every step, that they might be faithful witnesses to the Lord Jesus Christ, to His gospel, and to the written Word of God. And that they might "shed the light of Christ in the place of dark deeds, and bring the reformist rebels to a sanctified understanding of the way of Jesus, avoiding cruelty and unnecessary violence…and help prepare Scotland for such a spiritual revival that the gospel would spread like an unquenchable fire…"

Knox prayed long and fervently. So long, in fact, that Ransom's back began to hurt and his knees ache. But the young man considered it a kind of test. He would not shift his weight or complain. After all, what was a little stiffness in the legs compared to the unspeakable misery and torture his father might be enduring at that very moment?

Ransom had surprised even himself at his willingness to join Knox. He believed his mentor had been secretly hoping he would do so. But he also knew that Knox would not pressure him into deciding one way or the other.

Was it seeing the sheriff's notice on their door that had so steeled his heart? he wondered. Perhaps. Or was it his unending fear about his father's plight? He did feel it was now his turn to act the man and do his part in honoring his father's sacrifice for the faith.

But there was something else, and Ransom was embarrassed to admit it even to himself. When Catherine had so openly kissed him—not once but twice—he had experienced a kind of explosive and heroic energy. It was no matter that her parents sounded as if they had been sympathizers of Cardinal Beaton's—therefore full-fledged papists, making them enemies of Ransom and his father, and of John Knox as well.

Ransom tried to tuck that last, conflicting thought away in the remotest regions of his mind. After all, there were more pressing matters now. Like Catherine's affection for him. His actions would be observed from afar by the lovely red-haired girl. He was now sure of that. So he needed to show himself a worthy suitor, strong and full of courage. Striding into the forbidden castle would certainly accomplish that.

After Knox's protracted prayer, he and Ransom gathered up a collection of books and papers, as well as clothing and a small supply of food—as much as they could carry. Then they walked over to North

Street, where several of Knox's students were already waiting. Each of their parents, Protestant leaders in St. Andrews, had pledged that their sons would continue under Knox's tutelage.

The siege had been halted and a tenuous truce forged. Why Marie de Guise had decided not to storm the castle was unclear. But whatever the reason, the temporary lull was permitting the group to enter the castle under the watchful eye of the Catholic troops.

Ransom dutifully followed the black-robed figure of John Knox along with the other students as they approached the main gate. Next to him was a plump and frightened-looking lad, who looked to be a year or two older than he was.

"I'm Oliver Haggerty," the other boy whispered.

"Ransom Mackenzie."

"Oh," Oliver groaned, "I hope they don't shoot us at the gate…"

"They won't," Ransom said confidently.

"How do you know?"

"Didn't you hear what Master Knox said?"

They were now nearing the gate, and on either side of them were small groups of the queen's bowmen eyeing them suspiciously.

"We're in a truce," Ransom continued. "We'll be safe."

But Oliver looked askance at the crossbows at the soldiers' sides.

When Knox reached the far end of the drawbridge he turned and motioned each of his students inside—as if under the shield of his black robes, whose sleeves draped down from his arms like wings.

"Fear not!" he said to the boys as they filed past. "God will be your shelter—for His pinions are mightier than the stone and mortar of this castle. Don't eye the soldiers now, boys…eyes straight ahead…that's it…through the strait and narrow gate…do not fear those who can merely harm the body!"

Ransom was the last in. The heavy castle doors creaked behind him as they began to close slowly. Then they slammed shut with a reverberating bang, so loud that the ground shuddered, so loud it could have been mistaken for a clap of thunder from one of the violent storms that swept off the sea and crashed against the cliffs of St. Andrews.

Once inside, Knox shook hands with several serious-looking men. After a moment, he strode over to the boys and explained where they would stay.

The foretower, which overlooked the front gate, was off limits to them. If there were another attack from the queen mother's army, it would probably be there. The tower was manned around the clock.

Knox and his students were sent to another of the five prominent towers that, connected by the walled surround, made up the castle complex. They walked across the pentagram-shaped open courtyard to the far end. The Sea Tower, which overlooked the ocean, was a four-story structure that had been used by Cardinal Beaton as a prison. In the upper rooms there were well-furnished bedchambers for detainees of more noble birth or, on occasion, visiting bishops. On the first floor were crude jail cells for common prisoners, with a small hole cut in each cell's door for passing in food.

After Knox explained some of the history of the Sea Tower, he told the boys to wait on the first floor while he made sure that the upper rooms had been readied for them.

After their teacher left, Harold, a self-assured seventeen-year-old student, exclaimed, "The truth is out! Old Knox would have us locked up as his prisoners here!"

The rest of the boys belly-laughed at that. But their laughter died quickly when their tutor appeared at the bottom of the stairs.

"Come with me." He solemnly led the students under a gate to a square room. In the stone floor was a hole.

"Look down there," Knox instructed young Harold, the jokester.

He peered down into the black abyss.

"What do you see?"

"Nothing…it's too dark to see anything, Master Knox."

"Incorrect," Knox snapped back. "Can anyone tell Harold what lies beneath—in the darkness below the hole?"

There was silence. Knox surveyed the young faces. None had a glimmer of understanding—except one.

"Ransom Mackenzie," Knox called out. "What say you?"

"'Tis the Bottle Dungeon, sir."

"Aye. That it is."

Knox turned to face Harold again.

"What do you smell coming up from that hole in the floor—from the depths of the dungeon below?"

The student bent down, took a deep breath, then winced at the foul scent.

"Pheww!" He exclaimed, trying to be a little funny.

"And what do you smell?"

"Filth of a very bad sort."

"Aye—to the human senses, perhaps," Knox responded. "But to the senses of God, it is the sacred perfume of sacrifice."

The scholar stepped back from the hole and eyed each of the lads one by one as he spoke.

"In this very place, where we stand—many of God's children were imprisoned here. And here they prepared to meet the Lord of all creation—martyrs for the gospel of our blessed Savior, Jesus Christ."

Then Knox asked, "Name one of them—just one, my learned students."

There was silence. Knox looked again at Ransom.

"Mister George…Mister George Wishart," Ransom answered quietly, a little embarrassed to be seen as the teacher's pet so early.

"Aye, George Wishart," Knox replied in a low and distant voice, which caught a little at the name *Wishart*.

Harold was eyeing Ransom now with a look of disdain.

"Mark you well, my students," Knox said, concluding the impromptu lesson, "there is the learning that comes to the informed and well-read mind—in the comfortable, familiar rooms of the school. But there is also..." Knox glanced toward Ransom—"there is also the education of the soul—which comes only by a tutorial in the classroom of God. And though it comes with little luxury, that education is precious, my lads...precious in the sight of our Lord."

Upstairs, the boys were shown straw mats on the floor in a large room still hung with the red velvet draperies of the cardinal. After a supper of broth and bread with a small portion of meat, they were led in Bible study in the Gospel of John by their tutor. After prayers, each climbed under his rough blanket, and the lamps were turned off.

In the darkness, the voice of Harold was loud and taunting.

"You may be the pet of Master Knox, little Ransom boy—but you'll be my whipping dog by week's end!"

Ransom had never felt so lonely as he did then.

A moment later he heard Oliver next to him.

"Never mind him," Oliver whispered. "He has a bad bark...but not a very big bite."

"Is that you, Oliver, you fat little poodle?" Harold yelled angrily.

No one dared answer. Ransom tried to conjure up the image of his father's face to comfort himself. But he could not. His life before—everything he had known—was quickly changing, it seemed. And now he was on his own in a hostile and frightening new place.

All of his pretensions of courage and heroism—mostly intended for Catherine Fawlsley—were ridiculous and false, he felt. What if his decision to enter the castle with Knox and the students had been a terrible mistake?

Ransom lay on his bed of straw, as still as a stone, in the pitch-black room. He did not know how long he stayed awake, thinking of that and staring into the dark, until exhaustion finally took over and he fell asleep.

Chapter 11

When Ransom awoke to the call of John Knox to morning prayers, he did not feel any better about his situation. But in days that followed, he would at least find a small amount of comfort in the routine that quickly developed, and the relentless schedule imposed by his instructor.

Up by five in the morning, prayers until six. Then the students would make their way to the other tower along the seawall where the kitchens were located. They were assigned to the cook to help in the preparation of meals. He was a large man with a ruddy face and a pleasant disposition who appreciated the help—but when Knox was not present and the cook wasn't looking, Harold became Ransom's tormentor. He would trip the younger boy, mete out punches and shoves, and would often spill garbage on him and then demand he clean up the mess.

The insults and attacks were regular and monotonous. Ransom had managed to make friends with all the other students in just a matter of days, but none of them would confront Harold about the intimidation. Although Ransom was much smaller than Harold, who was two years older, he was beginning to feel he would soon have to stand up to his enemy. If he didn't, he thought, there would be no end to the harassment.

By the end of the first week, Oliver had overcome much of his fearfulness, and Ransom found him to be a cheerful companion. The two had formed a firm bond. Yet Ransom thought much about his former life outside the castle walls. He wondered what Philip was doing and what he might be thinking about his best friend's joining the ranks of the rebels. But his daydreams—which were usually relegated to the little pockets of time when he was not working, studying, or enduring the assaults of "Harold the Terrible," as Oliver now called him—would always end up with two images.

First, the face of his father, whose visage Ransom was now finding more and more difficult to recall to mind.

And second, the pretty face of Catherine Fawlsley. The fact that he could remember everything about her—how she smelled of flowers and scented soap when she bent her head near to kiss him, and the feel of her lips, and the tilt of her head—yet he was increasingly unable to recall the details of his father's appearance—all of that gave him a feeling of guilt and shame he could confide to no one. He had silently taken it to God during the many daily prayer times, but his father's image still remained shadowy while Catherine's grew more vibrant and enticing.

One day, Ransom and Oliver were finishing up work they were doing at the wall of the castle overlooking the sea. Several masons, their faces covered with gray stone dust, were working furiously to repair gaps in the walls there. The two boys had been assigned to help them.

Ransom's strength and agility made him a good mason's apprentice. He had quickly learned how to use the mason's hammer to split smaller pieces of stone to correct dimensions. Oliver's task was to scoop up the discarded bits, lug them down the steps in a wooden bucket, and dump them into the stone salvage pile in the courtyard. Others then had the task of sorting out small, uniform pieces of stone that could be shot from one of the several cannons perched in the castle's blockhouses.

Oliver complained incessantly that he was given the harder job, because it required him to clamber down the steep steps with a heavy bucket. So when the bell rang in the Sea Tower, summoning all of the students to another round of lessons, he was delighted.

"At last," he moaned, wiping the sweat from his face and fanning himself with his cap. "I thought that bell would never ring…Just to think that I would be excited to rush to one of Mister Knox's lectures!"

Ransom was brushing the stone dust from his vest and pulling his cap from his pocket, looking pensive.

"Why are they working us so hard right now?" Oliver asked ruefully.

"They need to strengthen the seawall."

"That's a daft bit of madness. There is no need for that—no one can attack from the sea side. The cliffs are steep—the walls are sheer—why the worry? I've carried so many of those blasted buckets that my back's about to go silly on me…"

"Oliver, you'd make a pretty sorry field general," Ransom said with a little laugh.

"Why's that?" Oliver said defensively.

"You're missing the thing that's right in front of your nose."

"And what's that, your generalship?"

"The seawall faces the sea…and ships come by the sea…"

"Then what they say about the truce ending must be true. What'll happen to us?" Oliver cried out.

"Dunno," Ransom replied quietly.

When the two students arrived at the great hall, the other boys were already there. Knox had not yet arrived. Ransom could never keep from glancing up at the hall's vaulted ceiling that soared to a dizzying height. Great oak beams crossed its width and joined other massive beams that ran its length. He wondered at the skill of the builders and tried to imagine how they could have constructed the timberwork at such an astounding height.

Several students were sharing conflicting stories they had heard about battle being joined again. One agreed with Ransom's opinion about what the work on the seawall meant. But Harold and another boy had heard something different.

"I tell you," Harold said, "that wee little Ransom, the teacher's pet poodle, is totally daft."

A few of the boys laughed a little.

"I say," he continued, "that the men who I worked with have talked with the men at the front gate—and they ought to know, after all—they say a peace is in the works. We will be leaving soon under a flag of truce. And all will be well—for every one of us…"

Then he swaggered over to Ransom and said, "Or—*almost* every one," and put him in a headlock and began to squeeze.

The younger boy grabbed his persecutor's wrist and slowly pulled his hands apart—and in a battle of strength, started bending Harold's wrist backward.

Finally Harold had to shove Ransom backward with his other hand to break his hold.

While he was rubbing his wrist, Ransom walked up to him, stopping just inches away.

"I know that right now you are taller than I am," he said quietly. "But I can remedy that. I'm not afraid of you…"

Before Harold could respond, John Knox strode in, books under his arms, his black robes flowing. He smoothed out his beard, straightened his cap, and ordered the students to take their seats at the long wooden table and bow for prayer.

After prayer, Knox launched into the first topic of the day—what he called "the heresy of the real presence of Christ in communion."

The students were visibly disappointed. They had hoped their teacher would comment on the rumors. But in characteristic style he stuck to his meticulously prepared lectures on weighty theological matters, regardless of the circumstances of his impromptu school.

"While Christ is a real and present force in the being of those chosen instruments of His—chosen ones such as yourselves," Knox intoned, "yet, my bairns, mind you this—that during the sacrament of holy communion, which our Lord does bid us to, the Lord Jesus does *not* appear as a real and physical presence in the property of the bread and the wine. Nay, that is the error of the Church of Rome. While we can agree with the papists that Jesus is present at communion—He surely is present *only in the persons of His followers,* but *not* in the physical substance of the elements of communion!"

For his part, Ransom could not understand why Knox would display such fiery agitation whenever the issues of the "real presence" and holy communion arose. Knox had been a priest of Rome and had practiced ecclesiastical law, but now he followed the doctrines of the reformers. Perhaps, Ransom thought, that turnabout was what made him so ardently defiant now against the Catholic doctrines of the sacraments.

But it was the next topic that fired Ransom's imagination—though he was alone in that. The other students looked bored and confused. Knox's second discussion was on the issue of predestination.

Knox explained how the apostle Paul had preached the perfect sovereignty of God in choosing and calling forth His church.

"Did not Paul say," Knox explained, "in Romans chapter 8, that those whom He has predestined, He has also called?"

As Ransom considered that, his mind became both excited and overwhelmed all at the same time. He squirmed a bit in his seat, and his face contorted in deep thought.

"Questions?" Knox asked.

Ransom slowly raised his hand. Oliver comically rolled his eyes. At the end of the table, Harold's eyes narrowed in an angry squint.

"Are we just puppets of God?"

"Puppets?"

"Yes…like those of the puppeteers who come from faraway places to the Spring Festival in the town. They sit behind the booth out of sight, but they pull all the strings. And the puppets dance. Are we like that?"

Knox's face took on a strange and intense look. He slowly walked toward Ransom. His gaze was so unnerving that Harold thought, gleefully, that the teacher was about to turn his favorite student into a pillar of salt.

"Not like strings…" Knox muttered. "No—but more like…more like clay."

"Clay, sir?"

"Yes. Clay."

Then Knox returned to the lecture podium and carefully turned the pages of his huge Coverdale Bible. He began to read from the book of Jeremiah, chapter 18—how God commanded His prophet to go down to the potter's house and watch his labors.

"And what did Jeremiah see there?" Knox explained how the potter was fashioning something on his wheel. "But the vessel did not come forth, and the design of the clay was spoiled in the hands of the potter," he said. "The clay did not respond to the touch of the potter. So then— who prevailed? Was it the potter, whose design was not fashioned in the end—or was it the clay, which had failed to be formed into the desired shape?"

There was a moment of silence.

Then a student's hand shot up. "The clay was the prevailing one because…it determined how the story ended."

Another hand went up. Knox nodded.

"But how can clay be greater than the potter?" countered another student. "The potter is the master—everyone knows that."

Ransom's eyes were riveted on his teacher.

"But that is not the end of the story, my bairns," Knox said. "The potter then took the lump of unruly clay and fashioned it into yet another vessel, as it pleased him to so do."

He carefully closed the Bible and turned to his students.

"God permits us all, as clay in His mighty hands, to respond or no—but always according to His perfect will. And though we may rough-hew the touch of the Master Potter, His design will prevail in the end. Yes, you may mark that well."

For a moment Ransom was lost in the thought, imagining the mighty fingers of God thrust into the clay of the earth. Kneading it, working it as a baker would bread dough.

How will God shape me with His great hands? What shape will I be?

Glancing over at his youngest pupil, Knox recognized something the other students did not, and could not. He beheld it with a look as fierce as molten fire—a look greatly misinterpreted by the arrogant Harold. The master was watching the unveiling of the mind and soul of a young man who he now believed would have a place—some place, but what, he did not know—in the events of the religious upheaval now beginning in Scotland. How could he deny what was suddenly so obvious to him? *This clarity of vision,* Knox thought, *must be from God Himself.*

It was all clear to the master now. Even in the mundane studies of Hebrew and Latin; in reading Calvin's *Institutes of the Christian Religion,* Luther's New Testament and his *Order of Public Worship;* in consuming the history of Christian martyrdom chronicled by Knox's friend John Foxe; in all of these matters Ransom had shown himself not only to be gifted beyond his age—but also drawn to them as if by some invisible force.

But Knox's thoughts were interrupted. One of the rebels was running into the great hall. Reaching Knox almost out of breath, he paused a minute and then whispered something in the instructor's ear.

Knox's eyes widened, and he slowly turned to his students.

"I must go," he said solemnly. "Harold, as the oldest, you are in charge of the safety and care of the students until I return."

Harold nodded and grinned broadly.

As Knox turned to follow the man out of the hall, he paused and glanced at Ransom. "Master Ransom, I need you to come with me."

Ransom almost stumbled in his haste. There was no thought of honor or recognition in his mind at that moment. As he tried to keep up with the long strides of Knox and the other man, he had only one thought.

He wanted to know where he could hide when the advancing forces attacked—and when the awful, final destruction of the castle would begin.

Chapter 12

From the upper level of the castle blockhouse, the men could look down to where the queen mother's soldiers and the deputies of the sheriff were still keeping watch on the street below, barring any further visitors to the castle. Everyone felt that something was about to give.

John Leslie and James Melville were arguing with John Knox.

Leslie, a sandy-haired man in his early thirties with almost transparent blue eyes, was enraged. His face, usually fair, was scarlet.

"If there is to be a fight, then we'll have at it—but our men have to see our common cause in defending the castle…and claiming our rights to Scotland. Claiming it for the Scots, and not for Marie de Guise and her French brood in Paris…nor for the popish father in Rome. But what do I hear from the two of you?"

Melville, as usual, was attempting to negotiate a compromise.

"All I say is that an honorable truce with concessions from Edinburgh is a far cry better than slaughtering the hundred men here who have been at your side all these months—"

"Concessions? You can expect none of that," Leslie exclaimed. "The only concession you'll get from Marie de Guise and her Catholic assassins is perhaps, if you are very lucky, the straw at your feet will be dry and not damp at your burning—that will make it a little quicker for you!"

"*Assassins,*" Knox interrupted. "That's a keen word—a word that the queen and her archbishop would no doubt attach to you, John Leslie, for the killing of Cardinal Beaton."

"I would have thought better of you, John, than that!" Leslie said with barely controlled rage in his voice. "Do you mean to distance yourself now from everything we have accomplished?"

"What have you accomplished?" Knox said carefully. "The execution of Beaton without any proper process—or even attempt at a legal process. No giving notice to the world of the charges against him, the deeds that warranted his execution."

"We knew them well enough," Melville said. "At least I tried to give Beaton a chance at repentance—but he would not—"

But Leslie would not be quieted.

"Then why did you join us here?" he cried. "Why? Here we—James Melville and others—laid hands on you in this very castle to call you to be a minister of the gospel and begin your preaching, after John Rough himself, from the pulpit, called you to that vocation. And now you dare to decry your own band of brethren? Are you with us or not in this enterprise?"

"I would hope," Knox replied, "to be with God in His enterprise…"

"Fine and fancy preaching," Leslie retorted, "but the lines are being drawn. Melville here believes there will soon be an attack—he wants to negotiate. I wish to fight. And I'm willing to die if necessary."

Ransom was in the corner, listening to it all and fearing to move a muscle. John Leslie's determination to fight to the death had sent a chill through him.

Leslie stepped closer to the preacher.

"But where does John Knox stand?"

"I hope to be exactly where God is standing. I saw His hand in the events leading to the capture of this castle. I neither condoned nor commissioned the killing of Beaton. Yet I thought some good could come from it—but only if the gospel was unshackled in this land so that hearts may feel the fire of the Holy Spirit of God. But all that, all of what is at stake, may have been forgotten during the long siege here."

"I will tell you what is at stake," Leslie said. "Not only the reformed religion of Christ, but the expulsion of the tyrants who rule us from France through a wicked agent in Edinburgh, and then chain our people's minds through the religious heresy from Rome. Most slaves have only one master. Our people have two. So—what would you have us do, Master Knox? What?"

"You, John Leslie, will undoubtedly do whatever John Leslie has in mind to do...and no persuasion from me will have much effect. But if you want my advice—all of you who had cause in the death of Beaton need to fall on your face and repent of the spirit of anger and vicious revenge in which that act was done—"

"Repent!" Leslie cried out. "I'd rather be killed where I stand first—"

"And that you may well be, yet," Knox snapped back. "I do believe the French fleets are coming—"

"Which is exactly why we must negotiate a truce," Melville interjected, "while we still have time, before the French arrive."

"And what if they do?" Leslie shot back.

"I fear God's judgment has turned against those in this castle who captured it with ungodly intentions," Knox said raising his voice.

"We shall prevail, I warrant it," Leslie shouted back.

"You do not see what I see," Knox rebutted.

"John Knox—the special prophet of God—is that it?"

"I cannot deny what the Lord has laid on my heart—"

"And I cannot deny what my eyes tell me," Leslie shouted. "We are protected by the thickest castle walls in all of Scotland."

"They will be broken as mere eggshells," Knox said in a tone of settled conviction.

"The armies of England are on their way, as we speak, to rescue us. The English Crown guaranteed it—and made good on the promise. The English have crossed over the borders. They have already won a great victory at Pinkie."

"You will never see them here at St. Andrews," Knox declared flatly.

"Leslie," Melville said, trying to mediate, "Knox may be correct—the English have been beaten back outside Edinburgh…"

"When did you obtain this report?" Leslie was clearly aghast.

"Just today," Melville replied quietly.

Leslie had no retort. He stroked his hand nervously over his sandy beard and walked over to the windows that overlooked the enemy troops down below.

"And you shall be delivered into your enemy's hands," Knox said to Leslie's back. His tone was that of a judge passing judgment from the bench.

"And you and I," Knox continued, now in a voice that reflected an awful resignation, "we shall be captured by our enemies…and carried away to a strange country."

Leslie slowly turned from the window. And then he spoke.

"I will die fighting first. I'd best be rallying the men." Before hurrying out, he glanced at Ransom, who was standing in the corner, wide-eyed. "And when the volleys start firing and grown men start crying—you'd best look after your bairns, Master Knox."

And then he left the room.

Melville was shaking his head. Knox pulled Ransom close and whispered, "Go tell Harold to move the boys down to the bottom level and sleep there—and have them pray well and hard for their safety this night. I will be spending the evening on the parapets…keeping watch."

Ransom ran back to the students and delivered the message within the hearing of them all, so that Harold would have no choice but to follow Knox's instructions explicitly.

That night, each student picked up his books, clothes, and bedding and lugged it all down the narrow stone steps to the sparse quarters on the first level, where the commoners' jail used by Beaton was located.

Harold threatened to lock Ransom in one of the cells in jest, but lacked the courage to carry it through.

After eating a few loaves of stale bread and smoked fish, the boys prayed together and lay down. The lamp was doused, and darkness surrounded them all. Every one of them knew that a great and terrible battle might begin any moment. And they could be in the very midst of it. Few of them slept very soundly, and there was a great deal of tossing and turning. Ransom thought he heard Oliver whimpering. But eventually the room grew quiet. Ransom finally fell asleep himself, but not until he had prayed to God that he would be of good courage during the time of testing. And that God would keep his father safe, wherever he was.

In the minutes just before dawn, in the gray beginning of light that was pushing back the blackness of a cloudy, moonless night, it started to drizzle. A slow, seeping rain came down, shimmering across the horizon and over the sea.

Up on the high walkway Knox was looking out onto the ocean with two others.

As the gray dawn started to break, they could see just a little bit better, out beyond the shallows. And what they saw jolted them to the core.

A huge fleet of ships was anchored in the firth of St. Andrews. They must have come in the night.

One of Knox's companions fetched his glass and scanned the ships.

"French men-o'-war...galleys...heavy cannons..." he exclaimed, his voice high and tense.

"How many?" the other shouted.

"Two, four, six...ten...fourteen..." the man said as he tried to count them. "Eighteen...nineteen..."

"This can't be," the other replied. "We've never seen a fleet like that in the firth...ever."

"Twenty...no...no...*twenty-one!*" He was almost gasping as he spoke. "By God's heaven I swear it—twenty-one French ships..."

At the front gate tower, one of the rebels fixed his glass on one of the towers of the cathedral, a few hundred yards away. In the first light he was now making out something...a great cannon that had been mounted there.

Whirling around, he fixed his gaze in the other direction, toward the towers of St. Salvators College. There he saw more cannons.

And they were all pointing toward the castle.

He dropped his glass and ran to the bell rope within the arches that overlooked the courtyard. As he frantically pulled to ring the bell he began to scream:

"Bombardment!"

From down in the bay, red fire flashed from the muzzles of dozens of cannons. Silence. But for only a second.

Then came the awful report, like the thunder of an earthquake ringing through the harbor.

Then the whizzing of cannonballs overhead.

At the top of the college towers, cannons exploded in brutal volleys aimed at the castle blockhouse near the front gate.

As the cannon shot began raining down, the castle walls started to blow apart, with stone and dust and smoke flying everywhere.

The bombardment kept coming, unending, smashing the tops off the castle structures, opening holes in the thick castle walls.

John Knox was sprinting down the steps to the bottom of the Sea Tower, where the students were sleeping.

But they were no longer sleeping. They were screaming, panicked, running in all directions as they heard the cannon fire and felt the castle shake.

Knox appeared at the doorway. "To the courtyard!" he shouted, "and then lie down—get away from the Sea Tower—stay away from the walls!"

But they never had time to carry out his orders.

There was an explosion. Part of the roof began to collapse. Timbers and stones came raining down.

Oliver, who was running behind Ransom, gave out a shriek. And then several large beams fell down, covering him.

Ransom ran back to where his friend was lying on his stomach. He couldn't get loose from the rubble. With several tugs, he managed to pull him free.

"Run—run!" Ransom yelled as he pulled his friend to his feet.

Oliver steadied himself and, though limping, began to sprint with all the speed of complete terror.

But then there was another explosion—louder—overhead. Ransom looked up.

The ceiling above him began to give way. It gave a terrible creaking groan and then collapsed. Downward. Down onto Ransom.

The last thing he saw was Oliver scampering ahead of him—through the doorway and to safety beyond.

Chapter 13

French troops were scouring the rubble-strewn grounds of the castle. The cannon bombardment had obliterated the defenses of the rebels. Once the walls were breached, the French troops who had been called to support Marie de Guise poured in. In the final minutes before the capture of the rebel leadership, a hasty attempt at negotiation was made. John Leslie scorned it, but James Melville pursued it, and the French command promised to provide humane and safe treatment for all of them—including John Knox—in return for their agreement to leave Scotland.

But, as the Castilians made their way cautiously into the open and showed themselves, the French captain barked out a shocking order:

"Chain them all—they are now the property of the Nation of France!"

At the other end of the castle, amid the caved-in ruins of the Sea Tower, several French soldiers were picking their way through the rubble. One of them saw something.

"There…over there!"

"Yes. I see him," another soldier replied, approaching someone trapped under the timbers and stone. "Just a boy!" he said after examining the seemingly lifeless body. "This is no rebel."

"Well, pull him out."

"We are not on the burial detail…Let them take care of the dead bodies."

The first man nodded, then gestured for the detail to make its way out of the Sea Tower and toward the Kitchen Tower.

After several long minutes of silence had elapsed, Ransom Mackenzie opened one eye, then the other eye. He tried to look around, but a flash of pain swept through his head. He could move his arms, enough to push at the timbers above him. But their weight was immense—they surely would have crushed him had it not been for a large square stone next to him that had caught most of their weight.

After a few minutes' thought, he grasped the edge of the stone with both hands and pulled with all of his strength in spite of the pain in his left ankle. He finally tugged himself loose from the rubble that had pinned his legs—but the pain was now excruciating.

He bit his own arm to keep himself from crying out. He thought he would pass out. After resting, and despite waves of nausea and pain, he pulled himself completely clear. But his ankle was impossible to walk on. And what if the soldiers returned?

Then he noticed the fireplace in what was left of the near wall of the room. He dragged himself on his belly, over to the iron fireplace poker lying there. He slowly lifted himself up, using it as a crutch. He finally looked down at his ankle to make sure his foot was still there, because the pain was so intense.

Each step made Ransom gasp. Dazed, hurt, and scared, he picked his way through the rubble desperately hoping to avoid the small contingents of French troops still searching the grounds.

He found a cannonball hole in the wall that connected the Sea Tower to one of the blockhouses. He passed his poker through first, then pulled himself through with his arms, trying to guard his injured ankle as he did.

Squirming through the hole and wincing with pain, Ransom finally flopped onto the wet grassy yard outside the castle walls. He stood on shaking legs. Pain was blurring his mind. He leaned on the poker and slowly hobbled around the corner of the blockhouse. Now he had a clear view of the front gate. But he was feeling dizzy…what he saw seemed trance-like and otherworldly.

Dozens of French soldiers and the men of the Queen's Sheriff were yelling at a group being led, in chains, down the drawbridge. Out in the distance, the French galley ships in the harbor were ready to receive their newest batch of rowing slaves.

A restless mob was being kept at bay by the soldiers. Some were shouting for the rebels to be released and shown mercy. Others were crying for them to suffer the same fate as their "heretic friend, George Wishart."

"Burn them!" someone shrieked.

Then Ransom saw the shuffling figure of a man with a beard, black skullcap, and black robes being led with his hands chained together.

It was John Knox. When he reached the end of the drawbridge and stepped into the mud of the St. Andrews street, his captors motioned for him to move along, down toward the harbor.

But he would not be hurried. He paused, looking over the steeples and buildings of the city he loved. Just for a moment.

Then he turned to the crowd, which had grown quiet as it recognized who he was.

"Mark ye this day," he shouted out, his voice echoing off the broken castle walls. "I, John Knox, shall return to Scotland…and I will once again preach the blessed gospel of Jesus Christ here in my homeland!"

One of the French guards took his staff and struck the scholar in the side. For a moment he doubled over, but then he straightened himself up, not glancing at the guard shoving him along. Knox took one last, fleeting glance at the streets of St. Andrews. Then he turned away and trudged down the path toward the harbor and the waiting ship.

Ransom caught no further sight of his mentor.

Ransom could have quickly blended into the crowd, except for his strange walking stick, torn clothes, and the trickle of blood that was making its way down his face.

But as he, still dazed, tried to make his way through the throng, a man's hand abruptly grasped his shoulder. It stopped him dead in his tracks. He dared not breathe or move.

He turned clumsily, leaning on the poker, and looked at the arm of the man. His chest. His face—and as he looked into the man's eyes, Ransom Mackenzie wondered if he was actually in the grip of an illusion...

"Don't say a word, my precious laddie," his father whispered. Hugh Mackenzie was glancing around at the mob; all eyes were still focused on the chained prisoners being led away. "Not till we're both safe at home."

He reached down and put his arm around Ransom's shoulders to help him keep off his ankle.

Ransom stared up. He didn't understand why he had not instantly recognized his father's face. But then it became clear. Hugh's countenance was now gaunt—his eyes seemed dark and sunken in his skull—his skin had an unhealthy, almost gray, tinge to it.

As the trickle of blood from Ransom's scalp started to drip off his chin, his father lifted his other hand to wipe it away. But his hand was wrapped in dirty rags, and at its end was an evil-looking blood stain, where old brown blood mingled with bright red as well. Hugh's smile faded into a grimace, almost imperceptible, for just an instant.

Then he smiled down at his son again, fighting back the tears that were coming now.

Whatever manner of deprivation and fear that Ransom had experienced, he now knew it had been eclipsed by the suffering his father had endured—endured in silence, and almost certainly alone.

That was what he was thinking as they held on to each other and slowly walked to the front door of the printing shop. The high sheriff's notice had been torn down. Hugh swung open the door, and they both walked in.

Chapter 14

"What did they do to you?"

Ransom was studying the grim injuries to the fingers of his father's hand. Stretched out with his leg propped straight ahead of him, he was watching Hugh Mackenzie unwrap and then clean the wounds.

"Finger screws," Hugh replied matter-of-factly.

Ransom looked confused.

"A finger screw is two plates squeezed together—tightened by a screw," his father explained. He gestured over to the printing press.

"Like our press. When the screw is tightened, the plate presses down...but instead of the paper...they wanted my fingers instead."

He was wincing as he applied salt water to the broken flesh around his swollen knuckles. His hand was almost twice the size of his other hand, and was a putrid black and reddish color.

"What did you tell them?" Ransom asked.

"The truth..."

"But...what?"

"That I knew nothing about the murder of Cardinal Beaton. That I was no conspirator. But that I believe that those who burn the followers of Jesus at the stake are criminals and deniers of Christ."

Ransom considered his father's answer.

"Is that why they hurt you? Or did they think you were lying—and didn't believe what you said about not being associated with the men who killed the cardinal?"

"Perhaps." Then he glanced over at the printing press. "Or perhaps it was a warning…"

"A warning about what?"

"That I should be careful about the great power of my printing machine. Not to use it to expose the wickedness of the queen mother. Or the heresy of the Church, which would punish men because they preach the Word of God…in the common language of the people."

"Were you frightened?"

"Yes." Then Hugh smiled and looked at his son. "Were you?"

"Oh, yes. All the time I was in the castle."

"But you see…the Lord in His mercy has watched over both of us."

Ransom looked down at his swollen ankle. Then he glanced over at his father, gingerly applying the rag to the ravaged knuckles of his left hand, dabbing at it ever so slightly.

"I'm sorry they hurt you, Da…"

Hugh stopped and wheeled around, so he could look his son in the eye.

"Do you remember, lad, when I told you how life can bring its crushing force, like the pressure of that printing press, down on us?"

Ransom nodded.

"The hand turning the press might mean it for evil. To crush us to the bone. To make us cry out in pain. But God can make it all for the good. God appoints us to be His paper in the press. That way…well… you might say that on our bodies is writ the message of the Almighty."

There was something in what Hugh said that triggered a memory in Ransom.

"Master Knox said something…"

"What did he say?"

Ransom brought to mind the precise words Knox had used in his lesson—there in the cavernous great hall of the castle. And how his voice, filled with an electric passion as he spoke about the sovereignty of God, had echoed off the stone walls. How it had seemed to reach all the way up to the heavy wooden crossbeams far above.

"Though we may rough-hew the touch of the master...His design will always prevail in the end."

Hugh smiled.

"Now you know why I wanted you to be taught by a man like Master Knox." But he also added silently, *though I did not know he was about to traipse his bairns into a battlefront...*

"What will happen now?"

His son's question brought Hugh back from his thoughts.

"They will come back for me. Have no doubt about that...And they will come for you as well..."

Ransom's eyes widened. He pressed his lips together.

"Which is why," Hugh continued, "we must leave this place."

"Where will we go?"

"I shall take my press. My equipment. My parchment and paper and ink, and all my tools. And I shall go to Edinburgh to see if I can establish a printing trade there."

"Right near the royal castle?"

"Yes—but that is also where I may find work for my trade. There is much business for printers there. I will change my name. Keep far away from the queen mother's palace at Holyroodhouse. I will keep myself safe...and when I know that it is safe for you as well, then I shall send for you."

"Send for me? Where will I be?"

Hugh gave a sigh. He stood up, and with his healthy hand he patted his son on the shoulder.

"I'm sending you away from here. This is no place for either of us now. I shall have you live with my cousin Hamish Chisholm."

"Where does he live?"

"Far..." Hugh said reluctantly.

"How far, Da?"

"All the way to the west—the Highlands."

Hugh could see his son's countenance had fallen.

"But Hamish is a good man. And his wife is a kind woman. A little like your own mum was…He has a daughter about your age. Can't remember her name. You will learn the life of the Highlanders. A rougher life than here in St. Andrews. But a life that is hearty, full of honest hard work, and the sights and smells of God's green earth—things you will ne'er forget, I wager. I just pray God it will all be for the best…"

At dinner Ransom was so dejected that he could hardly eat. His trip would begin in a week. He would travel with a trusted friend of Hugh's by the name of Finlay Ogilvie, a traveling tradesman and a tinker, and a sympathizer to the reformist cause.

In the next few days Ransom tried to walk a little, but his ankle was still stiff and painful. Hugh had him soak it every day with hot water and herbs.

As the day for his departure neared, Ransom wondered about trying to communicate with Philip—to say goodbye in whatever way he could. The two boys were now, it seemed, irretrievably fixed on the opposite ends of a great struggle. Since the battle at the castle, Scotland had been dividing into two camps. Philip's family was directly aligned with the Catholic powers that ruled from Holyroodhouse in Edinburgh, from the palaces in France…and of course, from the Vatican in Rome.

Hugh Mackenzie, associate of the notorious John Knox, and whose son had himself become a kind of rebel Castilian, was now considered throughout St. Andrews to be an unofficial member of the reformist plot.

So, it was not surprising when Hugh told his son he was to have no contact with Philip. Ransom was prepared to obey the order, though he was greatly distressed by the thought of never seeing his best friend again.

But then something happened. In Ransom's clever mind—as his father would say, "a mind like a budding lawyer's at court"—it would provide the loophole he was looking for.

Hugh had been gone most of the day, meeting secretly with some of his friends about his strategy for the relocation to Edinburgh and his plans for his son.

Ransom was home alone, moping about and wondering what would ever become of him, and trying to walk a little more on his sore ankle. He had heard a few things about the Highlands from some of his friends. It was a wild and empty place with few towns and almost no books to read. People lived like animals, with vulgar ways of speaking—and they rarely had anything worth saying anyway. They even lived in houses made of dirt. To Ransom's mind, his father was consigning him to the very remotest and most forsaken edge of the earth.

Hobbling about in the shop, he heard something at the door. Someone had passed a note under it—one made of fine linen paper, pale yellow in color. His name was written on the outside in red ink with a fine hand and an elaborate flourish.

He swung open the door and looked in both directions but saw no one nearby. And yet he sensed someone close nevertheless. Like a heart that beats, a breath taken—familiar rhythms, like those of a twin brother.

"Philip…is that you?" Ransom said in a hoarse whisper.

Around the corner of the shop, just out of view, he heard feet shuffle. "Philip?"

Down the street there were the *clip-clops* of a horse drawing a cart. And the bells tolling from the steeple of Holy Trinity Church. And finally, a voice.

"It's me…"

Then Philip peeked around the corner of the building.

"So…ye're alive after all," he said with a smirk.

"Aye," Ransom replied with a big grin. "Just hurt my ankle."

"Is that all?" Philip said, mocking. Looking around in all directions, he scooted into the shop and closed the door behind him.

"Where's yer da?"

"Gone for a while. Did you put this under the door?"

Philip nodded. Have you read it yet?"

Ransom shook his head. Philip laughed.

"What's the matter—are ye afraid it'll bite you?"

"I'll read it when I'm good and ready…"

"Ach—like the very instant I leave you alone, you mean…"

"Naw. I'm just glad to see you. I can read this letter some other time."

"Did you smell the paper? It has the scent of flowers and perfume and such all over it," Philip said with a guffaw.

Ransom's face was now pink and flushed. He wanted to change the subject.

"It's good to see you."

Philip didn't respond. He shuffled his feet a little and glanced at the door.

"I can't stay. Maybe I shouldn't have come. My da would skin me sure…Ye're a Castilian and a Reformist. And a rebel—ye're with those that hate the likes of my family–and the Holy Church in Rome…

"Don't go yet," Ransom said abruptly. "I don't hate anybody. And…I might not see you…"

"What do you mean?"

"I'm going away."

"Where?"

"Can't tell you that."

"Oh. I see it now. You don't trust me. Then maybe we are enemies, after all."

"No. Not true!" Ransom cried out. "We're blood friends, remember? *Against everything else in the world if need be!*"

Philip looked down and shrugged. Then he walked out without looking back.

Ransom hobbled to the front door to watch his friend as he walked away. But when he was a ways down the street, he stopped and shouted something:

"Friends...even against the cannons of the French fleet!"

Thought Philip did not turn back, Ransom could see him wipe his eyes. Then Philip broke into a run toward his home.

Ransom slowly closed the door, overcome with despair. Something had died, he was sure of it. But he could not locate exactly what it was, or where.

He took the note over to the table, eased himself down on a chair, and carefully broke the wax seal.

In a girlish and delicate hand, it read,

Dearest Ransom,

> *How very frightened I was at the news you were taken into the castle with those terrible rebels! Were you frightened? I would have been so upset by all of the cannons firing. You are brave, Ransom.*

> *I do not regret what has passed between us, Ransom. I dare not write anything else on that account. Except that my heart is not my own any longer. We shall talk soon.*

> *May you be kept in safety until we speak.*

> > *Catherine*

Ransom read and reread the letter, pausing to imbibe some of the hidden meaning. And to put the paper to his nose to smell the lilac perfume.

He read it again, stopping at certain points to analyze it further.

She writes my name thrice! he thought to himself, allowing himself a smile. *And she calls me "dearest"!*

But the phrase he returned a dozen times was, *"Except that my heart is not my own any longer. We shall talk soon…"* There was simply no denying her deep feelings for him. It filled him with a grand and almost silly exuberance.

He was unsure how long he lingered over the letter and memorized its phrases. But something dawned on him. Once again, he was plunged back into unspeakable and inconsolable sorrow.

How could he speak to Catherine about her longings…about her deep feelings for him? About his unrequited yearning for her? He was going to leave the next day, at the break of dawn, on his long journey. How would they talk?

Ransom resolved to leave the shop and walk the four long blocks to her home—and even display himself to Philip's family and father if need be. He was willing to risk that. He had to see her—speak to her before he left for that forsaken and terrible place called the Highlands.

At the very instant of his resolve, he heard the heavy footsteps of his father and the bang of the front door.

"Ye're on yer feet, I see…walking a bit better, aye?" Hugh said.

"Aye," Ransom answered quietly, turning to make sure his father did not see the letter he was slipping under his vest. Nor see his eyes, now beginning to flood over with the unrestrained emotions of youth.

It seemed certain to him now—deadly and absolutely certain—that there would be no last words of affection…no consolation of the heart… from Catherine Fawlsley, before his journey to the end of the world. An overpowering tide of loneliness swept over him as he hobbled up the narrow stairs to the rooms above.

Chapter 15

The next morning, Ransom was roused from his bed before dawn. By the time he had dressed and gathered his things for the trip, the gray light was just starting to break over St. Andrews.

He packed two bags. One, a large blanket, which he tied at the top with a leather strap, held his clothes. In the other, a smaller burlap sack, he packed the books he had mastered under the tutelage of John Knox.

Hugh stoked the fire and fixed one of his son's favorite breakfasts—mealie pudding, made of sausage, suet, and oatmeal, with just the right amount of onions and herbs. Ransom ate most of it silently as he contemplated being separated not only from his father again, but also from all of the familiar sights he had taken for granted in his hometown.

He thought about the harbor, with the excitement of new ships arriving and unloading their wares from around the world. And the festival held at the market square each spring, which drew merchants and travelers all the way from the continent. And St. Salvators College and the university. The school buildings damaged during the long siege against the castle were being repaired. Soon students would return to their studies there. But his hopes of entering the university seemed to be forever dashed. Instead, he thought, he would be living among savages in dirt huts.

But as his father helped get him ready, Ransom was thinking of Philip...and even more of Catherine. Her note was tucked inside his shirt. He would not let it be any farther away from him than that.

Hugh gave Ransom his favorite walking stick, made of hickory and carved in the shape of a lion's head at the end. He explained that the stick had been a present from his wife in the first year of their marriage.

"A right fine stick...your mother paid for it out of her earnings from stitching and sewing," he said wistfully. "And the lion's head was special to her, she said...because of the Scripture that calls Jesus the 'Lion of Judah'..." Hugh's voice wavered. How astonished he was that after all of the years without her, the wounds to his heart from her absence could still seem so present and so real.

"I wish she could have been here to raise you up," Hugh said, his voice trembling. "She would have been so proud...so very proud..."

He stopped talking and hugged his son. They heard a knock on the door. They knew it was time. Hugh gathered himself for the task. He shook hands with Ransom and patted him firmly on the shoulder. Then he gave him a final benediction.

"Let the Lord God be your guide in all that you do and say, and may He bless you and keep you, lad—until we meet up again..."

As Ransom limped to the waiting cart and slung his sacks onto the front bench, he felt all hollowed out and empty inside, like a fish that had been sliced up for dinner. The horse clopped one of its hooves down on the dirt and shook the reins lightly with a toss of its mane.

"I will send word for you and fetch you as soon as I can," Hugh said to his son.

On the cart bench holding the reins was Finlay Ogilvie, a bony man with one bad eye, a few missing teeth, and a floppy hat. His waistcoat had been the victim of several tears, which had been repaired carefully but with no eye for color of threads and patches. As Hugh and Ransom said their tearful goodbyes, Ogilvie maintained a constant, almost irritating grin.

His smile was an offense to Ransom. He wondered how this strange man could be so oblivious to the sad parting taking place right in front of him. So he kept entirely silent for the first few hours of the cart ride, as they left the outskirts of St. Andrews behind and took the road north.

As the cart made its way on the road the pots, pans, kitchen utensils, and small farming implements hanging from its outside gave off a symphony of clangs and gongs as the metal wares swung freely against the side of the large wagon in back. Despite Ransom's silence and the drudgery of the trip, Ogilvie still maintained his smile. Ransom had quietly promised himself he would say nothing to this strange man until spoken to. However, after several hours of hearing only the heavy hooves of the horse on the dirt road and a few whinnies and nickers, and listening to the clanging of the metal wares, he finally relented.

"Sir, can you tell me where we are going?" he asked without looking at him.

"Aye lad, I *can*..."

Ransom waited for an answer. But none came.

After a few moments he asked again, "Can you tell me where you are going?"

Ogilvie smiled. "Aye. That I *can*..."

After another full measure of silence, observing Ransom's look of total confusion, Ogilvie continued.

"You were a student of Master John Knox, were you not?"

"I was, sir."

"Then you should know the difference between what a man *can* do—and what a man *will* do." Ogilvie's smile revealed even more missing teeth than Ransom had surmised. "It is the difference between dreamin' and doin'—between sayin' so, and makin' it so..."

Ransom had to reluctantly admit that this strange traveling merchant had a point.

"Yes, sir. I see," Ransom said. "So I would ask you...*will* you, if you please, sir, tell me where we are going?"

"Never thought you'd ask!" Ogilvie exclaimed. "We are heading north to the lands of County Angus."

"Is that the road to the Highlands?"

"One of them," the cart driver explained. "It's a longer route—but it's a safer one. The other is due west, past the castles of Loch Leven…not a good way to go for you, lad. There are those in that region who would die for Marie de Guise—those who wait for her young daughter, Mary, to take the throne as queen of the Scots. They don't like us reformist folks, so we travel north to Glamis—and then west to the Highlands…"

"Glamis?"

"Yes. Glamis Castle. You've not heard of it?"

Ransom shook his head.

Ogilvie raised his eyebrows. But his smile seemed to hide something mysterious.

After a while Ransom could not help but inquire further about Glamis Castle.

"Is there something special about the place where we are going?"

"Special?" Ogilvie paused and stopped smiling. He glanced over and simply said, "Aye…in a manner of speaking…"

"I would like very much to hear of it."

"Well," Ogilvie began with the air of a man who loved to tell a good story and knew that his audience was bound to listen to him, "the first thing you must know is that the owners of that grand and opulent palace…they are the owners—yet are presently not—yet soon shall be, I have heard…"

Ransom could not understand the cryptic statement, and his face expressed it.

"Which is a manner of speaking," his companion went on, "that is to say…that the owner of Glamis castle was Janet Douglas, Lady Glamis, late widow of the Earl of Glamis. But the good Lady Glamis is no longer owner—nor could she be—as she is now residing in her eternal destination…"

"She's dead?" Ransom asked bluntly.

"Yes, sadly so. I knew her. Exceedingly fair of face she was…I did business with her family on many occasions. She particularly liked what I call my 'specialities'…pearl buttons and needlecraft tools from the Continent. Those are the items I keep locked up in my caravan there." He gave a nod to the wagon in the rear. "And I keep them in a well-hidden place at that…"

"What happened to her?"

Ogilvie let his smile fade a bit and seemed genuinely sad as he recounted it.

"Marie de Guise was the wife of James V, who was still alive back then and ruled all of Scotland. Some say that out of the darkness of her heart she put her husband up to it…though I believe he was every bit able to concoct such a cruel plot himself."

Ransom was now transfixed by the story told by his quirky traveling partner.

"Glamis has always been a beauty of a place. So the king has Janet Douglas arrested. 'Twas…nigh on eight years ago now that it happened. He has her seized and charged as a witch. I know well she was no witch, but it was a convenient ploy to call her so—and when the king calls it black, you dare not say white…so…they lead her to the stake and burn her alive. Then the king and his darkhearted queen take the Glamis castle for spoils and enjoy it for their own."

The burning of George Wishart had suddenly leapt into Ransom's memory. He had not thought of it now for many months.

"I once saw a burning…"

Ogilvie gave him a solemn look.

"Was it one of God's own elect, laddie?"

"Aye. It was George Wishart—"

"Oh my eternal soul," Ogilvie exclaimed, "the mighty preacher of Jesus' gospel himself!" He halted the horse and removed one of the floorboards where his feet had been resting. He pointed into the space. Ransom peered down and saw a compartment with a large Bible.

"Coverdale Bible." Ogilvie grinned. "I'm reading Isaiah…writ in the common English tongue!"

Ransom smiled a little as he recognized it as the very kind of Bible regularly read by John Knox and used by him in his preaching.

Ogilvie carefully set the floorboard in its place, snapped the reins, and as the cart jerked forward he continued his narrative.

"Well, the king had little chance to enjoy his new possession. He died a year or two later, and not long after that it comes out that poor Lady Glamis was no witch at all. And so the powers in Edinburgh decide to remove the stain of her name—they hold a grand type of proceeding with pomp and formality and such and declare her innocent…too bad it was eight years late! Well, soon, I hear, will come the official granting of the castle back to the kin of the late Janet Douglas…"

Ransom was considering the story.

"Who, sir, is in charge of Glamis Castle now?"

"That," Ogilvie said, with a sort of grimace, "is the second thing you must know, Master Ransom. The custodian of the castle for the time being is David de Blois Douglas. He is distant kin to Lady Glamis… chosen by the queen mother because of his connections to France. She presumed him an ally to her reign—but she is mistaken on that, by a long sight! In truth he hates Marie de Guise and her henchmen. So that is why your father and I believe you will be safe there for the night. And then tomorrow we will leave for the northern route to the Highlands."

"So, then he is a follower of Jesus and a reformist?"

"Not exactly," Ogilvie said, letting his voice trail off.

But Ransom's attention was no longer on the cart driver. Up ahead in the distance, he saw a great castle rising up on the plateau. It had a cone-topped tower at one end and several chimneys rising up from its five-story-high roofline. Massive in size, it had one long, stately road that led up to it. On the grounds, he could see numbers of servants and groundskeepers busy at work.

Ogilvie did not speak again until the cart was about to enter the road to the entrance of the castle. He pulled the reins back, and as the cart stopped, he turned to Ransom and eyed him intently.

"Sir David de Blois Douglas will protect your body from harm here," he said mysteriously. "But ye must beware…do *not* engage Sir David in any conversation on matters religious or matters metaphysical—you must *not* do so—d'ye understand?"

Ransom was taken aback by Ogilvie's severe countenance and the foreboding tone of his voice.

"Aye. I understand."

"Jesus says not to fear those who can kill the body only…" He turned to gaze down the long promenade, lined with trees and hedges, "but to fear those that can kill the soul."

Those words, spoken with unexpected authority by the tinker in the floppy hat, were still echoing in Ransom's mind as the cart slowly rumbled down the long road to the castle. As they neared it, the only sounds were from the cart's wooden wheels, the horse's hooves, and the pots and pans that were still clanking noisily.

Chapter 16

When Ransom and Finlay Ogilvie presented themselves at the great oak door of Glamis Castle they were greeted by a manservant. Ogilvie, as a common tradesman, would spend the night in the relative discomfort of his wagon. Ransom was slightly surprised that the tinker would not come under the roof, at least that of the servants' quarters. But he supposed that by staying with the wagon Ogilvie could keep a better lookout over his valuable "specialities."

The servant led Ransom inside. He said that master of the castle, David de Blois Douglas, was aware of his arrival, and that his room had been made ready. Ransom, carrying his bags, was led up a long, winding stone staircase to the second floor, then up another equally serpentine stairway, which grew increasingly narrow.

At the top, the servant led him through a wide room with a grand fireplace at each end and huge tapestries hanging down each of the high stone walls. Ransom could not help but slow down and stare as he gazed at them. They were exceedingly peculiar…the designs all seemed to be of a celestial nature.

Some had embroideries of the sun and moon. Others had what Ransom surmised were constellations with Latin and French words underneath.

"Come along, don't be dawdling, young sir," the servant said, chiding Ransom.

"Please—why do all the tapestries show the heavenlies?" Ransom asked.

But the servant only grunted at first as he showed Ransom to a bedchamber just off the main hall.

"What do you know of Sir David, the custodian of this place?"

"Only a few things—"

"No matter," the servant said, interrupting him. "You'll be learning of Sir David soon enough, I'll wager."

The servant pulled the heavy purple drapes closed over the high windows and lit the candles in the wall sconces.

"Prepare yourself for dinner," he barked abruptly. "The lady of the house, Mistress Jean Douglas, wife of Master David Douglas, will be dining with you in the banquet hall on the second floor." He turned to leave.

Ransom poured water from the pitcher into the bowl and washed his face and hands. It felt good to rinse the dust of his trip off. He fished into the sack of clothes until he found a white shirt with a starched ruff. He judged it to be sufficiently formal for a dinner with the gentry of the castle.

But Ransom was surprised when, on arriving at the long dining hall, he found the long wooden table set with only two plates. One plate was at the very end, closest to the mammoth fireplace, whose opening was taller than he was—and the other, for Ransom, was midway along the table's length. There was a blazing fire already set. And the huge logs burning within the maw of the fireplace were snapping and popping violently.

Ransom stared into the flames that were shimmering and licking up the flue. He was tired, and the warmth felt good. But he could not shake an uncomfortable feeling. Perhaps it was the sobering warning Finlay Ogilvie had given him as they arrived at the castle. Or maybe the strange tapestries. Or the brusque treatment by the servant. Whatever it was, even though Ransom was only one day's journey from St. Andrews, he already felt very far from everything familiar, and trusted, and safe.

"Laddie—come here."

It was the shrill voice of a woman. Ransom turned. Mistress Jean Douglas was standing before her plate at the end of the table, her arms crossed in front of her. She had black hair pulled back tightly in a bun and wore a black satin dress. There was a prominent mole on her cheek.

Ransom stepped over to his place at the table and bowed quickly.

"Sit down." Then she called out sharply for the servants to bring the food. There was roasted breast of pheasant, pea soup, several types of bread, and boiled potatoes. Ransom feasted, as he had eaten almost nothing on the journey, except stale bread and a piece of cheese with mold on one end. It would have been one of the best meals of his life, had it not been for the dismal company of Mistress Douglas.

After Ransom bowed his head over his meal, she inquired, "Saying your prayers, boy?"

Ransom said he was. With intruding rudeness she asked, "What did ye pray for, boy?"

He replied that he prayed for safe travel, for protection for his father—and of course he thanked his heavenly Father for the provisions of the meal he was about to eat.

"Did you bother to thank Him for those that are custodians of the castle, whose fields produced the food and whose servants are paid well to prepare it…did you, boy?"

With some embarrassment he shook his head no, but he offered her a word of thanks for "your kind hospitality."

Mistress Douglas seemed moderately satisfied with that. After several minutes of silence Ransom asked innocently, "Will Master David de Blois Douglas be joining us?"

But his question was met with a scowl from the woman in black.

"Of course not!" she snapped. "Mister Douglas is at work on his star maps—engaged in his library. Important work it is—not to be disturbed…"

Then she asked, "Don't you know of his work on the heavenly bodies and the celestial predictions of the ages to come?"

Ransom shook his head.

She began a long and detailed recital of David de Blois Douglas's background. He had been born and raised in Paris, where his father, David Douglas I, a transplanted Scotsman, was studying and writing on the peculiarities of natural phenomena. "His father wrote on the oddities of the natural and supernatural order—of such things as proven instances where the skies would rain great numbers of frogs and a variety of fishes. And other mysteries—such as the discovery of an entire three-masted ship, complete with the corpses of the entire crew, at the bottom of a mountain mine shaft."

Then she turned to Ransom. "Do ye find interest in unexplained phenomena and mysteries and the like?"

Something in Ransom wished he could deny it. But he did have a certain curiosity for such things. Mistress Douglas must have detected that in his expression, because something resembling a smile crept over her lips. She continued, now speaking even more rapidly.

As David de Blois Douglas grew older, she said, he wished to continue his father's discoveries into the unexplained mysteries of the cosmos. He pursued his studies at the University of Montpellier. That, she explained now in a hushed tone, was where her husband first met a person she called "The Master." Ransom was listening carefully, and after more of her rambling narrative he finally determined that this "Master" was a fellow by the name of Michel Nostradamus.

"It was in my husband's acquaintance with Master Nostradamus that he learned the art of astrology and the meaning behind the heavenly constellations…and their power in helping us to see into the future," she said.

She stopped. And she saw that she had Ransom's rapt attention.

"What room did the servant lead ye to for your bedchambers?"

Ransom told her.

After a pregnant pause she said, "Do ye believe in specters and spirits?"

"I dunno, Madam," he replied. "Why do you ask that, if I may ask you?"

"Nothing, perhaps. Just a trifling thing…"

After dipping her bread in the last remaining gravy on her plate and popping it into her mouth, she continued.

"It's just that…five hundred years ago…*this very night, I might add*…Macbeth of Glamis Castle, kin to the Douglases of this place, personally delivered a bloody death to King Duncan. Some say it was at the town of Elgin nearby…but others hold that the place of slaying was *here in this very castle.*"

She licked a couple of fingers and then made her final point.

"So, boy—some of our guests have complained that there are odd goings-on in the middle of the night—unexplained noises, apparitions— and it has been speculated that the specter of King Duncan is roaming the premises, looking for vengeance for his ruthless murder—"

Her sinister story was interrupted by a servant entering the hall. He bent down and whispered something in her ear. The woman's face showed utter surprise.

"He does? Master Douglas wants him? Are you sure?"

The servant nodded earnestly.

"Very well." With a wave of her hand she dismissed the messenger and turned to Ransom. She had the look of someone about to communicate a solemn pronouncement…the kind that royalty announces, sitting in high-backed, velvet-upholstered thrones, with attendants standing round.

"Master Ransom." He noticed that, for whatever reason, she had now ceased to call him "boy."

"You are to be the beneficiary of a great honor," she said, with her hands folded together in an image of officialdom.

"Master David de Blois Douglas wishes to see you—see you *personally*."

Then she rose. "You will follow me."

She quickly led the way from the dining hall up the stairways to the second floor, up two more twisting staircases, higher and higher. Ransom guessed that, when they finally arrived, it must be at the very top of the castle.

At the top of the stairs there was a dark wooden door with a large, black iron knocker. She knocked twice. A muffled voice on the other side said something. Mistress Douglas told Ransom to "stay there," and then she opened the door, entered, and quickly closed it behind her.

He could hear a few words exchanged. Then the door quickly opened, and Jean Douglas stepped past Ransom, barely able to squeeze past in the narrow confines of the winding staircase.

"You may enter. He will see you."

She gave him a brief glance, as if to underscore how undeserving he was of an audience with a great man like David de Blois Douglas.

Chapter 17

Ransom closed the heavy door behind him. The room was long and had high, vaulted windows—above the windows were high crossbeams. The walls were lined from top to bottom with shelves of books. A few chairs were placed between the stacks, and there were four round tables placed throughout the room. On each was a scattering of books and papers and what appeared to Ransom to be maps.

Standing in the middle of the room was a man of medium height, dressed in a shirt opened at the neck with sleeves pulled up to elbows, and the puffy silk pantaloons of the French style. Unlike the men of St. Andrews, who customarily wore their beards long and their hair closely trimmed, this man did just the opposite. His long tangle of reddish-blond hair flowed down to his shoulders, but his beard was short and well-trimmed.

"Come closer," he said calmly.

Ransom stepped up to the man. He saw he had the lightest color of blue eyes, almost transparent, very ethereal in effect.

"Did you have an ample dinner?"

"Yes, sir, thank you."

"Did you dine with Mistress Douglas?"

"I did, sir."

"And did you find her…agreeable? Pleasant to dine with?"

After a moment's pause, Ransom answered as courteously as he could, "Yes, thank you. Very pleasant."

"Well, then," the man said, "that would make you either a liar or a fool."

But after a moment's reflection the man added something else.

"Or perhaps it would simply make you a better man than I."

Ransom was stunned and unable to respond. But the man saved him from the silence by continuing.

"I, myself, find her company quite unpleasant."

Again, Ransom was dumbfounded, but the man pointed to the round table next to him.

"You are standing next to Cancer," he said.

"Pardon, sir?"

"The constellation of Cancer…that table contains my star maps and observations regarding Cancer. Appropriate for you…because Scotland is governed by the zodiacal sign of Cancer. Did you know that, lad?"

"No, sir."

"And this table," the man said, pointing to one of the other round tables, "this is for my work on Aries, which rules the fate of England."

Then he pointed to yet another table. "And this is my work on Taurus, the zodiacal sign for the affairs of Ireland. And that last table, over there, is for Capricorn—the sign in the heavenly regions for Wales. This is my work. This is what I do. What do you do, lad?"

"I am…I was a student…"

"Yes, I heard. A student of the notorious John Knox, according to that fool of a tinker Finlay Ogilvie."

Then the man walked up closer to Ransom, and looked him directly in the face, his pale blue eyes seeming to look right through him.

"Do not fear me, lad. I will not harm you. I despise those in Edinburgh…Marie de Guise and her minions…the popish followers who seek to harm your father, and Knox, and those other reformist rabble-rousers. So you are safe here. And your travel here shall remain our little secret…Do you like secrets, lad?"

"I...well...I suppose so..."

"Good. Then we have something in common, you and I. For I have devoted myself to unwrapping the secrets of the stars, and how they portend for the future. Did that teacher of yours—Mister Knox—did he bother to teach you of the heavenly bodies, the stars, the moon, and such?"

"I...I don't think so..."

"You have learned *nothing* of the moon and the sun and the stars? *Nothing?*"

"Well, sir—" Ransom stammered.

"Yes?"

"I did learn something..."

"Then tell me. Teach me," the man said with a sardonic laugh.

Ransom concentrated, trying to remember a scripture passage from his months of instruction with John Knox. In the Psalms. He thought it was Psalm 136, but he was not sure. Suddenly he was sorry he had not taken his studies in the Scriptures more seriously. How could he have known he would be tested in such a strange and unexpected way?

Then he recalled it and began reciting:

> *O thank the* LORD *of all lords,*
> *for his mercy endureth for ever.*
> *Which only doth great wonders,*
> *for his mercy endureth for ever.*
> *Which by his wisdom made the heavens,*
> *for his mercy endureth for ever.*
> *Which laid out the earth above the waters,*
> *for his mercy endureth for ever.*
> *Which hath made great lights,*
> *for his mercy endureth for ever.*
> *The Sun to rule the day,*
> *for his mercy endureth for ever.*

The Moon and the stars to govern the night,
for his mercy endureth for ever.

Douglas snorted. "And so—the point of that religious recital is… what?"

But before Ransom could answer, the man continued.

"The point is obviously—and this is why Knox and his bunch likely instructed you of it—the point is that they are still mired down in the medieval cosmology. They say they oppose the Catholic heresies—and so do I, but for a different reason. They want to replace the old religious dogmas with their own equally ignorant dogmas. Mind you—I want the Pope's rule over Scotland to end just as they do, but for a different cause. I want to open Scotland to the instructions of the new metaphysics—the esoteric mysteries—the hidden powers of the zodiac."

By now Ransom was lost in the ramblings. Douglas smiled and continued.

"So—do you not agree that I have pierced the real meaning behind those verses from the psalmist?"

"Well, sir—"

"Yes? Then, pray tell, what did John Knox teach you about that scripture? Tell me…"

"Well, sir," Ransom answered meekly, "that the true meaning of the verses is that 'his mercy endureth for ever'…that is why—or so he taught us—why it is so oft repeated in the verses."

"*His* mercy?"

"Yes, sir."

"*God's* mercy?"

"Yes, sir."

"But God created the stars and moon and everything in the sky. Did He not?"

"He did, sir."

"And for a purpose, no doubt?"

"Well…I suppose so, sir."

"And God's purpose must have been, then, to reveal something great in such a great design?"

"Yes, it would seem so…"

"And does it please God, from time to time, to reveal to mortals what will happen in the future? Did not the prophets of old predict the future?"

"Oh, yes," Ransom replied brightly. "They did."

"So it must be good for God to tell us the future?"

Ransom thought on that.

"Yes. I think so…"

"Then if God created the stars in the heavens, and God wants us to know the future, then we must conclude that God reveals the future in the skies. Is that not so?"

Ransom was now totally enthralled by Douglas's sophistry. He glanced down at the star map of the constellation of Cancer on the table next to him.

What if, he thought to himself, *my future could be found in the strange configuration of lines and points on that map? What would it be like to know when I will see my father again…or whether Philip and I will be friends again? Or whether Catherine will keep liking me?*

As Ransom was thinking on the wonderful mysteries that might be contained in the maps and charts, he suddenly recalled Finlay Ogilvie's warnings: "Do not engage Sir David in any conversation on matters religious or matters metaphysical…"

He wondered why Ogilvie had been so adamant. Ransom's father, and his tutor, John Knox, had often warned him of the dangers of false ideas and the vain speculations of men. But how could Douglas's argument, which seemed so logical and which spoke highly of God, be in any way dangerous?

Douglas was studying his young visitor.

"Perhaps these matters interest you," he added. "If you wish—perhaps you would like to stay a few more days. I need a young helper. We have great stores of food and drink. You could be quite comfortable."

Ransom thought back to his opulent meal. He did not know where he and Ogilvie would be eating next, but he was sure it would be no match for the meal he had enjoyed at Glamis Castle. On the other hand, Mistress Douglas made his blood run cold. And he had to admit that his conversation with Mister Douglas was giving him an increasingly uneasy feeling.

That was when Ransom's mind fixed on something Finlay Ogilvie had said on their journey. He had been reading aloud from his Bible, from the twenty-eighth chapter of 1 Samuel, regarding Saul's consort with the witch of Endor. The tinker had turned solemnly to Ransom and said, "Always flee from supernatural divination, young Ransom!" Now Ransom's mind was made up.

"You are so kind," Ransom said, "but we must leave for our travels tomorrow."

His host's countenance quickly changed. He turned to one of the tables and shouted over his shoulder, "You can find your way back to your room, I am sure…"

Ransom turned and headed for the door. By the time he reached it he thought of one question he wanted to ask Douglas, and it burned in his mind. He wanted to know whether he should expect any hauntings by the spirit of the murdered King Duncan in his bedchambers, as Mistress Douglas had suggested.

As he stood at the door with his hand on the black iron handle, he paused.

"Something else?" Douglas called out from his worktable without looking up.

"No…thank you…" Ransom answered reluctantly. "Good night."

He closed the heavy door and began walking slowly down the steep, narrow, winding staircase, wishing he could have asked that last question. But Ogilvie's warning had stopped him.

Now, he thought to himself, he would simply have to find out for himself. His hands were clammy and he found it hard to swallow as he wondered whether the metaphysical realities described by Mistress Jean Douglas might actually manifest themselves in some kind of apparition.

Chapter 18

The night was long for Ransom. He spent the shadowy hours in his bedchambers propped up with pillows, sitting upright, fighting against the urge to sleep. He let the candles burn through the night. And he opened the heavy window drapes wide so that his room would be illuminated at the very earliest chance—when the first light of day broke over the horizon.

But physical exhaustion finally took over. At some point in the late watches of the night Ransom fell into deep slumber in the canopy bed.

And then something woke him with a start.

At first, he couldn't tell what it was. But as he slowly awakened, he realized it was a sound, coming it seemed, from the other side of the door to his bedchambers. The sound someone might make if they were scratching long, dirty fingernails on the door. He had once heard that fingernails continue to grow on a dead man's hands even after he is buried. Perhaps those were the fingernails of the long departed King Duncan. Scratching on the door. Demanding entrance.

Ransom was frozen. On the one hand, he felt he must act...do something. On the other hand, he tried to reassure himself that perhaps it was nothing.

Then he heard the sound again. He snatched the candle that was burning low at his bedside, lifted it high, and slowly climbed down from the bed. He slowly walked toward the door.

The sound was getting louder. What more proof did he need? Surely, he thought, there was something…or *someone*…on the other side of the door.

He was almost to the door. His heart was pounding in his chest, so loudly that he was afraid the…*person*…on the other side of the door would be able to hear it.

The scratching suddenly stopped. Ransom halted, then sensed something down at the floor. With his candle in front of him, he peered down.

There on the floor was a tiny shape. Two little black eyes. A tail. Standing in front of a gap in the stonework of the wall.

The mouse was motionless, but only for a second. Then it scampered into the hole. A few seconds later, Ransom heard the scratching sounds commence as the mouse gathered more sticks and straw for its home.

He groaned out loud to himself, then trudged back to his bed. It was cold now, so he moved his legs back and forth to warm it up under the goose-feather bedding.

He had said his prayers many hours before, but now he thought it good to say them again. He was still praying when his eyes closed and he fell back asleep.

Before Ransom was even aware of the blinding light of morning that had flooded his room, he was awakened by a servant banging on his door and announcing that his presence was demanded by one Finlay Ogilvie…who was waiting out in the courtyard by the main entrance.

Ransom threw some water from the basin on his face, quickly dressed and gathered his belongings, and then hurried down to where Ogilvie was waiting. On the way, he could smell the savor of sausages and pork being cooked—fresh breads, too—wafting from the dining hall. He wished he could stay for just one more meal.

Neither Mistress Douglas nor the enigmatic David de Blois Douglas was there to say their goodbyes, which did not surprise Ransom. As

Glamis Castle disappeared behind them while they rumbled along in the cart, Ransom was tempted to tell his companion of his conversation with Douglas. But he felt guilty about it and decided against volunteering anything about his intriguing and baffling meeting with the man.

And for the next few days of their journey the matter slipped entirely out of Ransom's mind. Ogilvie knew the route well, and he headed them north by northwest to avoid the pockets of support for Marie de Guise—from Glamis through the high hill country, up to the River Dee. Ransom found the trip almost pleasant. They traveled a path north along the river, which seemed to change characteristics most dramatically. In places it was a wide and tranquil band of water, while elsewhere it narrowed and cut through the forested hills in a ribbon of splashing, surging rapids that spilled over rocks and shallows.

They left the River Dee and connected to a rough road that headed due west, finding a narrow pass through a small mountain range that took them several days to traverse. Ransom innocently concluded that the roughest part of the journey was over.

Finlay Ogilvie simply smiled at the naïve comments, as he usually did at almost everything, but did not tell Ransom that the trip would simply get harder from that point on.

The little cart and its two passengers rumbled on until they entered County Moray and headed into the Grampian Mountains, a high and impressive range that rimmed the eastern side of Loch Ness. There in a small village on the loch, Ogilvie did some trading, as he did at almost every town and outpost he encountered. He enlisted Ransom's help in bartering his goods, as he found that Ransom had both a sharp skill in negotiating and a smooth way with words. And his youthful, innocent appearance was an enticement to the customers. It was a task that Ransom took on but secretly disliked immensely.

After a good deal of selling, Ogilvie stocked up on food and provisions. Then he went to a blacksmith he knew from his travels, had his horse shod, and then paid for the use of a second horse for a few weeks, reluctantly leaving some of his "specialities" as collateral. Ransom asked him why he needed a second horse when the cart had already been lightened of half its goods.

Ogilvie looked at Ransom. Then he put his hand on the boy's head and said, "The climb is higher from this point on…unless you'd rather walk! We head due west into the high mountains of Ardmanoth…and of Affin Shire—these risings you've been climbing with me till now are but foothills!" And then he laughed.

As they headed away from Loch Ness with its narrow, deep waters as dark as night and frigid to the touch, Ogilvie launched into stories he had heard from the locals during his many journeys there. About the great sea creature that dwelt there in the hidden crevices at the bottom. And how Saint Columba, the patron saint of Scotland, had, it was said, actually seen the creature. As had a few of the villagers also—though several of them could not vouch for it, as they had been rather tipsy when they claimed to have seen it.

As Ogilvie spoke of the mysteries of the loch, Ransom once again thought back to his eerie discussion with Mistress Douglas and David de Blois Douglas…and the intriguing star maps Douglas claimed could tell the future.

"Do you think God can give us the power to tell the future?" he asked as the cart started on a particularly steep stretch.

"'Tis a queer question," Ogilvie replied with a chuckle. But after thinking it over, he remarked, "Indeed, the prophets of old were given that special power…but anything beyond that, I cannot say…"

The question continued to needle Ransom as they began the long and arduous journey into the Great Glen and into the lands even farther north. After lumbering up one pass, they spent several days following a narrow path through the mountain range and then down into the valley toward the glens that were their final destination.

The mountains had sides of mossy green that swept up to their tops like giant waves of earth, terminating there, high above, in outcroppings of sheer granite and jagged ridges. They towered around the two travelers, mere insects down in the valley by comparison, and surrounded them, embracing them like a mammoth cradle of rock and moss. The mountain range seemed to close into itself, overlapping, creating deep valleys filled with rushing streams. On either side of their valley path there were black, spongy bogs filled with scruffy vegetation and brilliant flowers. Ogilvie often had the two travelers dismount to give the horses a rest as they traveled along the valley floor.

At one point, Ransom was intrigued by something he saw just off the path. It was an animal skull of some type. By virtue of many months, or perhaps even years of exposure to the elements, it had a white, sunbleached appearance. But Ransom had forgotten the hidden mystery of the terrain, which looked for all the world like solid ground, but once stepped on would give way to soft, water-soaked bogs underneath.

"Help!" Ransom cried out as he felt himself instantly plunged downward. He was soon up to his chest in black, mucky peat and mud, which had a foul odor and was cold, and quickly oozed into his clothes and soaked his legs.

For a moment he actually feared he would disappear altogether.

But Ogilvie quickly came to his rescue, holding out a long pole he had fetched from the cart, and pulled Ransom out of the bog as he laughed out loud.

Later, when they rested for the night, the older man suggested that Ransom leave his clothes on, but dry them by the warmth of the fire. He could then put on clean clothes for the meeting, the next day, with the Chisholm family. That way he could then knock the dried mud off his clothes clean and save himself having to wash them in one of the nearby streams.

Ogilvie found a fine spot for stopping. It was next to a rock plateau, with large pockets of dry, soft moss to bed down on. They watered and fed the horses, and Ogilvie fixed a satisfying stew from salted rabbit meat. In front of the crackling fire, Ransom stretched out, feeling his clothing already starting to dry.

Up in the vast black sky, there was a dizzying panorama of distant points of white, sparkling light. Ransom was gazing up at the stars, some brilliant and twinkling, and some dull and carrying only the faintest trace of color.

Lying on the other side of the fire from Ransom, Ogilvie spoke a little more about the Chisholm family with whom he would be living.

"Now Hamish Chisholm, the father, is a good man—though he may take some gettin' used to. He be the overseer of the lands and cattle in the south belonging to the Laird of the Glen. Rhona, his sweet wife—you'll find her to have a great heart—and then there be their wee bairn, little Margaret. A sprightly one she is, but not so little anymore, I would suppose. She ought to be about your age now—as I recall she takes after both of them, she does—a fine face like her mother, but headstrong like her father. The Lord will keep you safe here. For now…"

Ransom listened politely, but his mind was not on his newfound family. He didn't want a new home, even if it was only temporary. Nor did he want to linger very long in this vast and wild place.

As he looked up into the constellations twinkling in the black void, he wondered how long it would be before he could rejoin his father, and Philip, and Catherine, and the life he had known. He wished he could somehow divine, from the brittle beauty of the faraway stars, something about his future.

He discreetly pulled Catherine's letter from his vest and turned away from the fire so his companion could not see. He was pleased it had not been soaked from the bog incident.

Ogilvie, as he did each night, announced he would lead them in evening prayer. Ransom slipped the envelope back into his shirt and bowed his head.

As the other man prayed, Ransom was aware of the smell of dark, wet wood burning slowly in the fire next to him. Somewhere in the dark an owl was giving out a haunting proclamation.

All he could do now was to throw himself on the gentle mercies of God…and hope that the time of his banishment to this faraway region could in some way be shortened.

Chapter 19

In the bright blue sky of late afternoon, on the side of the mountain along the edge of the valley, the girl was gathering sticks. In the distance she could see the white, stone-sided cottage and the smoke circling up into the sky from its chimney.

She was fifteen years old. Of medium height, she had a sinewy strong frame and a pretty face with bright ruddy cheeks, framed by long black hair that reached the middle of her back. She was wearing the drab brown woolen dress and high leggings of the Highland women.

The sticks had to be gathered together in bundles, tied with reed, and then carried to the small lean-to next to the house, where they would be thoroughly dried. After drying they would be used for kindling. This was her daily task.

Margaret Chisholm had a full bundle now, and she slung it over her shoulder. Hungry, she was interested in seeing what her mother was preparing for the family's dinner. With her load of sticks balanced on one shoulder, she began to run. She was picking her route, dancing and leaping from rock to moss to hard ground along a path that avoided the mire of the bogs.

She was in a bright and exuberant mood that day, and as she ran she began to sing a simple nursery rhyme in Gaelic:

> *Fosgail an doras!*
> *Fosgail an doras!*

Fosgail an doras, trobhad a-steach!
Fosgail an doras!
Fosgail an doras!
Ciamar a tha thus?

By the time she was almost to the stone cottage she noticed her father coming down the valley lane from the opposite direction. He was walking on foot with his staff in his hand, and behind him there was a cart pulled by two horses. Margaret had been told that a boy would be coming from the town of St. Andrews. He would be staying with them in their home in the glen. Margaret could see nothing good in that and loudly protested when it was announced. But her father quickly silenced her. She had stewed on the matter since that day.

And now the dread day had come. The stranger boy was here.

Margaret ran to the lean-to and stacked her bundle of sticks. Then she strode out to the dirt lane.

"My wee, fair lass," Hamish Chisholm called out in a booming voice, "*gradh mo chridhe!* Tell your mum our guests are here—make way for the meal."

Hamish was a tall, wide-shouldered man with dark hair and a curly black beard. He wore a rough brown kilt that wrapped around him and was slung over his shoulder. His knees, visible above his woolen stockings, were a ruddy red.

Margaret paused, eyeing the riders on the cart with suspicion. She saw Ogilvie holding the reins. Then she studied Ransom, sitting next to him.

The cart stopped, and its occupants dismounted. Ransom had not had time to change his clothes and was still wearing the clothing that had been stained a muddy black from the incident the day before.

"Look, Da!" Margaret cried out, "that boy's been dancin' with the bog!"

"Hush now," Hamish cried out. "Fetch your mum, lass—go to it…"

Margaret gave out an exaggerated laugh, and then ran into the cottage.

"Never mind her," Hamish added with a smile. "She takes after her mother."

After dismounting, Ogilive groaned as he stretched. Ransom pulled his two sacks and his father's walking stick from the back of the cart and reluctantly trudged behind Hamish and Ogilvie. He was struck by the small size of the cottage and its remote location in the valley.

How can anyone live in such a place? he asked himself as he entered.

Once inside he was quickly introduced to Rhona Chisholm, a strong-shouldered woman with a wide, pretty face and a cheery smile.

She wiped her hands on her smock, then strode over to Ransom and gave him a hearty hug.

Margaret was standing, stone-faced and with arms folded, in the corner.

The cottage was comprised of three adjoining rooms with no doors separating them. It had few windows. The kitchen had a central hearth for cooking, with a long iron chain hanging from the ceiling with a black iron pot dangling over the fire. There was one window near it, and it was open for ventilation. Next was a small middle section with a bed where Margaret slept, and lastly a bigger room at the end with a small fireplace and a bed for Mr. and Mrs. Chisholm, a small desk, a chest of drawers, and a wooden trunk.

Rhona Chisholm laid out a dinner of broiled red deer venison and flat potato scones. The three adults sat at the rough wooden table and laughed considerably at Ogilvie's tales. It was apparent the three of them knew each other well and that Ogilvie would travel that far to the northwest at least once a year.

After dinner Rhona fetched a bowl of hot water and led Ransom into the farthest room to wash himself. It felt good at least for Ransom to have the shelter of a house—even if it was as humble as this one.

Ransom donned his nightshirt, and Rhona prepared a straw mat with blankets and bedding next to the hearth in the kitchen.

"This will be for your sleepin'," she said with a smile, "close to the hearth—but mind the window," she said, pointing to it, "the animals crawl in sometimes."

Ogilvie had retired to his cart. Before dawn, he would be off for trading in a village a day's journey to the south. Then he would begin the long trip back across the mountains and toward the Angus, Perth, and Fife county areas.

Hamish was reading something at his desk. In her room, Margaret was pretending to sweep the floor, but was studying Ransom and her mother from the corner of her eye.

Rhona knelt next to Ransom's bed on the floor of the kitchen and instructed him to say his prayers, which he dutifully did. When he was done, she bent down and kissed him gently on the cheek and stroked his hair.

There was something in that gesture, perhaps in the tenderness of it, that took Ransom by surprise. And though he wanted to act the man, especially in his first encounter with this unknown family, his eyes began to fill with tears.

"Thank you, mum," he said, his voice quivering.

Margaret was standing now in full view of Ransom and Rhona and muttered something loudly enough to be heard.

"Cryin' like a wee lamb…"

"Ye'll get into bed or feel the switch, lass!" her mother called out.

Margaret jumped into her bed.

Rhona blew out the lamp and went into Margaret's room. The two talked softly together. Then he heard the two of them singing something quietly, but it was in Gaelic and he could not understand the words. Then they laughed and said prayers together.

As the light was doused in Margaret's room, Ransom felt a little bit differently about one important matter.

Perhaps this won't be that bad, he thought to himself. *At least for a while.*

Chapter 20

It could not be denied. Ransom was beginning to feel comfortable and even at home with the Chisholm family. Yet the work was long and hard, and even after many weeks of living in the Highlands he was not used to the rough living.

Hamish Chisholm he found to be a combination of a man both classically learned, yet also possessing the capacity for plain talk and fierce, blunt action. Several times he had Ransom accompany him on some of his shorter travels. And during those trips of a day or two each, Ransom and Hamish and several of his hired men patrolled the fields and lower mountains to the south of the Clashmore Glen. Hamish's job was as the chief cattle drover and captain of the "Glen Watch." His employer, and the owner of the cattle, was Colin MacDonald, a chieftain of the clan Donald, Earl of Clashmore, and Laird of the Glen.

The job of Hamish was to oversee the cattle and keep an eye out for marauding clans, who would quietly sweep into the valley at night under the towering shadow of the jagged Highland hills and then filch large numbers of the Laird's livestock.

"What will you do if you catch them?" Ransom asked Hamish as the small group huddled around the fire on the side of a slope and bedded down for the night.

A few of the men laughed coarsely and uttered some Gaelic comment under their breath—which Ransom could only surmise probably contained crude references to violence.

Hamish stirred the glowing sticks of wood in the fire and unpinned the silver broach that held the shoulder throw of his kilt. As he wrapped the long drape of wool fabric around his legs like a blanket, he answered.

"There is an old Gaelic sayin' among the Highlanders—that even the cold waves of the sea occasionally show mercy…but the rocks will always crush and will never bend, and so they have no mercy at all."

He added, as he lay down next to the fire, "I'd rather be like the waves…but God help me, sometimes I must be like the rocks." He took his long broadsword—with an intricate basket-hilted handle of woven metal and feather light steel blade—and tucked it close to his chest and under his arms, which he folded in front of him for sleep.

Ransom had seen another of Hamish's weapons—an imposing claymore sword which was nearly as long as Ransom was high. It was propped up against the wall in the cottage next to the fireplace in the room of Hamish and Mrs. Chisholm. But when Hamish was traveling fast and "prowlin' for poachers" as he put it, he preferred his broadsword.

Yet there was another side to this man who was his temporary mentor, master, and protector. Ransom soon learned that as a lad, Hamish had been schooled in the Lowlands and spent some time with his father on the continent. He knew Latin quite well, and some Greek. He knew Highland Gaelic of course, and would often speak it to his companions. Ransom found it to be a strange language, full of mysterious, guttural sounds.

As Ransom prepared for sleep he tossed the throw of his own kilt around him. On his second day with the Chisholms, he had been told to "cease wearin' his Fife County fancies" and to adopt the local dress. Rhona Chisholm had prepared a smaller kilt for him to wear. But when he tried to pin it himself, it nearly fell down past his knees.

Margaret, who was standing by, roared with laughter. In the first few days Ransom had come to the conclusion that her chief delight was to make him the brunt of her constant joking. She certainly was nothing like the young women of St. Andrews. They were cultured, delicate, and knew their place. But there in the Highlands, if Margaret was any example, the girls were rough and forward and spoke their mind in ways he found to be bewildering.

Yet he also had to admit, particularly after the passage of time, that his opinion of Margaret had slowly changed. He still found her rough lack of manners disconcerting. But on the other hand, he was beginning to find her to be a useful friend, if for no other reason than to stave off the loneliness of the glen. And occasionally he even found her to be a source of a great deal of fun.

One day they had been assigned a job by Rhona while Hamish was away for several days. They were to take the small two-wheeled cart and go over to the mountainside where there was a large stone and rock outcropping. They were to collect a cart full of rocks of a certain size and bring them back. Hamish could then use them to repair a portion of the outer wall of the cottage.

Not content to simply help Ransom, Margaret dared him to a feat of courage.

"I'd say ye're not man enough to take a dare from a girl—what say ye to that, townie boy?"

She flipped her long black hair back dramatically as she gave her challenge.

"I see nothing around here that scares me," Ransom shot back, and added a little manly laugh to cap it off.

"No?"

"No, indeed not!" he shouted back.

"The mountainside, then—are ye not scared of it?"

"Why should I be?" Ransom said, glancing down the long, steep path they had taken up from the floor of the valley.

"Well…" Margaret said with a coquettish smile as she walked to the cart and leaned up against it, "if you were to climb into this cart…"

"And why would I do that?"

But Margaret continued, struggling not to smile too broadly.

"If you were to climb in—and then I'd give ye a strong push down the mountain path we came up—would ye not be scared then, laddie?"

Ransom looked down the sloping side of the mountain pass. Then he looked at the cart. And lastly he glanced at Margaret.

Suddenly, though he did not know why, he saw in her face a look that was not boyish or rough at all. In her dark eyes, and in her graceful, ruddy face that was more womanly than her manners would let on, he saw something else…if for only an instant. She was smiling and giggling, making a grand gesture toward the cart.

So he climbed in. He pulled himself down low, thinking this might better protect him.

"Hold on!" Margaret called, and with a grunt she pushed the cart toward the well-worn path that led down the mountain.

"Don't jump! Hold tight!" she cried as she ran after him. The cart began to slowly rumble down the steep path.

Ransom poked his head out of the cart and waved victoriously back to Margaret, who was unable now to keep up. For a moment he felt a sense of courage and thrill, with the damp cool air of the Highlands rushing at his face, seeing the granite tops of the mountains all around him as he cascaded down. Soon the cart was traveling at a terrifying rate and beginning to leap over rocks—it would actually leave the ground and then smash down again. The green moss and rocks and scrub grass and everything on the ground was flying by.

At some point Ransom knew that he was in trouble, but there was no time to consider it as the cart took one last jolt up in the air over a large rock outcropping and became airborne.

Boy and cart separated, and Ransom somersaulted through the air. He hit the ground with a sickening thud.

He did not know how long he was knocked out. But when he started coming to, he found himself being cradled. Margaret had her arms around him and was moaning and crying. "My fine lad, oh no...*gradh mo chridhe*...please God, don't let him be hurt..."

She was holding him so close that he could feel her soft face next to his, and the hot tears she was crying were now rolling down her cheeks and onto his.

By the time Ransom had fully regained consciousness, Margaret had carefully placed his head down on the mossy ground and taken a step back.

Ransom groaned as he rubbed his head.

Margaret managed a half-smile, but resisted the inclination to make light of his injury.

"What was that?" Ransom said, still a little groggy.

"What d'ye mean?"

"What you were saying...something in Gaelic."

But Margaret did not answer him at first. She leaped to her feet and giggled, then reached down with her hands and took one of Ransom's hands in each of hers. Then she pulled him to his feet. Ransom was surprised at how slender and soft her hands were despite her life of hard work in the Highlands.

"'Tis nothin'," she shouted out, and then began to run over to where the cart was lying on its side, laughing as she did.

Out on the hillside Ransom was thinking back to that in the twilight between waking and sleeping. The night was clear and full of stars. As the fire next to him slowly crackled into embers, he found himself chuckling too as he thought of the cart ride and Margaret.

Hamish Chisholm must have thought it odd, because Ransom could see the shadow of the reclining man turn to look at him, then shake its head, and turn back to sleep again.

Now Ransom's mind began to race. *Where is my father—where are my friends right now?* What a strange thing it was, to him at least, to find himself in the wilds of a glen in the Highlands, sleeping under the stars with men who were armed with swords and so far away from St. Andrews.

As he drew his kilt around him tighter against the night air, Ransom prayed to God he would receive word from his father. And that it would be soon.

Chapter 21

The weeks in the Highlands had turned into months for Ransom. The winter swept into the glen quietly at first, with frost that hardened the mossy valley and froze the streams. But then the winds came and brought with them blinding snowstorms that descended with very little notice.

On one occasion Ransom, Hamish, and his men were caught on the high ground trying to make it home when the snows came down in a dizzying, swirling cascade and silently rained down a curtain of white so thick they nearly lost their way.

Those were the dreary months. Rhona could see that Ransom was growing homesick and tried to cheer him. She did manage to make the cottage feel like a home. Her cooking and hospitality was a wonder, particularly given her meager resources.

Every so often, when the valley was silent in the dead of the winter night, and the only lights were from the pale, luminous moon hovering just above the mountains, and a fire in the hearth that sent a golden glow from the few windows in their little cottage, the Chisholms would make music. And that lifted Ransom's spirits considerably.

Hamish played the pipes, Rhona the small whistle flute, and Margaret tapped the rhythm out on a small drum made of animal skin. It usually started with a simple ditty, but as they played Margaret would begin hastening the beat until mother and father had to beg for mercy and all of them ended in a good laugh.

Because Ransom had been formally tutored in languages, the classics, and theology, he was given the job of teaching Margaret. During the winter there was much less for the two of them to do outside, other than breaking through the ice that covered the stream and gathering water, and occasionally spear-fishing for trout that would be cooked for dinner. So during the days, for several hours at a sitting, Ransom would tutor her.

By then their friendship had deepened, and he found her to be a willing and enthusiastic student. He did wonder somewhat at Hamish's insistence on her learning to read and write, and to go on to try to master some of the subjects Ransom had learned. After all, back in St. Andrews, proper girls were better off learning the culinary arts, and needlecraft, and proper dressmaking and the dying of fabrics. Those were the arts of womanhood. The disciplines of book learning were not encouraged among the girls.

But Ransom did as he was told, and he found that Margaret had a quick mind and an almost insatiable appetite for his tales of life on the eastern coast of Scotland, in County Fife, in the shadow of the university.

She was mesmerized as he told what he knew of the murder of Cardinal Beaton and then described his experience in the castle during the great cannon siege.

"Did ye think that ye'd die?" Margaret asked, wide-eyed.

"Thought that maybe I would."

"But ye crawled out of all that ruin and terrible destruction…" Margaret's voice was building in dramatic crescendo.

"Aye. I did."

"And ye didn't die…"

"No, I didn't," Ransom said, a little embarrassed now, as he was aware that Rhona Chisholm was cleaning the great iron pot that hung over the kitchen fire and eyeing him.

"I'm glad ye didn't," Margaret said with a kind of quiet solemnity unusual for her.

A few feet away, Rhona stopped her cleaning and shook her rag out. In her eyes was a look Ransom could not, in his youth, understand. It was a mother's recognition of the turning of the seasons of her daughter's heart. Just as surely as the winter had come and taken the brilliant purple heather of the windswept mountainsides away, so this change had come—and had come in Rhona's own little family. She felt the warmth of recollection of her own feelings when she had been so young—mixed with the fear of all mothers, and a certain sadness too. Not just for herself—but more for Margaret. For reasons that could not be explained now but would become evident to her daughter later.

"I'm sorry we've heard no word from your da," Rhona said matter-of-factly, "but when the snows start to thaw—maybe then he'll tell us when he'll be fetching ye."

"Yes," Ransom said. "I would like that."

Rhona glanced at her daughter and saw something in her eyes. Margaret rose from the table quickly, and she ran out the door without looking back so no one could see the tearful passions in her face. She shouted, "Got to check on the sheep…make sure they've not fallen in the creek."

That was the last time they would talk about Ransom's father until several weeks later.

It was the occasion of a great gathering at the fine tower house of Colin MacDonald, the laird of the glen, nearly a full day's ride out of their valley and into the next mountain range.

MacDonald, as a chieftain of his clan, was the *fear an taigh*—the chairman of the social gathering of all of the clans and gentlemen under his keeping, a gathering called a *ceilidh*.

En route, Hamish rode on horseback next to the wagon that was driven by Rhona. Ransom and Margaret were in the back.

After hearing several references to Hamish being a "broken man," and what an honor it was that he should be invited to the clan's *ceilidh*, Ransom had to ask.

"What's a broken man?"

"Broke off from his clan," Margaret said quickly.

"The Chisholm clan first settled in the Roxburghshire in the south," Hamish added. "Then, about one hundred year or so ago, my people moved north…to the Highlands."

"All the men at the laird's castle, where we're headin'," Rhona said, "they'll be native men…men of their clans to which they belong…"

"Where is your clan then?" Ransom asked.

"Not here—not in this glen…" Hamish said.

"Why aren't you with them?"

But his question was followed by an uncomfortable silence. After traveling a few minutes in quiet, as the wagon rumbled and the horses' feet clopped on the path, Hamish spoke up.

"Do ye know why yer father sent ye all the way out here?" he asked.

"To keep me safe," Ransom answered.

"From who?" Hamish asked. This time his voice bellowed.

"Well…from those that hate the reformists and the Protestants—"

"And so yer father sends ye here!" Hamish thundered. "To the Highlands—where the Pope has more followers than in Vatican City itself!"

"Hush now, Hamish," Rhona admonished him.

"Well, where's the lie in it?" Hamish roared back.

"I don't understand…" Ransom said.

"What Mr. Chisholm is trying to say," Rhona said diplomatically, "is that you are safe with us—but that most of the clans in the Highlands have a heart for the Romish Church—and that when you attend the *ceilidh,* you'd best not talk about religion…"

After traveling a while further, Ransom still wondered about one of his questions.

"But why isn't your da with his own clan?" he whispered to Margaret.

"Because," she whispered back, "he became a reformist himself. He learned to read the Scriptures, and then he believed in the way of the reformers—and his clan threw him out. So he is here, in the glen of the MacDonalds, working for them. But he is on his own and has the protection of no clan…"

"Don't worry, laddie," Rhona said reassuringly. "The MacDonalds are not so fierce on religious matters—"

"Yes, but good fighters nevertheless," Hamish added, "and fought at the right hand of Robert the Bruce at Bannockburn…as they will certainly tell you at the *ceilidh*, especially the more they get to drinkin'."

After a moment's reflection Hamish said, "But Mrs. Chisholm is right—you see, the MacDonalds hate the Campbells—almost as much as, say, the MacGregors do—and because the Chisholms, my clan, have fought against the Campbells on occasion—well, that makes me welcome to the MacDonalds of this glen. So, by his hatred for another clan, the laird of the glen has seen fit to overlook the matter of my 'heretic' Christian faith…"

Ransom was trying to figure out the politics of the clan system. As he did, Hamish added a final thought on the subject.

"So you see—yer da is not as foolish as I made him out. Ye're safe here, more or less—don't take my jokin' for truth."

Then he added, "But don't be takin' my truth for jokin' either…"

Ransom was still trying to sort out Hamish's cryptic humor when they rounded a bend, and beyond the sloping edges of the mountains, he saw a large cream-colored stone tower house. The tall, four-story structure rose up from the edge of a large loch, the surface of which was still half frozen.

He could see, even from the great distance away, horses and carts and a large number of people gathered around the outside of the small castle.

"There it is," Hamish announced with a flourish. "Now, master Ransom, I warned ye—mind what ye say—for I've brought only one sword with me, and we're outnumbered considerably."

Ransom could not tell whether this was just one more of Hamish's jests, or whether he was deadly serious.

But he decided to err on the side of caution and remember that the comment came from a man who made his living chasing down cattle reavers—thieves—and putting his sword through them if necessary.

Chapter 22

After Hamish, Rhona, Margaret, and Ransom had arrived and quartered their horses and wagon, someone blew a stag's horn. That was the signal for everyone to gather in the great hall.

There were close to a hundred people gathered. Many rough-looking Highlanders, men wearing multiple swords, with faces that were worn red and leathery by the elements. Their wives, by and large a haggard lot, spoke loudly and heartily, and they had their many children with them, who looked every bit as wild as their parents.

Ransom stayed close to his little Chisholm family as the clans grouped together, all looking to the end of the room at something Ransom could not make out. Someone was speaking, and as he did, the clansmen were shouting out, lifting their swords, and swinging them over their heads. When a few of the men shifted their positions, he could see what they were all acknowledging.

At the end of the room was Colin MacDonald, the laird of the glen, a tall, lanky man. He was wearing a dark kilt with a ruffled shirt open at the neck. His hair was fiery red, matched by his full beard. On his head was a small cap with a long bird's feather protruding from it.

Bliadhna Mhath Ur! Bliadhna Mhath Ur! he was shouting, toasting the New Year with a large goblet in his hand. As he did, the other men in the hall yelled back the greeting and brandished their swords.

After the greeting the men and women were shown into the long dining hall, where a great feast had been prepared. A small group of clan musicians were already playing in the corner of the hall.

The children were ushered into the kitchen, where they pushed and shoved their way to secure places at the long table that was served by the servants of the laird. Margaret and Ransom elbowed their way to a place near the end of the table.

As they feasted on trout, rabbit, venison, and an evil-looking food made of animal innards, called haggis, the group of clan boys across the table began chiding Ransom for his peculiar form of speech, which was clearly something other than Highlander's.

"I'm from St. Andrews," he replied, eyeing the chief antagonist, who appeared to be about the same age and size as he. Next to him was a large, tall lad with a thick neck, a scruff of unkempt hair, and an unpleasant expression.

The boy across the table just smiled a thin little smile and continued to gobble up his food in great fistfuls, occasionally letting out a large belch, to the amusement of his friends. As they were nearing the bursting point, the boy across the table sat back.

"Say, townie lad from St. Andrews," he said, "do ye know ye're in the Highland territories—do ye know that?"

As his companions guffawed, Ransom managed a cautious smile and simply nodded.

"Well then—have ye seen a true Highland *sabaid* yet?"

Margaret turned toward Ransom and whispered, "Don't play his game, Ransom—ignore him!"

"Oh—tellin' wee secrets—just you two girls," the boy said rising from the bench and scooting over next to Margaret.

"He's no girl," Margaret shot back. "And he's braver than ye, Rory MacDonald—Ransom was in the battle at the Castle of St. Andrews—"

"Was he now?" Rory said, grabbing the back of Margaret's hair and pulling it so hard she cried out.

Ransom reached in back of Margaret and grasped the hair on the back of Rory's head and yanked it hard until he let go of Margaret.

The other boy shot him a grim look and called out to his friends, rubbing the back of his head.

"Come on, all of ye, let's go out to the courtyard and show the townie boy a Highland *sabaid*."

"Don't go—they plan to fight you…"

"I sort of guessed that," Ransom said wearily. Getting up from the bench, he followed the group of a half-dozen of Rory's friends.

Out in the courtyard, Rory told Ransom to follow them to see "what ye can learn from the Highlands."

The group of six was walking in a huddle about five feet ahead of Ransom. Then Rory gave a quiet signal to his compatriots. And in a flash, all six wheeled around and charged at Ransom furiously, swinging their fists, flailing and screaming.

Ransom, having anticipated the rush, ran to the side, but still caught the fury of half of the group, who smacked into him with wild force, knocking him to the ground.

The boys rolled in gales of laughter on the ground. Ransom wiped the blood from his nose and stood up. Rory leaped to his feet.

"Once more!" Rory called out to his crew.

"No—stop it!" Margaret called out from the side.

"Again!" Rory retorted. His troops quickly got up and scurried to his side.

"Yes—again!" Ransom yelled out to the bewilderment of the group. "But this time I want the biggest of you—I want *you*," Ransom said, pointing to the huge boy with the thick neck.

"No—I decide!" Rory shot back.

But by now the big boy was standing in front of Rory and said, in a low guttural voice, "No, I decide—and I decide that I go."

Ransom's huge opponent was a full fifteen feet away, and now he was grinning sadistically. He pawed the ground like a bull and charged, running wildly, grunting as he did, straight for Ransom. But Ransom was not waiting for him. Instead, he too had started running—directly toward the giant youth.

Margaret covered her eyes and muttered a quick prayer. But just as the huge boy was almost within reach, Ransom dropped down like a stone right in his path, covering his head with his hands.

His huge combatant tripped and went flying into the air, nearly doing a complete somersault. He smacked down onto the ground on his back. For the next few seconds he lay on his back, gasping for breath and making little movements with his arms and feet, like a mammoth beetle that had been tipped over onto its shell and couldn't right itself.

Ransom leaped to his feet. His body was sore, his nose still bleeding, but his pride was intact. Rory's gang struggled not to show their new-found respect for the boy from St. Andrews.

As Margaret and Ransom entered the door to the tower house, Margaret turned around, shook her fist at Rory, and cried out, "Ha!"

Ransom quickly pulled her into the castle, and the two headed for the dining hall together. They didn't speak, but Margaret was walking so close to Ransom that her clothes were brushing up against him, and she was glancing over to him with a mysterious and constant smile.

They could hear the din of the dinner conversation in the hall as the men were arguing about something. As they approached and peeked around the corner of the stone walls, several men with large goblets in their hands were yelling at each other.

"They're talkin' about some clans," Margaret said, acting as translator. Then after hearing some more of the argument, she added, "Talking some against the Douglases...but mostly against the Campbells."

"What are they saying?"

"Well—that the Campbells have gathered all their lands by trickery, one of them's sayin'—by legal tricks, and the cleverness of sheepskins…"

"Sheepskins?" Ransom asked.

"Contracts, he means," Margaret said, "writ upon the skins taken from sheep."

Then she added, "Don't ye use sheepskins in St. Andrews?"

"No—paper…" Ransom replied with a quizzical look.

Then Colin MacDonald stood up and put an end to the discussion. There was some laughter, and then MacDonald gestured over to Hamish Chisholm and invited him for a walk into the front hallways outside the dining hall.

"We've lost very few cattle to the reavers," MacDonald said to Hamish with a sound of satisfaction in his voice. "Ye're doin' a fine job at the watch."

"Thank you," Hamish replied without elaboration.

MacDonald halted and glanced around the hallway to make sure they were alone.

"Some of the clans are being pressed—from Edinburgh—to make our intentions known," MacDonald said.

"Intentions about what?"

"Now Hamish, don't play at me," MacDonald said. "You know full well it's been a full year of seasons since the death of Henry in England. The only man-child he has in succession is that sickly boy Edward. No one thinks he will live long…"

"Beggin' yer pardon, Master MacDonald," Hamish responded, "but I don't play at English politics or palace intrigue."

"Don't ye now?" MacDonald said with a slight air of cynicism. "Then why is that boy with ye all the way from St. Andrews…it is strange that Cardinal Beaton is murdered there, the castle taken by the reformist rebels, at least until the French siege—and then the boy shows up here…strange indeed."

"I see ye still have yer spies about the lands."

"Of course, of course. 'Tis the burden of the laird to know more than the clansmen he leads—which is why I speak to ye about the things I know. Ye're a broken man, and so that gives you a certain value to me. Not beholden to the MacDonalds here—nor to other clan hereabouts. And ye're also an educated man. Your advice is a higher coin than that of some of my commanders or even my chosen *tanist* who shall lead upon my death. So I need to solicit you close on a matter…"

"I'll do the best I can."

"Marie de Guise is moving little Mary, the future Scots queen, out of Scotland—to France I am told. For her protection. De Guise knows that the rebellion that started in St. Andrews is now threatening Edinburgh and Holyrood palace. And some of the clans have been approached by the Scottish Crown—as to where we stand…"

"On?"

"On siding with England, and Edward, and the Protestants—or with Mary Stuart, and France, and the Catholics…"

"But ye're Catholic—the choice for ye should be clear," Hamish said with reserve in his voice.

"Yes. Catholic. But for me there's more to it. I have no love for the English, God knows that. I have uncles who fought, not that long ago, against the English at Solway Moss—thousands of Scots slaughtered by the English Crown. Yet—our late Scottish king, some would say, brought it on himself, and the stink of his mistakes has plagued all of us. So now we are left with his widow, Marie de Guise, who would have us ruled as an outpost of France. For me, I simply want freedom for my clansmen. And I see the fires burning beyond the Highlands, Hamish—the fires of this reformist rebellion. Fanned by King Henry in rejecting the

supremacy of Rome during his life, and now in the cry for a new religion in Scotland after his death."

Then MacDonald locked eyes with Hamish.

"So—will our clan be better served, do ye think, by an alliance with
England now, before young Edward is crowned—or by throwing ourselves behind de Guise and the future Mary, Queen of the Scots?"

Hamish thought for only a moment before he spoke.

"I can only speak for my simple self...and not for the chieftain of
the clan, the laird of the glen," Hamish replied. "But for me, I have found
it...useful...to go on a matter where I find the truth to be—and to pledge
only to those who speak it."

MacDonald guffawed and waved him off.

"When the swords are drawn, Hamish, and the sides are chosen, I
don't believe ye will be spouting yer philosophies! Ye'll be using that fine
sword arm of yours to lop off the heads of yer enemies."

"Perhaps. But I hope to be doin' it on the side of God's truth, Master
MacDonald. For sure, that's a thing worth dyin' for..."

Chapter 23

1550—Berwick, England, just south of the Scottish border

The group of men were heading to the center of town at a full run. They had heard the story of the battle of the castle of St. Andrews and the French attack. And how John Knox, the preacher who was the spiritual leader among the rebels, was captured, along with others of the reformists, dragged off in chains, and enslaved in a French galley ship. Tied to an oar, and destined, it seemed, to row until he died a miserable death.

But the latest news about him was so remarkable the men now had to see it with their own eyes. A large group of folks from as far away to the west as Cawhill and Coldstream had come to Berwick to see—and to hear—this strange and magnetic man.

The men muscled their way through the crowd to the front. Up on a wagon was a solitary figure, and he was speaking in a loud and vibrant fashion. Under his arm was a large book, and his right arm was extended outward toward the crowd. His long beard reached down to the mid-part of his chest.

John Knox was preaching, his eyes aflame with the passion of his story, his voice ringing out like a church bell. He was explaining his recent defense of the Protestant reformed religion before the learned teachers and bishops at the cathedral of Newcastle.

"But I did tell those learned men—and learned they are, far beyond my education—*What good is such learning?* I told them, *if it keeps you from learning the truth of God's Word?* Better to be simple and foolish and correct than to be learned and wise in the eyes of the world, and yet so wrong that ye are consigned to everlasting hell!"

The commoners below him broke into wild applause, and several yelled out, *Huzzah! Huzzah!*

"My dear and native land, Scotland, I tell ye, is mightily caught between truth and error—between God and the devil—between the evangel of Jesus the Christ and the mere human customs of the Church— but mark me, all! We are all engaged in a battle for truth. Let us spare no arrows in defeating superstition, and greed, and corruption, and replacing it with the Holy Scripture and obedience to its righteous principles!"

When Knox's sermon was ended, a handful of the audience hung after and shook hands with him and thanked him for his preaching, including the commoners who had forced their way to the front. Finally, after the crowd had dispersed, Knox noticed that there were three men eyeing him from a distance. When he was alone, the men approached.

The three were clearly gentlemen and appeared to be dressed in the silk waistcoats and velvet hats befitting courtiers from the palace in London. He was correct.

"Mister Knox," one of the men said—a tall, handsome man with an immaculately trimmed beard—extending both of his hands to greet the preacher, "Well done, sir—very well done indeed."

Knox thanked them and inquired about their business.

The tall gentleman introduced himself as John Dudley, Duke of Northumberland.

"Since the English Crown has granted you permission to preach as pastor and teacher here in Berwick and Newcastle as well, we have been watching your progress very carefully," he explained.

"Very closely indeed," added another of the men.

"It is apparent that your sufferings during your long years as slave on a French galley have not made you infirm, but in fact, just the opposite, seem to have steeled your resolve to preach with boldness."

"Thank you kindly," Knox replied, "but I must correct you—I was a rowing slave not for *years* as you suggest, but merely for nineteen months..."

"Pish, pish, let's not quibble about a few months here or there—the point is that you are a true martyr to the new faith, to the reformed religion," the tall man continued.

"I do not mean any disrespect," Knox countered him again, "but I knew one of the *true* martyrs, George Wishart, and saw him with my own eyes endure death in the flames of his tormentors...I cannot, good gentlemen, ever consider myself a martyr in comparison—"

"Yes, but the point is," the other man said, interrupting, "that we bring you great tidings from the Privy Council."

Knox simply nodded, waiting for their explanation.

"We three are emissaries of Lord Hertford, the Lord High Protector of young Edward, king and heir to the English Crown, and of the Privy Council. We bear the full weight of their authority in the message we bring."

"What message?" Knox asked bluntly.

"The Crown of England requests your attendance at the Court of King Edward in London, good sir," the tall man said. He smiled, stepped forward, and placed a kindly hand on Knox's shoulder.

"And there, Mister Knox, to commence your official duties as one of the Royal Chaplains of the English Crown."

"And with the blessings of the people of England, I am sure!" the other man added.

"And to travel to Court with all deliberate haste," the third man added.

Knox was stunned. Overcome with emotion, he momentarily turned his back to his visitors and placed his hands behind his back in contemplation.

But the three men could see his hands and also his wrists, which were clearly visible beyond the edge of his black robe. There were the scars left by the iron manacles placed there for nearly two years while he was imprisoned on the French ship.

The tall duke studied the scars carefully. A military man himself, he did not wince at the signs of physical suffering. But in some way, those marks authenticated the choice of Knox, for pragmatic reasons if nothing else. He then spoke again.

"Good sir, will you consent to the appointment now—so we can begin making the preparations for you?"

After a few more moments of solitude, of thinking back to all of where the Lord had taken him and where he was now being led, Knox turned slowly and spoke.

"I will consent, gentlemen—God be praised."

"Excellent!" the elder man declared. "Now you must make provision for travel immediately. And you will need a staff. We can help you there, though the other chaplains often choose their own personal secretary."

"Yes, by all means select your own if you desire," the second man said.

"Do you have someone in mind?" the third man inquired.

Knox smiled—in fact, smiled so broadly that he took them by surprise, as he had gained a reputation as a somewhat sober, if not somber man.

"Yes," Knox replied quickly, "I do have someone in mind—the very person."

Ransom Mackenzie had experienced the long and tedious run of Highland seasons. From that winter at the great Tower House of Colin MacDonald, and then the dreariness of February and March, waiting for spring, and with it, the thaw of the lochs and streams and the rushing of clear water again, and the blooming of flowers over the valley and the return of the velvet-green moss of the mountainsides. And into the summer and fall, and then yet another winter.

There were times when Ransom lost track of the months, or even the year, of his life with the Chisholm family. The work was all-consuming. But slowly Ransom had grown strong in the doing of it, and had managed to slowly tolerate and finally adapt to the rough life of a Highlander. Hamish took him on all of his trips now through the craggy mountain trails. He had taught his young apprentice sword and fighting strategy Highland style. Though not exactly an expert, Ransom could handle a sword well. He learned to fell a red deer at fifty paces with a bow. And he was proud to finally outdo the more agile Margaret in spearing salmon with the three-pronged pole.

Ransom had become muscular in a sinewy kind of way, and self-assured in the wilderness of the glen. His handsome boyish face had grown manly, with a strong jaw, and he now was sporting the beginnings of a beard—though Margaret still teased him for it, as it was still uneven and had not filled in.

Margaret was fully a young woman, and Ransom had noticed what most of the other young men in the glen had also observed—that her quick wit, comely figure, and pretty face had made her the leading catch in the area.

But although several of the Highland men had approached Hamish for the privilege of courting Margaret, in deference to her wishes, he dismissed them all. Margaret had declared her heart to her mother in a very candid way, as well as to several of the other young women in the glen. And Ransom was perceptive enough to understand it. Margaret's clumsy and girlish infatuation with him had grown into a consuming passion. The fact that she had steadfastly resolved not to disclose the full extent of her feelings for Ransom until he did so toward her first, was testament to her fortitude.

Rhona was particularly grieved at all of this. Admittedly, she had grown to love and cherish Ransom. But for the longest time she knew that at any moment he might be summoned by his father and would leave the Highlands forever. That was no proper match for a Highland woman. Rhona and Hamish found that keeping Ransom away from the cottage—sometimes for weeks at end—as he tracked poachers with Hamish and his band had the practical goal of keeping Margaret and Ransom at arms length.

But they also knew that the day was coming when a decision would have to be made by Ransom. He would have to declare his intentions. He had hinted around the matter on more than one trip with Hamish, but never directly.

What they did not know for sure—but were able to guess—was the fate of Hugh Mackenzie during the months, and now years, of his silence. It seemed reasonable to assume that after arriving at Edinburgh, he may have been imprisoned, perhaps even killed, by Marie de Guise. Or perhaps he had been struck down in some accident, or by the plague that constantly beset Edinburgh, or by some other malady.

But Ransom seemed caught between two poles—between his growing affection for Margaret on the one hand, and on the other hand his desire to be a man of his own means and to search out for himself the fate of his father. And for the longest time Ransom had felt that his destiny was to be fulfilled somewhere other than amid the angular, granite-ridged mountains and green valleys of the Highlands. But he could not understand why. Except that as he had entered early manhood he understood that the choice was now his to make.

In the Highlands, there was still much superstition abounding. He had heard about *traibhse*—the "second sight" gift that some boasted of, to see some specter or vision of the future. He could not square that with Holy Scripture. From time to time he thought back to the astrology of David de Blois Douglas at Glamis castle, and Michel Nostradamus, whom he described as his mentor on the Continent, who believed that the future could be foretold in the sky. Ransom was resolved that such belief was as sinful as the ancient art of divination that many of the Highlanders—the Chisholm family excluded—still practiced.

But Ransom's sense of divine leading, if that is what it was, was much different. It was just a belief that something was to be revealed, and that he would know it when he saw it. Yet as the seasons wore on, Ransom had questioned that. He was led to the conclusion he needed to focus on the matters of which he could be certain. One was that God was not the cause of accidents or coincidences. Ransom's instruction at the feet of Master Knox, as he studied Scripture and God's dealings with mankind, had convinced him that the Lord was intentional and sovereign in His plan.

The other thing he was sure of was that he was in the Highlands now, and in the company of a young woman who had grown into a striking beauty and who clearly had affections for him.

It was that "other thing" that was leading him to conclude that, barring some unexpected occurrence, he should pray on, and then plan for, a time to express his intentions to Hamish Chisholm.

"Lord," Ransom said in his prayers one night, "let me know when the time is right. When I should discuss the matter of Margaret with her father…and announce my intentions."

And then he stopped. *My intentions…* he thought to himself. *But what are my intentions?*

Chapter 24

"Ransom, I was cleanin' the cottage…"

"Oh?"

"Yes, I was. And I found something…"

"And what might that be, Margaret?"

"It was an envelope."

"Is that all? By your tone, I would think it much more important."

"But much more than just an envelope…"

"How much more?"

"There was a letter inside…"

Ransom and Margaret both halted simultaneously.

Ransom looked out from the promontory point, from their high mountain view, down into the valley to the silvery glint on the surface of the long loch, far below.

Then he looked at Margaret. He was able to guess what she had found.

"If it's what I think it is," Ransom said, "that letter was from a long time ago. Another time. Someone who is not part of my life now…and besides…why are you digging around in my private things?"

"Hidden things…are usually hidden because someone is ashamed to admit something…" Margaret replied, with some hurt in her voice. "Is there something you want to admit to me?"

"No. And if there were—I would be slow to admit anything to someone who pries into something that doesn't concern her—"

"Doesn't concern me?" Her hurt was turning into anger.

"Doesn't concern me?"

Ransom stepped over to mend things with her, but she pulled away.

"I didn't mean exactly that…" Ransom said, trying to console her.

"A love letter to you…from this Catherine—whatever her name be—and that does not concern me? Well…if it doesn't concern me—then you are no concern of mine. Is that what ye're sayin', Ransom Mackenzie? That you and I are no concern of each other…And if that's it—"

Margaret's dark eyes flashed with passion and hurt, and were filling with tears.

"In case you haven't noticed, there is a long line of fine Highland lads that have come to our cottage, and they'd be askin' for me—or haven't you noticed?"

"Of course I've noticed."

"But—what? Ye just don't care about that? *It's no concern of yours*…is that the truth of it, Ransom?"

"No. That's not true. I care about you…care deeply…"

Margaret studied his face intently. For a moment, there was no conversation. Then she spoke.

"I'll not say it for ye—I'll not—it has to come from yer heart, Ransom. And I'll not try to put into yer heart what's not already there…I won't do it. I have too much pride for that."

The wind from over the mountaintops was picking up. And Margaret's raven-black hair was lifted a little in the air, floating around her face as if by some supernatural suspension.

Ransom stepped yet closer to her, and when she tried to turn away, he gently took her hands in his. She tried to look away to hide her tears, but he wouldn't let her go.

Then Ransom said something in Gaelic, and said it softly, into her ear.

"Gradh mo chridh."

"What?" Margaret said, her eyes widening.

"It's what you said that day when I took that bad tumble on the cart…down the mountainside. I learned what it means—*love of my heart*…"

Margaret smiled and wiped her tears. Then Ransom gently touched her face and kissed her on the mouth.

But something was moving, down in the valley, on the other side of the mountain, and it caught their attention.

There were two men on horseback approaching the cottage. Then they could see two tiny figures—it must have been Rhona and Hamish coming out of the front door. They watched as Rhona and Hamish greeted the two men on horseback. They dismounted and continued talking outside the cottage. Then Hamish left the group and walked quickly toward the path that the two had taken upward.

"I think we'd better go…and see what's happening," Ransom said.

Margaret nodded, and the two started descending as quickly as they could.

By the time Margaret and Ransom had fully descended and made their way to the cottage, everyone was inside.

There were two strangers seated at the kitchen table. One was a Scottish lowlander, a guide. The other was English, judging by his dress and manner of speech.

Rhona was serving them both some strong tea. Hamish was standing.

"Ransom. These men have come for ye…"

"My father—any word?"

The two men at the table both gave a confused look.

"No, lad. I'm sorry. No word from yer father," Hamish said. "But they have come for something else."

"What might that be?"

Rhona gave a quick side glance to her daughter, who was still back in the doorway, as if afraid to fully enter.

"We have come bearing an official message," the Englishman said, putting down his tea and turning in his chair to face Ransom. "From your former teacher, Mister John Knox."

"What?" Ransom said with shock.

"England negotiated his release from the French galleys. He has been in England preaching. And now the Privy Council and the Lord Protector—the Crown of England, young sir—have summoned him to London to be one of the Royal Chaplains."

The news was too astonishing to comprehend. After a few seconds, Ransom smiled and was able to respond.

"Such good news for Master Knox…that he is alive and well…and the recipient of such an honor!"

"The honor is not just his," the Englishman said, rising from his chair and approaching Ransom.

"What do you mean?"

"Just this," the Englishman continued. "That he has chosen a personal secretary."

The room was silent.

"And he has chosen," the Englishman finished, "you, Master Ransom. *You.*"

And then he added, "You must leave immediately for London. We will accompany you. We still have some travel time left in the day…Mrs. Chisholm has been kind enough to gather your things together."

Ransom thought he heard Margaret make a noise like a muffled gasp, or a whimper, perhaps. When he turned to face her, she was covering her mouth with her hand, standing stone-still in the doorway.

"I'm sorry this is so sudden," Rhona said, trying to sound matter-of-fact.

"God's blessings on you, Ransom," Hamish said. There was an unusual amount of emotion in Hamish's voice as he said that. So much so that Ransom found it hard not to become emotional himself. In that instant, he came to realize that Hamish, who had no son, had found one in Ransom in their many months together.

"Ransom, son," Rhona said quietly, "go outside and have a word with my daughter if you would…and comfort her heart in your goodbye, if ye can…"

Margaret was standing outside the cottage. Her head was ever so slightly bent forward, and her body was swaying a little. As if the slightest breeze, if it came along, would topple her to the ground.

"I'm so confused," Ransom said. "I can hardly keep my wits about me."

"I suppose," Margaret said, now in a voice so thin and distant, "that ye have no choice…"

"The Crown of England has summoned me—and Master Knox summoned me to London."

"No choice in the matter…" Margaret continued, her face a reflection of stunned disbelief, not directing her words to anyone or anything in particular. "Just like that…no choosing…a rider comes…and ye're off to London. Ransom, were ye ever real? Have ye been here with me…here in the Highlands? Was this but a dream? Or were ye just a wisp of smoke that curled around my life—and then is gone…gone?"

Ransom had no words to console her. And no way to make sense of it all. Except he knew that he must go to join his former mentor in London. Was this not, now, the divinely wrought destiny he had been searching for?

Ransom had only one thought—one word—a promise for Margaret. It was his only offering to her.

But before he could utter a single word, she saw into him, and interrupted.

"Don't think," she said, her faced now flooded with grief, "that I will wait for ye to finish in London and someday return…for I will not wait. I will not…"

In less than an hour Ransom was mounted on a horse, his bags tied to the saddle, and was ready to depart with his guide and English companion to the Court of the young King Edward.

Margaret had vanished.

Hamish clasped Ransom's hands with a powerful grip, and then gave him a small Highland sword in a leather scabbard. It was not, Ransom realized, for ceremony. It was for protection.

Rhona was crying openly and hugged Ransom's neck as he bent down from the horse.

Then, just as they readied to ride, Margaret came dashing around the outside of the cottage, carrying something.

She reached it up to Ransom, and he took it. It was a small, square glass box with a wreath of preserved heather curled in the middle of it.

"It was to be for yer birthday…" But she couldn't finish the sentence.

Margaret turned and began to run away—running, without turning back, in the direction of the mountain path they liked to take up to the "View of Kings," as it was called.

He carefully wrapped the glass box in a cloth and placed it in his bag slung from the saddle horn.

And then they started to canter in the direction of the end of the valley beyond.

By the time Ransom and his two companions had reached the middle of the valley floor, Margaret was at the top of the mountain path. And she watched the three men on horses until they disappeared out of sight. And she remained there even beyond that, until the darkness of night began to fall.

Chapter 25

For Ransom the journey south brought with it a mixture of two powerful emotions.

First, his separation from Margaret burdened him with an overwhelming sense of melancholy. In fact, because of that, at first he found it difficult to converse with his travel companions, even though both of them tried to be pleasant and friendly.

He was aware that he had been growing increasingly fond of Margaret, so much so that he found it difficult to imagine day-to-day life without her lively laughter, or her pretty face, or hearing her surprisingly strong opinions, and then debating them with her. Yet now, her absence, and not knowing if he would ever see her again, gave him a sense of mental pain and loneliness he had rarely experienced before. The closest to that emotion came when he had been forced to go away from St. Andrews, leaving father, friends, and home behind.

Yet at the same time there was a clear sense of growing excitement that was just under the surface. The first few days of travel he was so occupied with his sadness over leaving Margaret that he denied himself the luxury of imagining what life would be like as a young man in the Royal Court of London.

Then, as the trio traveled on horseback closer to the southern uplands of Scotland, toward the borders with England, the lowlander guide gave his adieu. He said he had to attend to certain matters in Stirling. The Englishman gave him a handsome fee and thanked him for his services.

Then he and Ransom continued on their journey, in a south by south-easterly direction, toward the borders.

When Ransom realized they were passing within thirty miles of Edinburgh, he pleaded with his English guide to take a short trip into that city to try to locate his father.

"Nay, I'm sorry," the Englishman said, with pity in his voice, "Master Ransom, you have told me your father lives there—but my orders come from the Crown of England—from the personal assistant to Lord Hertford, the Lord High Protector of England. I can't dally. And, you must understand the other risks."

"What risks?" Ransom asked.

"Marie de Guise has gained new alliances from France. As a consequence, England, at least for the present time, has withdrawn from its former strongholds here in the lowlands. To avoid a war you understand. If Madame de Guise were now to capture me, an emissary from the English Crown, in Edinburgh, she would hang me sure as a spy—not to mention what they would do to you, now that you are on orders to be the personal secretary to Mister Knox in London. I'm sorry, but we simply can't take the risk."

Ransom could understand the wisdom of that course, but his time in the Highlands had taught him something else. That there were occasions where great reasons required great risk—even reckless abandon.

He recalled one occasion on the mountain ridges with Hamish Chisholm and his crew of cattle watchmen, when Hamish and his two men had charged on a group of five reavers who had stolen several of the laird's cattle. Hamish and his small band wildly swooped down from their position with bone-chilling screams. Hamish personally dispatched one Campbell thief with a single sword thrust and injured another. Though outnumbered, Hamish and his two compatriots won the skirmish with sheer audacity.

For Ransom's part, he was quite willing to risk entering Edinburgh. He had survived the siege at St. Andrews' castle and had adapted to the rough life of a Highlander. He did not fear the forces of Marie de Guise. But the decision was his companion's to make, not his. And he had to abide by it.

Ransom was still mourning the decision to bypass Edinburgh as they entered the borderlands. Unlike the sheer cliffs and plunging valleys of the Highlands, or the flatlands of St. Andrews that rimmed the crashing waves of the ocean, this area was quite different.

It was early spring and the green hills were rolling and gentle. There were occasional placid lakes, and everywhere the flowers and trees were beginning to bud. As the days went by, the number of villages seemed to increase—they were tucked amid dales and woods, and the clearings that marked their outskirts were easily seen from the well-worn road they were traveling.

However, by the time they were deep within England, the Englishman began complaining of a great and sudden illness—so intense, in fact, that he feared he could not complete the journey with Ransom. He explained in detail the route that Ransom would travel during the remaining part of the journey.

"There is a village close by," the Englishman explained weakly. "I'll try to make it there. Here is your traveling fare. It ought to keep you in good stead for the days it will take you to arrive at London."

He handed Ransom a velvet bag containing silver shillings, sixpences, and one gold ducat.

"Now that you are in England, you have little to fear. Just keep to the main road. The only danger comes on the smaller byways. When you arrive at Stratford, go to the center of town and look for a wool dealer and glover...he goes by the name of John...he is a Protestant sympathizer and a supporter of King Edward. He will put you up, give you a meal, and then will see you on your way."

As they parted, the Englishman bid Ransom a labored "God's speed," and rode off, bent slightly over on his horse. Ransom's previous bravery now seemed to falter a little, momentarily, at the thought of traveling in an unfamiliar country, unattended.

After several hours of riding alone, Ransom was feeling more confident. He was glad for the experience of long hours on horseback, in bad terrain, during his time in the Highlands. It had readied him for the long trip down to London.

But his travel seemed to go slower than he expected. His horse was favoring a hind leg. The daylight was beginning to wane, and he was concerned about reaching Stratford before nightfall.

Then he spotted a sign that indicated a route to Stratford. It was earlier than he had expected. And it was not where his English guide had described. Ransom stopped his horse, got off, and inspected his mount's hind hoof. It had suffered a cut, and now was in need of cleaning and binding.

The sunlight was low in the sky and was now peeking through the woods. Ransom looked down the lane indicated by the sign. It was a small road, with a sharp bend that quickly caused it to disappear from view.

Ransom didn't feel he had much choice. He hopped back onto his horse and turned it down the little bypath.

When he had made his way past the bend, he thought he heard some rustling noise in the deep woods that cloaked both sides of the lane. Perhaps it was a deer or fox, he thought.

He listened closer. No more sound.

Then suddenly the woods exploded with noise, as two riders thundered from opposite sides of the woods, one stopping abruptly in front of him, and one directly behind him.

Then he saw a man jump out of the woods and present himself in front of Ransom, as he grabbed the reins of his horse in his gloved hand.

The man wore no hat and had long, straggly hair that fell down to his shoulders in a tangle. He had two swords dangling from his belt. His beard was unkempt, and as he smiled he showed he was missing a prominent tooth in both the top and bottom of this mouth.

"Good day to you, young sir," he growled. "We are the taxmen of these parts hereabout—please dismount and we will do our business as quick as you can say jack-o-the-woods."

"Taxmen?" Ransom said. "I am on official business of the Crown of England...I've heard nothing of this taxation..."

But one of the horsemen reached out and yanked Ransom from his horse, and he fell to the ground. As he did, the velvet bag of coins spilled out of his coat and dropped onto the ground. The man on the ground quickly scooped up the bag and laughed loudly.

"Crown of England, indeed—then this bag ought to be full of the coin of the realm, don't you think, men?"

The other men chortled coarsely at that.

Then Ransom noticed a movement out of the corner of his eye. One of the horsemen was slowly beginning to pull his sword out of his scabbard.

They mean to kill me where I stand, Ransom heard himself thinking. And then he heard the advice of Hamish Chisholm ringing in his ears— *"Never hesitate, lad..."*

Ransom turned and slapped the hindquarters of the horse whose rider was reaching for his sword. The horse leaped into a full run, taking its rider by surprise. He was now hanging off his saddle sideways and struggling to right himself.

"Full of clever tricks," the leader on the ground barked out. "Well, now ye'll feel the trick of my cold steel," and he quickly brandished his sword. Ransom pulled his short sword out of his belt.

The man was a fair swordsman, but after several thrusts and parries, Ransom noticed he had a stiff leg, which made him slow and ungainly. Ransom waited for a lunge and when the man was off balance, Ransom ducked to the side and stuck his sword into the man's side as hard as he could. The man fell to the ground, moaning and swearing loudly at his wound.

The remaining horseman had a pistol in his hand, and he was circling and trying to take aim at Ransom in the melee.

Ransom put his sword back in his scabbard, bent down, hiding behind his horse, and scooped up a large handful of dirt. As the horseman was coming alongside Ransom's horse on the other side, Ransom leaped up into the saddle with one hand, and with the other tossed the dirt into the face of the highwayman.

The man's pistol discharged, narrowly missing Ransom. The rider was choking and coughing.

But Ransom's horse had gotten the message. The sound of the pistol shot had so startled it that—bad hoof or no—it took off at a mad gallop with Ransom holding on tightly.

By the time the highwayman had cleared his eyes from the dust and the other rider had finally regained control of his horse and untangled himself, Ransom and his steed were completely out of sight.

He did not slow his horse until he was back on the main road to Stratford and had ridden far enough to know he had left the highwaymen safely behind.

He yelled out loudly in triumph as he slowed his horse to a canter. But then a dismal thought set in.

He realized he had left his velvet bag of coins—all of his traveling money—back with his attackers.

Now what do I do? Ransom wondered, as his jubilation faded into dismay.

Chapter 26

By the time Ransom had reached Stratford, his horse was hobbling so lamely that Ransom had dismounted and walked the last few miles on foot.

Stratford was a fair town, much smaller than St. Andrews of course, but bigger than any of the villages of the Highlands, and it was larger than most of the villages in the lowlands and along the borders.

As he led his horse into the town, he saw an abundance of businesses and shops, including bakers, smiths, weavers, masons, shoemakers, grocers, and saddlers. There was also an abundance of alehouses and makers of malt. And near the market crossing between High Street and Henley Street, just as he had been told, there was a sign: *WOOL-DEALERS AND GLOVERS.*

It was sunset, and Ransom quickly tied his horse to a post outside the wool dealer's shop and entered.

It was a large open room with several large, bloodied tables, with the hides of animals strewn over them. The room had a foul smell about it. No one was there.

Ransom called out, but did not receive a response. He walked farther into the room cautiously, and noticed through the back window that the proprietor had a small sheepfold in the back, which was encircled by a fence, with about a dozen sheep grazing. He noticed a figure of a man out in the back in the shadows of the last bit of sunset, who was heading toward the rear door of the shop.

After a few seconds the man entered through the door and was a little startled to see Ransom standing in the middle of his shop.

"May I help you, good sir?" he said with a quick smile.

The man looked to be in his late twenties, and was of medium size. He wore the leather, blood-stained apron of someone who made his business raising, killing, and skinning animals. He had a lively face full of expression, a nose with a graceful arch, and deep eyes that were widely set apart and that were examining Ransom to determine his business.

"Thank you, yes," Ransom began. "I have traveled so far...all the way from the Highlands of Scotland—"

"You don't say," the man said. "Imagine that—such an adventure for a young man as yourself! Always wanted to see the regions of the north," the man said. "Bit of the wild Scottish lands—raging streams and waterfalls—mountains of sheer rock, I've heard...who did you say you were?"

"Ransom Mackenzie," he said and extended his hand, which was shaken vigorously by the shopkeeper. "I was waylaid by highwaymen—"

"You don't say!" the man said, his eyes dancing and wiping his hands on his leather apron. "You've had a real adventure—but count yourself double-blessed by fate, lad. Not everyone comes out with his life. Did they hurt you?"

"Not a scratch," Ransom said with a burst of bravado. "There were three of them. I ran one of them through with my sword before I escaped."

The man was leaning back against the edge of the table, mesmerized by the story.

"And what did you say your name was, good fellow?"

Ransom repeated his name again. But there was no glimmer of recognition in the man's face.

"Were you not expecting me?"

"No, I can't say I was. But I have certainly enjoyed your company. Why did you think I would be expecting you?"

"Are you not a wool-dealer and a glover?"

"Most certainly—as you can see!"

"And is your name not John, sir?"

"It is, it is!"

"I am traveling to the Court of King Edward in London. I was told, while on my travels, to come to Stratford and here seek a man by your name and by your trade."

"By Jove's beard!" the man said, "you don't say—business with the Crown of England, no less. But I don't know anything about this...I'm very sorry."

Ransom was utterly confused. Had his English guide given him the wrong instructions? He looked outside. Night was falling. He was tired, his back ached from his tumble off the horse, and he was weak with hunger.

The man studied Ransom. "And what was your business with the Crown—if I may be so bold to ask?"

"Personal secretary to a preacher—Mister John Knox—who was recently appointed Chaplain to the Royal Court at London."

"A man of faith!" the man said energetically.

"Are you...are you then also of the reformist religion—the faith of the gospel of Christ? A Protestant sympathizer, as I was led to believe?"

"Well, I am a man...how can I say...a man who reveres the Creator of us all. The Almighty whose hand is seen in tranquil reflections on the quiet River Avon—and in the ever-changing clouds of the sky. But as for doctrine or disputations of this matter or that matter, I'm not much for that."

Now Ransom's confusion was complete.

The man paused. Then he burst out laughing and slapped the bloody table that was next to him.

"I know exactly what we have here!" he exclaimed. "A confusion of identity! Precisely. You said you were looking for a certain John, a wool-dealer and glover of Stratford..."

"Exactly," Ransom said, but with no more understanding than he had before.

"And my name is John, and that is my occupation—"

Ransom was still waiting for the explanation.

"But I have had, until just a few fortnights ago, a partner in this business with me whose name is also John. So, don't you see?"

"Yes, I think I do."

"The local folks were always mixing us up, so we adopted the names of John the first and John the second. I am John the second because I am two years his junior..."

"I see..."

"But his name is John Burke. Now he was in fact one of the reformist believers—but he has already left the business to me and gone to London. He says he wishes to be 'part of the work of God' in London, as he called it—his very words. I think the confusion of identities has been fully revealed."

But the man probed a little further.

"I am sorry Mister Burke is not here to greet you. Do you have a place to stay? I can walk you to the Red Horse Inn just down the road."

"I have no money," Ransom blurted out. "The highwaymen took it all."

"Yes. Of course. Stands to reason," the man said thoughtfully. "So here you are...night has set...strange new town...no lodgings...the adventure suddenly turns a bit dreary."

Ransom managed a weak smile and nodded.

After a few more moments of reflection, the man's face brightened and he slapped the table again.

"What say that you help me here at my business for just a while? I'll give you Mister Burke's bed and rooms—and meals fit for a king—and then, after, let's say four days' work in return for food and lodging, and oh, perhaps two, let's say three silver shillings for you to travel with, you can be on your way to London. How about that, Mister Mackenzie?"

Ransom took only a second to think it over. He had no other choice. He shook hands with the man. Now he was thinking about dinner and how soon they could eat.

"And what did you say your name was, good sir?" Ransom asked.

"Why, it's John of course," the man said with a laugh. "John Shakespeare."

Chapter 27

Ransom tried to take his short stint with John Shakespeare in stride. He told himself that Mister Knox would excuse his delay at arriving at Court, once he knew the full scope of the recent events in Ransom's travel, more particularly being set upon and robbed of his entire travel fare by highwaymen. To make matters worse, Ransom's horse had gone lame.

John boarded the horse in his small barn in back of the shop and attended to its injured hoof. Ransom allowed him to do that on the condition that John would not kill the poor horse—or skin it—as the man's occupation seemed to involve butchering and tanning the hides of almost every conceivable variety of animal.

John Shakespeare laughed at the thought but assured Ransom that the horse would be well taken care of.

And in the next few days Ransom came to see that his host was as good as his word. All of the things he said would be done, in fact were honored. The horse's hoof was carefully wrapped and the bandages cleaned, and the horse was well fed.

The meals provided by John were hearty, and there was always plenty to eat. The only complaint Ransom privately entertained was the room he was given for his stay. It was represented to be the former quarters of John's business partner, Mr. Burke. But if that were actually true, Ransom thought, then he could understand why Burke left Stratford in search of his fortune in London.

The room was actually a loft overlooking the shop, and was attached to the adjacent barn by a small pass-through door. It smelled like a stable, and Ransom had a difficult time going to sleep because of the noises on the other side of the door. The mice and rats would scratch and scurry back and forth. Night owls hooted from the rafters of the barn. And at the first break of dawn every morning, Ransom was wakened by the winsome—though unwelcome—cooing of mourning doves. Even in the Highlands he had never heard such an assembly of animal noises.

The spring rains were coming, and John and Ransom spent most of their time inside. After the first two days Ransom began to adapt to the foul scent of slaughtered animals in the shop. The first task that John assigned him was tolerable, but each job after that became more and more disagreeable.

First, he gave Ransom a tool called a teazel carder, which had a short wooden grip and a wide trowel-like attachment with a wide row of bristles. The tool was used to comb through the large piles of raw lamb's wool and clean it out. No sooner had Ransom mastered that than John assigned him the task of cutting the wool from the sheep with a sheep shearing knife.

The next day after that, John told Ransom to man the bucket for the animal innards as he gutted several large deer.

John was a hard worker, but also a nonstop conversationalist. As he worked side by side with Ransom he engaged him in discussions about every conceivable topic—though his favorite seemed to be hearing about Ransom's life before coming to Stratford.

He was enthralled at Ransom's description of his days inside the castle of St. Andrews, and how he learned a little of the stonemason's trade there while repairing the walls. He was amazed at his account of the cannon bombardment. He showed genuine compassion when Ransom shared his long years apart from his father and his inability to gain any knowledge of his status in Edinburgh.

Ransom's experiences in the Highlands were fascinating to John. Though his favorite was undoubtedly Ransom's tale of his short stay at Glamis castle, his meeting with David de Blois Douglas—and in particular the story, told to Ransom by the eerie Mistress Jean Douglas... how in ages past, near that very castle, Macbeth had cruelly slain King Duncan...and how his spirit was thought to still walk the corridors and parapets of the castle.

And when Ransom described the sounds of scratching near his bedroom door in Glamis Castle and how he thought it was the long deceased Duncan coming to pay a visit—but in fact was only a mouse building a nest in the walls—John roared with laughter. Ransom was tempted at that point to complain a little about the sounds of mice and rats scuttling through the walls next to his bed in the loft but chose not to. There was something very generous about his host, and Ransom did not want to slight that generosity by voicing such minor irritations.

John Shakespeare also talked freely about himself. In fact, he shared personal things in an easygoing way that seemed unhindered and unashamed. He spoke of his recent rise to a position of some leadership among the tradesmen in Stratford. And he talked about some of his other ambitions.

"You know what craft I would really like the chance to entertain, Ransom?" John asked one night at dinner. It was raining outside, and the mud roads of Stratford were turning into a long chain of ponds outside in the dark. The two were finishing dinner, and the logs in the fireplace had collapsed into embers.

"I would," John continued, "most heartily desire the craft of public polity—of statecraft. The art of governing."

"Politics?" Ransom asked. "Why is that?"

"But why would you question that, Ransom, of all people?"

"I don't understand..."

"Well, is it not true that you yourself are soon going to be venturing into the world of polity in the Royal Court?"

"Not really polity. My master is a Court Chaplain—an ecclesiastical position—and I will be his secretary, a merely ministerial title."

"But engaged in the Royal Court, under the auspices of the Crown of England—don't you see?"

"I do not see my work as political."

"When you sleep in the Royal Court and work for a man who is a Chaplain for the King of England, boy or no, *everything you do is political!*"

As he sopped his last piece of beef in the remaining gravy and popped it in his mouth, John added, "And in that, I truly envy you..."

Ransom had never entertained that thought before. After some thought he turned to John and clarified the matter.

"Or perhaps we could put it another way," he added.

"Which way?"

"That when God, in His divine plan, chooses to put John Knox in the business of the Chaplaincy of the English Crown, is not God then declaring that the business of English politics is also His business as well?"

John broke into a wide grin, laughing and clapping his hands together.

"Good show, Ransom! Spoken like a true politician!"

Then John grew a little serious, and gave the impression of someone who was about to share a great secret.

"You know," he said, "there is some talk among the leaders of the town that soon I may be appointed to a position of chamberlain. And after that, well, who knows? Perhaps some day to become town alderman—or take some other high public office..."

"I am sure you would be well-suited to any of those positions," Ransom said brightly, though he did not know the particulars of any of them.

"Such a position, together with my business ventures, would position me well to secure the hand of…a certain lady…"

"Who? Tell me who it is!"

"You've not met her. Her name is Mary Arden. She is a fine lady. Gracious and pretty. She is the daughter of Robert Arden of Wilmecote, a family of very good repute."

"I would be very happy for you."

"And you, Ransom, though you are younger than I—still, with your life as an adventurer and scholar and soon-to-be member of the Royal Court—surely you have a young woman in mind?"

It was a testament to John Shakespeare's friendly and hospitable nature that Ransom felt at ease sharing something of this. After all, the first night, when Ransom unpacked his things and moved into the loft for sleeping he came across two profoundly important belongings—one was the letter from Catherine Fawlsley, and the other was the little glass box with the heather within given to him by Margaret Chisholm. It seemed sad to Ransom that he had to leave both of the two young women he had cared for deeply, with no assurance he would ever see either of them again.

So Ransom told a few of the facts about his acquaintance with both Catherine and Margaret.

John thought on that and then spoke up.

"You had spoken of the star maps and astrologies of David de Blois Douglas at Glamis Castle—surely then, lovers would have their fates either matched or mismatched by the stars also," John continued. "And if that is so, then your two lady friends would both be as to you, as it were, star-crossed lovers and mismatched in the heavens."

"No, not at all," Ransom replied. "I am truly sorry now I ever told you of those profane beliefs of Mister Douglas. Scripture teaches that God's will is what moves the events of our lives, not the movement of the stars in the heavens."

"Well, at least there is one good match that even I can see," John added with a smile. "You are well-suited, Ransom, for the work of the Chaplain's office—you will soon be preaching as well as that master John Knox of yours."

When Ransom bedded down for the night, even though he had enjoyed the fellowship and conversation with his host, he was saddened by his thoughts about leaving Margaret. And he was almost equally troubled by the prospect of never seeing Catherine again. He tried to put both of them out of his mind as he fell asleep to the sounds of mice scurrying in the walls and an owl giving its shivering night call in the adjacent barn.

Chapter 28

When the last day of the week arrived, although Ransom was anxious to complete his journey to London and begin his work with John Knox, he still felt a measure of regret to have to say goodbye.

True to his word, John Shakespeare paid Ransom handsomely for his work, well enough to secure a coach ride, together with one night's stay over, en route to London. The horse was mending but was not strong enough to carry a rider, so it would be tied to the back of the coach.

The coach was scheduled to arrive at the market cross by midday. John said he would neglect his work for the first few hours, and he took Ransom for a walk along one of his favorite haunts. It was a quiet path next to the River Avon, a wide but very tranquil body of water. The sides of the river were heavily wooded, and the recent rains had released a rich, woody scent that, mingled with the wildflowers, gave the whole outdoors a wonderful fragrance.

They passed the time in talk until they had to make their way to the market crossing. Before too long the coach to London arrived.

"I shall see you again someday, I shall make sure of it," Ransom said. "And when I do, I shall bring you the latest Bible in the common language—if you are to be a man of both means and authority you will be wise to read what God has said on those matters!"

John Shakespeare shook his hand vigorously and watched him depart, standing and waving in the road crossing until the coach was out of sight.

It was somewhere during the last few miles of his journey to London that Ransom actually began to imagine the life to which he had been appointed.

He shared the crammed coach with a lady of moderate means who was a widow and was traveling with her two young children, and two men. One of them said he was traveling to London to settle the estates and lands of his uncle, recently deceased. The other was a businessman who was traveling to negotiate the purchase of a quantity of cotton.

The businessman seemed to know quite a bit about the politics of the Court and the reign of young Edward, now just shy of fifteen years of age. He shared considerable knowledge about the governance of the late Henry VIII, his break with the Church of Rome, and the current confusion over who would rule in the event that Edward, a frail boy, might soon die. Then he quickly added, "Not to impugn his Majesty's health in the least, mind you—may God save and protect the young King, now and forever. And mind you, I consider myself a loyal subject of King Edward."

As Ransom listened to his companion's backtracking and hedging, he suddenly understood one small measure of what might be in store for him. He presumed that he would be privy to great Bible scholarship, not to mention walking very near the center of power and privilege. Yet at the same time, he wondered whether the intrigue and complex politics of Court would consume everything. And he wondered whether it would be a place where everyone had to measure their words and guard their meaning.

Listening to his traveling mate, Ransom thought, *Perhaps John Shakespeare was right—perhaps everything at Court will be about politics, even the Chaplaincy of my good teacher John Knox...*

But whatever thoughts or worries Ransom had as he traveled in the crowded coach disappeared when the coachmen brought the coach to a halt. Ransom had only been told that he was to report to Hampton Court. He did not know what to expect.

But when he climbed out of the coach with his bags and looked at the palace buildings off in the distance, he could barely breathe.

The coach had stopped about a half mile from Hampton Court, at the guardhouse. The palace guards examined a letter of introduction that Ransom had been given by his English guide. Then they waved the coach off. One of the guards assisted Ransom onto a large, magnificent white horse. Then the guard mounted his own chestnut steed, carrying Ransom's bags as he rode. They cantered through the main gate and down the cobblestone road toward the great palace.

The buildings of Hampton Court were located on the banks of the River Thames. The huge complex of spires, peaks, walls, and courtyards was so massive that Ransom would be unaware that it was a riverside palace until days later, after an extensive tour.

"Your first time to Hampton Court, sir?" the guard asked.

"It is...and I am speechless!"

"A bit of history," the guard said, enjoying his opportunity to give a short explanation.

"Built by Cardinal Wolsey. But then, after his—let's say—his parting of ways with his late Majesty King Henry VIII, King Henry acquired Hampton for himself. The present king, by the Lord Protector and his Privy Council, has seen fit to give rooms to some of the Protestant chaplains here. Including your Mister Knox. I trust your stay here will be a productive one, sir."

Ransom was led through a mammoth stone entranceway and into a cavernous reception hall. He was told to be seated on a red velvet settee. He watched as courtiers, military men, and ladies in long rustling satin gowns with delicately brocaded designs and headpieces with pearls walked past him.

It all seemed an unimaginable paradox to Ransom. Just a few weeks before he was living in a humble cottage in the Highlands of Scotland with a man who made his living as the head of the cattle watch. And now he was to make his home in one of the most elegant and lofty palaces in all of England.

He was so enthralled with the flow of royal traffic that he lost track of time. But suddenly he was aware that someone was standing off to his side.

He looked over. And for a second he felt that he had to be dreaming.

It was Knox. More gaunt than he had remembered. His beard was longer now, and there were deep lines in his face, where his cheeks had been full and youthful before. And his eyes were more deeply set, now with slight bags under them.

But there was the same fire in the eyes.

Knox grabbed Ransom and gave him a crushing embrace. Both of them laughed loudly, despite the decorum of their surroundings, and Ransom thought he could see a little glimmer of a tear in his friend's eyes.

"By God's perfect grace, it is so good to see you, young man! Thank you for accepting the appointment as my secretary. We have so much work to do—so very much work…"

He immediately led Ransom up several stairways and down a series of halls to their apartments—with adjoining bedchambers, a large library, a small study for Ransom, and a much larger one for Knox.

After Ransom settled into his rooms, splashed water on his face, and changed into a clean vest and shirt, he met with Knox in his office. Food was brought in—cooked pheasant, fruits, an assortment of breads, and plum pie. Ransom feasted until he felt he could not rise from his chair.

Knox wanted to know everything about his life since the siege at St. Andrews Castle. Ransom talked at length about his travels and experiences that led up to his presence at Hampton Court.

"And what of yer da?" Knox asked. "What news?"

"Nothing," Ransom said with a sigh. "I would have thought that he had established himself in Edinburgh by now…and would have sent for me…"

"We'll pray for him together, here in our time together at Court—however long—or however short that may prove to be."

There was something in the way that Knox said that—something that gave Ransom the impression he believed their life at Hampton Court would be shorter rather than longer.

Knox explained the duties of his Chaplain's position.

"Preach to the king and his royal aides, the members of the Privy Council and so forth, two or three times a week, as requested. His Majesty, though still young, has expressed an impressive interest in the evangelical reforms I have advanced. And I will be working with his aides in suggesting modifications to the forms of worship—and as one of the six royal chaplains, I will review and give advice on various religious documents that are now being drafted—the Articles of the new creed of faith—and examining various and sundry religious books to determine if they warrant licensing for publication."

Knox explained that in each of these tasks, Ransom would be involved to assist him.

"And in addition," he added, "I have decided that in your spare time you will do well to begin an apprenticeship in the study of English law. Starting with the Great Charter. I have arranged for a master of law to tutor you for two hours per day."

Ransom listened intently, but he harbored a quiet sense of panic as Knox listed off the extensive activities and duties. *Will there be no time left at all for frivolity, games, sport, or gaiety?* he thought to himself. That was the kind of question, though, that was best kept to himself.

But he did have one question for his master.

"Sir, if I am here to assist you in matters of your ecclesiastical work—the Chaplain's position, Christian worship, and discussions of Scripture and such—why, if I may ask, most respectfully, why am I to also study the law?"

"You may ask. But the answer will be best learned in the course of time—have patience. And be willing to learn from the circumstances in which God has placed you."

And then, in a more somber tone, "Ransom, you were not brought here merely to indulge in the trappings of luxury. Far beneath the pomp and grandeur you see all around you, there is an earthquake at the ready, moving and rumbling—and soon to crack the earth open. England is a nation on the edge—and you and I, we will help to tilt it one way or the other."

Knox's pronouncement made little sense to Ransom. The exhaustion of his travel had overcome him. He asked leave from his mentor and climbed into his bed.

When he had rested, then he could try to figure out what Knox's dire prophecy was supposed to mean.

As Ransom drifted off, submerged in the soft goose-feather down of his bed, he had a fleeting thought… just a fragment of a thought…*I wonder what it's like to be in an earthquake…*

Chapter 29

It did not take Ransom long to adapt to the busy schedule of life within Hampton Court. John Knox led early-morning chapel services. Ransom would often fetch papers or books for him for the preparation for these lessons. That would be followed by a sumptuous breakfast, and then the day's correspondence, with Ransom taking dictation of his master's letters—addressed to the churches at Berwick and Newcastle where he still maintained his position as pastor.

Next would be a series of meetings between Knox and other aides of the Court. Three times weekly all of the chaplains of the Crown would meet collectively on ecclesiastical matters, and it was Ransom's job to gather whatever intelligence he could on the proposed agenda. Because Knox was the least senior of the chaplains, he was always the last to learn the details—or more importantly, the strategic import—of the gathering.

Then there was dinner, which was always so bountiful that Ransom soon learned to restrain himself lest he begin dozing off later.

By early afternoon, Ransom had his daily instruction in English law from a master of law, a thin, hunched-over man who was impatient and caustic. Though he could not prove it, Ransom did entertain the notion that the lawyer either did not care for Mister Knox and therefore cared less for his young secretary, or simply did not like Scots—or perhaps both.

Those lessons always seemed interminable, and when they were over, Ransom was then required to attend to daily Bible studies and the reading of certain theological texts suggested to him by Knox.

When all of that was completed, Ransom would work on the draft of a basic outline of Bible citations and commentary that might be helpful for the next of Knox's three weekly sermons to the Royal Court at Windsor Castle. Because each of his sermons would often run two to three hours in length, the research and preparation for them was always substantial. Ransom was always pleased when a few of his citations and thoughts surfaced in the course of one of the sermons—though more often they did not. And when that happened, Ransom often wondered what use he was to his employer if his labors did not yield any visible fruit.

In the evenings there were occasional events that were entertaining—balls and musical festivals. Knox would often make an appearance, but rarely participate. He occasionally commented to Ransom that while he could not condemn dancing as idolatrous—indeed King David danced before the Lord—he held it in cautious consideration because, if led by passion and directed to pagan purposes, it could in practice become so.

Yet even these colorful events did not please Ransom very much. He and his mentor seemed excluded from the inner circle of alliances and close friendships at Court. And often, by the evening, Ransom was so exhausted that he had little energy to expend.

There was so much study, learning, debating, and writing that Ransom's head would ache from all of his academic efforts. He soon yearned for what he was now beginning to think of as "real life," which existed outside the walls of Hampton Court. Out in the world where deer were hunted for food, and where families gathered around humble tables for dinner and talked in friendly conversation, and in the towns and villages where travelers and shopkeepers plied their trade in the hustle and bustle of market squares.

Perhaps, he thought to himself, what he really longed for was his old life as a boy in St. Andrews, with his father, his friend Philip, and the small-town flirtations of Catherine Fawlsley. But when he thought that he scolded himself. No matter how much he wanted to find his father, and no matter how much easier life had seemed before the horrible burning of George Wishart and the seizure of the castle, he had to remind himself of one thing. That his presence at Hampton Court in the company of John Knox was a matter of great honor. If his growth into manhood meant putting away childish things, then that was what he must do. Lingering in the past—or longing for something else—was not going to be helpful.

And then one day Knox told him he would soon be traveling into the city proper of London to deliver a number of worn theological tomes to be newly bound. Ransom was elated.

At last, he thought. *A chance to venture back into the real world.*

First, however, he had to assist Knox in a sermon he was about to give in the presence of the young King Edward himself, as well as the other chaplains and much of the Court. Knox had picked a topic that had been smoldering in his mind for years.

Ransom knew that to be the fact. He remembered Knox teaching on that subject to his "eager bairns" years before in the besieged St. Andrews Castle.

"I will be preaching on the sacrament of Communion," Knox announced. "And I have a feeling that the feathers of some may be ruffled by my words!"

Ransom thought that perhaps Knox, who always seemed ready for a fight, was precipitating a battle that simply did not need to be fought.

When the day for preaching arrived, they traveled together to Windsor Castle in a gilded coach sent for them by the king himself. Knox seemed especially pensive on the ride. Ransom could not have guessed that his mentor secretly hoped to avoid confrontation, but felt that it was his duty to rise and meet it when God had so clearly thrust him into the midst of it.

For his part, Ransom was taken by the spectacular luxury of the coach, as well as the silks and gold braids of the footmen and coachmen that rode along on the outside. As they passed milk women, farmers, and traveling merchants on the road, the commoners would bow to the coach because it bore the emblem of the Crown of England. Ransom suddenly felt a swelling sense of importance just being in the royal coach and heading to the presence of the king himself.

When they arrived at Windsor Castle, they were shown into a medium-size stateroom where red velvet chairs had been arranged in a semicircle. In the center of the very first row was a large red-and-gold-tufted throne chair. An ornate carved pulpit had been placed in the center of the room, facing the chairs.

The room was not empty for long. Soon, several members of Court and royal staff scurried in and took their seats. Then the Duke of Northumberland and his two military aides strode in and were seated. The other five royal chaplains entered, each with his personal secretary. A few more minutes elapsed. And a few more.

Several members of the Privy Council walked in and sat on either side of the throne, in the front row, leaving one chair also empty next to the king's.

Then two heralds stepped into the room, lifted their long, bannered bugles, and blew a golden-toned announcement that sent everyone rising to their feet and bowing low.

The Lord Protector entered with the young king and stepped aside, bowing, as Edward looked over the room, nodded, and was seated.

Edward, almost fifteen years old, had the Tudor reddish-gold hair and pale gray-blue eyes. He was dressed in a dark blue and purple velvet coat with matching soft hat, and white silk pantaloons and stockings. His thin face and frame did not look robust.

John Knox was announced by a member of the Privy Council, and he rose and took the pulpit. Ransom wondered whether he would adapt his demeanor and preaching style to the impressive array of luminaries who sat before him. But he should have known better.

The Scotsman launched into his lengthy sermon with the same kind of athletic force that he used whether he was teaching his students or addressing commoners in a country church in Scotland.

He explained the purpose and history of the sacrament of the Lord's Supper. How it had been instituted by Jesus Christ Himself at the Last Supper as He neared His time of crucifixion.

"Yet we must all mind this point, and mind it well," Knox noted, "that the Lord's Supper, as it is the partaking of earthly bread and tangible wine, so lifts us up, as believers in Christ, to those heavenly and invisible things.

What things?" he went on. "By that I mean the spiritual banquet that Christ has prepared. The earthly elements of the Lord's Supper are but tokens of the invisible spiritual nourishment that our Lord gives to our souls by faith in His Son. And therefore we are renewed unto both godliness and immortality—not by bread and wine, but by His Spirit."

Having introduced the case for the symbolic—and not the mystical—purpose of the Lord's Supper, Knox marched his argument directly into the center of the theological battle.

"The Papists use the phrase *Hoc est corpus meum*—'This is my body'—the saying of Christ at the Last Supper as He presented the bread. And a good saying it is—but it cannot mean that the bread and wine are transubstantiated into Christ's body and blood—never!"

Now Knox was leaning forward like the prow of a ship, plowing into the waves of clerical opposition and Church hierarchy.

"For Your Majesty, and my dear friends, it is not the presence of Christ in the bread that can save us—nay—but as Holy Scripture teaches us, rather, it is His presence in our hearts through faith in His blood, which hath washed out our sins and pacified His Father's wrath toward us because of our sins."

Ransom could see, out of the corner of his eye, that young King Edward was riveted to the sermon, his eyes squinting in concentration and his pale brow slightly wrinkled.

But it was the next line of argument that sent shock waves through the audience and horrified Ransom.

Knox reasoned that if the doctrine of the "Real Presence of Christ" within the bread and wine was false, then the mode of worship should not be designed to encourage such false thinking.

"To what do I refer?" he asked loudly. "I refer to the ungodly and idolatrous practice of *kneeling before the altar and before the bread and the wine during the Lord's Supper.* If the bread and wine do not possess the person of Christ, but they are consumed because of our remembrance of Him who died for us, then why do we bow before it? We should be seated erect and raised up through God's free promise of salvation by faith, and so should we drink—and eat—not as beggars—for by God's grace we are made rich in Christ!—but we should drink and eat as sons and inheritors whom the victorious King hath placed at His table. We are not slaves or servants, but we are children of the King. We are the redeemed of the Lord! We are the partakers of His spiritual kingdom!"

But Archbishop Cranmer was there that day, seated in the back of the room. Though he was viewed as a leader in the Protestant reforms by the English Crown, Knox's sermon had now infuriated him. His face was flushed with rage. Everyone in the audience cast a glance back to see his reaction—all except one.

Young Edward the King was still looking straight ahead, though fully aware of what was transpiring in front of him.

Cranmer had just finished his revisions to the *Book of Common Prayer.* While he had incorporated many of the features of the reformed faith, he had seen fit to keep the instruction to continue the old practice of kneeling before the bread and the wine during Communion.

And because King Edward had signed an edict that required every citizen of England to obey the new *Book of Common Prayer* during worship, that necessarily meant that anyone following Knox's advice would be guilty of rebellion against the Crown.

Ransom had mentioned this aspect of Cranmer's revisions. But he had touched on it only very briefly as he helped Knox to prepare for his sermon. But Knox had now made it the focus of his sermon—and had fired the arrow directly into the heart of the religious establishment of England.

When Knox finished his sermon, there was a dead silence.

Then the young King clapped politely. A scattering of mild applause followed.

Edward left the room with the Lord Protector behind him who, as he passed Cranmer, quickly whispered something in his ear.

Cranmer was arguing loudly in the back of the room with several of the other chaplains, while Northumberland, ever the politician, nodded politely to Knox and then left, deciding to avoid this fight for as long as he could.

Knox and Ransom left Windsor Castle without fanfare. Now Ransom was anxious for the next day, when he would be able to escape for a while into the City of London on his errand. As he figured it, the full strength of the storm would, by then, be blowing into Hampton Court.

Chapter 30

Ransom had half expected that Knox would cancel his trip to London in the wake of the scandal created by the sermon on the Lord's Supper. But that did not happen.

Instead, his mentor presented him with six very thick books on theology that needed binding and wished him well that day. The only other thing he said, other than giving Ransom directions to the bookbindery in the city, was to indicate that upon his return to Hampton Court, he would very much appreciate Ransom's help in preparing his defense, as he fully expected an assault from some members of the Privy Council, and assuredly from Archbishop Cranmer himself.

The quickest route to the city was on the river, by one of the royal boats. As the oarsman used his long pole to guide the boat down the Thames, Ransom started reviewing some notes regarding Knox's possible defense.

But it was not long before the pleasant scenery gliding past him along the river, and his joy at escaping the walls of Hampton Court, had taken over his senses. He began to daydream and stopped his note-taking. The only unfortunate part of his boat trip was the fact that it was a warm day, and the river was stinking more than usual with refuse. Otherwise, this travel would have been delightful.

At the end, he disembarked, asking the boatman for the general direction of the corner of St. Giles and Fleet Streets, where the bookbinding shop was located.

Because he had grown up in St. Andrews, by no means a small town, at least by the standards in Scotland, Ransom usually found himself considered to be a "city" lad. But nothing could have prepared him for what he experienced as he ventured into London from the River Thames harbor.

He passed through the fine Temple Bar and Blackfriars neighborhoods and then entered the crowded, noisy commercial heart of the city. The streets were narrow, boxed in on all sides by shops and buildings that seemed to reach dizzying heights—sometimes ten floors up into the sky.

On the cobblestone streets there was a human tide of thousands. Beggars and young street urchins in rags; well-dressed merchants; common street vendors calling out advertisements for their goods. Women would cry warnings from high tenement windows and then toss buckets of garbage and waste out onto the street, which would leave the cobblestones slippery with an everpresent thin film of refuse.

The noise of clopping horses and rumbling wagons, the beckoning of the commercial hawkers, the arguments of vendors with their customers, the hammering of carpenters and stonemasons, and the lively shouts back and forth between passersby, all combined to create such a din that Ransom found it hard to hear himself think.

There was a multitude of ale taverns, all, it seemed, with large wooden signs hanging in front that named it after a boar, or a horse, or a stag. Sometimes men were arguing, and in one case fighting, on the front steps of those establishments.

Ransom tried to scan every shop sign on both sides of the crammed street for the name of the bookbindery.

And then something caught his eye. On the second floor of a building was a small sign, in much need of repainting, that read:

FAWLSLEY GARMENT AND STITCHING

He stared at the sign. He continued to gaze up at it, so transfixed that a wagon driver with a squealing herd of pigs in the back heading for the slaughter had to yell for Ransom to "Lay by there!"

Narrowly missing being run over by the horses pulling the wagon, Ransom jumped aside into the arched entrance of the building. There was a narrow winding staircase immediately in front of him that led to the upper floors.

He did not question whether he should further investigate. As if pulled by some irresistible force, he slowly mounted the twisting wooden stairway with his two packages of books, one under each arm.

He knew there could be other Fawlsley families in London. Yet he also knew that Catherine said her parents were in London. And back when he was still living in St. Andrews at least, they supposedly were performing some trade or craft for the English Crown.

But then, Ransom wondered, why would they not still be at Court? Why would they now be within the City of London itself, in this dirty, crowded commercial area? Could it simply be that the proprietors shared the same surname but had no connection to Catherine's family?

By the time Ransom had reached the second floor he could hear the crying of babies and a man's loud voice, which sounded as if he might be intoxicated. There was a small oak door that led to the stitching shop, and it was open halfway. Ransom paused for a moment in front of the door. What exactly was he going to say to the proprietor?

But that question was about to become moot. As he reached for the door handle, the door swung open from the inside. A young woman was lugging a large bolt of fabric out of the door. It was awkward and she was having a hard time carrying it. She turned, and they were suddenly face to face.

She had a common scarf wrapped around her head, and her reddish-blond hair was tied in the back in a bun. The dress she wore was plain. The years had sharpened her features. The softness was gone. The beauty had remained, though now it had a worn and slightly wearied quality. But her eyes were still inviting, and her smile, no longer simply girlish or coquettish, had a womanly character to it.

"Catherine…Catherine Fawlsley?" he stammered.

She set the bolt of cloth down outside of the doorway and looked at him with slightly open mouth, her eyebrows arched.

"Ransom…oh, Ransom…is that you? Is it really you?" she cried.

She glanced back in the shop and quickly closed the door behind her.

"Oh, you are a Godsend…a dream come true!"

Ransom blushed a little.

"Catherine…I saw the sign outside. I thought it might be, perhaps, by some chance, might be you…"

"Just look at you!" she said exuberantly, studying his velvet waist-coat and hat from Court. "So much the prosperous man and—oh look!—you are sporting a beard!"

She stroked his thin beard with her hand.

"You look so very handsome—yes—quite the man, I must say!"

Ransom struggled to speak, but she interrupted his attempt.

"You are carrying packages, I see—are you on an errand in the city? I was on my way to deliver this bolt of fabric to a shop just down the street. It's not very far, but I seem to be having trouble managing it…I never was very strong! Not like you, Ransom!"

"Here, let me carry it," he offered.

"Such a gentleman. Still the courteous and kind Ransom…"

Ransom shifted both packages of books to his right arm, picked up the bolt of fabric with his left, and tossed it up on his left shoulder.

"Just follow me," Catherine called out as she descended with a bounce to her step.

Ransom had trouble managing the long bolt, which kept hitting the low ceiling of the staircase overhead. And both packages of books under one arm were heavier than he would have thought.

At the bottom of the stairs she was waiting for him. As soon as he appeared, her face lit up with a smile. The two of them quickly hurried down the crowded street together.

"Just imagine...the two of us running into each other, and here in London of all places. And after all this time. Oh, Ransom—I have truly missed you so..."

Ransom was trying to keep up with her while struggling with his load.

"Yes, Catherine...I have thought of you so often..."

"Have you? Oh really? You're not just saying that, are you? Truly?"

"Yes, it is true...I have had so many travels and experiences since we parted in St. Andrews—and always I seem to keep thinking back to you."

"Experiences? Tell me please—I want to hear everything!"

"Well," Ransom began, breathing heavily under his burden, "first I left St. Andrews after the cannon siege, and traveled north and stayed at a castle—"

"Here it is!" Catherine shouted out. "Here, let me carry this into the shop. You stay out here, I'll be right back."

She grabbed the bolt from Ransom and lugged it in. After a few minutes she came out, slipped a small cloth purse into her apron pocket, and carefully laced it closed.

"All done!" she exclaimed. "Now what should we do? Let's do something wonderful—I'm sure you can show me all kinds of marvelous entertainments. Where shall we go first?"

"Well, actually," Ransom began with hesitation, "I have these packages to deliver..."

"Oh, yes. Of course," she said, with a look of mild disappointment on her face. "And what did you say brought you to London?"

"I am the personal secretary to…one of the chaplains at Court. I am staying at Hampton Court presently."

Ransom felt immediately guilty that he did not mention the name of John Knox. But he knew Catherine was familiar with him and, given her family's Catholic leanings, she might take offense.

"How very impressive!" she said. "I always knew you would be a man of considerable means…and so you seem to be."

"Not really…"

"You're just being modest!" she said, linking her arm in his.

"You know," Ransom was trying to decide how much he would divulge in this first, brief encounter, "I…kept the letter…kept it with me through all my travels—and read it often."

For a brief moment, Catherine's face went blank. But she quickly recovered, smiled, and spoke up brightly.

"Yes…the letter…and tell me about the letter that you kept…"

"Why, your letter to me, of course—delivered to me by Philip, just before I had to leave St. Andrews…setting forth your affections…do you remember it?"

"Remember? Ransom, would you jest with me after we've been separated all of this time—would you trifle with my feelings so? Of course I remember it."

"I didn't mean to suggest anything untoward…you have to be assured of that."

"I believe you," she said, squeezing his arm a little tighter. "And it is good to see you. Things have been dreadful for us—"

"How so?"

"Well, my father was a tradesmen for Court. He summoned me down here because he thought I was a suitable age for work at the palace… but after I arrived…everything went so bad…and those terribly mean men in the Privy Council and the wicked old advisors at Court, they sent my father away. He says it was because of his support of the Pope and of Marie de Guise...and ever since we have been living in misery."

"I am so sorry—"

"Absolute misery! My father has had to get work in the feltworks across the river—in Southwark. And now he says we may have to move out of this part of London and actually move over there to live—can you imagine! Over there where there are criminals and brigands, and low types of every kind. And the houses are shacks and filthy—I've heard stories of the rats nibbling at the children's feet as they sleep!"

"How terrible!"

"If we cannot come up with the rent, then we will be evicted and have to move to Southwark—and who knows what will become of me then."

Catherine's voice seemed to quiver, and she sniffed a bit as her eyes filled with tears.

"Dear Catherine!" Ransom said, stopping and gathering her two hands in his. "I won't let that happen. I will try to figure something out. Perhaps there is something I can do."

"Oh, will you? Oh, Ransom!" she cried out and hugged him close, and put her cheek next to his and whispered in his ear, "I just knew you would be my hero—that you would come someday and help me..."

Chapter 31

As soon as Ransom returned to Hampton Court, he tried to locate his mentor, but could not find him. He considered that somewhat odd because Knox had instructed him to consult with him as soon as he returned from his day in London.

Ransom ate alone and went right to bed. But although he was physically exhausted, he could not sleep. He couldn't take his mind off of Catherine Fawlsley. Tossing this way and that, restless in his bed, Ransom thought of the way that her hair had brushed against his face before they separated…and the soft touch of her cheek to his.

But just as quickly he thought of his cowardice in failing to mention Knox's name. And he wondered whether he should risk an infatuation with a young women whose religious affections seemed to be so ill-defined, and so potentially at odds with his own reformist beliefs.

And then he would glance over at the glass box on the nightstand next to his bed.

The box and the simple heather wreath within it were his only connection now with Margaret Chisholm. And that was an undeniable fact. Margaret was in the Highlands. At the time of their parting, she had assured him that she would not wait for him merely on the chance he might return at some undetermined time in the future. Ransom could understand her feelings—what likelihood was there that he would ever be called again up into the wilds of the Highlands?

Yet if she did not want to be remembered, then why did she give Ransom the glass box to remember her by?

And there was another point also. What were the chances he would ever have gone to the Highlands in the first instance? Ransom knew that God did not roll dice to create encounters such as his with Margaret. Yet in the same way, then, wasn't God also the author of Ransom's surprise meeting with Catherine? And if that were so, then Ransom seemed to be caught in the middle, pulled between two equally powerful extremes. And which way he should go, or what choice he would make...or even whether he needed to make a choice...all of that was completely beyond his ability to decide.

The next day Knox announced himself. He was excited and talking quickly. When the two sat down in his rooms, he thrust a letter at Ransom to read. It was the letter, he explained, that had caused him to depart to a quiet place for the afternoon and evening to pray, making him inaccessible to Ransom on his return to Hampton Court, for which he apologized.

The wax seal of the Privy Council was on the edge of the letter. Ransom read it carefully, then reread it.

"This is a most remarkable turn of events," Knox began. "Not altogether unexpected. Yet quite promising!"

"Yes. Most promising," Ransom added.

"The fact that the Council is asking Archbishop Cranmer to defend his insertion of the kneeling reference in the *Book of Common Prayer* clearly means they are questioning his prudence and giving heed to my sermon."

"Without a doubt."

"Now then," Knox continued, "what other thoughts do you have for me?"

But Knox's inquiry was met with a blank stare.

"Come, come," Knox said with a snap. "What else do you have to say—in light of the Privy Council's letter?"

Ransom was tired after a night without much sleep. He rubbed his eyes and glanced at the letter again.

"They want you to respond with your defense after the archbishop gives his…"

"Yes. Yes. That's what it says. And so we shall. What else?"

There was a pause.

"This is the kind of refutation," Knox said, now with an edge to his voice, "the very type of work for which you were called here to Court—didn't I tell you that when you first arrived?"

"You did."

"Then give me the benefit of your learning and studying…and *promptly, please.*"

Suddenly Ransom realized that, despite his title of personal secretary to one of the chaplains of the King, he was still Knox's student. And Knox was the teacher.

Ransom looked again at the letter. Then a thought came.

"Well…there is a point to be made on the order of argument…"

"And that would be?"

"I have been taught by my master of law, Mister Crenshaw, that the order of proof in a proceeding…" Ransom stopped momentarily to think back to his lessons.

"That the order of proof begins with the proponent of a certain state of facts…so that, the proponent has the burden of proving such facts—and he who responds merely has the privilege, though not the burden, of disproving them—"

"And so?"

"So—the archbishop must prove the necessity for including the reference to the act of kneeling at the Lord's Supper. It is his burden to prove it…not ours to disprove it."

"Clever enough," Knox began, "but too clever by half—for if we simply rest on his failure of argument rather than the strength of ours, we will be seen to be forfeit whether it be well-reasoned in the law or not. Remember, laws, including the laws of argument, are things that men in power sometimes bend to suit themselves. Better to give a whole defense and trust the rest to God than to trifle with the fine points of who has the burden of this or that argument."

Ransom sighed. *Why does he ask my opinion if he already knows what he will do or say?*

"What else say you?"

There was another thought Ransom had. But he did not know whether it was any use to voice it.

"Yes?" Knox asked, deciphering Ransom's expression.

"There is one other matter—"

"Speak it out, lad!"

"I prepared some Bible quotes and points for your sermon on the Lord's Supper as you had asked."

"And I read them and rejected them, as I recall."

"You did."

"Which ones do you still commend to me?"

"Just one."

"Which one?"

Ransom gathered his internal fortitude and spoke.

"That Jesus Himself, we are told in the Gospels, did only *sit* at the institution of the Lord's Supper. We are never told that He ever *kneeled*…"

Knox leaned back, considering the point again. Then he launched into a possible counterargument.

"And what if it is argued that the absence of any reference to His kneeling is not proof that He did not kneel…in fact, if the Lord Jesus was already reclining, would that not mean that He may have also kneeled?"

Ransom could see his master was seriously considering his point. Now his blood was beginning to run. Ransom sat forward on the edge of his seat.

"Then we would argue," he continued, "that if God had intended kneeling to be an important act of worship at the Lord's Supper, He surely would have had His Son kneel and would have caused the writers of the Gospels to have said so…"

Knox's face was blank with concentration. Then there was a flicker—and then a full explosion of emotion.

"Well done!" he cried out. "Yes. I will work on that point. It is worthy of inclusion in my written defense. Indeed, yes."

Ransom was flabbergasted at Knox's imprimatur of approval. Buoyed by that, he was in the mood to continue conversing with his master on the point, but Knox quickly excused himself, indicating he had a difficult task ahead of him.

He needed to begin work on a letter to his churches at Berwick and Newcastle. "Surely," he said, "they will begin soon to hear rumors that the Crown seeks them to kneel at the Lord's Supper, but that I preach against it. I do not want to hinder or injure them—but what I will write to them on that matter I do not know…"

As Ransom reflected on the whole kneeling episode and Knox's courage in preaching such an unpopular position, he began to understand that his time of learning at the English Court might involve more than simply memorizing all sixty-three articles of the Great Charter, or helping his master complete his correspondence, or compiling Bible verses. That the lessons he was meant to learn were also ones of personal character. And that those might even be more important than the academic knowledge he was amassing.

He also knew he was struggling with a difficult lesson of character regarding Catherine. On the one hand, he knew his hesitation on account of their religious differences. Yet still, he argued to himself, he did promise to her that he would try to help with her family's desperate financial crisis. And shouldn't a man be true to his promises?

Although he was earning nothing near Mister Knox's forty pounds a year as chaplain, Ransom's annual salary of fifteen pounds seemed to him to be quite a lot of money—and more than enough to pay a small amount, perhaps a few shillings on a regular basis, to Catherine.

Ransom waited until the bookbinding had been completed and then he made his way down to London again. Still somewhat unresolved on the matter, finally he decided to look Catherine up again and pay her what he could. She was happy to see him, and even more delighted at the shillings he brought with him.

Knox's written defense of his position on sitting—and not kneeling—at the Lord's Supper met with an incredibly unexpected victory before the Privy Council. The Council affirmed Knox's position in the strongest terms. However, they also faced a practical problem. The argument had dragged on, and the *Book of Common Prayer,* printed in red-lettered text, had already been published—and at great cost to the English Crown.

In the end they ordered, with the blessings of the King himself, an insertion of clarifying language—called the *black rubric,* as it was printed in black so as to stand out.

The rubric in each prayer book stated that by advising worshipers to kneel at the Lord's Supper,

> *No adoration is intended or ought to be done, either to*
> *the sacramental bread or to the wine thereby bodily*
> *received.*

It was a political compromise of sorts, but Knox's influence at Court was now clearly evident. But not everyone was pleased. Powerful enemies were beginning to gather.

Busy with his schedule at Hampton Court, and shuttling back and forth to London as often as he could to see Catherine, Ransom could not see the storm clouds that were now building over his newfound life in England.

Chapter 32

1553

It is the luxury of youth to assume that those things that are shall always remain so. It is only with age and experience that one begins to understand the unstoppable and onward march of life, and the inevitability of change.

Over the course of many months Ransom had continued to help support Catherine's family, something he did not explain to Knox. Nor did he explain the growing affection between Catherine and himself. Unlike their encounters in St. Andrews, this was, as far as Ransom could judge, something much more mature, and certainly more real. That relationship, and the growing workload as Mister Knox's assistant, had completely enveloped him. He simply had not noticed the growing dismay on Knox's countenance; nor did he appreciate the full extent of the changes taking place.

But part of the reason for that was the elimination of Knox's position with the Court, and Knox's increasing absence from Hampton Court castle.

At some point, and Knox had not fully confided in Ransom why it was so, Knox's name was removed from the official roll of the King's Chaplains. Knox was not alone in that, however, as Chaplain Bradford, also a staunch reformer, was also removed.

Though Knox was no longer an official chaplain, he was granted the title "King's Preacher to the Churches in the North." It was something much closer to Knox's heart anyway, and he told Ransom exactly that. He would continue to receive his yearly stipend. And he would have access to his rooms at Hampton Court. But as of late he was now spending most of his time preaching at, and attending the needs of, the Protestant churches in Berwick and Newcastle and Kent as well. He occasionally took Ransom along, but more often than not had him stay behind. He explained to Ransom that he needed a trusted ally at Court, and he trusted no one more than his young protégé.

Ransom had proven his worth repeatedly. More recently, Knox had been charged because of his having stirred up several nasty controversies, the total sum of which could have resulted in his trial for treason. He had bluntly refused the "promotions" to a position as Bishop of Rochester, and later as Vicar of All Hallows, which had been masterminded by Northumberland as a means of minimizing his influence at Court.

Then there was his fiery sermon in the North that took aim at what he clearly saw was a growing conspiracy to replace the ailing young king with a papal sympathizer.

He was hailed before the Privy Council to answer those and various other charges. But Ransom had gathered intelligence within the Court as best as he could as to the identity of the main antagonists on the Council, and then helped Knox to prepare his case. Knox was vindicated in a majority vote of the Council. Though it seemed strange to Ransom that Knox did not celebrate his victory—and in fact he seemed almost more dejected than before.

At one point, Knox had returned to the castle from his churches in the North to finish his review of the new Articles of Faith being circulated by Archbishop Cranmer. During that visit Ransom found him seated in a chair in his rooms, reading a letter. Ransom could see that he was greatly distressed. His body was hunched forward over the table.

The letter was dangling at the ends of his fingers, as if it had a weight so great that it labored him to hold it up.

"This is a letter," Knox said, "passed on to the church in Berwick from a faithful friend in Scotland, and they in turn have passed it on to me. It tells us of what has been transpiring in our native land since we have arrived here in England."

Knox explained that Marie de Guise had been increasing her influence and power in Scotland. It was generally assumed that she would try to elevate herself into the political power of the position of Queen Regent of Scotland. She had also traveled to France with some of her Scottish nobles to meet with her two powerful brothers, Charles, Cardinal of Lorraine, and Francis, Duke of Guise, both of whom were close to the French king.

It seemed painfully clear that she was closing the loops tight between France and Scotland. Not only did that pain those Scots who craved independence from foreign rule, but it also spelled disaster for John Knox's dream of a nationwide Protestant church movement.

Then Knox turned to Ransom, uncommonly emotional.

"And there has been another burning...a soul by the name of Adam Wallace...for reading and teaching the Word of God," Knox said in a heavy voice. "The Bishops of Madame de Guise had him arrested in Edinburgh. And it says here he dared to baptize his own bairn, rather than having the Church priest do so, and taught against such practices as praying to the saints and belief in purgatory. And at his trial he produced his Bible, and said, 'I desire God's Word to be the judge between the bishops and me,' saying if they could show he had done anything against God's will as revealed in His Word, then he would willingly die for it."

"What was the response?"

"They cried out, '*Heretic! Heretic!*' And although one in their council, the Earl of Glencairn, tried to persuade against it, they still voted for death, and bound Wallace and led him to the top of the Castle Hill…and tied him to the post, lit a fire under him, and watched him burn."

Ransom was quiet, and then asked a question.

"You said this terrible thing was done in Edinburgh…"

"Aye, it was."

"Did the letter say anything else about the goings-on there?"

Knox put the letter down and looked straight at Ransom.

"No…and there is no news in this letter—nor from any other source that I know of—about your father…"

Ransom nodded silently.

Then Knox prepared to fully share his heart with his secretary.

"You must know, my friend, that death is closing in on our young king—and what I fear will happen then to this land is so grievous I can hardly bear it."

This was a shock to Ransom. He could not have guessed that the king's end was so near.

"When Edward dies, the forces of Mary Tudor will try to quickly crown her and institute Catholic rule. I know that Northumberland has his own personal designs, but Mary's supporters are very powerful. And she has the backing of Catholic Spain as well."

Knox's eyes were now looking through the crisscross lead-paned windows of his castle room and far beyond.

"I would have thought it impossible," he said with a catch in his throat, "that any land would become so dear to me as that of my beloved Scotland…yet…the troubles here in the realm of England are doubly more burdensome to my heart than ever were the troubles of Scotland."

Then Knox put the letter down.

"I received another correspondence, God be praised, from my dear friends in Berwick, the family whose daughter Marjory has been so pleasant and agreeable to my heart. She—and they—have lifted my spirits so often. Helped me out of my doldrums of despair…"

Knox had spoken occasionally about Marjory Bowes. He was thirty-five, but she was only seventeen. Ransom secretly wondered about such a match, but said nothing about it. What really stuck with Ransom was that even his mentor, the invincible John Knox, seemed to have found someone in whom he could delight, and whose company he enthusiastically enjoyed.

Why wouldn't he be entitled to the same privilege?

The next day Knox left early to ride to one of his congregations.

Ransom had the Court boatman take him to London again. The boatman tried to ask him about his frequent travels there, but Ransom simply smiled and tried to change the subject.

Catherine was waiting for him. She brazenly took his hand in hers and kissed it. Ransom was taken aback by her forward passion, yet at the same time he was in the grasp of affections so thrilling that he seemed to be at a loss to criticize her or find any fault in her.

"I want you to take me somewhere!" she said with a sly smile.

"Where?"

"Promise me first—that you will say yes. Promise me!"

"How can I do that when I don't know where you want to go?"

"Ransom—dear man—don't you trust me?"

"Well, yes, but…"

"Then promise me."

"All right. I promise. Now—what is the mystery?"

"I want you to take me to see the bearbaiting contests!"

Ransom was a little shocked, yet he also found it mildly humorous.

"Why in the world would you want to go there?"

"I just want to—wouldn't it be exciting to actually see the bears fighting?"

"I don't think they even permit women in to see such sport. And the types that frequent those kind of games…I don't think it would be safe for you…"

"Oh, you're simply no fun," she said with a slightly pouty mouth. After a few minutes she changed the subject.

"I have been thinking," she said. "With you at Court—and with your wonderous influence and power—"

"I have no great power, Catherine, you must believe that."

"With your great influence," she persisted with a smile, "and the fact that my father was once employed at Court—could you see your way clear to put in a favorable word on his behalf?"

"Oh…I am not sure…"

"Just a word—a simple word that he might be re-employed in the service of the Crown. It would mean that all of us could be taken out of this dreadful, dirty city—wouldn't you want that for me?"

Ransom grew quiet. Catherine could see he was struggling with something.

"What is it?" she asked, a little hurt. "Won't you tell me why you've become so pensive? Was my suggestion so evil—is that it?"

"No of course not," Ransom said.

But he would no longer talk on the subject. That was because Ransom knew he did not dare disclose the smallest detail of what he knew.

That the king was dying. That there would soon be a titanic power struggle for the control of England. And that Mary Tudor, an ardent supporter of the Catholic cause, could well be ruling the realm soon.

And he knew if that were to come to pass, then he would have to decide on whether to execute a plan that had been occupying his mind from almost their first encounter in London, and since the rekindling of his affections for Catherine. It was daring and risky, perhaps even foolhardy.

Because of that, Ransom knew he could not speak of it, at least not yet. It was, he had thought to himself, shocking enough that he was even contemplating such a plan.

Chapter 33

While young Edward, the king of England, lay dying in Windsor Castle, in the nation to the north, in Edinburgh, the Scottish queen mother, Marie de Guise, was seeking to consolidate her Catholic base of power. She had a keen political sense and had successfully formed an alliance with many of the Scottish lords and noblemen. Her young daughter Mary, the heir apparent to the Scottish throne, was still living in the safety of France with her relatives.

The queen mother's plan was simple: When her daughter Mary finally arrived of age, she would be installed as queen of Scotland with the blessings of the nobles. After that, while securing her grip on Scotland, they would wait—and when the timing was right and the throne of England became vacant, they would make their move. Her daughter Mary would demand recognition—based on her descent from Henry VII—not only as queen of the Scots, but of England as well. All of England, Scotland, and Wales would then be ruled by the French political influence of the de Guise family and the religious doctrine of the Roman Church.

To further this plan, Marie de Guise planned on installing, within the year, Frenchmen in positions of power in Edinburgh—in the departments of finance, in care of the Great Seal, and in the Scots' Privy Council as well.

Her trip with the Scottish nobles to France, though, had not gone well. She had promised French titles and lands to those nobles who supported her, but from that journey, at least, the noblemen had returned to Scotland empty-handed and skeptical.

And then there was the scandal of the Edinburgh printers.

Since the killing of Cardinal Beaton and the temporary takeover of St. Andrews Castle several years before, the Protestant radicals were getting increasingly bolder. Pamphlets were circulated on High Street, denouncing the corrupt practices of the papal structure in Scotland, the abuses of the Black Friars and Gray Friars, and the doctrines of the Church. Some included the words of songs and hymns that raised the reformist banner.

At the same time, political handbills were littering the Edinburgh streets, decrying the slow but insidious French takeover of Scotland. Many of them put new political refrains to old tavern songs, lampooning the current leadership of Madame de Guise, who held court just a few blocks away at Holyrood Palace.

The queen mother convinced the Scottish Parliament to enact stern measures against such treasonous publishing, and so they outlawed all printed "ballads, songs, blasphemies, and rhymes, whether in Latin or English."

But it had not achieved the desired result.

On this day Marie de Guise sat in the red-velvet-tufted, high-back chair in the Privy Council Chambers, surrounded by her advisors. Her face was labored in an exercise of calm. She had learned to mask her emotions. She had found it nearly impossible to keep control of the arrogant Scottish nobles and the defiant clan chiefs while also pulling France ever closer to the takeover of the nation, yet somehow she had managed it.

She had an implacable smile; her hair was perfectly in place, swept back and tucked neatly under her crownlike band of jewels. Her right hand was slowly fingering the strand of pearls that hung around her long neck—the only sign of her internal agitation.

"And yet," she said, continuing with her comments to the Council, "despite the Act of Parliament—*our Parliament*—that has outlawed these rancorous publications—these libels and heresies, vile and despicable, refuse of lies upon lies—do we not agree that they are so?—yet they continue unabated. It is embarrassing, is it not? So—what shall we do?"

"We must be careful," one of the advisors said with a tinge of apology in his voice, "lest we stir up the populace…a hornet's nest is best not swatted."

"So then, what are you saying? That we shall simply be stung?" she retorted with a hint of sarcasm.

"No, Madam, no," another advisor said. "Yet—it is a problem that has no clear solution at present. I would remind this council that it has been a full six years since the arrest and jailing of one John Scott, printer and rabble-rouser. That was followed by more of these scandalous publications, not fewer—thusly we then passed an Act of Parliament, and yet that has not stemmed the tide of these troublesome printings."

"Perhaps we need more trials for treason among these printers," she said.

"There are many lawful printers here in Edinburgh," another Council member put in. "And the trade is much needed here for commerce and for the affairs of government. I dare say that rounding them all up and locking them in the Toll Both jail will not solve the problem."

"The very point exactly," another advisor said. "Just a fortnight ago we had to release another printer who had been arrested. He had been languishing in jail for God knows how long—like the others, he was suspected of religious rebellion. Yet all that could be proven against him was that he had not secured the proper municipal printer's license."

"I will hear you further on this matter," the queen mother said with an air of finality, "and I will expect at that time an answer—on how to save the Scottish Crown from the stinging insults of these vile pests."

A mere four blocks away, just off of High Street and down a narrow, twisting close, a crowded, stone-cobbled alley lined with four-story tenement buildings and shops of the lower class of trades, a printer was cleaning up. But his shop was emptier than it should have been. His printing equipment had been seized by the Queen's Sheriff when he had been arrested.

Since his release from custody he had been forced to work during the day as a typesetting assistant at a more prosperous print shop, farther up High Street toward Edinburgh Castle. His aim was to save enough money to buy back his press out of the Crown's bailment. It was an insult to his decades of experience as a printer and a proprietor himself to work as an assistant in a competitor's business. But more than that, his long months in jail had left him plagued with sickness and disability. To work the long daytime hours in his condition was a daunting task.

At night the printer would trudge back over to his own shop, repair the vandalism that had occurred during his absence, and clean the racks of type, preparing for the day he could—once again—open his own printing and binding business.

Hugh Mackenzie sat down on a hard wooden chair in his printing shop, glancing occasionally at the door. He was waiting for someone to arrive. His entrance was one of the last doors toward the bottom of the winding, crooked close, down from the shops of several leatherworkers and almost to the end—where the leper hospital was.

His compatriots called it Leper's Close, though that was not its official name. The alley was so named not only because of the hospital, but also because of the stories in the Gospels of the lepers healed by Jesus.

Before his arrest, the reformist sympathizers would bring their pamphlets to be printed by him by night—or gather quietly in his upper apartment for secret prayer and Bible-reading and strategy sessions.

But since his seizure by the Crown, fewer of them came.

Hugh Mackenzie was waiting, but grew weary and began dozing off.

Then his shop door opened and a traveling merchant entered.

"Good evening," Hugh said. "Can I help you?" He was eyeing the man closely.

"Yes—perhaps you can. You are a printer…"

"Yes—though I am waiting for the return of my press."

"Well enough," the man said. "When it is back in your possession, I am wondering if you would be able to print me one of these…"

The merchant pulled out a piece of paper and a piece of dark chalk, and drew the outline of a fish.

Hugh smiled and slowly rose, extending his hand to the man.

"God bless you, my brother in Christ," Hugh said. "You are the one to carry my message north, then?"

"Aye. I am," the merchant said. "I go to several fishing villages along the western coast for my master. To secure contracts for the season's catch. I will make the side trip to the Highlands for you."

"Here is the letter," Hugh said, handing it over to the merchant with great care. "It is for my son, Ransom—last I knew he was staying under the care of Hamish Chisholm…head of the cattle watch for the laird of the glen, Colin MacDonald, just south of Glencoe."

"I believe I can find it," he said. "I will have a Highlander guide with me who is kin to the MacDonalds—anything else?"

"Aye," Hugh said, "bid him my deepest affection…and God's speed…"

As the merchant turned to leave, he thought of something and looked back at Hugh.

"And what if he is not there—if I cannot locate him…"

Hugh sat down, wearing a wearied look.

"Then...I dunno," he replied.

His mind knew full well the length and breadth of time that he and his son had been separated...and all of it without a single word of communication. Yet his heart could not bear the thought that the message might not find its appointed recipient.

"I just dunno..." Hugh added, with an inner exhaustion that had simply run out of words.

Chapter 34

Edward, the young king of England, was dead.

True to his political nerve and ingenuity, Northumberland, when Edward's death seemed imminent, had arranged the marriage of one Lady Jane Grey, a devout believer in the reformed faith, to his son, Lord Guildford Dudley. By no coincidence, Lady Jane was the only other blood relation of Henry VIII to lay claim to the throne of England—other than Mary Tudor, the powerful Catholic challenger, and young Elizabeth, daughter of Henry's temporary union with Anne Boleyn, of course.

With the cautious backing of the Privy Council, Northumberland had Lady Jane quickly crowned as Queen of England.

Though Northumberland had his own plans for Queen Jane, which involved making his son Guildford in king matrimonial, they were no match for Mary Tudor. Mary soon rallied the Catholic nobles, and then the countryside populace as well. It was clear she would be able to march into London and take the crown if she wished.

But that would not be necessary. Queen Jane's reign lasted only nine days. The Privy Council forsook their backing of Northumberland. Lady Jane, Guildford, and Northumberland as well were all arrested and taken to the Tower of London.

And Mary Tudor was queen.

Elizabeth was also taken to the Tower as a co-conspirator—though the case against her was clearly flimsy. During her temporary exile there, she etched into the glass of her prison window with her jeweled ring a self-assured ditty:

> *Much suspected of me*
> *Nothing proved can be.*

However, as concerning Jane, Guildford, and Northumberland, things were much more dismal. The only question regarding their executions was simply the matter of timing.

All in all, London was now a very dangerous place for reformist Protestants.

And so, it did not take Ransom by surprise when he heard the footsteps of John Knox echoing down the hall, growing nearer, and then stopping at his bedchamber door. And then the heavy knocking.

Knox was blunt—even more blunt than usual.

"Ransom, gather your things. Be ready to ride. We go to the North—to my congregations there. They will give us shelter and protection. I will determine then whether we stay in England...or go elsewhere..."

"Where else would we go?" Ransom said, trying to process the cold steel of Knox's determination to leave London immediately.

"Scotland is out of the question for the time being. And with Mary on the throne in London, the fires will soon be burning bright across the countryside...lighting up the skies and using the bodies of faithful followers of Christ as kindling. Perhaps we will go to Switzerland—Mister John Calvin has, through some intermediaries, suggested that I may benefit by meeting with him in Geneva. And well I might—I will need your help, as always. You have been a good and trusted helper—now hurry, lad, hurry!"

Within the hour Knox had arranged for two horses and was waiting for Ransom. They mounted up and began riding due north, away from Hampton Court, away from the City of London.

There was little conversation between the two of them. Knox seemed preoccupied. But Ransom knew the look on his face and what it meant. He was already trying to peer into the future, discerning where the hand of Almighty God was leading.

Ransom was struggling in his mind, writhing within. A deadly guilt now lay heavy on his heart. He was about to make his announcement…he had to do it soon, before he was too far out from London. But to confront his master and mentor with this news would be grievous.

Yet, he had decided to do it—and had been so firmly resolved in his mind, that nothing Mister Knox said or did would dissuade him.

It took Knox only a few seconds to notice that Ransom had stopped his horse.

Knox wheeled his horse around and cantered up to Ransom.

"Why do you stop?"

"I do not merely stop," Ransom said. "I ride back…back to London."

"What say you?"

"I must return to London…I am so sorry, Mister Knox…but I must return there. I can't go on with you to the North—"

"What takes you to London, where Mary Tudor and her allies seek to spill the blood of the faithful in the streets?"

"I am in love…with a woman…and she does love me…I am sure of it…and the match is the truest thing that my heart has ever felt."

"A woman—I am sorry…I didn't know…then we will both ride back to London and fetch her quickly, and she will join us in our ride to the North."

"That cannot be—all her kin is in London with her, and I am sure she would not…that…she would not desire to ride with you…"

Ransom regretted the words as soon as they left his lips.

"What manner of woman is this, who desires to stay back in the place most dangerous to the reformers? Would that make her a hero of incomparable courage?"

Then Knox thought more deeply on the matter.

"Or perhaps, would that make her something else altogether?"

Ransom could not answer. It was as if his tongue suddenly lacked the means to move—as if the muscles and ligaments had been severed.

"Speak up!" Knox said loudly. "Explain this madness—I implore you by the love I bear you in Christ—by the love I have shown you as a poor and humble replacement of a father for you. Speak your heart, for pity's sake!"

Ransom was now unable to defend himself against the emotional visage of Knox and his withering glance. How could he? Yet in that very instant, just then, there was a moment of clarity for Ransom.

This great and glorious gospel revolution—that was Knox's campaign, but it was not his. The battle for reformation of the Church and the new doctrines of justification by faith and the Scriptures for the commoners, all of it—it was for others. For the martyrs pure of heart, like poor George Wishart who was charred in the fires of Cardinal Beaton—or for the thundering prophets like Knox—or for the political schemers who meted out retribution and seized power, like the men who captured the castle in St. Andrews...

But it was not for Ransom.

He had chosen another path. He had discovered happiness and joy in the company of a woman. And for that reason he would stay behind. So now the die was cast.

Knox could see that his pleas would not reach Ransom's heart. The doors to that chamber were locked from the inside.

Before he turned and rode away from his young apprentice, John Knox said one more thing.

"Aye—and you did not confide in me about this love of your heart. Because you knew I would disapprove and would implore you against it...as surely I would...don't you know, Ransom? Deeds done in darkness never prosper—never."

Then Knox set his face to the North and rode hard in that direction.

Ransom watched him for a while. He thought he would feel something. But he only felt an overwhelming numbness. So now he needed to go to the one person who could make him feel alive again.

As he entered London, he had to dodge the groups of the queen's soldiers who were posted on almost every corner.

The streets were a cacophony of noise, celebration, and bedlam. Some Protestants were gathering their goods on carts and quickly exiting the city. But others, failing to believe the dire predictions of persecution, were content to sit in the doorways and windows and watch the melee. After all, if Mary Tudor was now queen, it was by God's hand—what would they have to fear?

Monks and priests, now that the evangelical radicals had been dispatched from power, streamed into London. Drinking bouts, once started in the taverns, were now spilling out into the streets.

Ransom finally made his way up the narrow stairway to Catherine's apartment and shop. He would tell her, once and for all, that he had made the greatest sacrifice of his life for her. He had left everything behind on the promise of her sweet affections.

But when he arrived, he was surprised to find that her mother and father, and Catherine too, were busy packing their goods and clothing in boxes and crates.

When Catherine saw him, she hurriedly exited and closed the door behind her.

"Ransom—whatever are you doing here?"

"I've come to tell you something…"

"Well then—tell me quickly…"

"Mister Knox and much of the Court have left the castle—but I have stayed behind. I have left everything for…for you, Catherine…if you will have me…"

Catherine smiled and turned ever so slightly to the side. Ransom could not make out the meaning of her strange reaction. In an instant he would understand.

"Things are so very different now," she said matter-of-factly. "With Queen Mary, everything has changed. My father, we are told, has been invited to be one of the queen's tradesmen."

Ransom stared at her, finding it difficult to understand Catherine's plain meaning.

"Ransom—don't you see, silly man—my family and I are going to Court. We are finally rid of these horrid surroundings. I shall wear silk again! And ribbons! And I shall go to some of the balls and festivals! Oh—can you just imagine?"

"And what...what will become of me?" Ransom stammered.

"Well...this apartment will be vacant...and because of your kind shillings toward the rent, it is paid up through the month's end. You can stay here. And I will send for you from time to time—and we can meet..."

"When? When will that be?"

"I really cannot say...but...oh, I didn't tell you something else..."

"What else could there be?"

"Your friend...is already here too. His father will be advisor to the Crown on matters concerning Scotland—and he is coming to London also. His family is taking beautiful furnishings—their house is practically a mansion."

"Who?"

"Why, my cousin—Philip, of course!"

"Philip is here?"

"Yes, I said that."

There was an awkward silence. Then Catherine brought their meeting to a close.

"You must let us finish packing—and it will be best if we are not seen with you as we leave. I will put one of the keys to the apartment under the black pot just outside the door."

"Catherine…" Ransom said, calling after her as she turned to the door.

"Ransom, have faith in my truest affections. Won't you, please? Now run along and wait until our wagon has pulled away. And then you may enjoy the whole place to yourself."

"How long before I hear from you?"

But Catherine did not answer.

Instead, she smiled and dipped her head quickly to the side coquettishly, then swept back into the shop and closed the door firmly behind her.

Chapter 35

The sun was setting over the craggy mountain peaks of the Highlands of Scotland. There were streaks of red and pink in the western sky, and the hills were still lush with the green of late summer. In a few weeks they would be awash in purple heather. Now in the final, waning hours of sunlight, a golden tinge was cast over the contours of the slopes that surrounded the little cottage down in the valley.

Hamish Chisholm sat with his broadsword laid on the table in front of him. His huge claymore—with a blade nearly as tall as he—was down from its usual perch, within arm's reach. His short sword was in its hilt.

Across the table, Rhona was rubbing her hands anxiously.

"Isn't Margaret due home?" Hamish asked.

"Yes…she will be…but I sent her on an errand so we could finish our talk."

"She's not a wee bairn any longer—she's a grown woman now. She deserves to be part of this…"

"And she will…but I need to give ye my heart on the matter."

"I already know yer heart…it's my head that's tryin' to figure this out…"

"Head 'n' heart…this or that…Hamish, ye're so stubborn that ye'll make me moonstruck with madness," Rhona said with exhaustion in her voice.

"I know what ye want me to do, woman—to run...to leave the Highlands and head due west to the Isles and seek refuge—run like a coward..."

"No," Rhona retorted. "I want you to live like a man—rather than die like a dog with a sword in your back. Do ye want to end up like the laird? And it doesn't matter who killed him—the fact of the matter is that they're blamin' ye and naming ye as the plotter—"

"No woman, it does matter. I know it was his nephew Murdo, because he is the one who stands to gain by it all. I told Colin it was a mistake to name Murdo as his clan *tanist* to succeed him—that he was the type that wouldn't wait for God to take Colin in His own appointed time. No—Murdo wanted the fine house and lands and titles of the laird, and he wanted them now..."

"So what if ye're right? Ye've said yerself that Murdo has made alliance with some of the Campbells, and he's using French mercenaries now to patrol his lands and cattle—they'll be comin' after ye, dear heart... we have to leave..."

"And what about Margaret?" Hamish asked.

"She'll be comin' with us."

"Margaret has other desires..."

"Ye're her da—ye must order her to come with us."

"She wants to answer this," Hamish said, lifting up a letter in his hand, "and in person."

"Ransom is not here. When we've settled safely in the Isles you can send a message to Hugh Mackenzie and tell him his son was last seen headin' to London."

"If ye care deeply about your daughter—and I know ye do—then in yer heart ye have to believe she would be safer in Edinburgh with Hugh than on the run with us—"

Rhona was starting to cry.

"I don't know that...I don't!" she said, holding back her sobs.

"Ye do—and ye have to let go of yer daughter now. It's time—no one in these glens will marry her now…she's turned them all down anyway…and with us she will be marked for death. Come now, my precious—perhaps it's time to let her go her way…"

"He's right."

The voice came from the doorway. It was Margaret.

Hamish looked at his daughter, with the dying glow of the last sunlight behind and all around her as she stood in the open door—and he saw the woman in her.

"What'll ye do down there?" Rhona asked.

"Like the letter from Mr. Mackenzie says—help him with his printing shop."

"And what do ye know about any of that, pray tell me?" Rhona snapped back.

"She knows how to read and write—and Ransom said she was a quick student in book studies and language," Hamish said with a smile.

"And no thanks to ye!" Rhona said curtly. "Hamish Chisholm had to make sure his daughter was the only lass in the glen with more education than the laird himself! And now she'll be leavin' me—and never to be seen by these poor eyes again I fear…"

Margaret swept over to her mother and hugged her.

"As soon as I get to Edinburgh I will send word to ye," Margaret said brightly.

"Now, lass—I have not yet decided…" Hamish said reluctantly.

"Yer da has not yet decided!" Rhona parroted.

"Well, I have!" Margaret retorted.

"Watch yer tongue with yer da!" Hamish said firmly. "I'll sleep on it…and pray on it…and give ye my word in the mornin'. And I'll also give ye my word on our running away like wee little fawns to the western Isles tomorrow too!" Hamish said to Rhona.

Margaret was not pleased. She went to bed pensive and angry.

Hamish and Rhona whispered quietly together in bed that night. Hamish said he felt he likely had to let Margaret go to Edinburgh. After all, it seemed like a fair trade. That Ransom was taken in by them in Hugh Mackenzie's hour of need—now Margaret could be taken in by Hugh as danger loomed over the Chisholm family.

Rhona wept in Hamish's big arms, and he comforted her.

For the longest time they did not speak, but she lay against his chest, seeking consolation.

Then Hamish whispered his deepest love to her in the old Gaelic and kissed her. And they fell asleep.

At some point in the early hours, as the dark of the cool night slowly lifted and the gray of dawn was breaking, Hamish woke with a sound.

He couldn't be sure, but it sounded like a horse.

He slipped out of bed, careful not to wake Rhona, and quietly passed Margaret's bed, glancing over at the slumbering shape under the quilt.

The Highlander wrapped on his kilt and donned his boots, buckling his broadsword to his waist, hilting his short sword, and fetching his massive claymore.

Once outside he glanced around the cottage. One of the horses was missing.

"Thieving marauders!" he muttered. Then he looked out into the distance. He thought he saw a shape—perhaps a horse and rider—on the crest of the hill.

He mounted his horse and rode hard to the north, toward the hill.

But when he arrived he saw only a riderless horse standing nearby, shaking its mane. Hamish looked at the horse—he realized it was not one of his—in fact it belonged to Geordie, one of Hamish's closest friends and his trusted helper on the cattle watch. He knew something was terribly wrong. He slid his broadsword out and dismounted. He walked in a semicircle around the horse until he discovered Geordie's body lying face down in the boggy ground, dead.

He could not have known that Geordie was riding hard to the cottage to warn Hamish and his family of the impending massacre. But he never made it. He was intercepted by Murdo and a dozen of his French mercenaries.

And now, as Hamish groaned in grief over his friend's body, Murdo and his gang rode down from a nearby bluff, galloping straight for Hamish.

Hamish sprinted over to his horse and grabbed the reins in one hand and with the other, gripped the handle of his broadsword hard. But he knew he could not mount the horse and outrun Murdo's gang. But at least he could try to warn Rhona.

He let go of the reins, and with his other hand he pulled his claymore out of the saddle and stuck the tip of it into the ground, handle up. With the flat of his broadsword, he swatted the horse's hindquarters, sending it back in the direction of the cottage.

Three of the mercenaries dismounted and cautiously approached Hamish.

Murdo was on his steed, smiling.

"Geordie here must have been in on the murder of my uncle—along with ye," he said sarcastically. "Otherwise, why else would we have killed him?"

"I'll tell ye why ye killed him," Hamish said loudly. "Because ye're a coward and because ye've got a dozen of yer French assassins to do it for ye."

By now the nine French horsemen had surrounded him.

The three on the ground were each nervously balancing a sword in their fighting hands.

"Don't just stand there!" Murdo shouted. "Lay into him, lads!"

All three rushed toward Hamish. He picked the biggest one and, as he had once demonstrated to Ransom, rushed him with a screaming ferocity but, at the last second, dodged and then tripped him, sending him facedown.

Before the fallen man could lift his head off the ground, Hamish plunged his sword into his back.

Hamish crossed swords with another opponent, knocking the weapon out of his hand. He tried to run away, but Hamish grabbed the little dagger out of the hilt in his sock and flung it. It stuck in the man's back and he went down.

But the third Frenchman was now on him and stuck his sword into his leg.

Hamish grunted in pain, and then whirled around and plunged his broadsword into his assailant's ribs, lodging it there firmly as the man fell back.

"Horsemen—take him down!" Murdo cried frantically.

Hamish limped over to his claymore, which was stuck straight in the ground waiting for him, and grabbed it with both hands.

The first rider charged. Hamish swung in a fierce, slashing arc and took off his sword hand.

A rider galloped from behind. Hamish ducked his swing and then grabbed him and pulled him off his horse. Then he two-handed his claymore down onto the man's neck with a deadly blow.

But one of the Frenchmen was a bowman, and he fired an arrow that tore into Hamish's back.

He staggered. One of the Frenchman dismounted and rushed in with his sword. But Hamish had one blow left…and delivered it with his claymore to the man's head.

Two more dismounted and charged him. Plunged their swords into him.

Hamish had a prayer on his lips—for the safety of his wife and daughter—but it was never uttered.

He gasped and then took his last breath where he lay with the smell of the soft, fragrant Highland earth in his nostrils.

Murdo then ordered the rest of the men to slaughter the occupants of the cottage.

By now Rhona had awakened, saw Hamish's riderless horse, and grabbed a dagger.

She plunged it into the belly of the first Frenchman who burst into the cottage. She turned to warn Margaret in her bed. But she was quickly overpowered by the rest of the gang, and moments later lay dying on the floor of her home.

Outside, Murdo yelled, "There's a daughter in there—kill her too!"

Chapter 36

On the second floor of Hugh Mackenzie's shop, the candles in the wall sconces were burning low. There were two men with him, and one of them was talking.

"Hugh—are you listening to me? Have you heard anythin' I've said?"

"Yes, I have," Hugh replied. "I was just thinkin'—there was a time when this room once had a dozen reformist Christians—men strong of faith and stout of heart. Now there's only three of us…and one of us sounds like he's raising the flag of truce…"

"Mind who ye're talkin' to," the man retorted. "Who visited you in jail? Who helped you locate your printing press in the sheriff's lock-up?"

"Hugh," the second man chimed in, "I'm sure you meant no disrespect. We know you've suffered for the faith, jailed twice since arriving in Edinburgh…and the second time for longer than I can count…"

"I don't count that suffering, lads," Hugh said quietly. "Nay—what I call suffering is what they did to poor Adam Wallace up on Castle Hill…"

"Hugh, that's what I'm talkin' about," the first man said. "It's been two years since the burning of Wallace. Things are changing. All I am sayin' is that we should give the queen mother and the Privy Council a chance—change comes hard…"

"What change?" Hugh asked. "I see no change—not in the things that really matter."

"Many changes—favorable signs," the first man countered. "In St. Andrews, the new archbishop—Hamilton—he is no Cardinal Beaton. He is working for reforms—legislation has been passed—you know what I am talking about—sixty-eight statutes passed—sixty-eight! Designed to eliminate the abuses of the Roman Church here in Scotland. Now priests are prohibited from maintaining concubines and mistresses—and no longer able to endow their bastard children with the treasuries of the church. All clergy are required to be knowledgeable on matters of doctrine and understanding of Scripture. Even the teachings from the sect of Martin Luther on justification by faith seem to have some influence on the new catechisms—"

"Concessions, negotiations, conciliations—" is this really what we have been fighting for?" Hugh asked.

"What are you sayin'?" the first man said with a hint of curiosity. "That you would support rebellion? Treason?"

"Only this—that I was slow to warrant a full-scale battle for the truth of God's Word during my years in St. Andrews. But I am older now—perhaps wiser—I pray so—but we must not stop the printing of our pamphlets nor our work on distributing Bibles to the commoners in the common tongue—nor our efforts to bring preachers of the gospel into Scotland."

"What happened to your friend Mister Knox?" the second man asked.

"After his release from the galleys, I believe he became a pastor down in Berwick," Hugh replied. "I was set to ride down and try to find him, but then I was arrested…"

"I heard he was made one of the king's chaplains," the first man added.

"Well, with Mary Tudor on the throne," Hugh noted, "any Protestant with a sane mind will leave England—and do so at a full gallop. I'm sure Knox is on his way to the Continent by now."

The second man studied Hugh's sallow face and noticed the trembling of his hands.

"We should leave you to your rest," he said. "You look a fright—are you sick with the fever?"

"I'll be fine."

"Any news from your son yet?" the other man asked.

Hugh shook his head. He knew that for all the infirmities of his flesh he had to endure, the emptiness in his heart was the more intolerable.

For Ransom life in London had taken an ugly turn. The only work he could find was across the river, on the south bank of the Thames, in the filthy, dark, hopeless district of Southwark. Because of his experience with John Shakespeare in skinning animals he was able to secure a job in a tannery, next to a slaughter yard. The flies were so dense that sometimes the sky seemed black with them. Payday was a fearful time. With little sheriff's protection in the area, thugs and criminals would lie in wait for men who had just been paid. Those who were only robbed and left to flee toward home penniless, but alive, were considered the lucky ones.

This was the section of town where Catherine's father had worked in a felt factory. Now Ransom could understand Catherine's revulsion at her father having to work there. Ransom thought that perhaps God was giving him retribution for not caring more for the plight of her family.

After three weeks at Court, Catherine, true to her word, sent a messenger to Ransom. She met him in a small, inconspicuous park in the fashionable area to the west of the Temple Bar section of London. She came dressed in a new yellow and blue dress, and was friendly and talked incessantly about the happiness she had in her new circumstances. But she was unpleasantly direct about Ransom's appearance.

"You are such a sight!" she exclaimed at his clothes, which, though he had washed them, were still tinged at the cuffs with blood. One of his boots had a tear in the side.

"And your smell is most unpleasant!"

"I am sorry," Ransom replied, with mild irritation. "I bathe...but I can't seem to get the smell of animal hides off of me..."

"Perhaps a more perfumed soap..."

"I have no money for expensive soaps."

"Here," she said. Then she fished in her small beaded bag and pulled out a single shilling.

"No, I can't take it," Ransom insisted.

"Don't be silly," she said. "You helped my family. This will be your recompense."

Ransom paused. She urged him to take it. As Ransom took the shilling, though he could not exactly decide why at that moment, he had never felt quite so humiliated in his life.

"Now you can smell sweet when we next meet!" she said with a laugh.

"When will that be?" he said.

Catherine rose to her feet and brushed off her dress.

"When do you think?" he repeated.

"I am not sure," Catherine said with a little sigh. "We are so busy. But I will send for you again..."

Then she kissed the tips of her fingers and placed them gingerly on his lips, and then turned and walked to the carriage and the driver who was waiting for her.

"Catherine," he called after her. "I've given up so much..."

She paused only for a moment. Then as he approached the carriage, she said, "And you still have the chance of gaining so much..."

As Ransom made his way through the city, back to his sparse apartment, he was only thinking of the bleakness of his present situation. He had no thoughts for the state of governance in England. That simply had no appeal for him.

But it should have.

Mary Tudor, quick to put down a fledgling rebellion against her, rounded up more than a hundred persons suspected of supporting—in word or thought if not in deed—the doctrines of the rebels. Then she had them all executed. Lady Jane Grey and Northumberland, her father-in-law, were taken from the Tower of London and beheaded.

In the countryside, there were ominous signs of the coming calamity. A priest was thrown into the Colchester jail for preaching against the mass. A man in Sussex was imprisoned for questioning the "Real Presence" of Christ in the bread and wine of Communion. Archbishop Cranmer was relieved of his duties, and then brought to a proceeding with two other prominent Protestants to voice his reformist beliefs before a throng of a thousand of Mary Tudor's shouting supporters. When he did so he was condemned as a heretic.

The stage was being set.

The ancient, dreaded Acts for the Burning of Heretics, which were first passed in England one hundred and fifty years before, were now being revived by Mary Tudor's new government.

As Knox had so dreadfully predicted, the cruel fires would soon be lit.

Chapter 37

The two families, Philip's and his cousin Catherine's, had gathered for a holy day feast at the fine house of Philip's father in the elegant section of London's residential area—where the lanes were lined with tall stone mansions and the lawns with massive gardens and scrolled gates.

Philip was strolling through the house with a punch glass in his hand, and he walked over to Catherine. She was chatting excitedly with two English soldiers who were part of the contingency of the palace guard invited to the gathering.

"May I deprive you of the company of my fair cousin for just a while?" Philip said with a smile. The two soldiers smiled politely, and Philip took Catherine's arm and escorted her out to the back colonnade, which overlooked the vast terraced gardens in the rear.

Torches were burning at the corners of the veranda. Inside the mansion, roving minstrels were playing light, pleasant tunes that were drifting outside through the wide French doors that had been opened.

As he looked over the gardens fingering his crystal cup, Philip cast a polite smile at his cousin.

"Philip," Catherine said, "you have been in London for months, I think—and this is the first time you have greeted me. Now you must invite my family over more often!"

"We will, be assured of that. I apologize for not seeing your family sooner. We have been so very busy—my father has been having me help in his government work for the queen. Nothing important—just small personal matters I attend to for him. How are you enjoying London, cousin?"

"It is so very agreeable," she replied brightly, "now that we are in the fine section of the city—but, of course, it is nothing like this most wondrous house of your family! It is so beautiful here, and the gardens are so well-tended. Just smell! The fragrance is almost intoxicating!"

"It is a fine house," Philip said.

Then he paused for a moment.

"St. Andrews does seem so far away. I think I am missing it already—don't you?"

"Oh, no! Not at all—there were none of the splendors that we have here—the fine palaces and parties, and games, and fabrics for dresses from around the world. How can you possibly miss that dark, stuffy old city up there on the coast?"

She looked at Philip, but his glance was now far beyond the gardens of his family's London estate.

"So tell me," she said, "all the gossip from the Crown—they say that Queen Mary is going to wed the Spanish prince—is it really true?"

"Why, cousin Catherine," Philip said with a smile. "Haven't you become the woman of politics—since when have you ever cared for matters of polity?"

"Since coming to Court," she said. "I see that all the really important women know something about palace secrets and state intrigue!"

"Well, if you must know, it appears she will marry the Spaniard—and there are many, including my father and others, who fear that in so doing she will alienate Scotland. And then any hope of uniting the crowns of England and Scotland under the Holy Roman Church will be dashed on the rocks."

But Philip hesitated. He realized he had already said more than he should have. After a moment of silence, he approached his real reason for talking privately to his cousin.

"Tell me, Catherine—what are your intentions?"

"About what?"

"I know all about you—and I know about Ransom. I even know he is living in the rooms previously inhabited by your family, down in the merchant part of the city…"

"So—there are no secrets!" she said coyly.

"Not when your father works for the Crown," he replied. "So tell me cousin—does he seek your hand?"

"Of course he does!" she gushed.

"And do you—and more importantly, does your father consent?"

"Ransom advanced us funds to survive in our very dark days. It would be rude to just dismiss him out of hand."

"That's a far cry from marrying the man—"

"Who said anything about marrying him?" she exclaimed. "Heavens, cousin—just imagine that! How could that ever be? A reformist—a radical—with the bloody stink on him from the slaughter yards—how could you ever think I would marry such a person?"

"Have you ever told him that?"

"What interest do you have in this, cousin?" she said slyly. "What has he ever done for you? He was part of the rabble in the castle in St. Andrews—an ally of John Knox, the hater of the Church of Rome—and he even worked with the Protestant chaplains before King Edward died. He told me that himself! So—why would you care about him now?"

"Because," Philip said, looking down, "he was my friend…once…"

"And I was just a silly little girl once in St. Andrews…flirting with boys…but those days are gone. I've changed."

"So—what about Ransom?"

"I wish him no harm, if that's what you mean."

"Regarding any question about your affections for him—there seems to be much in what you have *not* said," Philip noted. "You must know that his presence in London—it is dangerous for both of us. If it was learned by the Crown that we knew of his work for the reformers and that he still lingered here and we did not report him—it would be a disaster."

"Then," Catherine said coldly, "perhaps we should report him—that is—if you really think we must, of course."

Philip tried to manage a confident smile at his cousin's suggestion. But he couldn't. Instead he decided to disclose something held among his shadowy fears—and about the cruelty that would soon become national policy.

"There is a movement—not just from the queen, but from her advisors as well—to cleanse England of corrupt heresies. And the people who propagate them. Protestants will be hunted down and forced to recant their mistaken doctrine. They shall be given the chance for a pardon. But I fear they will be stiff-necked and rebellious and will refuse to recant. The burnings are already being planned."

"Did you just say—a chance for a pardon?"

"Yes…if they recant…"

"Well then," Catherine said with a strange sense of finality, "there is the end of the matter. Now, if you will excuse me—I have two handsome palace guards waiting on my return."

She curtseyed, turned, and walked back into the lights and music of the mansion.

The days melded one into another for Ransom. It had now been weeks since he had heard from Catherine. One day, after the sun had already set, he dragged himself home through the noisy, crowded streets of London and up the stairs to his rooms. He paused for an instant as he inserted the long key into the lock of the door. He sensed something…and turned slowly to the side. He peered into the shadows of the unlit hallway.

"Who's there?" he asked.

No answer came. So he turned the key in the heavy door lock. But he thought he heard something again, and so he called out again. But this time there was a reply.

"It is I…" the voice came, out of the shadows.

"Who?" Ransom asked. His heart was beginning to race.

"You once called me a friend…and I also, you…"

Philip stepped out of the shadows. It took Ransom a few seconds to recognize the tall young man. He was dressed elegantly. His look and bearing had the air of confidence and standing.

"Philip?" Ransom said. He grinned broadly and stepped quickly over to embrace him.

But Philip stepped back.

"No…no shows of friendship, Ransom. It is too dangerous. I do not know who spies me out, now that my father is working for the Crown."

"How have you been…you look splendid…" Ransom said, grasping for a way to convey the lost years during which he had so many thoughts about his friend.

"I shall be direct. Forgive me for that, Ransom. But time is short."

Then Philip reached out and placed several silver coins in Ransom's hand.

Ransom looked at the money and shook his head, adding, "I have too long accepted the kind gestures and coins of others…I cannot…"

"You will not win this argument with me," Philip replied sternly. "You must take this and leave—leave England now."

"That is something I cannot do—"

"Then you will burn. They will set you on fire like the others. And you will die an agonizing death."

"I am no longer part of the reforming rebellion," Ransom said with a sudden flush of embarrassment. "I have left that behind…"

"Catherine will not have you—no matter what your intentions or plans—she will not. She will play you on until she is bored of it…but know you well what I say. My cousin will not have you. And that is that."

Ransom did not want to believe it. He searched Philip's face for some glimmer, some hint of his motive to have lied in such a cruel fashion. But he found none.

"Then all is lost…" Ransom said, in a voice that was barely audible.

"You can still flee from London."

"Why? Why would they hunt me if I have forsaken the cause of Knox and the other Protestants?"

"You may have left Knox and the others, but the troubles of these days have not left *you*. There is a list…"

"What list?"

"Of reformers and sympathizers to the Protestant cause…"

"Why would I be on such a list?"

"Think, man, think! You were a secretary to the chaplaincy of John Knox himself. I have seen the list with my own eyes, it was on my father's desk—compiled by the advisors to the queen. The former chaplains and former Protestant bishops and archbishops who still remain here, Cranmer and the others, they have all been rounded up—arrested—the burning posts are at the ready. The fires will be blazing. They hunt for you, Ransom—and I am in danger of execution myself by even warning you…"

There was a sorrowful catch in his voice as he spoke. Ransom stepped forward to his friend, but Philip waved him back.

"Leave the city—flee from England—I will not have your death on my conscience. I will not," Philip said, holding back tears.

Ransom looked at the coins in his hand.

"Why? Why have you risked so much to help me?"

Philip turned and glanced down the stairs to make sure that no one was there. He made a half turn to Ransom and spoke the last words the two of them would ever have together.

"Like you...I have studied the doctrines of my Church. I am instructed that Christ, the King, is also the Captain of mercy...is that not true?"

But he did not wait for Ransom's reply, for he quickly scurried down the narrow staircase and then disappeared.

Chapter 38

Hugh Mackenzie had managed to pay the bailment for the release of his printing press. His two friends from Edinburgh brought a wagon around to the Toll Booth offices of the queen's men at the bottom of High Street and loaded it on their wagon. The sheriff's guards eyed them carefully, knowing that printers were a highly suspicious class of tradesmen—particularly as of late. Then Hugh's friends brought it over to his shop under cover of darkness, and the three of them carried it, disassembled and in three sections, inside. Hugh was of little help, however. His sickness had not abated, and he was getting weaker.

"Why don't you see a physician, for heaven's sake?" one of his friends asked him before they left for the night.

But Hugh simply shook his head. He did not say so, but he had paid his last Scottish ryal, worth a full thirty Scottish shillings, to get his press back. He had only a few sixpences left. Paying for the services of the local physic was out of the question.

After they were gone, Hugh tried to begin reassembling the vertical screw mechanism of the press to the floor braces and table plate, but he was far too weak. Outside, the air was cool and damp, and a drizzling rain was falling down on Edinburgh. The cobbled streets were running with rainwater, and the only people out were a few late-night tradesmen, and those still lingering at the taverns and inns. A chill ran through him.

He took the burlap cloth that had covered the press and wrapped it around himself. He was shivering—his knees buckled and he slowly sank to the floor.

Just a wee bit of a nap, he thought to himself. *Have to get some rest... then I will get to work in short order...*

He fell asleep on the floor, too weak even to lock the door.

He was still fast asleep when the door opened and then was softly closed. The visitor was drenched with rain, and put something down on the floor of the shop and walked slowly over to Hugh, gazing down at him.

The visitor's hand lifted off the burlap tarp. And then the hand was put to his back to see if he was breathing—and he was—and then that same hand was placed on his forehead, and his burning fever was immediately detected. And with that the visitor, in a voice that was soft and had an almost musical quality about it, but with a touch of sadness also, said, in Gaelic, *"Blath,"* and then added, *"Dragh,"* noting the severity of Hugh's infirmity.

Hugh was wakened, but he was shaking with fever and nearly delirious. He was helped upstairs and laid on the floor with bedding and a blanket before the fireplace. Then a fire was built in the fireplace, and there were rags, dampened with water, applied to his forehead and neck, and sips of water all night from a wooden cup.

Some time during the night the fever started to break. By the coming of dawn he started to come around again. But when he did, he saw the visitor bending over him. In the dusky shadows of first light, he gazed up at the outline of the figure, with its dark hair, oval face, and dark, beautiful eyes—those of the woman who had discovered him on the floor and had cared for him through the night.

Hugh uttered the name he had not uttered for so very long...though the name had belonged to the face he had never forgotten.

"Susannah." Hugh whispered at the visage of the woman who leaned

over his bed on the floor. *"Susannah,"* he said again, repeating the name of his long-dead wife.

"Nay," the visitor said. "I'm not Susannah."

Then the woman stood up and walked over to the window and drew back the drapes. Early light of day flooded the room.

She bent down close to Hugh so he could see her face.

"Who are you?" Hugh asked, summoning his strength.

The woman smiled, pulled back her dark hair, and flipped it over her shoulder.

"My name is Margaret Chisholm—kin of Hamish Chisholm."

"Hamish...Hamish Chisholm...of the Highlands?"

"Aye. He would be the very same—and I am his daughter."

It took Hugh Mackenzie a while to put together who Margaret was. And how she came to be in Edinburgh and, in point of fact, how she came to be in his very shop. Margaret explained how her family had received the letter he had sent to them, asking for Ransom to have leave to travel to Edinburgh to help him there. But she also told him how Ransom was no longer there, but had been summoned to London to serve under a certain John Knox, for the good pleasure and service of young King Edward, recently deceased.

But she did not confide everything in him—at least not then. She kept to herself how she had not waited for her father's blessings for her trip—but had, just before dawn, quietly gathered her belongings, placed some pillows under her covers, slipped out of the door of their cottage and, mounting one of their horses, started riding south. She had been oblivious to the catastrophe about to befall her father and her mother.

As Hugh questioned her about her travels and prodded her about the dangers of such a journey as a young woman alone, she tried to minimize the hardships she had encountered along the way. Then she turned the subject to Ransom and his position as a secretary to one of the king's chaplains.

"Have ye not heard from him, then?" Margaret asked, trying to be nonchalant.

"Nay, not a word. I have long wondered where he was…how he was faring…having no idea he was with Knox…"

"And the situation—in London?" Margaret asked. She had only heard fragments of information from others on her travel to Edinburgh.

Hugh explained what he knew. About Edward's death, and how Queen Mary had quickly assumed the throne. Stories of the coming persecution of Protestants in England, he said, were already starting to make their way across the border and up to Edinburgh. There was a sorrowful look that swept over his pale face, as he recalled once again that Ransom could still be at risk of arrest—or even death.

Margaret tried hard to hide her concern as well, but she pursed her lips together and wrinkled her brow.

"Ye're an angel sent of God for sure," Hugh said with a weak smile, "to tend to me like this." With that he reached out and touched the sleeve of her dress.

"Why…lass…ye're soaked wet to the bone. Your dress is still full of last night's rain…"

"Oh, its nothing," Margaret said. "I think the fire is drying me out a wee bit."

"Do ye have dry clothes with ye, lass?"

"Well," she replied, "I have a sack of clothes downstairs on the floor, but I'm afraid that it all got drenched as well…" And with that she gave a little laugh.

Hugh thought for a minute. Then he directed Margaret to a trunk at the end of the room.

"There are some of Ransom's old clothes—when he was a lad—still in the bottom of the trunk," he said. "But they should be able to fit ye close—put them on and see."

"Thank you, I will," Margaret said with a excited grin. "That will be perfect."

She tried on Ransom's vest and blouse and long stockings. They fit her well enough. It felt good to be warm and dry.

Margaret fixed some gruel for Hugh and suggested that she knew some remedies for reducing fever. He was thankful for all of her gracious help, but he had a lingering question for her. If his letter to her parents had asked for Ransom to return and help his father but Ransom had already moved to London—then why had Margaret taken such a long and perilous trip by herself just to personally deliver that message?

Hugh intended to pose that question to her, but before he could, they both heard the door downstairs open. Then someone was shouting for Hugh Mackenzie to show himself.

"Ye're so weak, why don't you let me see who is there?" Margaret asked.

"We are from the Sheriff of Edinburgh!" the voice said loudly. "Come out, Mackenzie!"

Hugh motioned to Margaret to be silent, indicating that he—and he alone—would be the one to engage his visitors. "Coming...coming, gentlemen..." Hugh called down the stairs weakly. He supported himself on a walking stick and slowly made his way down the stairs, laboring with each step. Margaret stood just out of sight at the top of the stairs, listening intently to the conversation.

"I'm sorry to take so long," Hugh said, "But I have been sick and was abed when you came by."

"It's not the plague...or fever...is it?" one of the men said curtly. "Ye're required to mark your door with a red cross, mind you."

"Nay...I don't think it 'tis," Hugh replied.

"Are you alone in this shop?" another of the Sheriff's men asked.

"Why do you ask? I was released by Her Majesty's guards...I was cleared of suspicions...except for that matter of my printer's license. And I've remedied that..."

"We're not here about such trifles as a license," the first man growled.

"Do you have a son, kin of your blood, by the name of Ransom Mackenzie?"

Hugh paused and took a deep breath.

"I do indeed."

"And is he with the heretic John Knox—be he with that Protestant rebel? Speak up now, quickly, and tell us!"

There was a strained silence as Hugh struggled with his answer.

"Look you," the other man snapped, "we have certain information that comes from the Crown of England, so, mind you well, don't play the idiot with us—or ye'll be taken to a place where ye'll never see the light of day."

"Now tell us true!" the first man shouted. "Where is your son, man—and where is that treasonous Knox?"

Hugh was about to speak. To refuse to divulge any information about Ransom, though he knew it would probably be the end of him. But before he could utter a word, he saw the eyes of the two sheriff's men fix on the bottom of the stairs. Hugh slowly turned around and beheld Margaret, still dressed in Ransom's clothes. But she had also swept her hair up on her head and put a cap over it. She was standing there with her hands on her hips, trying her best to emulate a mannish swagger.

"Da," she announced, straining to the lowest octive, "what do they want with me?"

"You!" the first man shouted. "Are you Ransom Mackenzie?"

"Well now," she answered in her most baritone voice, "why else would I be wearing his clothes!"

"Don't play the smart lad with me," the man barked back. "Or I will lay hard on your back the manners your father here failed to teach you."

"No need…no need…" Hugh begged.

"Now," the man continued, fixing his eyes on the figure in front of him, "were you in England in the company of one Mister John Knox, formerly of the town of St. Andrews?"

"Nay, never," Margaret answered. "And that is God's own truth."

"Never?"

Margaret shook her head emphatically.

"Step closer," the man said, beckoning with a finger.

Margaret took a step out of the shadows.

"Closer," the man said.

Margaret took another small step.

"A soft-looking lad you've got there," the man said with a sneer. "You'd best put him to work and make the man of him."

"I do rightly see what ye mean," Hugh said.

Without apology or further ado, the men turned and walked out, slamming the door behind them. When at least a minute of silence had passed and they were sure they were gone, Hugh and Margaret erupted into laughter. He collapsed into a chair and took both of her hands in his.

"Oh, it's been so many years since I've seen yer da and yer mum," Hugh said, thinking a bit. "But sure as the rose blooms ye have yer mum's fair face, ye do." And then after some further reflection he added, "And ye also have yer good da's pluck!"

Chapter 39

Getting ready for a hasty departure from London, Ransom hurriedly gathered his things. But he stared at the pile of books on the floor. There were texts used by Knox to tutor him. Selections from Augustine's *City of God*, and the writings of Jerome, and a Latin-into-English translation of the New Testament, and writings on the teachings of the sect of Martin Luther. He also had Knox's own copy of John Major's book *Predestination*. It was signed by Major himself on the inside, where the author, an instructor of Knox at St. Andrews, inscribed, *To my good friend and former student, John Knox.* Ransom struggled with whether he should take the books with him.

If I am caught, he thought to himself, *they will use this all as evidence to destroy me.*

But he also struggled with another thought. In a way, it was an even darker and more odious fact—one Ransom could hardly bear to admit to himself. It was the fact, true and undeniable as it was, that he had abandoned his mentor, John Knox. He had done so willfully and intentionally. Ransom had turned against him and all that he had worked for. And in so doing, he felt as if he had betrayed his father as well. Worse even than that, Ransom had actually admitted to Philip in their conversation together, "I am no longer part of the reforming rebellion. I have foresaken the cause of Knox and the other Protestants…"

His mind was spinning. If he had been a traitor to the Protestant cause, then why drag with him on his journey the written proof of what he had once believed and supported? Why hang on to the reminder of his own pitiful failure…especially if it could be used as the kindling wood for his own burning?

As he exited through the door, he gazed, one last time, at the pile of books he had left lying on the middle of the floor. Then he glanced over at the fireplace, where he had set on fire the long-treasured letter from Catherine. It was now smoldering in black ash. As he closed the door, Ransom felt it was the death of something. There was shame and guilt about it, there was no denying that. So he tried to put his mind on other things.

With the shillings he had, he was able to secure a seat on the next coach out of London. His fare would carry him as far south as the town of Lewes, nearly to the Channel coast. It was not to the north, as he had hoped, but it was his quickest exit from the city. Then he would figure out how to get to Scotland.

On the ride there, which was many hours long, he kept to himself, turning his face to the window. He tried to focus on the passing scenery. But his mind would not be quieted, as it was haunted by a continuous parade of pictures, and voices, and remembrances.

He thought back to his last conversation with Catherine. What a fool he had been. He had been kept on a string, just as surely as if he had been a marionette, and she, the puppet master. Yet he could not blame her. She was as she was…and as she always had been. It was Ransom's own failure to exercise propriety that was the problem. Why had he allowed himself to have been so mesmerized by her? Was it just her beauty? Or perhaps something else? Had he willingly allowed her skillful fancies to inflame his passions—and then take him over and so capture his will, slowly and deliberately? As if he were like a freeman who, ever so slowly, was making bargain after bargain with his own conscience—until finally he had placed his own sense of good judgment in the cold chains of slavery.

And he thought on his friend Philip. Amazingly, although Philip—
or at least his father—belonged to a regime that now seemed destined
to persecute and ravage Protestants, yet it was he who had warned him
to escape London while he still could and then extended him the funds
to do so.

Ransom thought back to the last comment his friend had made.
Without knowing why, Ransom felt the razor cut of its truth slice through
his heart, and rend it wide open. *Christ*, Philip had said, *was also the
Captain of mercy.* Ransom wondered why that statement hurt most of
all.

That question continued to plague him. Because it was so troubling,
he would try to find some distraction on the landscape...the great
rounded piles of golden hay on the countryside. The milkmaids walking
down the lanes, balancing buckets on the yokes slung over the back of
their shoulders. The very young children frolicking and playing, seemingly oblivious to great weight of care that adulthood would bring—
and uninformed, in their innocence, of the terrible wickedness and cruelty of the human heart.

But it was not until he had almost reached Lewes that the realiza-
tion came like a white flash of lightning. The thought, burning hot into
his mind like the flames of a fire, would not...could not...be extin-
guished. It was not Knox, or his father, or anyone else he had truly
betrayed; it was someone else. He quivered and quaked so greatly within
his soul that he feared that his body and limbs would begin to palsy,
and that the passengers with him would see it.

I have betrayed Christ, he muttered, but whether it was in his mind
or truly spoken aloud, he did not know. He was like Peter, the disciple
of Christ who, at the cock's crow, denied his friend, Messiah, and Savior,
not once—but thrice.

The crush of that truth bore down like Wormwood, the dark meteor
of bitter judgment from the book of Revelation, falling down from the

heavens directly onto him and burying him under it. Had he ever been truly faithful to Jesus the Christ—ever? Had he ever been transformed by the message of His suffering on the cross and stupendous resurrection—or had he simply assented to it, carried along by the faith of his father and by the electric passion of Knox and others? Even Hamish Chisholm and Rhona and the winsome, dynamically beautiful Margaret—they all had something about their faith that seemed so personal...and true.

The coach arrived at Lewes, and Ransom climbed out with his sack of clothes. He was so dejected and forlorn that he could hardly put one foot in front of another. As he shuffled to the center of town to see if he could find lodging at the cheapest inn, he noticed a large crowd had gathered.

Citizens were talking loudly, gathered in a semicircle around something. As Ransom pushed his way to the front he saw the object of their attention. There was a tall wooden post fixed to the ground. Gathered around the base of the post were straw and sticks of wood. Next to the post, off to the side, there were more bundles of wood. Three armed men of the High Sheriff of Sussex were there, dressed in full array, with padded vests and helmets. Two had swords, and the third was a billman, who carried a long spear with a sharpened blade on the end. One of the swordsmen had a man in tow, his feet and hands bound. The sheriff's guardsman in charge stepped forward with a piece of paper in his hand. He began to read.

"May it be known to all here present, that the accused—one Derek Carver of Sussex, a brewer by trade—has been found guilty by Her Majesty, Queen Mary of England, through her duly authorized deputies and agents. He has been found guilty of housing various and sundry prayer meetings among Protestant rebels in his house, and is guilty also of permitting, there and then, the public reading from a forbidden Bible published in the common English tongue. Unless he relents of his treasonous actions and false doctrines, he shall forthwith be punished in the flame for his contemptuous violation of Her Majesty's law."

The sheriff's guard turned to Carver and asked him something, but Ransom could not hear it clearly. He surmised he was asking him to recant his beliefs; if he did, he would be fully spared from the ordeal planned for him.

But Carver's answer could be clearly heard by all.

"I will never go from these answers I have given, as long as I live!"

"Then you shall not have long to live," his captor retorted. He ordered the other two men to secure him to the post.

The guard produced a large Bible, which he explained had belonged to Carver.

"And it shall join the other forbidden Bibles," the guard said, indicating the barrel next to him, "which shall be set to the torch as Mister Carver soon shall be…" and then he tossed the Bible in.

But Carver reached out with his arms, even though his hands were still bound, grabbed his Bible out of the barrel, and cast it out toward the crowd. It dropped onto the dirt. Ransom Mackenzie looked down at his feet. The Bible had landed directly in front of his boots.

He stared down at it. The murmuring of the crowd suddenly stopped, and a silence descended over the scene. Then it was broken by one of the sheriff's guardsmen.

"You there—fetch that," he yelled to Ransom, "and put it in this barrel."

Ransom looked down at the Bible again.

"Are ye deaf?" the man yelled. "Pick it up and throw it in this barrel—and make haste!"

Bending down, Ransom picked up the Bible and held it in both hands. But he did not walk it to the barrel. He stood where he was, holding onto it with a firm grip.

The guardsman unsheathed his sword, took a step toward Ransom, and pointed the tip of the sword toward him. "Bring it here, you daft little worm—before I cut it out of your hands with my blade!"

"Peter," Ransom said quietly to himself, "even Peter got a second chance."

"What are ye mumblin'? Are ye defying me to my face?" the guardsman now bellowed, his face scarlet with rage. "I shall not be sayin' this again—yield up that book!" he cried out.

But Ransom looked over at Derek Carver, an Englishman he had never known or met. Carver stood there, hands and ankles bound, but his eye was now fixed on Ransom.

He gave the slightest little nod to Ransom—and Ransom back to him.

Then Ransom turned to face the crowd in back of him and held the Bible up to the sky with both hands. As he did he remembered a Psalm he had learned during his first month of tutoring with Knox. He began reciting it with a powerful voice, still holding the Bible high:

> *The princes persecute me without cause,*
> *But my heart standeth in awe of thy words.*
> *I am as glad of thy word,*
> *As one that findeth great spoils.*

As Ransom finished, a man in the crowd about the age of his father stepped up, reached up also, touched his hand to the Bible, and then began speaking. He called out,

> *Thy Word is a lantern unto my feet*
> *And a light unto my paths.*

Then another man from the crowd reached up to the Bible with his hand and yelled out, "The Word of God." And then another, this time a woman, did the same—and then another man. And then other men and women joined them—all of them reaching up to the Bible, holding it aloft, and calling out, "The Word of God!"

The guardsman looked back at his superior, hoping to get the command to begin wading into the crowd, swinging and slashing. The billman nervously gripped his spear, getting ready to charge in.

But the sheriff's agent knew they were understaffed for a riot. Besides, he was under orders to see this execution through. He was not about to disobey the Crown of England. He stepped up quickly next to the guardsman and whispered, "Stand down, now—we have a man to burn here. There'll be plenty of time to round up sympathizers later. Let's tend to Carver's burning…"

They took Carver and tied him to the post. Then they piled the bundles of wood high around him, nearly up to his neck. The guardsman with the sword grabbed a lighted torch, lit the fire at the bottom, and stepped back. The wood had been taken from a drying shed in town, and the kindling exploded immediately with fire. The flames leapt up high, engulfing Carver's face.

"O Lord, have mercy on me!" he shouted out in the midst of the roaring fire.

The older man standing next to Ransom pulled down his arm which was still holding up the Bible. "Lad, ye need to take the Bible and make your escape while ye still can—where do ye head?"

"I'm not sure," Ransom replied, "but I must get out of England."

"Indeed ye must," he replied. "I have a horse—it's yours—follow me and we will get ye off and wish ye God's speed."

As the two of them hastened toward the man's stable, Ransom turned around and looked back at Carver. Mercifully, the billowing smoke had already overcome him. His head was dangling down as his body was being consumed in the blazing inferno.

Chapter 40

In Edinburgh, Margaret had been caring for Hugh Mackenzie, trying to nurse him back to health. He had been feeling only slightly stronger. In order to buy him cures from the apothecary, she took on a position as a scullery maid and housekeeper at an inn situated at the top of High Street, near Castle Hill.

With Margaret's help at night, Hugh had been laboring over his printing press, reassembling it. He had accepted her help reluctantly at first, but found her to be a useful and talented apprentice. He was also surprised to find that she had learned reading and writing and had been tutored by Ransom at Hamish's insistence. Hugh decided that Margaret could help him set the type, and perhaps could even be taught to operate the printing press. Now all they needed was to secure printing orders from customers.

From some Protestant sources at the port of Leith, who in turn sent word through reformist merchants traveling to Edinburgh, Hugh eventually learned that John Knox had fled England, bound for Europe. It was speculated he would make landfall in Dieppe, France, and then head to either Germany or Switzerland. But when Hugh asked whether Knox was traveling alone, or whether he had been seen in the company of an assistant, no one could say.

One day Margaret was glancing over Hugh's ledger.

"I have an idea, Mister Mackenzie," she said, "how ye can start up the shop again."

"So, first ye learn how to assemble the press. Then ye learn typeset—and now ye are managing my books," Hugh said with a wry smile. "Why soon ye'll be takin' over my printing business, whole cloth and all!"

"I don't mean any disrespect," she said with a hint of apology to her voice.

"Nay—let fly—what do ye have in mind?"

"Well," she said energetically, "ye have all the names of yer old customers here—and their addresses."

"Aye—but they've all gone to other printers since the time that I was arrested and thrown in the sheriff's filthy gaol..."

"Would they take ye back?"

"Why would they?"

"Perhaps," she mused, "because ye'll give 'em a cheaper rate."

"Will I?" he asked.

"Ye must!" Margaret said. "And we'll promise that the printing will be done a day earlier than their current printers too—that should turn their heads!"

"Will we do the printing job a day earlier?"

"Of course!" she said.

"And how will we do that?"

"By my workin' hard and your exceeding wisdom in the print trade."

Despite the lingering illness he could not shake, Hugh Mackenzie had found mirth and joy with this Highland lass. He never had a daughter, but if he ever had, he would not have wished for one better than Margaret.

"I cannot go to the streets, lass...I am too weak still. I cannot meet the customers."

"Then I will!" Margaret exclaimed. "We will print a letter of introduction announcing our terms—both the lesser price and the quicker printing—and I will deliver it by my hand to each of yer old customers."

Hugh nodded and laughed a bit at her enthusiasm. But his laugh turned into a deep hacking cough, and his coughing continued until he found it hard to breathe. Margaret brought him a mixture of honey and lemon juice she had prepared for his coughing, which was now coming on every day. She noticed the beads of sweat on his brow. His skin had taken on a grayish-yellow tint.

"Let me work on the letter of introduction—let me do that," she said. "Ye must save yer strength. And we must pray for yer better health…"

"And for Ransom," Hugh added with a raspy voice. "For my son…"

"Yes," she said with an intense look in her eye. "For Ransom as well."

Ransom had decided he could not trust any of the established inns along the way. So when he passed near Stratford, he thought that he could perhaps search out John Shakespeare and obtain a night's lodging and a meal with him.

John was in his shop cutting lambskin; he would later stitch it into gloves. When Ransom walked in and pulled his cap off his head, John gazed at him for a moment, then broke into a broad grin and called out his name.

"Ransom Mackenzie—look what the river Avon has brought in!"

The two men shook hands energetically. Ransom put down his sack and the Bible and at John's insistence, pulled up a chair. He explained he was hoping to spend a night and share a meal with his friend, for which he would pay him an inn's fare for the privilege.

"Nay—there'll be none of that!" John exclaimed. "Not for near-royalty that ye are, Ransom—having come from the Court of King Edward… or…that is to say, the Court of the *late* King Edward, God rest his soul…"

Ransom explained what John could already surmise—that Mary Tudor's ascension to the throne had caused him and all other Protestant leaders in London to flee.

"I do not wish ye to be put at risk," Ransom said. "If my being here is unsafe for you, friend, I will sleep tonight off the road and under the stars. There is still enough of the Highlands in me for that..."

But John would hear none of that and fixed a hearty meal for both of them. As they dined together, he was quick to share the most recent developments in his trade and life. He was now prosperous enough, he said, to take on a helper, which he would be doing shortly. He was also now assured of appointment to the position of town chamberlain, something he had earnestly hoped for. It would be, he said, a good start to his career in politics.

"What side will ye take, then, on the matter of the burning of heretics?" Ransom said.

Suddenly their reunion had taken on a solemn tone, and the familiar smile vanished from John's face as he answered.

"Just this," John said, lowering his voice and bending over the table toward Ransom. "The fires of Smithfield, and in Sussex, and Chichester... nasty they are. But they are burning bright for *one reason*—and *one reason alone.*"

Ransom was listening intently, for he had never heard John's mind on the subject before.

"The reason is this—they have found Protestant heretics there..."

"Well, yes, of course," Ransom added with a little confusion.

"If I am chamberlain of the town," John continued, "then I will simply make sure no Protestants are found. And I will be sure to tell the Protestants to hide well enough so I cannot find them—thusly—no burnings!"

Ransom smiled a bit at his naivete. Then John asked him how he had been faring in the troubles of the times.

He did not share many details, the beginning and end of the matter.

"I went to London not knowing why the Lord had sent me there—and while there, I lost my way. Though I had bungled it terribly, by God's grace, and by His divine will, I have been given a second chance—to believe in His Son Christ with all my heart and soul, where He resides this very day by faith—and to serve Him as Lord, to which I am now committed."

"Ye're too hard on yerself, Reverend Ransom," John said with a mischevious smile. "Lay back a little."

"I cannot," Ransom replied, and as he said it, he smiled at his friend.

Then after a moment's silence, John Shakespeare asked, "So how does that work exactly…about God's second chance…He being God and all?"

Ransom thought on that and recalled his lessons with John Knox in the castle at St. Andrews.

"A long time ago, I was instructed on the matter of God's will," Ransom said. "And I was told something from God's Scriptures that I have since come to believe as truth in my own life."

"What might that be?"

"That we are like a lump of clay on a wheel that has the capacity to refuse the Potter's loving hands—but when we are spoiled, He can remake us still. God's divinity shapes our ends, John, rough-hew them how we may…"

"Righter and sweeter words spoken I have yet to hear!" John exclaimed. "I will remember yer wisdom, and pass it down to my wee children—when they come—and come they will as soon as I am wed to my blessed Mary Arden—which is to be arranged shortly."

Ransom congratulated him warmly. The two talked for a while longer and then Ransom turned in for the night.

The next morning before leaving, Ransom offered Derek Carver's Bible to John Shakespeare, and explained Carver's burning and how Ransom came to be in possession of it.

"I must fulfill my promise that I once made to you—to give ye a proper Bible..."

"Nay, ye'd better not—my being a ranking member of the town polity. And now that Queen Mary sits on the throne, an English Bible like that in my house could be the very end of me!"

Ransom was somewhat disappointed, but said he understood.

"Besides," John added, "by yer telling of it—how ye came to that Bible, or should I say, how it came to you—it seems that perhaps ye were meant to carry it yerself for a remembrance of that poor soul at Lewes who burned. Maybe that Bible was meant for ye, Master Ransom—more than me."

Ransom agreed, and the two shook hands.

"Besides," Ransom added, "now I still have a reason to visit you again, to give you a Bible when these lands are free again for the reading of it!"

"Where do ye go now, lad?" John said, calling out as Ransom trotted off on his horse.

"Where the Lord leads," Ransom said. "That will be good enough for me."

Chapter 41

Although Ransom's parting words to John Shakespeare may have rung out with triumph and certainty, inwardly he grappled with a profound dilemma. Where to go? What was the divine will of the Lord on such a matter?

As he rode, he knew he needed to choose a direction and, with the fires of anti-Protestant burnings close at his back, he needed to do it quickly. He decided to fast for the entire day and devote himself to prayer while he traveled north out of England. At first he considered a return to St. Andrews. After all, it was the town of his upbringing and youth, where he had witnessed the martyrdom of George Wishart and had survived the onslaught in the castle while receiving the teachings of Knox. There was also another fact, and it lay heavy on Ransom's heart. St. Andrews was the place where he had last seen his father and was given his final embrace before their sorrowful separation.

But as he prayed and meditated on that, a verse of Scripture rose up slowly into his memory, like the form of a traveler appearing out of the fog. It was from the book of Acts, chapter eight. "At the same time there was a great persecution at Jerusalem over the congregation. And they were all scattered abroad in the regions of Judea and Samaria." Could it be, in a similar way, that the fires of persecution that burned in St. Andrews actually served to send Hugh Mackenzie, and Ransom his son, and even Mister Knox and his reformist allies, out into the far regions so as to spread the gospel of Christ even further? And if that were the case, would that counsel against returning? Beyond that, Ransom had to admit that there was nothing in that town to which he could really return—no home, no friends, no mission that he knew of.

Then Ransom considered riding up to Leith, Scotland, the port city that lay at the end of the firth that led to the open waters of the ocean. It would be a sensible destination if he were to venture over to the Continent in hopes of locating John Knox. The idea became fixed in Ransom's mind, as he rode north on a course that took him many days of hard riding.

Mulling over the possibility of shipping out of Leith as he rode, Ransom was finally happy to see the rolling hills of the borderlands that separated Scotland from England. As he entered the lowlands of Scotland, he thought on how he would have to secure employment in that harbor to earn the wages he would need to book passage by ship to Europe. He knew there was no way of knowing how long it would take to accomplish that. And the voyage would be long and possibly dangerous, but he was willing to accept the risk. Yet there still remained two nagging questions about his plan.

The first was a practical one. How could he hope to locate Knox? Was he prepared to scour the entire continent? To learn a half dozen new languages in order to carry on the necessary conversation with the locals as he traveled through the half dozen countries where Knox might possibly be residing? He knew that Knox had pastored a congregation in Berwick—perhaps they would know where on the Continent he had settled. On the other hand, Berwick was now to the south and east of him, as he had already entered the borders of Scotland. Was it really advisable to cross back into England again, now that he had safely escaped the country?

But the second question was even more troublesome. Would John Knox be willing to accept him back? At their last encounter Ransom had shamefully abandoned the work of the Reformation. He had no reason to believe that Knox, who had no patience with disloyalty, would still view him as a fit associate.

As Ransom struggled with those queries, he saw a sign post for Leith. He knew he was only a half-day's ride away. Just underneath that sign there was the placard for another city. He knew that the other city lay just south of Leith and must be passed by on the journey. The sign read,

EDINBURGH

The name of that city jolted Ransom so suddenly in his mind, it was as if he had been thrown from his horse and landed hard on the ground. Why had he not thought of Edinburgh earlier? After all, it had been the intended destination of his father. Perhaps his father was there still. Or maybe someone there knew of his whereabouts or his fate. He had been forced by his English guide to bypass Edinburgh on his way to London several years ago. But now Ransom had no earthly master— no letters commending him to this place or that. He was now free to assume any risk and head in any direction. And Edinburgh lay just an hour or two away, and lay directly in his path. The more he thought on it and petitioned God for the certainty of His Holy Spirit on the matter, the more certain he became. Edinburgh it must be—and Edinburgh it would be.

As he settled the matter just one black cloud remained over his spirit. He knew exactly what it was. And he could not deny that it was there. The only answer Ransom could give on this particular distress was that, perhaps, God was asking that he sacrifice this one, overpowering desire for reasons known only to God Himself. For as Ransom headed towards Edinburgh, he also knew where he was not heading...

The night before he had thought on that other place and the person who lived there, though in truth, he had also thought of it every preceding day as well, and even every hour—from the moment that he had his conversation with Philip before leaving London. Last night he had slept in a field. It was a mild autumn night, and the moon was full and bright and yellow in the sky above him. It was so bright he could not sleep, though his body was tired from the day's ride.

In the late, still hours of that evening, as the yellow glow of moon-light washed over him, he turned to his sack and fished something out. He held it up against the night sky and looked at it in the pale illumination of the moon. It was the glass box that had been given him. He looked at the moon's rounded shape through the crystal panes of glass, lining it up so that it shone through the middle of the heather crown inside the box. Of all the consequences of his betrayal and his double-minded carnality in London, of his blind, ill-fated obsession with Catherine, this one consequence had grown—day by day and hour by hour—to be the most insufferable. His heart ached for someone else—and he longed to be near her, to hear her laugh and to relive that one fleeting kiss on the high mountain of the Highlands. To hold her in his arms as he did, with the wind blowing up from glen and lifting her black hair ever so slightly—and covering their faces with it like a veil.

But she had promised not to wait for him. He could not fault her for that. But who could he fault now but himself for the abysmal pain he felt in his heart? Now that he was clear-minded and his spirit had been revived afresh, and he was recommitted to God, now that his sight had been restored—like one of the poor blind beggars healed by Christ—he must live with the cruel realities his sight revealed. The ugly truth seemed to be that the only things he had left of her now were this glass box and the saying of her name. But to speak her name was almost too exquisite a pain for him. Yet he could not refrain from it. In his longing, he said it out loud, to the balmy night, and to the moon:

Margaret...

As he fell asleep that night he was still clinging to the glass box.

He was thinking on that as he approached the city of Edinburgh. He had left in the Highlands the one woman he loved most truly, to then pursue in London the one woman who treated him most foully. It seemed now that his loss of Margaret was the awful price he would pay for having played the world's worst fool.

He stopped his horse and looked off in the horizon. He could see the spires and tops of the buildings of Edinburgh spreading out before him. The structures of commerce, and five-story tenements, and the steeple of St. Giles Cathedral lined the elevated rise of High Street. Up to the right, at the very top of the city, rising up above it all like a dark stone fortress cut out of the hardest rock, lay the castle.

As Ransom headed down the path to the city, he had no way of knowing what was awaiting him there.

It was the first day of September. Edinburgh was the city of the Queen Mother, Marie de Guise, who was about to secure to herself the added title of royal Regent of Scotland. As she had every year before, she would celebrate that day—Saint Giles' Day—with a procession along High Street to and from St. Giles Cathedral—in full Catholic regalia, with herself, in a gilded coach, at the very front.

She was accompanied by Black Friars and Gray Friars, by priests who carried banners of the Roman faith, and who blew trumpets and beat drums of celebration. And just behind the queen's coach was carried a statue of Saint Giles in a movable shrine, carried by various supporters of the faith.

Marie de Guise had not counted on opposition that day, though she should have. A few months before, the Archbishop of St. Andrews had executed an elderly priest, named Walter Myln, in that city. The old man had begun preaching the reformed doctrines and was promptly arrested, then burned at the stake. Although the queen disclaimed any prior knowledge of it, the growing Protestant presence in Edinburgh did not believe her.

The Protestants, it appeared, were about to rise up in concert. Two reformist pastors had begun preaching openly in Edinburgh. A reformist group calling themselves the "Lords of the Congregation" had begun meeting. They bound themselves to a "covenant" that pledged them to "minister Christ's gospel" and to also "renounce the congregation of Satan"—by which they clearly meant the religion of Marie de Guise. They called for the right to practice the Protestant form of worship, including the use of the forbidden English *Book of Common Prayer,* which had been composed by the Protestant leaders, including Knox, during the young King Edward's reign.

Oblivious to this revolt fermenting in her own capital, the queen mother led the processional up to the St. Giles' Cathedral. After the celebration of the mass in honor of St. Giles, she led it back down the royal mile with great pomp to the end of High Street. At the Canongate market cross she dismounted from her coach, flanked by her palace guards. She walked out with regal command, touching her lace and jeweled bonnet slightly. Then she swept her black velvet cape aside to avoid the mud of the Edinburgh street. Escorted by her guards, she walked toward the front door of the home of a rich burgess who was hosting a dinner in her honor.

The street was jammed on both sides with onlookers. Many were cheering and calling out. Marie de Guise paused and turned to the cheering crowd. She laid one hand on the large ruby encased in an ornate gold starburst pendant that hung from her neck by a heavy gold chain. With her other hand she gave a restrained royal wave. Then she disappeared inside the house.

But within the onlookers, there were those who were not smiling or cheering. They had heard about the burning of Walter Myln and of the covenant of the Lords of the Congregation. And as the statue of St. Giles resting on the platform of the processional shrine was set down on the street directly in front of them, one voice yelled out in protest. And then another. And yet another.

And that is when it all began.

Chapter 42

The skies had darkened, and it was threatening to rain.

Ransom had made his way through the crowds of High Street, all the way up to the top, near Castle Hill. Trying to locate his father, he had inquired where he might find the most prosperous printer in the city, thinking that was a logical starting point. He was directed to the shop up near the castle. The queen mother's procession had by then begun its descent down the steep incline of High Street and was nearing the market cross where Marie de Guise would exit her coach. The shrine of St. Giles would be set down on the street behind her coach.

When the riot broke out, Ransom could hear the yelling echoing up the steep royal mile that led to the castle. He was poised to enter the printing shop and begin his inquiries but was distracted when he heard the noises down the street. In a moment, the owner of the printing shop was outside standing next to Ransom, showing obvious displeasure at the commotion that surrounded the procession.

Down at the Canongate market cross, Protestants in the crowd were beginning to yell, "Down with the idol! Down with the idol!" Then several of them dashed over to the shrine and lifted up the platform housing the statue of St. Giles. The friars and priests, sensing a riot, fled. From inside the house Marie de Guise looked out through the window in horror. She immediately dispatched one of her guards to hasten up to the castle and fetch her French soldiers who were quartered there.

The Protestants lifted up the shrine and then tipped it over, dashing it down on the street. Then they proceeded to smash it down again and again until the head and hands of the statue were broken off. Catholics ran to the shrine and struggled with the Protestants. Soon the street was filled with yelling combatants who were laying blows around them with fists and bottles and clubs.

Now the rains started to come down on Edinburgh. Up near Castle Hill, across from Ransom, as if oblivious to the riot down the street, a slim figure of a boy, with the hood of his cape pulled over his head, was exiting a book bindery that had just decided to do business with the printing shop of Hugh Mackenzie. The owner of the printing shop near Castle Hill, as he stood next to Ransom, recognized the boy and glared at him in disgust. During the past week he had seen him scurrying up and down High Street, garnering new customers for Mackenzie. It was bad enough that Mackenzie—a former laborer in his print shop—was now competing with him. But to add insult to injury, the owner, a supporter of Marie de Guise and a royal printer, had heard of Mackenzie's reputation as a reformist.

Suddenly, there was the sound of the heavy hooves of the horses of the French castle guard. The guards were pouring out of the castle. They wore bright metal helmets that were being splattered with the rain now pouring down. The guards were carrying short spears for mob control and were galloping down the cobblestones past Ransom and the printing shop owner on one side of the street, and the boy with the hooded cape on the other.

The printer raised his hands and began yelling to the captain of the guard.

"Over there! Over there!" he cried, pointing to the boy on the other side of the street. "He works with the Protestant rebels—he works with Mackenzie, the Protestant printer!"

The French captain reined his horse back and signaled for the rest of the guard behind him to halt.

"Come here!" he yelled in a thick accent to the boy. The boy slowly walked over to the captain on the horse. But just as he came up alongside the captain's horse, he dodged out into the street and ran to the other side.

The captain ordered one of his sergeants to give chase, while the captain and the rest of the guard whipped their horses into a gallop, and headed down to the riot at the bottom of the street.

The boy disappeared down a steep set of stairs and into a narrow alley. Seconds later the sergeant dismounted and ran down the stairs after the boy, pulling his sword out of its sheath as he ran.

But Ransom had heard the printer's words—"He works with Mackenzie, the Protestant printer."

In a burst of excitement and fear, Ransom now sprinted after the French soldier. Down the stairs and into the winding close that was barely the width of two men, he gave chase after the guard, who was running hard and was slowly gaining on the boy. At a turn of the close that led both to the left and to the right into other darkened alleys, the boy hesitated and then dashed to the right, out of sight. But it was a costly hesitation. The guard was closing rapidly and sprinted into the alley to the right and also disappeared in the rain that was falling down in a shimmering curtain of water.

Ransom was not going to lose them—no matter what. He had to get to the boy before the guard did…he must…He turned the corner into the alley at the right, and as he did, he pulled out the sword that Hamish Chisholm had given him.

He saw that the soldier had the boy pinned down on the cobblestones under him and had his sword at the boy's throat. The French sergeant was yelling out in broken English, "Your name…your name…give your name!"

"Ransom Mackenzie!" the boy called out. "That is my name…"

"Good!" the soldier cried out. "Now I know the throat it is that I will cut!"

But Ransom was almost on him. From behind he could see he was wearing metal armor, both front and back. There could be no room for error now. He made a last leap toward the soldier, whose arm was raised to slash the sword crossways over the boy's throat. Ransom swung his sword hard and hit the side of the soldier's neck. He tumbled to the side, bleeding and dazed, and collapsed.

"Who are you? Where is my father? Where is Hugh Mackenzie? Tell me now!" Ransom was yelling at the boy lying on the wet cobblestones in the shadows.

"Answer me! And why did you call yourself Ransom Mackenzie?" Ransom yelled to the boy's face. The heavy rain was cascading down on them in ribbons and sheets.

"Because," the voice from within the hooded cape said in a Highland lilt, "'tis a very bonnie name, 'tis…"

The figure in the cape sat up and pulled back the hood. Her black hair fell down around her and onto her shoulders. Ransom blinked. For an instant he seemed to be dreaming…He was back on the high mountain overlooking the Highland valley below…in the lush velvet green of the rugged glen. And Margaret was there with him.

"Are ye tongue-tied?" Margaret asked softly, smiling at him. "Can ye speak, townie lad?"

Then Ransom knew that what he was seeing was real. That the miraculous was there before him, cleverly disguised in the trappings of the ordinary, in the rain, and in a nameless, winding close in the city of Edinburgh.

And in the shadows of that narrow alley, as the sky opened up and showered them with a drenching waterfall, Ransom pulled Margaret up and to himself, and when their lips were so close they were nearly touching he answered her.

"Yes, I can speak," he said. And then he whispered, "*Gradh mo chridhe...*"

And then he pulled her closer to himself and kissed her on the mouth.

But Margaret turned abruptly and cried, "Look out!"

Ransom saw the soldier lunging, his sword thrusting at him. He blocked the sword with his, knocking the French guard off balance. Then he plunged his sword into the soldier's throat.

"Murder! Rebels! Protestant rebels!"

The voice was coming from a woman leaning out of a tenement window several stories above them. Three soldiers who had entered the alley in search of fleeing reformist rioters heard the warning and began running toward Ransom and Margaret, their swords drawn.

"Quickly!" Margaret said. "I know all of the alleys here—follow me!"

She took his hand and the two darted together down the cobblestone close, turned quickly down several stone stairs slippery with water, into another alley—and then, in an instant, they were gone.

Chapter 43

In the apartment above his printing shop, Hugh Mackenzie lay in bed, weak and sweating. He was feverish again, and his illness seemed to have returned with a vengeance. His lungs were filling up with sickness—his chest was heavy, and it pained him when he coughed.

The rain was now slowing outside. Ransom and Margaret looked around cautiously as they approached the front door, and seeing no one around, quickly entered. They found Hugh in bed. Margaret stripped off her damp cloak and checked his forehead.

"He's burning up," she whispered to Ransom, who was standing behind her. Then she lit a candle. The sun was going down and the room was gloomy with shadows.

"Who's there?" Hugh said weakly.

"'Tis I, Margaret," she replied.

"And who else?" Hugh asked.

Ransom stepped out of the shadows and into the candlelight. Hugh looked up. At first the expression on his chalk-pale face was blank. But then, in the sudden recognition of the long-lost son who had returned at last, after years of separation, his face flooded with emotion. Hugh Mackenzie smiled, then smiled wider, and then closed his eyes and began to weep unashamedly, his shoulders and chest heaving as he cried.

"'Tis Ransom," his son said, kneeling next to his bed. "Your son—returned to you, Da. I am here."

"Ye are—oh, ye are indeed," Hugh said, his voice trembling. He lifted up his hand and stroked Ransom's beard and patted his face. "There's a good lad—my good lad. God's answered my prayers—more than answered…" Hugh looked over at Margaret and took in her face. "More than answered…"

Margaret dipped a rag in the water bowl and wiped his brow.

"He's sore ill again," she said.

"I can see—terrible sick, but…"

"What?" she whispered back as the two stepped away from Hugh's bed.

"But the castle guard was alerted to you and to my father—you'll both be tied to the riot…and…" His face grew somber.

Then Ransom paused. Margaret took his hand in both of hers. "Ransom, what is it?"

"I just killed a man…maybe two. Both of them Castle guards. Of the queen mother. And there were witnesses in the close who saw me."

Margaret squeezed his hand and laid her face against his chest for a second and looked up at him.

"Ye saved my life, Ransom Mackenzie. Ye killed those who would have killed me."

"They'll hunt me down for sure," he said. "There will be no peace in this city for us. We have to leave—and be quick about it."

"Yer da—he's too ill to travel."

"He will be taken by the queen's men for sure. Then he'll be a dead man—what choice do we have? We must go now…"

As soon as darkness fell, Ransom scurried out of the shop. Margaret tended to Hugh for the several hours he was gone, but Hugh's condition seemed to be worsening. Ransom arrived back to the shop close to midnight. After some convincing of who he was, he managed to negotiate a modest price for the press and the equipment in the shop. Hugh's friend and his wife bid him God's speed and said they would be especially praying for his father.

Ransom and Margaret loaded their meager belongings in Hugh's wagon and carefully carried him into the back and laid him down, wrapped in bedding. The rains were gone, the clouds were cleared away, and it was a balmy, starry night. Ransom's horse was hitched up to the wagon and at Hugh's suggestion, they rolled out of Edinburgh by a small side road that avoided the main gate at the Toll Booth crossing.

After traveling several hours, they finally stopped in a quiet grove of trees in the countryside. Hugh's breathing was labored and raspy. Ransom told Margaret to nap while he stood watch over his father.

Ransom and Hugh did little talking, until at the last Hugh reached out and touched Ransom's hand, surprising him a little by it.

"She's...bonnie lass..."

"That she is," Ransom said with a smile.

"Ye're a fool...if ye don't...take...her hand..." he said, gasping for breath between words.

"Be still, Da. Save your strength."

"So...don't...be...a fool," Hugh said, trying to manage a smile.

"I won't be a fool. Don't worry. I thought I lost her sure—I'll not lose her again."

"That's...a good...lad," Hugh said weakly. Then he added, "Proud of ye lad...so...proud..." Hugh was taking long, labored breaths. Then he said he needed to rest. Ransom kissed his father on the forehead and tucked the blankets around him. Ransom dozed off and on next to his father for the rest of the night, praying each time he wakened. Then something, perhaps a sound—like the breath of the gentlest wind blowing through the branches—woke him up. He looked around, having forgotten momentarily where he was. Then he reached over and touched his father's brow. But it was cold, uncommonly cold. He held his hand to his father's chest. But there was no breathing. No movement. His father was as still as anything he had ever touched. Ransom called his name and tried to wake him. But Hugh was gone.

At first the shock of it numbed Ransom all over. His mind searched for something to do...anything...how to save him. But there was no saving now of the frailty of the flesh. There was only the hope of the spirit. He began to weep. As he did, he remembered the words of his father, when he was a boy in St. Andrews—that when the forces of life crush down on you like the great turning of the press—*that*, Hugh had said, *that is the true test of the man.*

When Ransom was able to clear his mind a bit, he prayed out loud and thanked God "for receiving my da into the glorious splendors of Thy Kingdom...where he shall walk and talk with the Savior...and the Savior shall wipe away his every tear..."

It was only after he finished praying that Ransom was aware Margaret had wakened and had quietly come up from behind, and gently wrapped her arms around him. On the wagon, Margaret held him until the light began to break over the Scottish lowlands with the coming of the dawn.

Chapter 44

There, several miles outside of Edinburgh in the countryside, Ransom and Margaret said their tearful goodbye to the earthly remains of Hugh Mackenzie. When the light of morning broke, their wagon was sighted by a tenant farmer, a short, nimble-looking man with a ruddy face and leathery looks, and his wife, a round woman with a pleasant smile. They worked the land for the local Laird. They lent them shovels, and gave them a hand in digging a grave for Ransom's father, and they laid him to rest on the outer curtilege of the laird's property. They placed a simple wooden cross to mark the spot. Ransom took his short dirk and carved the initials of his father in the cross, the date of his passing, and the words "Psalm 16." He dared not carve his father's full name, for he had heard stories of the graves of the Protestant dead being dug up so their corpses could be burned publicly as heretics.

Ransom took the Bible he had received from the martyr Derek Carver at Lewes, and over the grave he read his father's favorite psalm:

> *Aforehand saw I God always before me,*
> *For he is on my right hand, that I should not be moved.*
> *Therefore did my heart rejoice, & my tongue was glad,*
> *My flesh also shall rest in hope.*
> *For why? thou shalt not leave my soul in hell,*
> *Neither shalt thou suffer thy saint to see corruption.*
> *Thou hast showed me the ways of life:*

Thou shalt make me full of joy with thy countenance.
At thy right hand there is pleasure and joy for evermore.

The farmer's wife invited them into their tiny cottage for a meal, and to rest a short while if they could. Without any home or definite plans for their destination, Ransom and Margaret cautiously took them up on the kind offer.

She set out a humble meal of salted beef and bread, and added a few carrots, which she tossed in a pot of boiling broth, and then ladled into rough wooden bowls. Ransom asked if they would mind if he said a prayer over the meal. The farmer's face flickered a little with a curious smile, but he said no, he wouldn't mind. All four bowed their heads as Ransom thanked God for their food and for the kindness of their hosts.

After some conversation about Hugh Mackenzie, and background of his family, and a Mackenzie the farmer once knew—but who Ransom did not think was direct kin of his—and about Hugh's final illness, the conversation turned to some of the current events in Edinburgh.

"What brings ye out of Edinburgh and headin' to parts unknown?" the farmer asked. His wife's eyes widened and she threw a glance over at her husband.

"Well," Ransom said, and took a short breath and then continued. "The current dismay and disorder in Edinburgh, for one thing…"

"Yes, I heard," the wife chimed in. "Riots and all manner of commotion—and the statue of St. Giles dashed to the ground—"

"Aye," the farmer said, *"to the ground."*

"And the queen mother nearly attacked…" the wife added.

"I do not believe she was harmed," Ransom said. "But there was considerable noise and public disturbance over it."

"And her French soldiers then attacked…attacked a few of the onlookers," Margaret said, glancing over at Ransom.

"Aye. Nasty business. Nasty," the farmer said. Then he paused, looked down at the last piece of beef on his wooden platter, and snatched it up. After he finished chewing, he cleared his throat loudly, as if preparing for a significant pronouncement.

"I do see that ye pray…uh…well…not in the manner of the old religion," he said.

"No, I do not," Ransom said. "I am a follower of the reformed faith, sir. I approach the throne of God boldly, as Holy Scripture says. Because Christ Jesus, my Savior, has prepared the way for me to do so…by His blood on the Cross…Christ Himself being my mediator."

There was a short silence.

"Such a sayin'—'tis a curious thing," the farmer said.

"Aye, most," the wife added.

"We have always followed the old ways of the Church," the farmer said.

"Aye, 'tis true," the wife added again.

Ransom, after another lapse in the conversation, spoke up.

"We do not mean to cause offense, you being so kindly in your hospitality…"

"'Tis no offense," the farmer said. "We've heard from here and there about the goins-on—and the rebels—and the queen mother—and have both wondered about the reason behind it all. And what manner of doctrine these reformers preach that would cause such commotion." Then the farmer's face grew grim. "And we've heard of the burning of an old man somewhere not a year back…"

"It was in St. Andrews," Ransom said. "The priest's name was Walter Myln. Burned for preaching the Protestant gospel."

"A priest, ye said?" the farmer replied.

Ransom nodded.

"Well," the farmer added, "I burn the laird's fields to make 'em fallow…and I burn the ruined hay, for 'tis worthless." Then after thinking a while he added, "But I wonder how burnin' a man could change his heart and soul on such matters…"

"And 'tis a man's heart and soul that God is after," Ransom said, "and 'tis where, by our faith in the Savior, He then sets His rule as King—"

"King, ye say?" the farmer remarked. "I'd say Her Highness in Edinburgh would be curious of any talk of kings, aye?"

Ransom was prepared to launch full-bore into the discussion, but the farmer's wife cut in before he could do so.

"And…might I be askin'…are ye both…well, in a manner of speakin'…are ye intended for each other?"

Margaret blushed and looked straight ahead, twirling her fingers slowly together.

Ransom looked at the farmer's wife, with her round, pleasant face.

"'Tis an honest question, it truly is," he said.

After a short silence, the farmer cleared his throat. Ransom turned in his chair to look at Margaret, who was still staring straight ahead. Her fingers started twisting a little faster.

The farmer's wife's eyes opened the widest yet, and her mouth opened in unabashed expectation. She was about to say something, but she noticed her husband raise a dirt-stained finger straight up in the air. She stopped and no word came out.

"Margaret Chisholm," Ransom said, with a solemnity she had not heard from him before.

"Yes…Ransom Mackenzie?" she answered very quietly. Her hands were now quiet and in her lap.

"Do you know, here in the presence of these witnesses—these kind folk who have harbored us and shared their table with them—do you know, Margaret, that my heart is truly for you, and for no other?"

Margaret paused and looked over at Ransom. And in her face Ransom beheld her joy, beaming and radiant, yet also a kind of strained anticipation, like that of a child who, upon seeing some amazing new thing for the first time, cannot contain the seeing of it.

"Oh, yes—I do believe that," she said, and placed her hand unthinkingly over her heart.

Ransom stood up, walked over to Margaret, and fell to his knees next to her, taking one of her hands.

"In the presence of these witnesses, and before the God Almighty who has brought you to me," he said in a voice halting with emotion, "I ask you, Margaret Chisholm—will you be the bride of my youth, and the wife of all of my days, and the love of all my life?"

Margaret's hand clutched for an instant at the rough fabric of her dress over her heart. Then she nodded, began to tear up, and spoke.

"Aye, Ransom—I will be yer bride—and yer wife for all yer days. And I will gladly be yer love, and ye will be my life—and my love—and the honor of my house. Before God I say aye—oh, I do say aye!"

Chapter 45

With Margaret's acceptance of Ransom's proposal for marriage, the farmer's wife burst into an explosion of applause and laughter. Her husband smiled and nodded in satisfaction that his humble little cottage, and his good will, had brought forth so unexpectedly such an occasion for joy.

Ransom rose, bent over, and kissed Margaret gently, then kissed her hand. The farmer strode over and shook Ransom's hand vigorously and slapped him on the shoulder, then pulled him aside.

"I would think," he said quietly, "by yer wife's manner of speakin' that she is a Highlander…"

"She is."

"They have, I have heard, their own way of makin' a marriage—and I cannot help ye there…"

"No, I understand."

"But I think it's a right thing that ye marry quick—so in the mornin', first thing, I will do what I can."

The farmer's wife quickly escorted Margaret out of the main room, into the bedroom, and closed the door behind them.

"Ye and I will make our beds here before the fire," the farmer said. "And in the morn it will be done as proper as can be…"

The two of them spread some blankets on the wooden floorboards and lay down before the fire. In a matter of minutes the farmer was snoring so loudly that the floor was vibrating. Ransom could not sleep.

He stared at the closed door that led to the bedroom, where Margaret was sleeping on the goose-down bed with the farmer's wife, on her last night before she would be wed. His mind raced and he could not still it. Hours went by, and he turned this way and that, until the fire had collapsed into embers and finally into ash. It all seemed to be rushing past him—the loss of his father...his betrothal to Margaret...the beginning of a life together that had no geographical direction and even less money. He needed to have a plan for himself and Margaret. *How shall I support her? And where shall we go? How can I ensure her safety in such a dangerous time?* he asked himself.

Margaret, in the soft bed with the farmer's wife, was lying stone still, but also wide awake. She could hardly believe the manner in which it had all happened. And then, all of a sudden, her throat began to tighten and her eyes flooded over with tears, as she thought on the fact that her mum and da would not be present at her wedding; that she did not know where they were, and they did not know about the marvelous marriage that was about to take place. Mostly, however, she was feeling desperately guilty about leaving the family cottage in the Highlands before the break of dawn...slipping away like a thief, without so much as a farewell or a God's speed from her parents. Yet she knew that the hand of the Lord had guided both Ransom and her to Edinburgh, and to each other. She would have to take consolation in that.

At some point in the very late hours of the night both Ransom and Margaret both fell asleep. When Ransom awoke in the light of morning he looked over to where the farmer had been sleeping, but he was gone.

He rose and went outside. There was a mist still rising up from the fields and a damp chill, but the clouds in the sky were parting and patches of blue were showing through. He had not fixed on answers to all of his questions, but one thing had, he believed, been revealed to him— and as soon as he could he would share it with Margaret.

Then off in the distance, he saw two riders. He watched them closely, and at long last he recognized one as the farmer on his large plough horse, with a bag slung over the side. Next to him was a man who appeared to be wearing the cloak of a Black Friar.

When they were almost up to the cottage, Ransom could see that the Black Friar was an ancient-looking man with long wisps of white hair that floated out from the sides of his head, which was bald on the top, and a face that was saggy with wrinkles. Ransom thought he looked so old that it was a wonder that he had been able to withstand the rigors of the ride.

The farmer dismounted and, with Ransom's help, the two gingerly lifted the old friar off his horse.

"This is Friar Scott, formerly of Stirling," the farmer said. "Now he lives in the abandoned friary a few miles from here. He has consented to seal your marriage."

Ransom, with a little embarrassment, took the farmer aside.

"Please know how glad I am at all that you and your good wife have done for us," he said, "but I cannot, good sir, have our wedding sealed by a Black Friar. As I explained, Margaret and I are Protestants…"

"Aye—as he is also," the farmer said with a smile. "He was the superior to a Black Friar named Kyllour in Stirling—have ye not heard of him? Back when King James was alive, and ruled with Marie de Guise, his wife." Then he turned to the Friar and said, "Isn't that so, Friar Scott?" The farmer spoke loudly so the old friar could hear.

"Aye, it is," he said as he shuffled over to Ransom. "I helped Friar Kyllour write the Passion Play that spoke the evangel of Christ most forcefully…and we had it performed before His Majesty one Good Friday morn. But it outraged the king…so poor Friar Kyllour was put to the torch. Begged His Highness, I did, and the Archbishop too…not to burn Kyllour…but could no' prevail. Shortly after, I was sent away to the country but was not burned myself…an odd thing 'twas…why was I not put to the torch also?" And with his last comment, his voice trailed off.

The farmer tried to break the somber mood with a wide grin and a slap to Ransom's back. Then, bearing a sack filled with fresh heather he had picked on the way, he helped Friar Scott into the cottage, and Ransom followed.

In the bedroom, behind the closed door, the farmer's wife was readying Margaret, who was trying on a plain white muslin dress with puffy sleeves. There was a stain of drab grey along the hem from mildew, and the farmer's wife was trying furiously to remove it with a damp rag.

"Never mind that," Margaret said with a goodhearted laugh, "'tis a miracle that ye're letting me use yer weddin' dress—and it fits so perfectly."

"Oh, I was a slender reed of a lass when we wed—not as bonnie a lass as ye, mind ye well—but I was a sight, I was!"

The farmer's wife then took a strip of tartan and quickly stitched it to one shoulder of the dress, doing it with the blinding speed of fingers that had learned their craft well during decades of weaving and sewing. She slung the rest of the tartan across Margaret's breast. Then she stepped back and admired the bride. Lastly, she brushed Margaret's long dark hair, oohing and ahhing as she did, and secured a small knot of heather over one ear.

Ransom was standing ready in the main room of the cottage. The old friar was standing, his wrinkled face bearing a mild expression of appreciation for the chance to see a simple blessing unfold in front of him, despite such times of turbulence and trouble. Next to him was the farmer, who had taken the time to wash his hands; from an old trunk he had fished out his pipes, which he shouldered and was now ready to play.

But when the farmer's wife stepped first into the room and the farmer blew the first shrill and soulful notes from his pipes—and Ransom looked and saw Margaret in her white wedding dress, her face aglow with a joy indescribable, he had to struggle hard to keep himself from crying. It was, he thought, almost too much to believe that he had so played the fool, had walked away from the work of God so inexcusably in London, yet now was so blessed with a woman of virtue and beauty and character. *It must be God,* he thought. *For only God could fashion such good out of the ashes of such ruin.*

The friar began. He announced the presence of God through His Son Christ at their joyful event. That the mystery of man and woman was meant to reveal the mystery of the Church, Christ's body. As Christ shed His blood to cleanse the Church and save it, so must the husband keep the wife pure, and shed his own blood, if necessary, to protect her and save her from the ravages of the world.

Then the friar, who had some knowledge of Highland custom, bent over and whispered something in the farmer's ear. He nodded and stooped down and unbuckled Ransom's boots, then rose and untied the laces of his shirt.

"As we untie these strings," the old friar said, "'tis to remind the husband that he is bound no longer to any of the things in this world, save one—and that one thing is his bride, Margaret. And likewise she shall be bound before God to Ransom and to him only."

Ransom and Margaret pledged their undying love and loyalty to each other, and Ransom slipped a pewter ring borrowed from the farmer on Margaret's finger, and then kissed her full and long on the mouth. The farmer then blew the room full of shrieking bagpipe music, and the farmer's wife laughed and cried. And the old friar smiled.

Late in the night of that evening, when all in the house were asleep except for Ransom and Margaret, he sat on the edge of the bed. She reached out and swept her slender hand over his bare back.

"What is on yer mind?" she asked softly.

"Three things…"

"And what might they be?"

"First, the grace of God…"

"A fine thing," she said.

"Second, the place of our traveling tomorrow…"

"I'll be glad hearin' of that," she replied.

"And third…" Ransom turned and looked at her, slowly taking in her reclining figure all the way up to her face as she lay on the bed next to him.

"Third?" she asked.

"Your beauty, my love…all of your beauty…"

Chapter 46

1558—Geneva, Switzerland

John Knox was hunched over in his study, finishing some of his notes. He was honored to have been asked to contribute to the translation of the Bible into English, and he hoped that soon the Geneva Bible would be ready for publication. Knox stopped and rubbed his eyes then glanced out the window, taking in the steeple tops of churches, and the highest of them all—the old Cathedral of St. Pierre, where Knox now regularly preached to the Protestant exiles who had fled Queen Mary Tudor's wrath and sought the safety of Switzerland. He and his wife, Marjory, had enjoyed Geneva. It was a lovely city. Many of its streets were divided by the Rhone River in a series of bridges, and much of the city could behold, as Knox could now, the blue waters of the Lake of Geneva.

But Knox's mind was not on that picturesque city. Instead, he was thinking about England and Scotland, and dwelling on the birth pangs of the Reformation that were being felt back in his homeland.

But his thoughts were interrupted by a noise at the front door. His wife, Marjory, holding their two small infants, was greeting someone. There was a man's voice, and it was loud—so loud that the two infants started crying. Marjory poked her head into his study, trying to talk above the crying of the two babies in her arms.

"John, it's your publisher—he's very upset—he wants to see you immediately."

"Thank you, dear," Knox said, rising, "I'll speak to him,"

Suddenly the publisher appeared in back of Marjory, waving a sheaf of papers and edging his way past her and into the study. As he did, she slipped out of the study and closed the wood-paneled door with a spare finger.

"John, please forgive me for barging in," he said, "but this simply cannot wait."

"Ye've frightened my wee bairns," Knox said with a raised eyebrow, "dinna ye hear them cryin'?"

"Apologies—many apologies—but these letters," he said and lifted them up in front of Knox, "they keep coming in—protesting, denouncing—your last tract I published for you..."

"Ye knew what ye were in for, didn't ye?"

"Well, not like this—anyway, you just wouldn't listen to me about my suggestions for revisions in the first edition. Perhaps now you will listen to me. And as we get ready for the second edition, we have to tone down this treatise of yours against ungodly queens."

"Tone down, ye said?"

"Yes, exactly."

"That's a tall order—my dear wife complains to me that I'm incapable of any such toning down...ye should ask her."

"John. Please. There need to be some...modifications..."

"What do ye propose?"

"Changing the title, for instance. Just listen again to the title you picked for the first edition—*The First Blast of the Trumpet Against the Monstrous Regiment of Women.*"

"The title cannot be changed."

"Well then, certainly the theme of the tract must be reduced in its rancor and vehemence—"

"The theme," Knox said firmly yet in the same controlled voice, "is not revolutionary. All I was saying in that work is that God has made it plain in the Bible that man is to be over the woman in authority, and this includes the authority of ruling nations."

"But other Christians, loyal Protestants," the publisher said, waving the letters in his hand, "have pointed out those women were granted authority by God in the Old Testament..."

"And I have distinguished those examples," Knox countered, "Deborah and others mentioned—have ye not read the work that ye yerself have printed, man? I wrote that God can—and occasionally does—grant that a woman may rule a nation but only 'by singular privilege and for certain causes,' that is exactly what I wrote. And I added that in all such exceptions, such a woman of authority must be manifest by God's hand, and must be a follower of the gospel of truth—and not—"

"Not a Jezebel, you mean?"

"Yes. I used that word for Queen Mary Tudor of England—and we shall use it again in the second printing. We must because it is true. And to write the record clean, I called her *'that horrible monster Jezebel of England'*—and such as she is for setting aflame more than three hundred Protestant saints because they would not retreat from the gospel of salvation of Jesus Christ as writ in God's Word."

"John," the publisher said, imploring his celebrated author, "leaders of the Reformation, men true and good, are now coming out against your treatise..."

"I have read their letters," Knox said quietly. "John Foxe, as an example. He took the time from his travels in chronicling the stories of Protestant martyrs to write me. And I have written him back, admitting that perhaps the emotions of my heart had overrun me in the writing of the tract. But I cannot retreat from the truth of what I wrote there."

"Yes, and John Aylmer," the publisher continued, "the personal tutor to the late Lady Jane Grey—just consider his advice, John—all he suggests is that you should have limited your attack to Marie de Guise in

Scotland and Mary Tudor in England. But by making an attack on all female sovereigns—on the idea of queens ruling nations—well...you risk giving grievous offense..."

"You mean offense to the next queen of England, don't you?" Knox asked, already knowing the answer.

"There are rumors, John, that Mary Tudor is dying—and the heir to the throne is no manly king, sir, but a womanly queen. Elizabeth, as we both know. When Mary Tudor is dead I would like to be able to return to my beloved England. But how will I be able to do so if Queen Elizabeth knows I have published your work, which seems to condemn all sovereign queens?"

"Well," Knox said with a sigh, "we shall learn soon enough what Elizabeth thinks of my *First Blast of the Trumpet*..."

"And why is that?"

"Because, my good publisher, I have long desired to return to England, and then go on to Scotland—assuming the rumors of Mary Tudor's impending demise are true—and to that end I have written to Sir William Cecil, Secretary of State for England—asking for permission to enter England under a guarantee of safe travel."

Then Knox smiled at his publisher, "So we will see soon enough, my friend, whether I am loved there—or whether I am hated."

In England, Sir William Cecil and the Earl of Sussex were riding hard and had made few stops as they made their way, followed by an entire company of soldiers, to Hatfield Castle. That is where Elizabeth had been residing, biding her time ever since she was transferred out of the Tower, and later out of house arrest in Woodstock, by order of Queen Mary Tudor.

Elizabeth had been out riding with two of her attendants. It was a clear day but cool, and she was wearing a thick cloak trimmed with lynx fur and a matching fur hat that was cocked smartly on her head and that hid most, but not all, of her fiery red hair. Riding sidesaddle with the expertise of a seasoned horsewoman, she slowed her mount when she saw Cecil, Sussex, and the military escort approaching from over the sloping hills.

Then she halted her horse altogether. Her two ladies stopped their horses directly behind her. Elizabeth knew there were only two explanations for Cecil's official visit. Either the dying Queen Mary Tudor, in her last grasp at heinous revenge, had ordered that she be arrested and readied for the executioner's axe—or it was something else—something deliciously and spectacularly different. Cecil gave the word to the Earl of Sussex and the military escort to hold back as he approached.

"Good madam," Cecil said, almost out of breath as he reined his horse in close to Elizabeth, "I bear you news from the Court of Queen Mary of England…"

"What news, pray tell?" Elizabeth asked, in more of a husky whisper than in her usual vibrant voice. There was a pause, as Cecil's horse shook its reins and gave one stomp on the ground.

"The news, madam," Cecil said, "is that Mary Tudor, Queen of England—is dead. You, madam, are rightful heir to the throne—long live the queen!"

"Long live the queen!" the troops shouted from their mounts.

Elizabeth was given little time to pack. Cecil told her he would send servants back to collect her personal items. She could not, he emphasized, risk dallying at her present residence in light of possible threats from former supporters of Mary Tudor. "Your home here is indefensible," he said. "You will be far safer at Court—in Whitehall Palace. Besides— you are Queen—you shall be crowned there."

As they rode together, Cecil began recounting to Elizabeth the nature of the business of the realm that needed attention. When they had ridden a full hour, the two of them began discussing Scotland.

"And what is your assessment," Elizabeth asked, "of the reformist rebels and the Lords of the Congregation? Shall they soon prevail over Marie de Guise?"

"Our agents in Edinburgh assure us," he said, "that Marie de Guise and her French alliance are growing more unsteady every day. The Protestants now talk of forming armies, of a full civil war, if she does not grant their demands for religious accommodation."

"And with the toppling of Marie de Guise—so would the French presence on our island disappear."

"Yes, madam, true enough—but we do need the partnership of the Protestants there to see it through."

Elizabeth was silent for a few minutes.

"My brother Edward, our young king who, alas, died too soon, was a Protestant…and I have always considered myself a follower of the new, reformed religion…yet…"

"Madam?"

"Yet—there are among the Scottish Protestants…a dangerous sect of preachers. I fear that they shall have no king or queen, but will have a church and a Bible over all."

"You fix on certain of their preachers, madam?"

"Well, that runagate John Knox for one. There are others—but Knox is certainly of concern."

"Yes. To be sure. Your wisdom on the matter is refreshing," Cecil replied diplomatically. "And yet…"

"Yet?"

"There are certain matters in common between the reforming church in England and in Scotland—or at least, certain mutual interests that can bind our two lands together, madam, at least for the time being, and for as long as it shall benefit England—and shall please you, of course, Your Highness."

Cecil did not, however, share with Elizabeth the fact that in his coat pocket he bore the letter of request from John Knox asking for safe travel into England in order to preach. Cecil had read excerpts of Knox's *First Blast of the Trumpet*, and he knew it would outrage his new queen as soon as she learned of it. He decided to keep the matter of Knox's request hidden from the queen so that the preacher would be denied entrance into England by benign neglect—rather than by a direct, sovereign edict, which could jeopardize England's anticipated courting of Scotland's Protestant lords.

As for Knox's incendiary *First Blast of the Trumpet*, Cecil decided not to educate Elizabeth on that matter either.

She will learn of it soon enough, he mused. *But better that it come from some advisor other than me—after all, I fancy having my head remain atop my shoulders...*

Chapter 47

Ransom first told Margaret on their wedding night, and then in more detail the following day, that they would travel to Perth. It was centrally located, roughly the same distance from Edinburgh and Stirling, and only slightly farther still from St. Andrews. It was south of the Highlands but north of the troubled lands most occupied by the queen regent and her forces. It was a handsome city, he had heard, and prosperous too. But most important of all, he had heard that it had become a town with a hospitable climate toward Protestants. So on the first day of their married life, Ransom and Margaret thanked their hosts, put a shilling in the hand of the old friar, and set off for Perth.

By all accounts it proved to be a wise decision, at least from everything that Ransom and Margaret could see. For a while the two of them were able to settle into a tranquil and uneventful life in Perth. The town was a very old and distinguished one, dating back hundreds of years. It had straight, sensible streets that were laid out in predictable square blocks; there was ample room between the many clean, well-kept houses, and the town lay near the banks of the River Tay. Margaret was delighted with life there, particularly when she compared it to crowded, noisy Edinburgh, with its grim row houses and filthy tenement buildings jammed with an overflow of humans and lined with walls black with grime.

There was a wide, lively market street with a variety of shops—

leatherworkers, pottery and pewter craftsmen, and even a fine fabric shop specializing in silks. The highest structure was St. John's Kirk—a towering cathedral with elegant stained-glass windows and high oak arches. There were monasteries of the Black and the Gray Friars in the town, and the great Catholic Charterhouse. But recently, Perth had also attracted large numbers of Protestant leaders and sympathizers. Some had fled the religious hostility of St. Andrews and Edinburgh. Others, who were already Perth residents, had become emboldened to declare their loyalty to the reformist gospel and the cause of the Lords of the Congregation. As far as Ransom and Margaret could see, there were no immediate signs of turmoil, despite the obvious presence in Perth of both sides of Scotland's religious war.

Ransom's training as a lawyer at Court in London had proved beneficial in his move to Perth. He quickly began supporting himself as a notary apostolic, drafting and negotiating land charters and property transfers. The large number of Protestants in Perth flocked to him, especially when the word traveled over the town that he had been the personal secretary to John Knox himself. But Ransom, still ashamed over his abandonment of his former mentor, avoided discussing the subject. Even so, with his busy law work he was soon able to rent his own law rooms in the building next to his family house, which he was also soon able to afford to buy.

For Margaret's part, though she missed the lush greenery and rugged mountains of the Highlands, she quickly adopted Perth as her home. As soon as Ransom and Margaret settled into their house, Margaret, who at that point was still uninformed about the tragic fate of her parents, began making plans to send a message to friends of her family in the Western Isles in an effort to try to make contact with Hamish and Rhona and tell them of her marriage and her newfound life in Perth.

Margaret loved the business of managing their new home. It was a good-sized two-story house, with a coat of whitewash covering the laid-stone walls. She had a wooden fence around her backyard, and the soil of it, she soon discovered, was quite suitable for planting a fine vegetable garden.

One day the Earl of Glencairn strode into Ransom's law-office rooms. He was a stately man with gray hair, and he wore an expensively embroidered coat with the collar trimmed with fox fur, and a velvet hat. He had the manners of a man well-acquainted with the Edinburgh Court. Ransom was familiar with stories about Glencairn's political background. He had also heard that the earl had been, at least in times past, somewhat of a puzzlement to the staunch reformers.

The earl greeted Ransom warmly and got directly to the point. He had, he explained, been a previous though hesitant advisor to Marie de Guise but had consistently urged her to exercise toleration toward the new Protestant cause. But now he had finally decided to formally join the leadership of the Lords of the Congregation. He had chosen sides. There was no going back, he said. He was visiting Ransom to solicit his aid as a legal advisor to the Protestant Lords. Ransom said he was honored by the invitation but would have to pray on the matter.

Later that night, Ransom spoke of the meeting with Margaret. She had made a fine meal and had cleared the table. She paused in front of the fire, which outlined her silhouette, and ran her hands slowly over her belly.

"Does it show?" she asked.

"Not yet," Ransom answered, half listening as he worked at the desk in the corner of their main room.

"No?" she said with a bit of a pout to her voice. "Doesn't show at all?"

"Only to those who know you very well..." he said with a smile.

He put his quill down, and turned to face her. He explained the meeting with the Earl of Glencairn.

"'Tis a great honor," she said. "Why would ye doubt the invitation? Why hesitate?"

"To make sure that the proposed association has the blessings of God. I know enough about the Lords of the Congregation to know that some are true men of God, seeking to spread the evangel of Christ and win souls and birth freedom in Scotland—but there are others, men who desire only power and wealth, and who would use the cause of Christ, or any other means for that matter, to achieve it."

"How will ye truly know," Margaret said, "if ye dinna meet with 'em and find out?"

Ransom had to smile at that. He had had the same thought himself. Margaret's counsel settled the matter. Two days later Ransom traveled to meet with them in the great hall of the castle of the Laird of Dun, where he was presented to the Lords of the Congregation. He was greeted with such a warm and exuberant welcome that it took him by surprise. The Earl of Glencairn was there, and the Master of Maxwell, Sir Hugh Campbell—the Sheriff of Ayr—together with several Protestant preachers, including John Douglas, a former Carmelite Friar, and of course, the Laird of Dun, who hosted the meeting.

They advised Ransom of the progress they had made in trying to force Marie de Guise, now officially queen regent, to retreat from her hostility toward their movement. They had, as they explained it to Ransom, taken several signal steps. They had filed petitions with Marie de Guise demanding that she reform the corrupt practices of the churchmen under her authority; that she suspend the dreaded laws against heresy and permit the taking of Communion under the English form of practice; that she permit public preaching and allow Christian worship to be conducted in English and not just in Latin. Their demands had been met with cool detachment, however. So the Lords proceeded to draft and then nail to the doors of friaries around the countryside "beggars summons," demanding that the wealthy Black and Gray Friars turn their huge poverty funds over to the poor for whom they were supposedly intended.

"'Tis clear to all," the Laird of Dun said firmly, "that the queen regent ignores our pleas while she makes a good face in public."

"There is room for hope," the Earl of Glencairn countered, "that her goodwill will extend to a genuine toleration of our reformist religion—"

"It seems that yer blind hope for royal tolerance springs as hot as the torch Marie de Guise uses for burning preachers," the Laird snapped back.

"Gentlemen," one of the preachers said interrupting, "we may disagree on where the queen regent's heart is—but let us get to the reason for bringin' Master Ransom Mackenzie here tonight."

"Exactly," the earl said, turning to Ransom. "Ye studied with him—worked as his personal secretary—and have been his trusted aide," he said. "It is time to summon John Knox back to Scotland—and who better to write the letter of invitation to Mister Knox than ye, Master Ransom Mackenzie?"

For a moment, Ransom felt his face so flush that he wondered whether the whole assembly of men standing around him could detect his embarrassment. He could not lie—that was out of the question. But was there some manner of diplomacy, he wondered, that could extract him from this excruciating request? Or must he simply admit, in that august assembly of Protestant leaders, how he must not...could not...be the messenger of such an important matter to John Knox, because he had failed his mentor at a most crucial moment.

"So—what say ye to that, Master Ransom?" the Earl of Glencairn asked. "Will ye be our emissary to Mister John Knox?"

Chapter 48

The assembly of Scotland's most notable Protestant leaders gathered around Ransom, awaiting his response. As he looked over the faces of the men, he noticed, for the first time, the presence of Sir James Stewart, one of Scotland's most powerful, and political, Protestant lords. Stewart had elbowed his way to the front and was eyeing him closely.

Ransom said a quick, silent prayer for guidance, wisdom, and candor. He took a deep breath and then began to speak.

"Gentlemen," he began, "I am greatly honored by your invitation to be present today, and to be privy to your discussions of such great moment and import. I am also humbled that you would ask me to author a request to John Knox, inviting him back to Scotland to aid in the work of the Reformation here." Ransom paused, looked over the semicircle of faces, and continued.

"But I am afraid I will have to decline your invitation—respectfully, of course—but decline it I must."

There was an audible response from the men. Someone muttered, "Outrageous," and another complained about "this audacious upstart…"

The Earl of Glencairn, as always, was seeking to preserve the order of the assembly, and raised his hand in an effort to quiet the group. He was only partially successful.

"Please, men, let us hear Master Ransom further on this matter," he pleaded. Then he turned to Ransom.

"Please shed some light on your reply, good sir. It has taken us all by surprise—do ye not believe that we can gain much by your master's presence here?"

"I do," Ransom replied. "I have great respect for Mister Knox."

"Then what is the impediment?" Glencairn asked with bewilderment in his voice.

"It is not Mister Knox, nor my disagreement with your strategy to summon him here—but rather…that I am perhaps the least likely person here, or anywhere else for that matter, to be able to persuade Mr. Knox to come, or to go, or to do anything. I am, to be frank, of low esteem in Mr. Knox's eyes—and thus any one of you would be better suited for this task than I—"

"Posh, posh!" Glencairn said with a chuckle. "Yer humility is wasted on this assembly, good Ransom—though it is refreshing to see that such a virtue still exists among at least one Protestant in this realm!"

A few of the nobles smiled at that. But Ransom's expression made it clear that he considered it no joking matter.

"Please, gentlemen," he said with urgency in his voice, "please know my heart on this matter—this is no pretense of humility. What I share with you is a genuine expression of disqualification for this task. Plain and simple—I, while in London, departed ways from Mister Knox in a manner that grieves me to this day—"

"On matters of doctrine?" one of the onlookers asked loudly.

"No, not at all, praise God," Ransom responded quickly.

"Then corrupt morals, is it?" another shouted out bluntly.

"No, sirs, not in that way…it was something else…"

"Then what?" Stewart said abrasively. "And be quick about it, or else by the time ye tell us yer secret we'll all have forgotten why we came here in the first place."

There were a few coarse chuckles, and when they died down Ransom spoke.

"Good sirs, some five years ago when Mister Knox beckoned me to leave England upon the rise of Mary Tudor to the throne and go with him to the Continent—well—I refused…"

"Ye wanted to stay behind and be martryed?" Glencairn asked incredulously.

"No, not at all. But I felt a deep affection and loyalty for a certain person in London…though I soon learned my affections had not been wisely placed…nevertheless, my last contact with my mentor and teacher was under those unfortunate circumstances. It burdens me to tell you this…but I feel I must…"

There was a momentary hush, and then James Stewart strode forward.

"Then why should we ever trust ye to be part of this proud assembly?" he asked. "Having cleft yourself away from the one whose authority was over ye?"

Ransom looked down at the stone floor, feeling a sense of disgrace wash over him. But then suddenly something flashed through his mind—and as it did, he now believed it needed to be said.

"That is for you, not me, to decide," Ransom said. "But I would ask you a question, Sir James."

Stewart's expression changed as he realized he was about to be questioned by an unknown young lawyer, whose credentials of loyalty were still a matter of dispute.

"'Tis a mark of my great patience," Stewart said, "that I will allow ye to ask me yer one question…"

"Very well, then," Ransom said quietly, but firmly. "Is it not correct that you still are employed as an advisor to the queen regent, Marie de Guise, yet you are here with these Protestant conspirators who oppose her—does that mean, sir, that like me, you have 'cleft yourself away from the one whose authority was over ye'?"

Stewart stood speechless. He knew that in order to answer the question he would have to give a definite answer on his intentions—on whether he still wanted to work a political compromise with Marie de Guise, his stepmother, or whether he would now leave her Court in Edinburgh altogether and band himself with the Lords of the Congregation.

In the back of the group, one man laughed out loud. A few of the other lords smiled, still struggling not to offend Stewart.

"I take great offense at that," Stewart said, pointing his finger at Ransom, "and will not stay here to be offended further!" He then started pushing his way through the group. Several of the leaders scurried after him to appease his wounded sensibilities. Meanwhile, the Earl of Glencairn walked quickly over to Ransom and began escorting him to the door.

"Master Ransom, I fear yer usefulness at this meeting may have come to an end. Yet, I will be in contact with ye—we still have matters to discuss."

As Ransom trudged to the door alone, he felt a hand on his shoulder. He turned around and saw a middle-aged man, dressed very humbly, whom he did not know.

"Master Ransom, allow me to introduce myself," the man said with a smile. "I am Paul Methven."

"I have heard of you," Ransom said eagerly. "You have been an outspoken preacher in Scotland of late. It's a pleasure meeting you."

"Don't be downhearted by the response from Stewart," Methven said. "He couldn't tell you on which side his breakfast bread is buttered in the morning unless you first tell him who it was that buttered it!"

Ransom burst into laughter, and Methven joined him in a hearty chuckle.

When the humor died down, Ransom looked at Methven with a sad look.

"Thank you for your goodwill toward me," Ransom said, "but the truth is…I just don't think I am worthy of being here in this assembly of leaders in the Reformation cause…perhaps it was a mistake for me to have come."

"Nonsense," Methven said. "You know—you remind me a little of someone else I know."

"Oh?"

"Yes, but it would have been many a year ago. Maybe you have forgotten. A man called by his peers to the charge of being a preacher of the gospel of Christ—but when he was called to do so, at first he refused, and all he could do was to run into a corner and weep and cry out that he was simply not worthy of such a task."

"Whom do you speak of?"

Then Paul Methven smiled. As he gave his answer he patted Ransom on the shoulder.

"Why it was none other," Methven said, "than Mister John Knox, of course."

Chapter 49

In the chill of November a merchant—a Protestant supporter by the name of John Gray—set off from Scotland by ship. He was bound for the Continent, and eventually to Rome on trading business. But he agreed to carry a letter to Geneva en route.

John Knox was home when the letter came. Gray was thrilled with the prospect of meeting Knox, and the Scottish preacher invited him in for a warm drink and a meal. He introduced Gray to Marjory, his wife, and then proceeded to open the letter.

It was from Sir James Stewart and the Earl of Glencairn. "If you will," the letter read, "bestow on our effort both your presence and your wisdom, God will surely shine upon the cause of the Reformation in Scotland. The time is ripe. The fire is struck. The metal is to the forge, and the Lord will surely be the great Smith to hammer and fashion a land free for the preaching of the gospel of Christ..."

After Gray left, Knox sat with Marjory and shared the letter. She did not hide her mixed feelings. She had longed to return to northern England and the pastoral village of Berwick where she and Knox had met. Her family was still there. But so much had happened since those days. And she and John had made a good home in Geneva.

"So it's to Scotland then?" she said with a bit of weariness to her voice. "And not to England as we had hoped?"

"Dear wife," he said with a mood of rising agitation, "I did desire to traverse England first before going to Scotland—but I have written to Sir William Cecil, Queen Elizabeth's Secretary of State—"

"I know, dear."

"Not once, or twice."

"Yes, John…"

"But *thrice—thrice!* And nary a single reply! All I was asking was a warrant of safe travel through England. And in my third letter—"

"But you threatened him, dear—you made threats against the Secretary of State."

"Not personal threats, mind ye," Knox said. And then having thought a little on it he added, "'twas not the threat of John Knox—I merely threatened him with the fiery and awful judgment of God if he neglects to do the right that is clearly in his power to do—"

"But John, dear, did you not lay the burning of the martyrs in England at his feet?"

"Aye, I surely did—he was Secretary also under Mary Tudor when it occurred. He could have protested—he could have stopped it."

Marjory sighed. Then she heard the babies waking from their nap in the next room. As she turned to tend to them she added, "I fear I'll never see England again."

"No, dear," Knox said rising and kissing her gently on the forehead. "My precious wife, we shall go to Scotland—but also to England as soon as the Lord in His mercy allows—I promise it."

When she disappeared into the nursery, Knox stepped over to the large window with its many square panes of glass separated by leaded latticework. He looked out at the steeples and cathedrals of Geneva, and out to the wide Lake of Geneva beyond. He thought of the dark, tranquil lochs of the lowlands of Scotland, tucked deep within the soft green rolling arms of the hills. He knew it would take months for him to ready for the trip, for the sailing to Leith. But he also thought of something else that prodded him on and created a sense of urgency. He thought of the many souls that inhabited St. Andrews, and Edinburgh, and Perth, and Dundee, and throughout the countryside.

"To Scotland I go," he whispered, "and woe unto me if I preach not the evangel of Christ when I am there."

The cool of the fall in Scotland gave way to the dark winter. And then to spring. In Edinburgh, Marie de Guise, queen regent of Scotland, was wracked with sickness and had to be carried into the meeting room on a long couch shouldered by four servants. They set it down on the ground gently in front of the table where the Privy Council was already seated and then quickly departed. While the whole Council had assembled, some of her advisors, like James Stewart, had been excluded. She knew he was consorting with the Protestants. But she also knew that he was an opportunist and could be turned this way or that—depending on the wind, or tide, or the climate of the times. Nevertheless, though she had allowed him to stay at Court, he could not be trusted to be part of her inner sanctum of strategy.

None of the Council members gave any expression of concern at her appearance. But they all knew she had been fighting a long weakness of body and running fevers. Despite her frailty, they all smiled confidently at her.

Marie de Guise sat upright. She was not about to let her deteriorating physical state minimize her dedication to the course of action at hand.

"This preacher at Dundee…" she began, and then cast an expectant glance over at one of the Council. "His name…"

"Methven, Madam—his name is Paul Methven," one of the members said politely.

"Yes—well—he is a blight. And a provocateur—he preaches in defiance of my edicts about public displays of Protestantism. Have I not ordered the provosts of Perth and of Dundee and like towns to suppress this heresy?"

"Your Majesty," one of the councilmen said meekly, "we have communicated your orders—"

"And what reply? Tell me!"

"They say," the advisor continued, trying to choose his words carefully, "that while they can make such preachers kneel and bow before you…they cannot find a way to make them violate…turn against…or should I say—"

"Out! Speak it!" she said sternly.

"They have no way to force such men to break from their consciences on such matters of faith—"

"How long," she shrieked, "must I endure such insolence!"

Her burst of fury was an amazement to them all, considering her apparent weakness. But such was the strength of her inner resolve. And that was clear to every member in the room.

"You shall publish a summons to this Methven," she said, "to produce himself and face the charges of criminal heresy and treason."

"Many of the towns—Perth, St. Andrews, Dundee—they increase with the reformist rebels daily."

"That is because," she retorted in a fiery tone, "I have followed your silly advice about trying to deal with these Protestants—to negotiate—but now that is ended. It is time for action."

"And what would Your Majesty suggest?" one of the councilmen asked.

"You shall issue a general summons for appearance to the Protestant preachers of each of those towns—"

"All of the preachers in all three of those towns?" one of them asked incredulously.

"Are there so many?" Marie de Guise asked in a mocking tone. But as she looked at the faces of her advisors, her self-assured sarcasm evaporated.

"I am afraid," one of them answered, "there are."

"I care not!" she exclaimed. "Set a date for their appearance before me. Designate the royal castle in Stirling. Tell them to get hence to Stirling and there be examined by my Council and myself at the certain date. We shall put the fear of God into them, I swear it—this Protestant rabble shall not usurp the royal succession. I will preserve the throne of Scotland for my daughter, Mary Queen of Scots, with my very last breath."

Chapter 50

Several Months Later

"I may as well have called myself a devil-worshiper and an idolater," Ransom muttered, finishing the last slice of breakfast gingerbread. He was filled with gloom again over the course of his life. Even quite a few weeks after his meeting with the Lords of the Congregation, he could not help turning it over again and again in his mind.

"Ye're stretchin' the truth, I'm sure…" Margaret said, pushing her plate back without having eaten a bite.

"Aren't you hungry?" Ransom asked, looking at her full plate of food.

"Got the queasies," Margaret said, rubbing her pregnant belly. Then she pushed her plate over to Ransom, but decided to reach over with her finger and scoop up a little dab of honey that lay on the edge and licked it off her finger.

"Are you sure?" he asked, diving into the bread and dipping it into the small bowl of honey. Margaret nodded and then continued trying to encourage her husband.

"As I've said before, ye told the truth to those gentlemen about yer partin' with Mister Knox—if gentlemen they were, which I question because of the way they treated ye. So, what else could ye have done? Besides—it's been many a week since that meetin'…"

"You should have heard their outburst against me…" Ransom said, reliving the scene again. But then, with a mood of resignation, he added,

"Well…what's done is done. I just wonder how it may be affecting us now…I think I may be losing clients…and with you carrying our wee bairn…"

"The Lord'll take care of us," Margaret said.

"Dear woman," Ransom said, "what does it mean that you feel sick when you're so long with child?"

"My mum always said it means twins—but others say it means ye'll have a boy."

"Twins…" Ransom said, his voice trailing off.

"Don't fret so," Margaret said, "we'll not starve." Then her mind drifted off to something, and she looked at Ransom.

"I sent a letter to my cousin up in the Western Isles. Heard nothin' and 'tis been a month and a moon. I long so to learn of my da and my mum…"

"I could make some inquiries—some of the traders who come through Perth head up that way."

"Naw," she said. "Let it be. I'll wait—I'll hear back soon enough."

There was a knock on the door of their house. Ransom got up and answered it. Margaret could hear him talking with someone at the door. Then he returned with a letter in his hand.

"'Tis for me?" Margaret said anxiously.

"I'm sorry, but no," Ransom said. "It's from the Earl of Glencairn." He eyed the envelope suspiciously, turning it over and looking at both sides.

"Open it, my husband!" Margaret said loudly. "It could be important."

Ransom broke the wax seal. Margaret watched his face for some hint at what was inside as he read silently. Then he put the letter down and threw a quizzical look at his wife.

"What is it?" she asked.

Ransom's face broke into a smile. Then he broke into a laugh and grabbed the letter again to reread it.

"Don't torture me so!" she said. "What does he say?"

"It appears the Lord God has a sense of humor."

"Whatever do ye mean?"

"Do ye remember my telling you about Mister Paul Methven, the preacher who befriended me after the meeting with the Lords?"

"I do..."

"Well, the queen regent has issued a summons against him," Ransom explained. "He has been preaching the evangel of Christ over in Dundee. Now Marie de Guise has summoned him to appear and to give his defense in Edinburgh on charges of heresy and treason—"

"How can you say 'sense of humor' over something as grave as that?"

"Just this—Glencairn says Methven is traveling here to Perth—that all of the Lords of the Congregation are assembling to support him in the matter—but that he has declared he shall not decide which course of action to take until..." and with that Ransom smiled, "until he consults with me as his legal advisor. And that he shall not take any other advice from any of the Protestant leaders until he hears my counsel first!"

Margaret was beaming.

"So," she said sidling up next to Ransom where he stood, "The great Protestant Lords support this Mister Methven."

"Aye, that's true," Ransom said.

"And Methven supports ye, Ransom Mackenzie."

"Aye, by the grace of God it appears so."

"But who," Margaret asked with a twinkle in her eye, "do ye support, Ransom Mackenzie?"

Ransom turned his head slightly, eyed his wife, and then wrapped his arms around her.

"Why I support *you*, my dear Highland lass!"

"Then does that mean then," she said with a mischievous turn of her smile, "that I may advise the Lords of the Congregation on matters of policy and such—seeing as I have the support of the whole lot of ye?"

Ransom laughed, but a little too heartily. Margaret's smile began to fade. She gave him a glare that conveyed much of what was behind her beautiful dark eyes.

"Tell me now, dear husband, do ye doubt I could?"

"Could what?"

"Address the great Protestant Lords?"

"Why would you ask such a preposterous thing?"

"Do ye mock me then?" Margaret said, as she stepped back, with a combination of hurt and indignation. Her pale skin flashed pink around the cheeks.

Ransom reached out to take her back into his arms, but she moved a step away and glared again.

"What is it, dearest?" Ransom asked, having a strong inkling of what lay behind her response.

"Just that—well—I was wondering—do ye consider me part of the 'monstrous regiment of women'?"

It took Ransom only a moment to make the connection between Margaret's comments and the papers that lay on his desk.

"Margaret, have you been looking at the letters on my desk?"

"I see nothin' wrong in it. They were out and plain to see—besides, isn't that what your Mister Knox titled his tract—the 'monstrous regiment of women'?"

"'Tis true, he used that phrase—and if you read those letters from several reformist leaders which are being circulated about, then you'd know they feel he used such language unadvisedly—but I think Knox meant to challenge the cruelty and corruption of Mary Tudor in England and Marie de Guise in Scotland, both women monarchs...and yet..."

"Yet what?"

"Yet…I would not have used such a title…for fear that it would have been like a cannon shot rather than a flag raised. A cannon sends everyone scurrying for cover—a flag requires a thoughtful decision whether to salute."

"Perhaps Mister Knox should have consulted ye."

"I hardly think he will ever consult me on anything again."

"Because ye left him in order to stay in London and pine after—*after that scheming tart, Catherine!*" she said with a flash in her eyes.

Ransom laughed, pulled her over to himself, and covered her face with kisses.

"Why, oh why, did I not simply stay in the Highlands with you when I had the chance? I must have been daft to leave you behind…"

"No," she said, "'twas the way of the Lord, I know it. But I pray to Him nightly that we not be separated again unless it be by death…and may that be a whole lifetime away."

Ransom kissed her full on the mouth. She had the taste of honey still lingering on her lips.

"Well," she murmured in his arms, "if ye'll not tell him—then perhaps someday I'll have to give Mister Knox yer advice myself."

As Ransom held her tight, he thought back to his meeting with the Protestant leaders. After he had refused to pen the letter to Knox, he later heard that Stewart and Glencairn had sent a letter to him themselves, begging that he return to Scotland and join their cause.

Perhaps, my good wife, we shall face up to John Knox sooner than we had thought, Ransom mused to himself.

Chapter 51

Much like the first meeting that Ransom had attended in the great hall where the conclave was being held, all of the Protestant Lords and reformist nobles and leading preachers were there. But this one was different. There was a nervous energy and a kind of dire anticipation that hovered in the air as the men filled the room.

The Earl of Glencairn called them to order, and the Laird of Dun said a prayer for wisdom and unity of purpose. Then they immediately set out on the first order of business—how preacher Paul Methven should respond to the summons that had been issued against him by the queen regent and her Council, which ordered him to appear and defend himself against charges of public heresy. Ransom had conferred privately with Methven upon the preacher's arrival in Perth, inviting him to stay in their home, but had not made his position known yet.

James Stewart and several of his allies jumped into the discussion.

"He must obey and produce himself at the appointed time—'twould be foolhardy to do anything else," Stewart pronounced. "But I have the full confidence of my position at Court that all will be well…"

"How can ye know that?" one of the nobles yelled.

"Several reasons, gentlemen," Stewart continued. "First, I know the queen regent and her advisors—and how she thinks on a matter. Second, I propose that I escort Master Methven myself. My personal presence shall be a guarantee of his safety. And third, ye all have spoken of tryin' to convince the queen regent in some measure away from her Catholic manners and more toward the new religion—well, here is yer chance. I canna think of a better man to preach to Marie de Guise than our friend Paul Methven here."

A number of men gave out loud "amens." Stewart stepped back into the crowd with a satisfied look.

"I'd like to hear from my counselor," Methven said with a smile, "Mister Ransom Mackenzie."

Ransom stepped into the middle of the room. Before he could speak a few of the Lords cleared their throats loudly. Ransom ignored them. He placed his hands behind his back, took a short pause, and then commenced to speak.

"I beg to differ with such an esteemed gentleman as Sir James Stewart," Ransom began, "but differ I must."

There was a loud and disagreeable murmur in the crowd.

"Mister Methven dares not obey this summons. I know that Sir James says he knows the queen regent. I do not dispute that he once knew her mind on certain matters—but it is clear that of late he has been excluded from her inner chambers and from her present strategies—undoubtedly because it is known he consorts with the Protestants behind her back. For that reason, the second argument—that Sir James's presence can guarantee Paul Methven's safety—must also be rejected."

The murmurs were getting louder. But Ransom pushed forward in his argument.

"And thirdly," Ransom said, "as to Marie de Guise being open to our Protestant gospel, I have much to say on that. It is widely known that John Knox wrote to the queen regent, setting forth the merits of the reformed gospel, and salvation by faith, and the Protestant form of worship. It was, I am told, a very cordial and diplomatic letter—uncharacteristically diplomatic for Mister Knox."

With that several members of the meeting laughed loudly.

"And yet, what was the queen regent's response?" Ransom said firmly, his voice ringing out in the great hall. "She called it a 'lampoon'! Yes, good gentlemen, she ridiculed a noted Protestant preacher and called his appeal a crude joke—a silly entertainment. Such is the state of her mind and heart on such matters. Did not our heavenly Captain, the Lord Jesus Christ, tell his own disciples that, when they came upon a town that rejected the truth, to knock the dust of such a place off their sandals? That, gentlemen, after much prayer and meditation, is my mind and soul on this matter."

The Earl of Glencairn turned to Methven and solicited his response. Methven surveyed the faces of the men in the room and then spoke up. As he did he walked over to Ransom and stopped when he was about an arm's length away.

"Master Ransom," he began, "I do not wear sandals—in Scotland it is too damp and cold for such footwear!"

The crowd chuckled at that.

"Though I know the Highlanders do wear something like that—you'll have to ask your pretty Highland wife how they manage that in February!"

Ransom smiled, and then Methven brought his thoughts to conclusion.

"But men, I do own some fine leather boots—and Ransom, I am ready to knock the dust of Edinburgh Castle and the queen regent's Holyrood Palace off those boots—and to follow your counsel, good sir."

There was much nodding of heads and amens from all but James Stewart and his allies. Glencairn then led into the second order of business—the matter of the queen regent summoning all of the preachers of Perth, Dundee, and St. Andrews to show themselves at Stirling Castle for an interview with her and her council.

Stewart charged into the middle of the room and pointed his finger at Ransom.

"If ye'll be straight-minded and true," he bellowed, "then ye'll have to advise the same for this summons as well, right? Ye must be of the mind that the summons for all of the preachers must also be disregarded and disobeyed!"

He paused to let the implications sink in. The faces in the entire room reflected the same thought—that a mass disobedience would be an invitation to civil war.

"Yes, gentlemen," Stewart added. "I see by your looks that ye know full well that what's good for the goose is good for the gander—that if all the preachers must show themselves before the queen regent, then so must Mister Methven. And so I say that we reconsider Mister Methven's plight and reject the foolishness of this Ransom Mackenzie—or else," he added, "we must decide to all disobey—and let the wind carry this matter as it will."

"You make a wrong comparison," Ransom said above the din now building in the room.

"Wrong, ye say?" Stewart bellowed.

"Yes, wrong!" Ransom shouted back. "The summons against Methven is criminal in nature. I've considered its language. It is a formal charge. It is a prelude to an execution by fire or sword, and on that I will stake my life. The queen regent will give no fair trial—she will simply make the pretense of a hearing so as to give her men time to search for wood and straw for the burning."

"But what of the other summons for all of the preachers of the towns?" one of the nobles yelled out.

"It is merely general in nature," Ransom continued. "It implies no charges, makes no accusations. But it does order an appearance. If all of the preachers disobey such a general warrant for appearance, then Marie de Guise will use that as an excuse to commence a war against all Protestants, claiming a general insurrection has begun. Gentlemen," he concluded, "we must send all of our preachers to Stirling Castle—except Mister Methven."

There was much shouting and yelling and raising of hands in the group, so much so that no one saw the massive oak door to the great hall open and close.

"'Tis just too bad that your master, John Knox, is not here!" Stewart shouted. "I dare say he would not counsel that all our preachers be walked into a lions' den—"

"Sir James," a voice rang out from the back, "why don't ye ask Mister Knox yerself?"

The room was stilled, and suddenly men parted and the figure of John Knox strode to the center of the room. There were shouts of joy and embraces between Knox and several of the men. After the greetings, Glencairn finally regained order and cautiously asked Knox to give his counsel on the matter under discussion.

"The advice you have received," he began, "not to disobey such a general summons for all of your preachers—'tis not faulty, though it is in need of refinement."

"And what change would you make to Master Ransom Mackenzie's counsel?" one the of the lords called out.

"Only this—that ye all accompany yer preachers as one large assembly—as a show of strength—but carry no armor nor weapons. And send a message ahead to the queen regent, telling her so. That way she cannot claim that ye're a hostile army in disguise and use it as an excuse to attack ye."

The whole of the group nodded vigorously, applauded the decision, and praised God for the result. Stewart struggled to smile and find a way to cast the whole episode, somehow, as a victory for his prudent advice.

The final bit of business was to chose a messenger to announce their intentions to Marie de Guise. The group decided on Erskine of Dun.

After the assembly adjourned, Ransom tried to step toward Knox to speak to him, but the crowd surrounded him and soon he and the lords and nobles all exited the hall together, engaged in lively conversation, leaving Ransom alone in the hall. Even Methven, delighted with the opportunity to meet Knox, had left with them.

As Ransom climbed on his horse to ride back to Perth and to his pregnant wife, and to the warm hearth and fire burning there, he was thankful for the way he had been used by God in the meeting. But there was now a lingering uneasiness about it, like a root bitten into that had promised to be sweet, but turned out to be bitter, dark, and distasteful. And he knew that it had to do with his mentor, Mister Knox, and the confrontation he now felt was inevitable.

Chapter 52

Following Knox's advice, the Lords of the Congregation sent an emissary, one Erskine of Dun, to Queen Regent Marie de Guise. Dun was not selected because of his boldness. To the contrary, he was chosen because of all of the Protestant leaders he was the meekest and the most courteous. He was never known to have said a rash word or utter his mind out of anger. Erskine of Dun was to bear the message that the large assembly of Protestants who were marching to Stirling were unarmed and were doing so in obedience to the queen regent's command. The largeness of the group, moreover, was simply due to the fact that the preachers so summoned to the Castle at Stirling were being accompanied by both their flocks and the entirety of the Protestant leadership.

But Ransom joined the assembly at Stirling, then rode straight home. He arrived back at home in Perth several days earlier than Margaret expected. When he trudged into the house, she could see by his face that he was burdened.

"Ransom, ye're home!" she exclaimed. "I'm glad to see ye, dear heart, but what ever happened at Stirling?"

"Nothing—a great event of nothing! Rancor and confusion within our ranks. I swear that the seed of the Protestant gospel will never take root in this land so long as the lords and nobles keep digging it up out of strife—"

"Strife over what?"

"Our messenger, Erskine of Dun, a kind and gentle man, sent a message back from his meeting with the queen regent. She outfoxed the poor man by saying she had changed her mind—and that we were not to arrive at Stirling but were to disband so she could think on the matter and come to some new accommodation of our religious demands."

"Why is that so bad?"

"Because Erskine did not know enough to demand that she formally withdraw her summons in writing and under her royal seal—without that, we were still bound by her order to appear."

"Surely ye argued the point to the great lords."

"Of course, but to no avail. Even Knox agreed with me that it smelled and looked for all the world like a trap. But the moderates, together with the men of the wide and comfortable middle, prevailed—and so it was decided by a vote of the majority that we should all disband and return to our towns and homes and await some further order from the queen regent."

"Well, at least there was no blood that was spilt."

"True enough."

"And something else, dear Ransom."

"Aye?"

"Mister John Knox, it seems, has agreed with you twice since his arrival in Scotland." She smiled, reached out, stroked his beard, and then hugged him.

"Also true, but I'm still troubled…"

"Ye look for things to fret over, Ransom," Margaret said. She studied his face and then asked, tenderly, "What is it, my dear husband?"

"He avoids me. Mister Knox turns straight away from me when I try to approach him. I want to make this better between us, but he will not engage me—the look in his eye says that I left the work of God when he needed me, and so I am disqualified."

"Do ye need Mister Knox's royal seal to do what God calls ye to do, Ransom?" Margaret asked in a voice that was rising, which let her husband know the question was merely rhetorical—as the matter was certainly settled in his wife's mind.

"I'm beginning to question a great many things," Ransom said with heaviness in his voice, "given the way things work here in Scotland… amid such a divided and confused church…"

"I think ye should make the Lord Jesus the Chief of yer clan," she said tenderly, "and then do what He says. And John Knox and all the great Lords of the Congregation will just have to decide whether Christ has made them part of yer clan or not—but it seems that God has called ye to do a powerful work—with or without Mister Knox or the Protestant nobles…"

Ransom stroked her pretty face and framed it with both of his hands.

"I'm blessed to have you at my side," he said. "Your words are like a breeze from the Highlands, cooling my mind and settling my heart."

But as they prepared for bed that night, Ransom was still pondering the decision of the Protestant assembly to disband merely on the spoken word of the queen regent. He could not shake a sense of foreboding.

He tossed and turned that night but finally fell asleep just before the morning broke. He thought at first he was dreaming when he heard the banging. Margaret had wakened before he had and had to shake him several times before he awoke.

"Ransom, there's someone at the door!" she said in a strained whisper. "Wake up!"

He stumbled out of bed, threw a coat on, and made his way down to the front door.

There was a young messenger standing in the doorway. Ransom recognized him as an aide to one of the Protestant lords.

"I know it's early, Mister Mackenzie," the young man said, "but I have been sent to warn each of the Protestant leaders here in Perth. Erskine of Dun arrived in the middle of the night—"

"Erskine?"

"Yes, sir, he says he was detained at Stirling Castle by the queen regent, but he escaped—"

"Tell me quickly."

"After he sent his message from Marie de Guise that it was her desire that the Protestant assembly refrain from entering Stirling but instead disband and wait for her further order, Erskine says she reaffirmed her prior order and then sealed it—she's ordered all the Protestant preachers appear before her—"

"Appear by what date?" Ransom interjected abruptly.

"Midday of yesterday," the young messenger said with an anxious look.

"I knew it!" Ransom said in an explosion of anger.

"What is it, dear?" Margaret said as she slowly made her way down the stairway.

"The queen regent's betrayed us—used poor Erskine of Dun as the bishop in her chess game—and has conveniently moved those muddle-minded Lords of the Congregation as if they were the pawns!"

"Marie de Guise and her Council have outlawed all of the Protestant preachers for disobedience to her command," the young messenger said rapidly, "and anyone who would 'harbor or assist them'—those were the very words of Her Majesty's edict, according to Sir Erskine…"

"Knox—have you informed him?"

"Aye," the young man said, "first off—"

"And?"

"All he said is that he will preach at St. John's Kirk—within this very hour."

Then the messenger dashed off to deliver his urgent news to the next member of the Protestant assembly.

"I must be off to St. John's for Knox's sermon," Ransom said.

"We'll go together," Margaret said.

They dressed and rode over to the cathedral. Though it was a Catholic structure, the Protestants had been using it frequently. The outnumbered priests and friars could only sit back and watch nervously. When the Protestants would vacate it—as they did after their sermons and worship services—the priests would then file in and conduct the mass.

Knox, in his long black robes and four-cornered hat, mounted the high pulpit, an ornately carved wooden perch that reached up and then outward over the sanctuary. Ransom—and the whole of the assembly of those present—expected him to preach against Marie de Guise and her abuse of power and her corruption of her God-ordained office. But he did not. Knox stroked his beard with his left hand, and with his right he placed his huge Bible on the corner of the pulpit.

After offering up a prayer on the words he was to share in the name of Almighty God, and after a petition for a blessing on their gathering, he began.

He preached on the subject he had already prepared. He spoke to the cathedral that was filled with expectant faces on the sin of idolatry.

"Has not," he thundered, "God spoken on the sin of idolatry? That we must be separated from idolatry? For in God's holy Word the apostle Paul says, 'Ye cannot drink of the cup of the Lord and of the cup of the devils. Ye cannot be partakers of the Lord's table, and of the table of the devils.'

"Of course God has spoken," he said, answering his own question. "And so would every idolater in this land thusly agree—and so would every idolater cry out, 'But we trust not in idols!'

"To which I say this—that if anyone here, or anyone anywhere, puts his trust in things other than God and thusly does contrary to God's

word, even if he says with his lips, 'But I do this thing in God's honor'—
nevertheless God says, 'You are idolaters!'"

"Mark this, brethren," Knox continued. "Many make an idol out of
their own wisdom or fantasy." The preacher made a sweeping gesture
toward the altar that was populated with statues of the saints. "But God
plainly says, do not do what 'seems good in your own eyes to do'—but
rather, 'Do what thy Lord God hath commanded thee to do.'"

When the sermon was completed and the assembly dismissed, there
was quiet as they filed out of the cathedral. Up at the front, at the altar,
a priest appeared with two altar boys at his side.

Erskine of Dun and several of the Protestant nobles swept up to Knox
and immediately engaged him over the newest outrage from Marie de
Guise. The Earl of Glencairn hurried over to Ransom, who introduced
him to his wife. Glencairn smiled and commented on the "much reported
beauty and wit of Margaret Mackenzie," and then turned to Ransom
and solicited him to join the group that would be meeting at the store
of a prosperous Perth merchant down at Merchant Cross.

A neighbor couple who lived in the house next to Ransom and
Margaret offered to take her back home in their carriage with her horse
at the back. Ransom thanked them heartily, gave a quick kiss to
Margaret's hand, and then scurried with Glencairn to the meeting place.

But when the cathedral was almost empty, a thirteen-year-old
Protestant boy who had heard Knox's sermon was still sitting in the
second pew from the front. The priest and the altar boys were preparing
for the mass. A few of Knox's followers were still milling around at the
entrance of the cathedral, glancing at the priest.

"'Tis idolatry!" the boy shouted out.

The priest, not believing his ears, turned slowly to eye the boy.

"'Tis idolatry!" he yelled again.

The priest walked down to the boy, snatched him out of the pew by his shirt, cuffed him smartly on the side of the head twice, and then returned to his duties at the altar.

The reprimanded boy ran down the aisle and outside. But in a flash, he returned with a large rock in his hand and with several Protestant men close behind. The boy ran up to the first pew and lobbed the rock straight at the priest, who ducked. The rock hit one of the statues squarely, knocking the marble head of a saint cleanly off its shoulders. Then the men behind him started pelting the altar pieces and the statues around the cathedral with stones. As the rocks flew, the priest and the two altar boys escaped into the robing room.

The crowd in the cathedral grew. Then someone shouted for them to go over to the friaries a few blocks away. The crowd ran over to the buildings occupied by the Black and Gray Friars, and to the Catholic Charterhouse, and forced their way in. They broke every statue and then began looting the supplies of fine linens and rich bedding and large stores of food.

When Knox was told of the riot as he and the other leaders were meeting at the merchant's shop, he attributed it not to his sermon or to any authorized act, but to the "rascal multitude," which had exceeded all biblical mandate.

A few days later, when Marie de Guise heard of the events in Perth, she simply smiled. Though her health was declining, her mind was fully intact—and her political judgment, she told herself as well as her advisors, had never been better. When the Protestant preachers had failed to appear as her warrant had ordered—which of course was her intention—she dispatched nine hundred French troops to the town of Perth. The riots at St. John's Kirk would only be seen as a further substantiation for her use of military force.

So while Knox, Ransom, the Lords of the Congregation, and the other Protestant nobles and leaders met at the Market Cross to strategize, the

French legions of Marie de Guise were already marching straight for Perth.

The fires of Scotland were no longer limited to the burning stakes at St. Andrews and Castle Hill in Edinburgh—the flames were now spreading into full civil war.

Chapter 53

"What are we going to do, Ransom?"

Margaret's question barely hid the panic of a mother-to-be who was worried not only about her husband and herself, but about the unborn life she carried as well.

Ransom had just returned from the gathering of Protestant leaders and had been sharing with his wife the newest military intelligence they had just received.

"Our spies say there are nearly a thousand French soldiers stationed just outside of Perth. I don't know if the queen regent is also sending troops from the other direction—if so, it wouldn't be prudent for you to try to escape in that way."

"What do ye mean 'for me to try to escape'? I'll not be leavin' yer side no matter what!"

"Margaret, if there are no troops on the other side of Perth—and we'll know straightaway if that is so—then I can make passage for you with some of the other women who are heading out of town—"

"Ye're not hearin'," she pleaded, "with either yer heart or yer ears. Remember what the good Friar Scott told us. Untied we are from everything but ourselves and God. I'll not be separated from ye…"

"I don't want you in the middle of any harm," Ransom said in a plaintive voice, "for your sake and that of our wee bairn."

"Please don't let us be torn apart, Ransom, *please*…"

Margaret was weeping openly and grasping Ransom's hands in hers.

"All right," Ransom said, wiping the tears from her face and kissing her, "at least we can wait until the Earl of Glencairn arrives. He is gathering Protestant troops to protect Perth. He'll tell what he has learned from his reconnaissance—and the strength of the army he has put together for us."

"How do we know that the troops won't attack before then?"

"I have heard that the French soldiers are waiting for the arrival of the cannons and artillery from Edinburgh—they want to hit the town with cannon fire before they charge."

"Cannons?" Margaret said with a gasp.

She looked up into his eyes. She saw behind his self-assured look that he was troubled with the seriousness of their state. Margaret remembered Ransom's tales of the ferocity of the cannon siege on the castle in St. Andrews.

"Perhaps not—maybe there'll be no war at all," Ransom said. "It all depends on the army that Glencairn and his men are able to assemble. I think the queen regent is too smart to wage a battle in Perth that she's sure to lose…"

"And what if she thinks she can win?"

"Negotiations, perhaps…"

"And then—if no truce is made?"

"Then the siege begins. But before then, you and I will pray for peace. But we'll brace our little house here just the same…"

So Ransom helped Margaret down to her knees, and the two of them prayed together against the cannons, and against the iron-tipped spears of the French troops and the blood and fire and devastation of war.

Then they rose. Ransom went out to the shed and gathered his mallet and all the loose timber planks he could gather and all his nails. He set planks across all of the windows of the house and hammered them tight. Then he gathered every wooden tub and pail he could find, filled them with water, and set them in the four corners of the house, both upstairs and downstairs.

"If the French make it into town and fire the houses, you'll have to douse it down with water quick. But if it spreads, then make your way out of the house and find a house that hasn't been fired. Hide yourself there—don't show yourself until you see our Protestant brothers in the streets."

Margaret was shaking her head ever so slightly and breathing slowly.

"Do you hear me, wife? Will you do as I ask?"

"And where will ye be?"

Ransom did not answer, but took her hands and squeezed them tight,

"So ye're going out with the rest of them to die, are ye?" Margaret said, her voice trembling, but with a look as hard as the granite mountains of her youth.

"I'll be going out in the morning when our army arrives—but not to die—I'll pledge you that…"

"And ye can pledge, now can ye, what only God can decide?"

Ransom put his hands on her shoulders and gently pulled her face close to his.

"I'll not be dyin'. Mark it well, my lover…I'll not…"

Ransom made a bed for Margaret on the first floor of the house that night. Though it was spring, there was a damp chill in the air, and so he made a fire in the hearth.

Then he walked over to a trunk, opened it, and then fished through some blankets and papers until he reached the bottom. He retrieved something from the trunk, closed it, and walked to a chair he had posted by the locked front door, and sat down there. Margaret looked up from her bed on the floor, and saw in Ransom's lap the reflection of cold metal that was catching the light from the flickering fire.

He was holding the sword Hamish Chisholm had given to him so long ago in the Highlands.

"Wish my da was here," Margaret said quietly.

"So do I," Ransom said. "So do I."

Chapter 54

There was a mist in the air in the gray dawn as Ransom woke with a start. There was the sound of men, many of them, marching through the street outside his house, just before daybreak. There were voices and shuffling feet and horses. Ransom unbolted the door, cracked it slightly open, and saw the men with weapons and horses—many of them, too many to count. Some of the horses were padded and armored for battle. Most of the men were helmeted and had small arms, but some carried the long spears that the Scots used to repel heavy infantry charges.

Then the young Protestant messenger ran up to Ransom's door in a feverish excitement.

"Thousands, thousands!" he cried. "Mister Mackenzie, just look at them! From Fife and Angus, Mearns and Dundee, sir…"

"Where is Glencairn?" Ransom cried out.

"At the front—ye're requested to join him and the others there."

Ransom turned. Margaret was sitting up from her bed on the floor, her arms outstretched. Ransom knelt down, wrapped his arms tight around her and kissed her, placed his hand over her belly and prayed a blessing over the life hidden there, and rose.

"I'll return to you, my darling bride—if you count anything I have ever said to you to be true, then count this as true—I'll walk through that door to your arms when this is over."

Then Ransom stepped out with his sword in his hand, telling Margaret to bolt the door tight and open it for no one save him.

He quickly ran down the street to the wide, flat green on the outskirts of town. The Protestant army was gathering there. He spotted Glencairn, Erskine, and the others, and started toward them. But suddenly he felt a hand on his back. He turned quickly around and saw a man standing toe to toe and eye to eye with him.

It was John Knox.

"The sword of the Spirit?" he said, gazing down at Ransom's sword. "Or perhaps the sword the apostle Peter used to lop off a soldier's ear?"

But before Ransom could answer, Knox produced a long, two-handled sword. Ransom recognized it from his boyhood days in St. Andrews. His mentor had once showed it to his students and said it was the weapon he had used to guard George Wishart on his preaching tours through the countryside.

"Let us both pray that these will not be used today," Knox said.

"And that the sword of the Spirit will prevail in the land," Ransom added.

"Aye, a good word," Knox said with a smile, "a good and true word, Ransom."

Then the preacher beckoned his former student to walk him to the meeting of leaders that was forming in front of the army on the green.

"I was much disconcerted that ye abandoned me," he said solemnly, "for such frivolity as a girl whose family openly consorted with that murderous and bloody Queen Mary Tudor of England," he said. "And so I did decide, when I finally made my way over to Geneva, to never partner or associate with ye again, lad—never."

But then Knox stopped and wheeled around to face Ransom.

"But then I kept coming upon the story of the apostle Paul and his young liege by the name of John Mark—an impetuous youth who accompanied Paul on his missionary journeys and into much danger. But his youth and foolishness prevailed, and John Mark abandoned the work of Paul—he deserted the mission of the gospel."

Knox smiled and took Ransom by the shoulders.

"But, I also read in Paul's letters that he speaks of that very same John Mark—he summons the lad and says he is 'very profitable' for the work," Knox said. "Does he not say that very thing in his second epistle to Timothy?"

Ransom nodded silently.

"Now, who did the changing, I wonder...John Mark only? Or perhaps old Paul too, his instructor."

Then Knox broke into a wide grin and said, "Ransom, my friend, ye are very profitable for the work of the reformation in Scotland—do ye not know that?"

Ransom could not speak—for if he did, he feared he would weep out loud, as his eyes were already filling with tears.

"Steady now, man, steady," Knox said straightening up. "There is still a stern work ahead of us. And we make our way to the battlefront..."

The two men strode quickly to the gathering place at the front of the troops.

"Mister Knox!" one of the lords called out. "I hear the queen regent has now placed a bounty on yer head!"

"'Tis true," he remarked. "But I only hope that the bounty is promised to be paid only with those coins that have the queen regent's face on them..."

"And why is that?" another leader called out.

"Because," Knox said with a wry smile, "no one in this realm wants a tyrant in his pocket—and thusly I shall be safe indeed!"

His good humor was a quick antidote to the tension that had been gathering, and all the men had a hearty laugh. Then someone asked about the numbers.

"Three thousand!" Glencairn called out.

A cheer rose up from the leaders. It was explained that their initial intelligence had been confirmed. There were nine hundred French soldiers posted outside the city. They had seen some of the French troops reconnoitering on horseback already. It would be only a matter of an hour or so before a fast rider would take the news to the queen regent's military headquarters. Even with cannon fire to soften up the Protestant defenses, Marie de Guise would be sending her French legion into a slaughter.

"They will have to negotiate," Glencairn said. And so it was agreed by all that attempts at mediation would be warranted. Within a few hours three French officers and a court advisor accompanied the queen regent's French ambassador in a slow ride out to the middle of the flat grassy field. They were bearing a flag of truce.

The Protestants picked Glencairn and four other leaders. Knox, it was generally agreed, was too inflammatory a figure to place into the negotiations. Knox suggested that Ransom act as his second and accompany the Protestants to consult on the language of any truce. But someone noticed that one of Marie de Guise's negotiators was none other than Sir James Stewart himself. Caught in the strange world of competing political interests, Stewart was now being used by the queen regent to garner favor among the very same reformers with whom she knew Stewart had been consorting. Because Stewart had harbored ill feelings against him, Ransom would not go.

So he stayed behind and sat down on the grass, placing his sword next to him. The troops rested on the green, waiting for the outcome of the negotiations. Ransom struck up a conversation with a young man who looked to be in his late teens. He was from Dundee and had been wearing a helmet slightly too big for him, but now he felt he could set it down on the ground and breathe easy. As the two talked, the young man pulled a piece of paper out of his pocket and showed it to Ransom.

"Mister Mackenzie sir, do ye read French?"

"I do some," he remarked.

The young man gave him what appeared to be a wrinkled and yellowed pamphlet printed in French.

"My cousin in Dieppe sent it to me, but I canna read much French, sir—except that it claims to be the words of a great prophet—and everyone is talkin' about his prophecies for this very year—"

"Prophecies?" Ransom asked. He studied the paper and translated it out loud to the young man.

"There shall be difference of sects, altercations, murmurings against ceremonies, contentions, debate, process, feuds, noise, discord..."

When Ransom read the name of the supposed "prophet," he could only shake his head with disbelief.

"This man is no prophet of God," Ransom said. "His name is Nostradamus."

"Ye know of him?"

"When I was a boy, I once stayed in a castle of a disciple of his—and heard of his blasphemies."

"But he has prophesied truly has he not?" the young man asked.

"No he has not," Ransom said. "Vague charges are made here—a charlatan's trick—remember your Bible? The wizards of the Pharaoh were able by trick to appear to copy the true miracles of Moses' God..."

"But he charges we will have 'murmurings against ceremonies,'" the young man said, his eyes wide, "and so we have in disputing the Catholic mass, is that not true?"

"My friend," Ransom explained, "when I was a boy and saw George Wishart burned, that year Martin Luther himself died. And before that by tens of years, Hamilton was burned in St. Andrews, and before him, Tyndale was burned to death. And before that, Martin Luther nailed his Ninety-Five Theses on the church doors of Wittenberg. This battle has been waged for a hundred years. Nostradamus did not see that in the stars—he simply saw it all around him and wrote it as if it were prophecy—for the unwitting and the unlearned, and the spiritually confused."

But as Ransom looked in the young man's eyes, he realized he knew almost nothing of what Ransom had just been expounding.

"Do you have a Bible, my friend?"

The young man shook his head no.

"Can you read?"

"I can in English, sir."

"Do you know where to get a Bible?"

"Aye. My father has one at home. He died and left it to me."

"Then read it, sir," Ransom said with a smile, "and ask the Lord to give you His Spirit to understand it—and look for the person and the promise of Christ in everything you read there. And you will find all the truth you will ever need."

Then Knox caught Ransom's attention. He was summoning him to join the others. The negotiating team was riding back from the center of the field where they had just met with the queen regent's envoys.

"Now it will be seen," Knox muttered under his breath, "whether there will be peace—or war—and we'll hear the price of each."

Chapter 55

"Marie de Guise and her French allies have offered terms," Glencairn said to the group of Protestant nobles. "And we made it clear to them we had no lust for blood. If they'll simply give us toleration for the practice of our Protestant beliefs, then they'll find no more loyal subjects than we—"

"What terms did they offer?" one of the nobles yelled out.

"The Queen's French troops will be withdrawn from Perth and will return to Edinburgh…"

"Aye, that's a start!" one of them said.

"No Frenchman is allowed within three miles of Perth…"

There were some rude comments made about the French influence at Court; that term was considered a good measure.

"There shall be no punishment of any citizen of Perth for having taken part in the recent commotion in the town."

"Ayes" rose up from the group. Then someone asked, "Tell us—what'd they require of us?"

"Only that we disband our army—simply that and none other."

There was immediate consensus that they had struck a pretty bargain and should quickly take their agreement back to the French captain and the ambassador.

"Sir James Stewart surely helped us from the other side," someone commented.

But there was a small detail that troubled Ransom.

"Did they agree to 'withdraw the French troops'—is that how they put it?"

"Aye, exactly," Glencairn replied.

"But should not the demand have been that the queen regent withdraw *all of her troops,* be they French or any other?"

"But our spies say that only French troops are allied with de Guise against Perth—they saw them with their own eyes!"

"Yes, but that is not my point," Ransom said, trying to interject one last word of caution. "What would it harm us to press the matter—for the queen regent to agree to withdraw *all* of her troops—and to further agree that *all* of her soldiers—not just the Frenchmen—not come within three miles of Perth?"

A few groans rose up from the nobles. Glencairn tried not to insult Ransom's desire for completeness in the truce. But it was clear that, having escaped the slaughter of combat with the queen regent's forces, Glencairn and the others were in no mood to quibble over particulars.

"Nay," the earl responded, "with all respect, master Ransom, I'll not be pressing for that—unless any of the nobles here believe I should…"

There was an embarrassing lack of any voices in favor of Ransom's suggestion. Even Knox believed the terms should be accepted—and quickly—as the Lords of the Congregation, once the truce was struck and the troops disbanded, were headed for their next strategy meeting.

"Then those terms shall be our terms—and the truce is agreed!" Glencairn announced. The group gave a hearty cheer.

As the group broke apart, a few of the military commanders approached the reclining Protestant volunteers and thanked them for their courage and willingness to fight for the cause. Then they were all ordered home.

Knox approached Ransom.

"Ye're straining at gnats," he said. "I do believe the truce is a good one. But never mind. I will need ye with me at the convocation being called."

"Where is it?" Ransom asked.

"We leave straightaway for St. Andrews. The leaders are gathering there."

"I thought the archbishop there has threatened you…"

"To make the matter plain," Knox said with a grin, "he threatened to shoot me on sight—and to do so personally! But I'll not be missin' the chance to keep my appointment with divine destiny. Though I was chained and dragged off to a French galley ship those many years ago, I believed God promised me that He would return me to Scotland… and to let me preach the evangel of Christ in St. Andrews again."

"I wish I could be there to hear it," Ransom said with a burdened look.

"What d'ye mean?" Knox said, with a wrinkled brow, his eyes searching Ransom's face.

"I made a promise of my own, to my dear wife, Margaret. She has been distressed by the recent events here in Perth. And she is great with child…I told her that when the threat of battle was over, I would return to our house here in Perth and care for her."

Knox studied his former student cautiously, as Ransom added, "I pray you and the others will not hold my absence against me."

"Mister Paul Methven tells me," Knox said, "that ye have a beautiful Highland lass for a wife. And that she walks in the grace and knowledge of Christ."

"True enough," Ransom added quickly. "I'm much blessed by her."

"Tell her I look forward to our first meeting. Now go to her, with all of the blessings of the Protestant Lords. I will vouch for ye at our meeting in St. Andrews. My own wife and wee bairns will be joining me soon—my heart longs for them. Farewell, Ransom—I'll send word to ye at the convenient time."

Then Knox turned and disappeared into the departing crowds.

Ransom hurried back to his house and burst into the front door with the great news of the truce—that the queen regent had abandoned her plans for an attack on Perth—and without a single shot being fired or a drop of blood on any blade.

Margaret was ecstatic and pulled her husband to her and kissed him all over his face.

"Ye see how all yer worryin' has come to naught," she said with a laugh, between kisses.

"*My* worrying?" Ransom said in a tone of mock disagreement. "What about *you*, dear heart?"

"'Tis my callin' to be the *heart* of our little hearth," she said with a smile. "But ye are the *head*. The heart is sometimes permitted the worries and cares the head is not."

"Such a pretty argument," Ransom said, chuckling, "from such a pretty bride. I would have thought you had studied the canons of law with me—to be able to make an argument that so twists the rules of logic and common sense—"

Margaret laughed, grabbed a broom nearby, and tried to swat him, but he blocked it, belly-laughing so loudly he could hardly fend her off. When he did at last, he gathered her up in his arms.

"How I love ye," she murmured in his ear. "My soul would have died, and I couldn't have swept up all the pieces of my heart for breakin', if ye had not returned to me."

Chapter 56

When Ransom arose the next morning the house was cool. He quietly slipped out of the goose-down bed, threw a cloak on, and descended the stairs. Seeing there was little kindling left, he went out the back door and walked to the lean-to in the back where their firewood was stacked. That is when he spotted them.

Ransom squinted and, through the side yards of the row of houses, he was able to spy a group of soldiers standing on a street corner. They were too far away for him to be sure, but it appeared they wore neither the red capes nor the burnished brass helmets of the French legions. He took a deep breath and exhaled with relief. He returned to the house with an armful of wood.

Must be a band of Protestant stragglers…some of our forces, he mused. *They had better get out of Perth before someone cries that we have broken the truce.*

Margaret was up by then and had begun preparing for breakfast. But something in the back of Ransom's mind drew him to the front door. He unlocked it, and the heavy iron slide bolt made a little clanging sound as it hit the stop.

Margaret had fetched two of their good pewter plates. She was planning on using them for their breakfast in celebration of the peace treaty that had been struck and that had saved their little house and kept her husband from danger. But she sensed something in Ransom's cautious and deliberate movements. She took a step toward Ransom and unthinking, clasped her hands together over her heart.

With the front door unbolted, Ransom opened it slowly. He stood in the doorway only an instant. Margaret could not see past him. He quickly closed the door and turned to his wife. She could see the look on his face. As she came to the door, Ransom slowly opened it only a crack, just enough for her to look out.

On each street corner were half a dozen armed soldiers posted. Indeed they were not dressed like the French legions. They were arrayed like Scottish troops. But they were also carrying the ensigns of Queen Regent Marie de Guise and the French crest. Ransom knew immediately what had happened.

"She's betrayed us," he snarled through clenched teeth, "*again*. She withdrew the French troops all right—but in the darkness of night she has filled Perth with her personal Scots guards—Catholics all, and loyal to her Court."

Margaret was staring into her husband's face, still waiting to hear what it all meant—for them.

"She intended all along to pull back her French soldiers and then replace them with the Scottish troops—she has taken us all captive. The queen regent has the whole town of Perth in her grasp."

"What do we do?"

"Wait," Ransom replied tensely.

"For what?"

"To see if they start rounding up the Protestants and the leaders. If they do, we shall hear their boots coming to our door very soon."

When the news got to the Protestant leadership, they had all reached St. Andrews—all except Ransom, of course. John Knox arrived early, followed by the Protestant nobles and the Lords of the Congregation, and the preachers like Paul Methven; the Master of Maxwell was there, along with Erskine of Dun and the Earl of Glencairn. When James Stewart heard of the queen regent's trickery, it finally pushed him over the edge. He stormed out of Edinburgh, publicly proclaiming that he was leaving the Court of Marie de Guise and would be aligned, from thence onward, with the Protestant cause.

As the leaders gathered in St. Andrews under iron gray skies and a wind that whipped the ocean into whitecaps that crashed on the shore, every one of them knew this was a decisive moment.

The coals of the Great Smithy were glowing white, and the metal was ready to be shaped in the Craftsman's hand. But what would be wrought? For the men who gathered that day, it seemed clear that before the ploughs could be fashioned for planting, there would need to be swords for fighting.

It was decided that the Protestants must now be united in a single, concerted cause, and there could be no rest until its fulfillment. Scotland was destined for a full-fledged gospel Reformation, not just from the bottom to the top, but also, most assuredly, from the top to the bottom.

And so, they believed, it was time for Marie de Guise, Queen Regent of Scotland, to go.

Knox had long grappled with the idea of Christian revolt. Though his ideas would have seemed radical to his colleague John Calvin, Knox had come to the conclusion that the Bible countenanced—in certain narrow circumstances—God's faithful people deposing those evil tyrants whose rulership seemed corrupt beyond redemption or repentance.

A full-fledged army would have to be mustered. Glencairn's three thousand hastily recruited volunteers had been able to halt the queen regent's progress toward Perth at the front—at least temporarily—until their ill-advised truce terms permitted her Scots guards to slip into Perth through the back. But now, it was agreed, they would have to brace for

a nationwide civil war. That meant a professionally trained army with
military leadership and a huge amount of funding.

That meant an urgent envoy to England—and to Elizabeth the queen.
Knox and several of the leaders jointly penned a letter that would be
sped by messenger to Sir William Cecil, Queen Elizabeth's Secretary of
State, pleading for assistance.

After the meeting, Knox announced he was leaving to take the short
walk over to Holy Trinity Church and there deliver his scheduled sermon.
All of the men urged him to abandon his plans. The archbishop had
several armed men posted near the church, and had threatened to assas-
sinate Knox if he so much as uttered one word of preaching in public.
But Knox would not be dissuaded. He had been waiting to fulfill God's
promise that had been such a comfort to him during his time of wretched
imprisonment on board the French galley ship. Now was his chance.

Someone suggested a large armed escort for him.

"Nay, men!" he said loudly. "I desire neither the hand nor the weapon
of any man to defend me. The only thing I crave is an audience to whom
I may preach the truth of God's word."

It was agreed he would be accompanied by the Lords of the
Congregation, but they would be unarmed. And so the group, with Knox
in the lead, clutching his large Bible to his chest, walked quickly down
the streets of St. Andrews, first along Market Street, then turning on a
small side street and over to the corner where the town kirk, the Holy
Trinity Church, faced South Street.

The archbishop was already there, standing outside, dressed in the
robes and in the tall, pointed bishop's cap of his full Catholic authority.
He held his vicar's staff in one hand; the other was clenched tightly
behind his back. He was surrounded by several dozen French soldiers.
When Knox approached leading his entourage, the archbishop moved
forward just a step and parted his lips as if to issue a warning. But Knox

never slowed and, throwing a stern look in the archbishop's direction, he and his followers quickly flooded into the church.

Knox mounted the pulpit and laid his Bible down on it. The entire floor of the sanctuary was filled up, and every seat in the balconies along the sides of the church was taken. The archbishop entered but had to stand in the back along with his soldiers. His best French marksman, carrying a long-barreled firelock culverin, stood next to him at the ready, his weapon already primed with gunpowder and loaded with a deadly iron ball.

Knox waited for absolute silence to descend over the assembly, and then he spoke.

"Jesus," he thundered, "went into the temple with a whip of cords. And the Gospels say He drove out those who bought and sold there, sayin', 'It is written, My house is a house of prayer, but ye have made it a den of thieves!'"

"Is not our Lord our ensample, the perfect design, of the restoration of the institutions of religion to their proper purpose and the reformation of the central cathedral to God's express command—the command that we love Him by obeying His commands and honoring His Word in all things?" Knox was making bold, sweeping gestures, sending his black cape flying around his arms as he did—taking on the appearance of some great bird of prey.

"There is corruption of religion in this land!" he proclaimed. "God's Word is held captive and secret from the people—while the edifices and offices of religion amass their wealth and power on the backs of the poor and the ignorant. This corruption shall not stand! And if ye be the people of God—as I know many of ye to be—then ye will take the cords of truth and drive out the money changers, and restore Scotland to the business of the pure form of worship and adoration of Christ our Savior, and reform this land for the hearing of the gospel of salvation!"

By the time Knox had finished his sermon, the archbishop had slipped out the back, and with him, his French marksman and his soldiers. No shots were ever fired. But the archbishop hastened to Marie de Guise, who was staying at her palace at Falkland, to advise her of the intolerable activities of Knox and his radical Protestant friends.

When she asked for his advice on how to respond, the archbishop did not hesitate.

"War, good Madam," he answered curtly. "War!"

Chapter 57

For the first day, Ransom and Margaret never left their house. It was a blessing, they both agreed, that they had sufficient stores of food and water. Ransom would watch the streets from the spaces between the planks on the windows. The queen regent's Scots guards would regularly rotate their corner posts. And now larger numbers of soldiers were appearing on horseback, patrolling the streets.

"The number of troops seems larger than I first thought," Ransom remarked, peeking between the boards on the second-story window.

"How many, do ye think?" Margaret asked.

"Several hundred at least…maybe more."

"What will they do?"

"One of two things. Either they are here simply as a show of force…to intimidate us. Remind us that Marie de Guise is in control."

"Or?"

"Or the troops will start going house to house and begin enforcing the new crackdown against Protestantism."

Suddenly there was a loud knocking downstairs.

Both of them froze and stared at each other. A silence. Then more banging.

"I'll answer the door. You stay up here," Ransom said in a hushed voice. "Be ready to hide yourself."

Margaret grabbed his arm as he started toward the stairs.

"Look at me!" she said in a hoarse, frantic whisper, pointing to her belly. "How am I goin' to hide myself?"

"Maybe it'll be nothing," Ransom said, trying to reassure her. He squeezed her hand, gave her a confident nod, and disappeared down the staircase.

A few seconds later she heard him talking with someone at the front door. The voice in the doorway was that of a Scot, sure enough. But was he one of the queen regent's soldiers? She listened more closely as she stood at the top of the stairs. It sounded as if Ransom was letting the man inside. She could hear the heavy footsteps of the visitor in the front room. She listened, now convinced the man was a Highlander.

"Margaret, please come down," Ransom called.

She slowly worked her way down the stairs. When she had made it to the bottom, she saw the man talking to Ransom. He turned to face her.

He was red-bearded and was wearing a small cap with a feather and a clansman's cape and kilt.

"Ye're from the Highlands?" Margaret asked anxiously. "And do ye have a message from my da and mum?"

"I do have a message in that regard, aye," he said solemnly.

"How did you get past the soldiers?" Ransom asked. "They're posted on every corner."

"I'm a clansman from the Western Isles. We're thought to be warm to the French—and we are loyal to the Catholic cause, as I am. Perhaps, Mister Mackenzie, ye would take me to be a blasphemer and a idolater?"

"I take you only as a man who has traveled a long and perilous journey to share news of my dear wife's family—and that, sir, would make you a friend," Ransom said quietly.

The clansman nodded and turned to Margaret.

"Takin' yer state of bein' with child and all," he said, "ye'd best sit down..."

"I'll stand, good sir, for whatever news ye have…"

But Ransom saw something in the bearing and mood of the visitor. He turned to his wife.

"Margaret dear, sit down. I believe our friend here has something to tell you."

Margaret sat down, but her eyes never left the clansman.

"The news is this," the visitor said. "Hamish and Rhona, yer kin, were plannin' to leave the Highlands and join some of us Chisholms in the Western Isles—"

"Plannin'?" Margaret said, interrupting. "Did they not arrive?"

"Nay, they dinna arrive," he answered. "So I took some men and traveled to the glen where yer home was…as I had been privy to some tales of a slayin' in that valley most horrid…leastwise accordin' to the tellin' of it…"

Margaret let out a little whimper and clasped her hands over her mouth.

Ransom stood behind her chair and gently placed his hands on her shoulders as the clansman continued.

"And so I arrived there with my men. And I surveyed the house… and learned of the dreadful doin's of that place. And I saw…I am sorry, Margaret," he said, lowering his voice. "I saw only the two crosses of their graves. They'd been slaughtered by that devilish Murdo, nephew of the late laird of the glen, and his French mercenaries."

Margaret gasped. And then gasped again as she choked on her sobs. Ransom bent down next to her and held her tight.

"'Tis bad about the news, I know," the clansman said. "But there's one shinin' thing in this—and ye'll both be glad at the hearin' of it."

"What is it?" Ransom asked, hoping for some kind of consolation for his grief-stricken wife.

"I took revenge, and it was sweet—we killed the men that did this terrible thing."

Margaret stopped her sobs and wiped her face. She slowly rose and walked to the stairway.

"I can say this, lass," the clansman said with some measure of pride. "I put the sword into the belly of that rotton Murdo myself. And he cried like a wee sucklin' to be saved from it—but I spit in his face, I did, and then stuck him through again."

Margaret was at the bottom stair, half turned to face the clansman. "Sir," she said almost in a whisper, "I don't care for yer revenge...it won't bring back my da or my mum. I am tired of the dyin'...and tired of swords that make for dyin'...and tired of the fires that are lit for dyin' and the wars that will now be fought for all of it...tired...I'm tired..."

She slowly mounted the steps, shuffled over to their bed, and lay down on it, her eyes wide open in a blank stare.

Ransom offered food and lodging to the clansman, but he waved it off and left. Then Ransom slipped up the stairs and sat with his wife through the night. She was not crying, or talking, or doing anything else, just looking off in a kind of trance.

In the morning, Ransom awoke in his chair where he had slept next to her bed. He kissed her gently and said he would make breakfast for her and bring it up so she could eat in bed. But Margaret shook her head.

"You have to eat," Ransom said.

But Margaret shook her head again.

"Not only for you, but also for our bairn...think of our baby..."

"*Coma co-dhiu*," she said almost inaudibly. "*Coma co-dhiu*..."

He offered her food several times that day, but she never left the bed and refused any food or water. Each time she would simply murmur the same words—*Coma co-dhiu*."

From his days in the Highlands, Ransom knew what she was saying. And it grieved his heart.

"*I care for nothing*," she was saying.

Chapter 58

While Glencairn and James Stewart started building their Protestant army, Knox and a preacher by the name of Robert Hamilton had been sent on a secret mission to England. They would attempt to secure the financial and military backing of England for the civil war that now seemed unavoidable.

The place of the meeting would be Berwick, just across the border of Scotland. The two Scots sailed from St. Andrews, making landfall first at Holy Island. But Knox was known widely in the area and was immediately recognized. Any hopes of absolute secrecy for their rendezvous had been destroyed.

By the time that the conference was convened at Berwick Castle, neither Sir William Cecil nor Sir Henry Percy, another high-ranking member of Court, was willing to be present. Knox and Hamilton had to settle for James Croft, Governor of Berwick. The meeting was cordial enough, but the terms seemed difficult.

"We need English troops and money for our cause against de Guise and the French," Hamilton said bluntly.

"Of course you do," Croft said, sipping wine from a silver chalice. "And what does England get for this act of national charity?"

"Ye will have the assurance that Scotland will not be controlled by France," Knox said. "France has been the enemy of England. If we lose this struggle, the French will be at your border."

"We have a peace treaty with France," Croft said matter-of-factly.

"Aye, and roosters have wings," Knox replied, "but no matter how their wings might promise otherwise, they'll never take flight—neither will the French keep the peace."

"France will never honor that treaty," Hamilton added.

"How do we get around the difficulty," Croft said, his eyes almost squinting in deep thought, "that England, in negotiating with you Protestant gentlemen and with your Lords of the Congregation, will be striking a bargain with a group that has no lawful or governmental authority? Her Majesty would be entering into a treaty with a mere band of rebels—nothing more..."

"Then let the queen herself," Knox said with a smile, "pick the Scottish Protestants that she—and she alone—thinks are most worthy of mediating the treaty between England and Protestant Scotland. And from the queen's selection, we will then make the final pick of those who will negotiate the terms. In the queen's wisdom, I am sure she will find those Protestant Scots who are vested with the proper authority."

Croft smiled blandly at Knox. He had heard of Knox's *First Blast* and his obnoxious habit of picking fights and naming names. But now, the English Governor thought to himself, there just might be a way of securing a treaty with a Protestant—and non-French—Scotland.

"I will convey your thoughts to Sir William Cecil," Croft said, concluding the meeting. "And then—we will see..."

In the days that followed the clansman's visit, Margaret finally rose from bed. She started taking some food, but not much. She rarely talked. Ransom began worrying about her ability to bear their child to delivery. She began looking pale and listless. He became so worried about her that the presence of the queen regent's soldiers in Perth no longer occupied his mind.

One night, as Ransom slipped into bed next to her, he noticed her staring out into space again. Then she rolled over on her side, turning away from him.

After a long period of silence, Margaret spoke up.

"Take it away."

"What?"

"Take it away."

After a pause, Ransom answered.

"I cannot."

"Why not?"

"Because I cannot take the pain from your heart, my love. If I could, then I would. But I cannot."

"Ye saved me once before...ye killed the French soldier in Edinburgh to rescue me...why can't ye now?"

"Only God can heal your heart and soul."

"Then ask God to do it."

"I have..."

"Then why won't He?" she said in a small, breathless voice.

"I dunno," he replied. "I cannot answer that. Perhaps if you pray yourself..."

"I canna do that," Margaret said plainly. "There's no prayin' left in me."

After another moment, Ransom said something else.

"The wee bairn. You must get strong for our wee bairn."

Margaret was silent for a long while. Ransom grew fearful and impatient, but held his peace. Then Margaret spoke again.

"Ye know what the Highland midwives used to say?"

"What did they say?"

"That if ye learned of a death of your family or kin while ye were in the last of yer being heavy with child...then it meant that yer babe would be born dead..."

"Superstitions—nothin' more," Ransom said. He placed his hand on her back and rubbed it gently. "The Lord will take care of our wee little one—"

"Ransom," Margaret said in a faint voice.

"Yes?"

"I've not felt our babe kick me at all today...not once..."

Chapter 59

The fall of that year in Scotland gave way to an early winter. The rains were often mixed with winds that carried cold, swirling snowfalls.

Within the Mackenzie house in Perth, the dismal news that had marred Margaret's pregnancy earlier was relieved by one happy occurrence—she was soon restored to the confirmation of the life within her. She started receiving, once again, kicks small and regular.

Ransom would watch his wife's shuddering belly and commented, with some measure of mirth, that in His divine sense of humor, God was correcting Margaret's Highland superstitions with proof positive of the budding life she was carrying. His wife would smile at that. It seemed that the darkness that covered her view of the world when she first learned of her parents' death had begun to depart.

Yet, though Margaret had always been a woman of extraordinary inner and outer strength, she continued to look pale and drawn. Her size had increased considerably, and she was feeling nauseated much of the time.

The presence of the Scots guards continued in Perth, though the numbers seemed to fluctuate dramatically. After the first few weeks, Ransom decided they might not pose a direct risk to the Protestant leadership there. He had learned that a large Protestant army was being raised, and that Knox and the others had corresponded with the Court of Queen Elizabeth of England, and that a meeting may have been attempted. It seemed clear to Ransom that Marie de Guise now had bigger problems than a mere uprising in Perth. Indeed, her grip on Scotland now appeared to be at risk of collapse. All of these suspicions were confirmed when Ransom was summoned to a meeting of the leadership at Cupar. Up to then he had stayed close to home. But now he assured Margaret he would be gone only for a day—and the gathering was of the utmost importance. The future of the Reformation in Scotland was hanging in the balance. He must go, he said.

Ransom arranged for a midwife to stay with his wife.

"There'll be no daylight for me till ye come back," Margaret said, trying to manage a smile.

"And there shall be no joy for me till that day." He kissed his wife and placed his hand gently on her. He whispered a prayer for *m'eudail* as he did. Margaret smiled and placed her hand on his hand over the life within her. She too prayed a blessing for *m'eudail*—"my darling child."

Ransom grabbed his satchel, kissed Margaret again, shook the midwife's hand, and then departed through the front door.

At Cupar the blood of the Lords of the Congregation was running hot. England had pledged an intent to support them—though unofficially—and several thousand Scots loyal to the Protestant gospel had already been raised. Their spies had reported back that Marie de Guise had retreated to her powerful fortifications at Edinburgh Castle. At the same time she was attempting to consolidate all of her French forces at the nearby port of Leith.

"'Tis clear," the Master of Maxwell stated without a shred of reservation in his voice, "that the queen regent means to make her stand in the blockhouses at Leith, thinkin', no doubt, that if we attack she can more than withstand us."

"And if she does withstand an assault—then what?" Sir James Stewart asked.

"Then," the Master of Maxwell continued, "I calculate she will await the troops she has summoned from France. And when they arrive, she will mount a war on our Protestant Reformation from the coasts at County Fife and St. Andrews in the East to the outer isles in the west, and having slaughtered us through the middle of Scotland, she'll no doubt send her French murderers and mercenaries down to the borders—burning and killing and raping as they go…"

"Then it appears," John Knox exclaimed, "that Leith shall be the Rubicon of our Reformation."

All agreed, but there was a question from the Protestant nobles about the creation of the controlling document for their Reformation.

"And what of the *Book of Discipline* that shall govern Scotland's worship of God and the polity of our Scottish citizens?" someone called out.

"We are working on it presently," Knox replied. "Commissions have been granted to myself, John Winram, Subprior of St. Andrews, Master John Spottiswood, and several others to draw up the *Book of Discipline* for the creation of a Christian commonwealth and for the governance of it in Scotland. I will be asking Master Ransom Mackenzie to assist in the drafting as well."

With that he nodded to Ransom, who nodded back, overwhelmed at the honor.

One of the nobles asked about the status of help from England for the Protestants, and from France for Marie de Guise.

"I can answer that," the Earl of Glencairn called out. "Admiral William Winter of the English navy has already set sail from England, bound for St. Andrews. He captains no less than *fourteen* ships!"

The entire assembly burst into spontaneous applause, with shouts praising God and enthusiastic huzzahs.

"And what of the French?" someone yelled out. "What of the ships sailing here to aid Marie de Guise?"

The groups quieted to a hush. Glencairn gave the answer in a more subdued tone.

"Our spies have disclosed," he said, "that the French have a large fleet on their way to Leith—"

"How large?"

"Sixteen ships."

There was a stone-quiet silence for a few moments as the immensity of the coming conflict began to sink in.

Outside of the great tower house where the meeting was taking place, the wind was rising to a shrieking wail. A bad winter storm was beginning to sweep onto the eastern seaboard of Scotland. As the wind moaned and the tall windows of the tower house rattled and sparks from the great fireplace swirled in the hearth from the updraft, the leaders of the Protestant Reformation were all thinking the same thing.

When the storm finishes its raging...how many of the approaching warships will survive the tempest? And will the surviving troops be from England...or from France?

Chapter 60

Out at sea, Admiral William Winter was captaining the flagship of the English fleet bound for St. Andrews. In his quarters he was trying to read the map and weather charts scattered over the varnished wooden table. But the veteran sea captain was barely able to stand upright. His first mate was standing next to him, summoning the presence of mind to deliver a message to the admiral.

"Beggin' the admiral's pardon," the first mate said, "but you wanted a report on the loss of our fleet—"

"Aye, Mister Johnston, what say ye on that matter?"

"I regret to report that six of our ships have disappeared in this blasted, horrible nor'easter, sir…"

"*Six?*"

"Yes, sir. We couldn't change direction quick enough to search the waters for survivors…I fear, sir, that all six ships are lost, and lost with all hands…"

"That leaves eight ships, including our own."

"Yes, sir—but if I may say this, sir, we may be blown aground on the shoals if we do not make landfall soon…"

"According to my calculations, St. Andrews is dead ahead, due north…"

The first mate had no reply. He knew that even Admiral Winter, with all his vast experience on the worst of seas, had his limits. And the black, blowing, snowing, starless skies over them had not permitted any reckoning with a sextant, because a sextant required the ability to shoot the stars. So Winter was forced to bank on his personal calculations and his lifetime on the oceans of the world.

"Do we sail forth, sir—or do we turn back?"

The admiral stood up as the ship rocked wildly, the glowing lanterns in his quarters swinging back and forth.

"We sail forth, Mister Johnston," Winter replied with no trace of indecision on his face, "to St. Andrews."

"Aye, sir," the first mate replied, struggling to stay upright as he made his way to the door.

Admiral Winter had not told his first mate the secret parameters of their journey. That he had received instructions from Queen Elizabeth, conveyed to him by Sir William Cecil, Secretary of State, that if his mission failed, or if he was captured by the French and even tortured by them, he was to claim the venture was a product of his personal judgment only. Under no circumstance was he to say that his venture to St. Andrews had been directed or even authorized by Queen Elizabeth. That official directive would only come when—and if— England and the Scottish Protestant leadership entered into a formal treaty of cooperation and mutual defense. Until then, if Winters and his men were taken by the French, he knew they would be summarily executed as spies.

He stood up, grabbing his long wool coat and strapping on his admiral's hat. Then he walked out onto the rolling deck of the ship, with the brunt of the nor'easter blowing snow and sleet into his face. He made his way up to the wheel, where a sailor was struggling to keep the ship on course. The sailor acknowledged the admiral—but Winter was not paying attention. His eyes were searching the black void ahead of the ship—out in front of the prow where the icy waves were bursting and spraying.

Winter watched and waited, steadying himself against the movement of the ship's deck under him, without a word. Then his head dipped slightly, his mouth opening, and his eyes fixed on something ahead.

"There it is!" he cried out. "The lights of St. Andrews."

The sailor looked ahead. His face lit up and he cried out as well.

"God save you, Admiral Winter, sir, it is indeed! As I live and die those are harbor lights!"

All eight remaining ships made it safely past the breakwater and into the safety of St. Andrew's harbor. They anchored fast for the evening. And when dawn broke, and the storm was lessening and sunlight began to stream through the spaces between the gray clouds, the French troops saw eight men-o'-war, bristling with cannons, flying the colors of England, anchored offshore. In less than an hour the order was given to retreat. They took their arms, horses, and light artillery and headed straight for Leith to join the rest of the army of Marie de Guise.

St. Andrews had been wrested from the control of France and the queen regent without a shot being fired.

What Admiral Winter did not know—but soon he, the Protestant leadership, and the queen regent would all come to hear—was the fate of the French fleet. The storm had devastated it, either sinking or driving back to the Continent a full three-fourths of the sixteen ships. Only nine hundred French soldiers had succeeded in making the journey from France to Leith.

The news reached the queen regent first. Though she was unable to rise or walk on her own because of her advancing illness, she was still resolute.

"War shall begin at Leith," she whispered to her Council. "And—God willing—it shall end only when the forces of Knox and Glencairn and Methven and the other heretics are crushed…crushed forever…"

In Cupar the next morning, word had already reached the gathering of Protestant leaders that a fleet of English ships had anchored in St. Andrew's harbor and had sent the French troops scurrying. It was seen as reason enough to celebrate, but with reservation. For it also accentuated the tenuous alliance with England. Ships had been sent to Scotland, for certain—but more for show than battle. Until England and the Protestant leaders reached a formal treaty, England would not enter in a full military engagement. A date—just a few days hence—had already been selected to discuss those terms. The place had also been picked. The negotiations would be held in Berwick, just south of the Scottish border.

It was decided a contingent of Protestants would be sent immediately. John Knox cornered Ransom after they had risen early and took him aside.

"I must confide in ye," he said. "Something about this meeting in Berwick."

As he spoke, Ransom noticed he was sweating heavily, looking pale and tired.

"First is this…I shall not be attending…"

"Why not?" Ransom asked. "Such a treaty with England is the only way we shall ever win our right to preach and teach the gospel freely here."

"Aye, indeed it is," Knox replied. "But I have suffered as of late with fevers and sickness. I have not spoken of it to most of the others. Just to Methven and Glencairn. But the lack of sleep and cares that burden me have overwhelmed this poor, frail body. And then there is the second matter…"

Ransom waited, having no idea what he was referring to.

"The fact is," Knox continued, "that I have made myself a mischief in the eyes of Queen Elizabeth. It is said that my name is one of the most despised to the ears of her Court—"

"No, I am sure not," Ransom protested.

"Aye, 'tis true—and I regret nothing of my writings and my preaching. But I also know I shall be useful to England as long as I am still useful to the Scottish Reformation. So, here is how I shall resolve it…"

Knox took Ransom by the shoulders.

"Ye shall go to the treaty meeting at Berwick. Ye shall be my eyes and ears and shall demand what I would demand. And ye shall agree to what I would agree. That is my heart's cry to ye, Ransom. I know yer good wife is great with child—have ye made arrangements?"

"I have a midwife with her."

"She's a good lass…she'll understand the importance of this thing I ask of ye…"

Ransom had no excitement over the task given to him. His only thought—his single burden—was of his pregnant wife and the future of his family. He found a room in the tower house to write a letter to Margaret, and arranged for a messenger to speed it to her in Perth.

In it, Ransom wrote of his love for her, and his prayers for her safety and that of their child. He asked for her forgiveness and indulgence for a longer absence than he had promised. But he was convinced, he said, that the hand of divine destiny was sweeping over Scotland. And so he wrote,

> *I am sure that I am to be in Berwick and offer whatever meager wisdom and counsel I have for the cause of the evangel of Christ in our land. But I am equally sure that the God of all grace—who knows all things—also knows the greatness of my love for you. And nothing shall befall either you or our wee precious one in my absence. God knows that I am but dust—and without you, the wind would scatter the dust of me till there would be no finding it.*
>
> *Your loving and most faithful husband,*
>
> *Ransom*

Chapter 61

Berwick was several days travel from the family home in Perth, where Margaret and her midwife were awaiting the day of delivery.

Ransom arrived at Berwick accompanied by Sir James Stewart, Lord Ruthven, and the Duke of Chatelherault who, like Stewart, was a recent defector from the queen regent's Court. Those three were the leaders of the negotiating team, though several other members of the Lords of the Congregation also traveled with them. Ransom had little trust for the spiritual judgment of that trio, feeling as he did that they were aligning with Protestantism for political—not theological—reasons.

But at the same time, Ransom, upon praying on the matter during the entire journey by ship to Berwick, came to one simple conclusion. God could—and often did—use both prophets as well as profaners— preachers as well as politicians—to work His inscrutable will. The Bible was full of such examples. It appeared to him, therefore, that if this uncertain "stew" was God's own recipe, then it was not his place to complain about the ingredients He used.

Queen Elizabeth sent Sir Thomas, Duke of Norfolk, to negotiate for her. Though he was accompanied by a retinue of English nobility, it was understood at the outset that he, and he alone, had the authority to strike a bargain for England if any would be struck.

The first term was easily agreed to. In return for English support of Protestant Scotland, if England was attacked by France, then the Scots would send their own army to aid England. But the next question was this—exactly what support would England give to the Protestant Scots?

Stewart called for a full English army to attack the French at Leith and drive them out of Scotland.

"Well enough," the Duke of Norfolk replied, "but what kind of nation are we giving birth to? This John Knox of yours seems to write and preach of common citizens having the right to remove their own leaders—what kind of anarchy is that?"

"Mister Knox," Ransom interjected, "believes that God installs kings and queens and that He also brings them down...and sometimes He uses His faithful people to accomplish that. Mister Knox also believes that the best government is one maintained by a righteous commonwealth of faithful believers in Christ. Nevertheless, monarchs also may rule, assuming they are guided by God's holy Word."

"Well, thank goodness for that!" the Duke exclaimed with a loud laugh. "You can thank Mister Knox for allowing Queen Elizabeth to continue ruling in England!"

Ransom was not amused, but the Protestant leaders enjoyed the joke. When the chuckles subsided, Lord Ruthven suggested that because the Duke of Chatelherault was an heir to the Scottish throne, Scotland would not be without a monarch. Anarchy, he assured the duke, would not reign in Scotland.

"Of course," Stewart added, "Mary, the daughter of Marie de Guise, claims herself to be queen of the Scots..."

"Well, she is still in France," Norfork replied. "Let us all hope for the sake of the simplicity of our plan that she stays there..."

In the end it was agreed that England would send an army to aid the Scottish leaders of the Reformation in expelling the French from Scotland, dethroning Marie de Guise, and restoring the Scots to their ancient heritage of liberty. It was also agreed that any fortifications taken over by the English would be surrendered to the new Scottish government.

Ransom reviewed and approved, on John Knox's behalf, the final document, which was titled the Treaty of Berwick. It was sufficient, Norfolk said, for England to give its pledge of direct military intervention. The following day, an army of nine thousand English soldiers began marching toward the border and then on to Leith. Just outside of Edinburgh, the English army joined up with several thousand Scottish soldiers raised by the Earl of Glencairn and the other Protestant nobles. As the armies amassed, the decision had been made that an all-out siege against the army at Leith would now begin.

Within the immense fortifications of Leith, Marie de Guise had an army of four thousand. After the naval disaster, the massive reinforcements from France that she had hoped for had never arrived.

As the armies of the Protestant cause gathered on the plains outside of Leith, Ransom Mackenzie had booked passage by coach. To his delight it would make a stop at Perth before heading to St. Andrews.

But at their home at Perth, Margaret was already experiencing labor pains. Her midwife, Jean Macleod, a woman young for that art but highly skilled and very knowledgeable, placed her hands on Margaret and pressed gently.

"What is it?" Margaret said between gasps of breath.

"Not what ye expected..."

"Is something wrong with my wee one?"

"Nay," Jean said, "but 'tis not one..."

"What d'ye say?"

"Only this—that 'tis not a 'one' but a 'two'!"

"Two?" Margaret exclaimed between her panting. "Two?"

"Aye, I can feel two, 'tis sure," Jean said, then added with a smile, "Do ye want me to keep pressing to see if I can come up with three instead?"

Margaret laughed, but her laughter suddenly turned into moans of pain.

"No," Margaret said between contractions of pain. "No…two is fine enough…for sure, it's been Esau and Jacob…fightin' inside of me!"

Then Margaret looked over at her midwife.

"My good Ransom is helpin' to birth the nation of Scotland…as I am birthing his twins it seems…" But then she moaned in pain and her eyes began to fill with tears.

"My da and mum will never know their Margaret had twins," she cried.

"They're watching down from heaven," Jean declared. "Now ye have to mind yourself, lass…keep to the task, love. We may have a new nation—or we may not—but what matters now are the two newest citizens of Scotland that ye're carryin'. And ye are the only one in the world that can bring them out…"

Margaret gripped the ropes on the sides of the bed and her moans turned to screams. The time had come—the deep mysteries of the profound but fleeting pain of the flesh as it presents the wrinkled little faces of those who were ordained by God before time. Margaret pushed with the inexplicable courage of motherhood, the wonder unchanged from age to age, as the tiny travelers slowly turned their way out of the quiet of their dark enclosure and toward the light.

"He's coming! I see him!" Joan cried out as she placed her hands on the head of the first infant.

Miles away, the armies of England and the Lords of the Congregation had begun to send the initial wave of infantry rushing toward the fortified walls and battlements of Leith.

Several dozen foot soldiers, pierced through with the arrows from the French long bowmen who were shooting down from the castle parapets or struck by cannon shot, had already been downed.

On the fields of Leith, men of the English and Scottish army were dying where they lay, many of them partially buried under rubble, wet sod, dead horses, wagons, and piles of exploded earth. Others were lying on open ground, struggling to get up but slowing bleeding to death before they could.

As the Protestant forces regrouped for another assault, there was a momentary quiet over the fields of battle.

The only sound that could be heard was the voices of a few of the dying men as they called out for their mothers.

Chapter 62

The siege of Leith had dragged on for several days by the time Ransom finally reached his home in Perth. The Protestant troops had sent wave upon wave of infantry armed with long spears and swords to the walls of the French-controlled castle, but a full-scale attack had not yet been mounted. Then days turned into weeks of skirmishes, attacks, and counterattacks. When the Protestants dug trenches to prepare for a closer assault, the French counter-dug their own around the castle perimeter.

Finally, William Cecil conveyed the order for a full attack. The English and Scottish soldiers that had survived were ready to put the battle to a final, bloody end. The English cannons were loosed, blasting down several of the French-controlled towers. Then the English longbowmen let fly a hail of arrows that rained down on the French watchposts. The trumpet was sounded and the charge began, as thousands of soldiers raced toward the walls of the French outposts.

Dozens of soldiers carried scaling ladders to climb up to the top of the walls. But the ladders proved to be too short. Soldiers attempting to climb the ladders were killed as they stood helpless against the walls several feet from the top, with the French firing down on them at will.

Again, the English and Scots retreated and regrouped. Several hundred more English soldiers arrived from the north of England to reinforce the assault. It appeared that the siege of Leith would grind on without the hope of any clear end in sight.

Yet it would all end—but not because of the excellence of military strategy or even the bravery of the soldiers who had raced into the arrows and cannons of death. The siege would finally halt because death would come to Queen Regent Marie de Guise. Bloated, swollen, and racked with fever, she knew her end was near. Propped up in a chair in Edinburgh Castle, she sent for her advisors and friends—to say farewell. She sent for Sir James Stewart and the Duke of Chatelherault and, during a lull in the hostilities, they both were allowed entrance to her private quarters.

She begged their forgiveness for any wrongs she had committed against them, but she also added that she forgave them for their wrongs against her. To the end, in a hoarse whisper, she continued to plead for them to continue an alliance with France, though she was smart enough to know that too much had happened, too much blood had been shed, and too many fires had been lit against too many Protestants for that to occur.

And so Marie de Guise died. Queen Elizabeth hastily authorized Sir William Cecil to negotiate a peace treaty for the ending of the hostilities. Under the terms, France was to retreat from Scotland forever.

John Knox was already summoning the leadership to call a new Scottish Parliament. The first order of business would be the passing of an act officially declaring Scotland to be a Protestant nation. It would be just as Margaret had said, the birth of a new Scotland.

But back in Perth, Ransom and Margaret had more intimate concerns about a birth of a much more personal nature.

Andrew and Philip, fraternal twins, so named by Ransom and Margaret, were consecrated just days following their births. John Knox presided over the ceremony, where the parents declared in the presence of the Protestant community of their town that they would raise the two boys in the nurture, admonition, and instruction of God's Word. The infants were strong and healthy. Everywhere he went, Ransom beamed, telling everyone he could the good news of the "bonnie lads my bonnie wife has given me!"

There was a welcome relief during that time. The treaty between England and Scotland gave the Protestant cause a powerful new ally. And the death of Marie de Guise and the removal of all French armies from Scotland after the Siege of Leith brought with it the promise of peace and religious liberty for the practice and the preaching of the Protestant gospel of Christ.

For Ransom, who had hoped to return to the quiet disciplines of his practice of law, changes came. He received offers to teach at both St. Andrews and in Glasgow as well. And Knox quickly pressed him into service, to assist with the drafting of the *Book of Discipline.* In the end he accepted a teaching post in Glasgow, while in Edinburgh he began work with the new Parliament leaders on issues of religious and public governance. Knox, ever the man to burn his candle at both ends and whose own health was not much improved, even urged Ransom to help edit his writing of his *History of the Reformation in Scotland.* But Ransom had to respectfully decline the honor. That was hard to do, as Knox had recently suffered the death of his wife, Marjory, and Ransom did not wish to unnecessarily add to his burden.

Ransom's greatest task, he had told both Knox and his colleagues, was to not stray too far or too long from his home in Perth, from Margaret his Highland love, or from his two infant sons.

Meanwhile, Margaret took immediately to motherhood. To Ransom's amazement, except from the circles under her dark eyes from lack of sleep for the first few months, she seemed to gain back her youthful, untamed beauty. And, in a strange way, there was even an added glow about her. Yet, despite her full-time responsibilities mothering the two boys, she was always interested in the politics of the day and quizzed Ransom incessantly on the newest developments from Edinburgh. She was particularly amazed when Ransom told her that the Lords of the

Congregation had actually *welcomed* Mary Queen of Scots to Scotland, entreating her to leave France and settle in the Palace at Holyrood as their monarch.

Knox told them she was not to be trusted. But the Protestant lords firmly believed, Ransom explained, that the eighteen-year-old Mary, once away from the control of the Catholic French Court and settled in Scotland, could be converted to the Protestant gospel.

And so, the day came when Mary Queen of Scots returned to Scotland. Ransom was in Edinburgh at the time and was present to witness her procession. Then he returned home to Perth.

When he slipped in the front door of their home it was dark. Upstairs he could hear Margaret singing. He listened closely, and then grinned as he recognized the tune. It was the Gaelic nursery tune she had learned in the Highlands.

> *Fosgail an doras!*
> *Fosgail an doras!*
> *Fosgail an doras, trobhad a-steach!*
>
> *Fosgail an doras!*
> *Fosgail an doras!*
> *Ciamar a tha thus?*

"For a minute," Ransom said quietly as he came up from behind and wrapped his arms around her, "I felt as if I was back in the glen with you and you were a girl…wearing a sprig of heather in your hair."

Margaret was rocking their infant boys in their two cradles, one hand on each, as she sang. She stopped and turned to Ransom.

"Well," she replied in a whisper, "if it isn't the wee townie boy come to see his two brawny lads."

"And come to kiss his bonnie love as well," Ransom said, squeezing her tight, "and to hold her so close he can feel her heart beating..."

He kissed her neck, and cheek, and then her mouth, and held her for a long time. When they pulled apart, they looked down and saw that the infants were fast asleep.

They tiptoed downstairs together, and Margaret set a plate for him at the table with a large bowl of stew. And then asked him about the business of Scotland. Ransom recounted the work on the *Book of Discipline,* and the innumerable petty quarrels among the leadership in the new Parliament. Then she asked about Mary Queen of Scots.

"I saw her procession going down the royal mile of Edinburgh," Ransom said.

"By heaven's gate ye didn't!" Margaret exclaimed. "What was it like?"

"Opulent...a little shocking...and, I fear, it does not bode well for the future..."

"What do ye mean?" she replied. "How can a queen's procession mean anythin' at all like that?"

"The people adored her—that was clear—celebrations and bonfires everywhere, singing and shouting. She made her way down the mile in an open carriage. Over her head a host of servants held a purple velvet canopy with gold fringe. The servants were dressed in yellow satin suits with black masks, like Moors. And girls dressed like the pagan goddesses and figures of Greece leaped and danced before her."

"Well," Margaret replied, "ye can't judge anythin' by such merriment."

"Perhaps not. But along the way, some Protestants were burning an effigy of a priest in protest of her coronation. She halted the procession, stood up in the carriage, and demanded that the effigy be taken down and the fire put out."

"Did that surprise ye?" Margaret said. "She is a Catholic, is she not?"

"She is."

"So?"

"So—we have a Catholic queen—born of a Catholic mother who burned Protestants—who now rules Scotland, even though this is an officially Protestant nation," Ransom replied, spooning stew into his mouth.

He swallowed and took on a pensive look.

"Margaret, my love—have you ever heard of a more explosive, dangerous marriage in all the world than that?"

Chapter 63

1562

The uneasy "marriage" between Mary Queen of Scots and Scotland had became neither easier nor more matrimonial as time wore on. In the two years following her accession to the throne she had attempted to consolidate her power in a land that had been fragmented by quarreling clans, by wars between Catholicism and Protestantism and, of course, by competing rivalries between past alliances with France and new allegiances with her enemy, England.

No sooner had Mary Queen of Scots begun her reign than James Stewart, her bastard half-brother, became one of her Court advisors. He went through the motions of urging her to convert to Protestantism. She laughed heartily at that and, in quick-witted fashion, suggested that if Stewart converted back to Catholicism she would see to it that the Vatican would make him a Cardinal. Stewart did not raise the issue again.

But for John Knox, Ransom, and many who remembered all too well the burning of the gospel reformers under Marie de Guise, Mary Queen of Scots was just another religious catastrophe waiting to happen.

Efforts were made to negotiate a cooperative relationship between the Catholic queen and her Protestant Parliament. So Mary agreed to accept as a religious reality—and not undermine—the official Protestantism of Scotland. In turn, she would be permitted to participate in her own personal Catholic masses administered by her own priest—but never in public, and only in her Edinburgh Palace when she was present, and with no other attendees. But those who grew to know her understood that the red-haired young queen—with her delicate beauty, quick wit, and penchant for reckless living and luxurious possessions—had her own ambitions.

She would never bow and scrape to the likes of Knox, and she often told James Stewart exactly that. Mary stated frankly she considered Knox to be the most dangerous man in her realm. But she also knew how to ply her Protestant advisors with benefits and titles, thereby creating a rift between Knox and his group on the one hand, and the moderates who supported her reign on the other. She started out by quickly granting James Stewart an earldom, increasing his power, prestige, and pocketbook.

It was no secret that Mary harbored ambitions for a unified Scotland and England under her rule. But in England, Queen Elizabeth was constantly vigilant and watchful of her. For that reason she relied greatly on her intelligence chief, Sir Francis Walsingham. This cautious and paranoid advisor with a well-trimmed moustache and beard, darting eyes, and a fondness for wearing black, whose shadowy figure could be seen lurking never very far from Elizabeth, had developed a labyrinth-like spy network in England; in Ireland, where Elizabeth was encountering mounting resistance to the creation of the Church of England; and in Scotland as well. And in Scotland, his spies were watching Queen Mary—whom Elizabeth did not trust—as well as John Knox, whom Elizabeth still hated but of whose usefulness she was still convinced.

Meanwhile, Mary's boldness had become bolder. She had tried to find any cause to banish, or even execute, John Knox to weaken the Protestant cause. So she had repeatedly summoned Knox to the Holyrood Palace and conducted a series of combative "interviews" with him—in hopes of catching him in some slip of the tongue upon which she could base charges of treason or insurrection.

Before each of the interviews with the queen, Knox consulted with Ransom. In preparation they discussed theological contentions that might arise, and points of law and political protocol. Twice their meetings were held in Ransom's home at Perth. Knox seemed to enjoy the company and wit of Margaret as much—perhaps even more—than his consultations with Ransom. By then, Knox had been without his wife for two-and-a-half years and still seemed somewhat overwhelmed by the loss of Marjory. He would laugh heartily at Margaret's Highland humor and would rave about her cooking and gracious hospitality.

Knox's health seemed always precarious. Yet he still pushed on with a breakneck schedule of preaching across the country, strategy sessions with Parliament, and meetings with the Protestant leadership over how to implement in practice the revolutionary structure set forth in the *Book of Discipline*. But whenever Knox visited Ransom and Margaret in Perth, he would dote on little Andrew and Philip, and then he would brag about his "own sweet bairns." Knox had asked Margaret's midwife, Jean MacLeod, to help with raising his children, until he finally got the help of his late wife's mother, who moved into his home to take over those duties.

Despite her attempts to trap Knox during their interviews, Mary failed on each occasion. And in one, Knox's scolding of her became vociferous—he thundered that he was unlike her counselors and advisors who spoke nothing but soothing, flattering words to her even though the commonwealth of Scotland was neglected and was wasting away. "Nay," Knox continued, "I am come to do none of that, but to only preach the evangel of Christ—and in that I address but two things—repentance and faith."

The queen was reduced to tears in front of her own Privy Council. Knox apologized on the spot.

"I have never delighted," Knox said to her, his voice suddenly softening, almost to the point of becoming tender, "in the weeping of any of God's creatures. I can scarcely abide the tears of my own boys whom my own hand must, from time to time, correct—much less, madam, do I rejoice in Your Majesty's weeping..."

But as the young queen wiped her eyes with the silk handkerchiefs provided by her lady in waiting, there was a look in her eye—and it was not lost on Knox, who caught it. Her dazzling blue eyes were fixed on him, as if he were a red deer at the chase, and she was the huntress on one of her trips through the hills of Scotland by horseback. She would, it seemed, put her arrow through this untamed, unkind prophet's heart, and would not rest till it was done.

Their eyes locked. Knox knew somewhere in the quiet center of his soul that Mary was not through with him. He had the overpowering feeling that this young, reckless, beautiful queen would not rest until she had been avenged on him for her tears. But what he did not know then, but would soon come to realize, was that his protégé, Ransom Mackenzie, would soon be within the queen's crosshairs as well.

Chapter 64

It was the end of the summer of that year. For several months, Queen Mary had been riding throughout the countryside with her entourage. She was an excellent horsewoman, and she traveled on her own horse into the west and southwest of Scotland, visiting the local castles and estates—being toasted and feted by the clan leaders and nobles and enjoying the thrill of the chase. She had special "Highland" outfits designed for the occasion—spectacular embroidered hunting gowns with plaids and velvet collars and gold lace.

But there was more involved than merely her love of the sporting life or her addiction to the balls and masques held in her honor in the great halls of the Scottish Highlands and Lowlands. Mary had picked a route that would take her through the heart of those regions where her political and religious support was the greatest. Even though she had promised otherwise, she participated in conspicuous masses in each of the castles. When word got back to John Knox, he addressed her "idolatry" and her betrayal of her solemn word as queen in a series of heated sermons.

That was when the whole affair began. During Mary's long absence that summer, her staff, Catholics all, loyal to the Queen, and having been given complete freedom to publicize their rites at Holyrood Palace, began arranging for large masses to be said illegally in the chapel, attended by numerous courtiers. The queen knew of it but turned a blind eye.

While a priest was readying for another mass at Holyrood Chapel, news of that reached two Protestants, Patrick Cranston and Andrew Armstrong. They raced over to the chapel and found the priest preparing as celebrant and setting the altar while twenty-two parishioners were in line, waiting to take Catholic Communion and witness the mass in Latin. Cranston and Armstrong forced their way through the Catholic guards and confronted the priest, threatening to lay waste to the entire chapel if the mass went ahead as planned. But they were unable to stop the proceedings.

Agreeing with Knox and the other strict reformers, the Protestant Parliament charged the various participants at the chapel with violating the ban of public displays of the mass.

When Mary returned to Edinburgh she was outraged. She promptly convinced her Privy Council to issue criminal warrants against Cranston and Armstrong, charging them with "felonious and intentional invasion of the Queen's Palace and for spoliation of the same."

What happened next was only partly known to Ransom at the time, though it would be made clear later. He knew that, with the trial date of Cranston and Armstrong fast approaching, John Knox had circulated his own personal letter to every Protestant supporter he could locate—though oddly, Ransom did not get one. The letter was written by Knox, and he never denied it. But it had been done hastily. Knox had failed to seek counsel from anyone on its language before sending it—and particularly not from Ransom Mackenzie.

In the end, it was that letter that provided Mary Queen of Scots with her long-awaited chance. It appeared to the young monarch that she now had the poison-tipped arrow to finally bring down her hated prey.

One evening that summer, Margaret was in the kitchen. She was readying the two boys for their weekly bath. They were both in a large wooden washtub filled with water. As she was singing to and scrubbing the two-year-olds, Ransom was standing back and watching.

"You know, dear Margaret, I am making more money now than ever," he noted thoughtfully.

"Aye," Margaret said, slightly out of breath as she separated the two boys, who were now flailing at each other. Andrew, with a quivering little lip, was on the verge of crying. She then handed him a wooden spoon and cup, and a little wooden sailboat to Philip. Peace had been momentarily restored.

"'Tis true. God Himself has blessed us. More ways than we can count on fingers and toes," Margaret said, still kneeling next to the tub.

"And with that blessing," Ransom continued with an air of authority, "it is incumbent on me to therefore bless you…"

Margaret stopped her playing with the boys and half-turned to her husband.

"Whatever do ye mean?"

"Jean Macleod, your midwife, helped poor John Knox after he lost his wife. She helped for many months to raise the boys till his mother-in-law could take over the job…"

"I know that. But what's that to us?"

"Just this. I think it's time—considering our station in life—to take on a children's nurse and a housekeeper as well."

"Whatever for?" Margaret said, her voice rising a bit.

"So that you can have help with the boys—and help with the house—and attend to matters of society with the other women in town."

"Do ye have some complaint of me, my dear Ransom—of the manner of my raising our wee sons?"

"Of course not," Ransom quickly replied. "You are the best mother that has ever trod this earth."

"And of my housekeepin' and cookin'—what of that?"

"You know what I think there, my love. Mister Knox has often bragged of yer meals after eating here. And Reverend Methven too."

"Then if ye would," she said with a bit of an edge to her voice, "please do not speak of a nursemaid or housekeeper again. 'Tis hurtful to my heart, Ransom. Truly 'tis."

Ransom was dumbfounded.

"I don't understand…"

"'Tis not a surprise ye don't," she snapped back.

"What is it?" he said, trying to delicately pursue the cause behind her hurt.

"Do ye want to know?"

"Of course."

"Ever since ye have taken on more work in this new government of Scotland, I've seen less of ye. And whenever I do, it seems…well…'tis as if ye don't care for what I have done and who I am. Ye are tryin' to make me into something I am not—I am not like the fine society women of Perth and Edinburgh and Glasgow, with fine china this and silver that—not pewter, mind ye, but real silver…And they are forever havin' parties and socials—and meetings where they are speakin' all the time but never really sayin' their minds—do ye want me to be like that? Or do ye want me to be the way I really am—just a simple Highland lass who loves her home and husband and kin?"

Ransom bent down next to her at the side of the wooden tub.

The two boys were squealing and splashing and trading loud declarations of "No!" and "Don't!" with each other. Andrew, the quieter one, with fine features and brown hair, was pointing his finger at his brother. But Philip, red-haired and wild, grabbed his brother's finger and yanked on it. Andrew cried out, but Margaret intervened again and quieted them.

Ransom's clothes were now soaked. Drops of bathwater were dripping from his raven-haired wife's hair and face. He wiped the drops off and kissed her.

"Listen to me, Margaret Mackenzie," he said softly. "Ye may be a beautiful Highland lass—and a prize of a mother and housekeeper and wife—

but there is nothing simple about you, dear heart. *Nothing*. In fact, if that confused, selfish band of politicians in Parliament had half your wit and cleverness we would have our new government established by now."

Margaret eyed him closely for a minute, then smiled.

"D'ye mean it—or is it just yer clever way with words to try to woo me?"

"I've never been more serious," Ransom said, smiling back. "You are the blessing of which I am utterly undeserving. And let God Himself judge my heart if I am deceiving you..."

They kissed again, and then both grabbed a slippery, naked boy out of the tub and began drying them off. When the boys were in bed upstairs, Ransom and Margaret slipped quietly downstairs and sat together on the front step, enjoying the night air. It was balmy, and the smell of flowers and evergreens and sod filled the air. The stars were out like chiseled diamonds, cold and hard in the black sky above.

"That puts me in mind of David de Blois Douglas," Ransom said, "who said the stars can predict the future. He was as lost a poor sinner as I have ever known...as if he were a log just drifting on a river."

Margaret thought about that for a few seconds.

"'Tis a good thing the Lord God doesn't tell us all the future for our lives ahead of time."

"Why so? If we knew the future we could avoid the mistakes of our foolish past."

"Well," Margaret said, "maybe so—but the burden would make us go mad, I think—the knowin' of it all, rather than just the livin' of it..."

Then she added, "I wouldna want to know when ye will depart this old world, Ransom—not at all—if I did, my heart would fix on the thought of it and wouldn't let go, and I would just wither up and die. There would be nothing left of me...I'd be like the empty shell of a bug."

Ransom looked into her eyes. Then he put down his logic, rhetoric, and systematic thought. He saw his lover and the mother of his sons sitting next to him, and he knew, then, that she was right. That the knowing of it all was not the only thing. But there was also the "livin' of it" too.

When they went to bed the moon was shining bright and cast a pale illumination into their bedroom.

They talked for a while with their heads next to each other on the goose-feather pillows in the moonlight. They talked about the boys— how different they were. Margaret still referred to them as her "Jacob and Esau." Andrew was the contemplative one. Sure of himself, but studied and deliberate. Philip was impulsive and bold. They wondered what life would hold for them.

Margaret asked about the progress of the Scottish commonwealth envisioned by the *Book of Discipline*.

"It all seems to have ground to a halt," Ransom said with a sense of exasperation. "The scheme of government is a grand one—local representatives elected by the people of each parish, responsible to the people—the rule of conduct established by God's own standards—but it's all just slowing down, tripping and hobbling like—"

"Like a lame horse?"

"Exactly. And for two primary causes—money and power, and the love of both. The nobles don't want to part with their entitlements and wealth. And the queen, of course, will not help us raise revenue for the very system of ruling that will diminish her power."

After a pause Margaret asked about a message that had come to their door that day.

"It was from Knox," Ransom said. "Said he must talk to me on the morrow. About a letter he wrote—and about Queen Mary—and what he called 'the most perilous threat against me yet to occur.'"

Ransom said that was all he would know of the matter until he learned more from Knox.

His eyes were growing heavy, and he was in the twilight between dreaming and waking when Margaret spoke. It startled him and he was suddenly wide awake.

"If the Lord should take me afore ye," Margaret said softly, "then ye must do something for me…"

"What?" Ransom whispered.

"Some part of me, some memory—something—ye must take it back and bury it in the Highlands…"

Then she turned toward her husband in the pale light, and with an urgency in her voice she spoke again.

"Ye must promise with yer heart and with yer soul that ye'll do it."

Chapter 65

Before leaving for his meeting, Ransom tried to question Margaret on her strange comment in bed the night before. But she would not discuss it. Changing the subject, she said only that, regarding the mysterious matter with John Knox, she felt "unsettled in her spirit" and felt that it did not bode well for her husband. Ransom assured her he would be sensible in approaching the issue—whatever it was—and would return the next day.

The conference with Knox took place in his house in Edinburgh, located at the bottom of the royal mile. Knox lived on the second floor. His mother-in-law was tending to his children, and Ransom heard them chattering and playing noisily in the adjoining room. He hugged Ransom warmly and offered him a seat at the large oak table in the main room, which was surrounded by small paned windows and overlooked the main thoroughfare of the city.

The two men spoke of personal things first. Knox asked about Margaret and the boys, and Ransom shared that they were prosperous beyond any expectation, and healthy and happy too. He noticed the creases in Knox's face and the bags beneath his eyes that now seemed to be a permanent feature of his countenance and asked about his health. Knox explained that he had a bout of apoplexy from which he seemed slow to recover. Then both of them commiserated about the sad state of the new commonwealth of Scotland, which lacked both the financial means and the political will to become a reality.

"'Tis a shame," Knox opined, "that all we wanted to accomplish—the support of widows and orphans and the poor, the schooling and education of all the boys and girls of Scotland, and the rigorous application of the Word of God to the ruling of this nation through godly, elected representatives—it all seems to have come to a halt."

Ransom nodded and expressed his frustration in his dealings with Parliament.

Then Knox finally began to address the matter at hand.

"My contacts within the Court tell me I should be warned that my letter alerting the church of the upcoming trial of Cranston and Armstrong has come into the hands of the queen. And into the possession of her most secret council—her inner cabinet."

"With what effect?" Ransom asked.

"Just this—it is quite possible they will use it as a pretense for charges of treason against me."

"Are your sources reliable?"

"Assuredly."

"Is there any indication as to the timing of such charges?"

"Only," Knox replied, "that they will likely come before the New Year."

Ransom asked if Knox had a copy of the letter. Knox went over to a carved black-oak dresser and pulled it out and showed it to Ransom.

After he had studied it for a while, Knox broke in.

"What do ye think? Is there substance there for such odious charges agin' me?"

"I wish it were not so," Ransom replied reluctantly. "But the truth is, John, that if they want to blast away at you, this may be ample cannon fodder for Mary and her cronies."

"But I was merely alerting the good Christian people of Scotland of the fact of the trial of Cranston and Armstrong—and to come and show their support of their fellow reformers."

"That may have been your intent," Ransom said, "but the prosecutor of the Crown will seize not on the intent of your heart, but on the words of your letter."

Ransom tapped his finger on the copy of the letter in front of him. Knox took the letter and studied it for a few minutes himself. Then he put it back down on the table.

"I should have asked ye for yer counsel—or that of the other leaders. I discussed the letter, but no one read the language before I sent it out."

After a moment's reflection, Knox added something.

"But then again—perhaps it's for the better. If I am tried and convicted, better there be only 'one for sacrifice' than the whole lot of ye if ye had read it aforehand and approved it…"

Ransom caught the reference to the long-dead George Wishart. But he shook his head in response.

"There shall be no executions over this letter, John, if God wills, and if I have any defense to make for you," he said with a smile.

Knox smiled back. He was going to say something in reply. But he did not get a chance.

They could not then see it, but a man with a long coat and a hat pulled down over his head had been walking along the cobblestones of the street below. But he had stopped and looked up at Knox's second-story apartment.

Everyone in the city knew where Knox lived, as he kept it no secret. The man on the street could see his profile as he sat next to the window. Next to him was Ransom, and his head was also visible. The man chortled to himself. He could kill both of them with a single shot.

The man looked around. Other than the crowds of people heading up or down the royal mile on their way to shops, he saw no one capable of catching him. He could fire away and then slip into the narrow winding close nearby before he was stopped.

The man carefully pulled out a loaded blunderbuss from his coat. Glancing around one more time, he quickly raised the barrel up.

But just before the gun fired, a man across the street saw the would-be assassin and yelled out a warning.

"Look out...he's shooting!"

The assassin's hand reacted as the shot was fired. It hit the window next to Knox and Ransom with a spray of shot.

The window pane shattered. Ransom and Knox fell down onto the floor. Down below they could hear the yells from passersby. Though he had missed his shot, the conspirator had safely escaped down the alley and disappeared.

The men sat on the floor for a moment, stunned. Knox's mother-in-law poked her head out of a doorway. In the background Knox's children were all crying.

"Take no heed," Knox assured her. "The danger's passed."

Ransom and Knox shook the glass out of their clothes and picked it out of their hair and beards. Knox added his own wry postscript to their close brush with assassination.

"I believe we have just received confirmation on one thing," he said with a little smile. "Having employed an assassin who was a poor aim, the queen now shall have no choice but to try me for treason and kill me by the slower but surer method."

Chapter 66

Upon his return to Perth, Ransom did not tell Margaret about the shooting in Edinburgh for a full two days, for fear that it might upset her. When he finally did explain it, she scolded him passionately. But then, in her tears, she said that perhaps it was a blessing in disguise.

"I do believe," she said, "'tis a fulfillment…"

"Of what?" Ransom asked.

"Of my feeling of doom," she replied.

"But God spared me—and John as well."

"'Tis just the point," she answered, growing more assured of her own argument as she explained it. "My spirit was witnessed to that there would be grave danger—and there was—but now the danger has come and it has passed, like the passover in Egypt in the Old Testament—and ye are safe. So all's well!"

Ransom was not going to argue the point. But he did say that Knox's legal and political troubles were not over—at least not yet. And that the queen might still issue criminal charges—capital ones at that—against Knox. If that happened, he explained, he would need to assist his friend and mentor in his defense.

As the summer disappeared and faded into fall, the heather bloomed once again on the hills outside of Perth. The air became chilled and full of the scent of damp wood burning in fireplaces and the smoldering fires on the fields to make them fallow.

The letter that had been the subject of Ransom's discussion with Knox was not entirely forgotten but had certainly been put aside, as the matters of daily life—both the mundane and the pleasurable—now occupied his attention. Perth held a market fair that year, and it was a source of delight for Margaret and the two boys.

As Ransom strolled with his family through the wide Market Cross, past the booths displaying wares from the Continent—fine dishware, linens, and embroideries for the women, and well-crafted iron hand tools and books for the men—he couldn't help but think back to his youth in St. Andrews. And to the annual spring festival that was held there. And to his boyhood frolics with his friend Philip. Ransom wondered vaguely what had become of Philip since the death of the queen now popularly referred to as "Bloody Mary." He wondered whether, with the rise of Elizabeth I, Philip and his family had fled England, as he once did when a queen antagonistic to his faith arose.

And Ransom wondered also what had ever became of his fellow students from the besieged castle in St. Andrews—the pleasant and loyal Oliver, and the tormenting Harold. And then there was the journey north, and the mysterious keeper of Glamis Castle and his most unpleasant wife. And he thought about the strange but protective tinker who guided him on his long trip to the Highlands. Ransom could also not help but ponder the ultimate fate of the beautiful but heartless Catherine.

"What are ye thinkin'?" Margaret asked playfully as she elbowed her husband while keeping the two boys in tow.

"About all the faces," he replied.

"Of who?"

"Of those I've met—encountered along the way. Up to now…"

"And what have ye considered?"

"One thing, my dear wife—one thing…"

"And what is that?"

Ransom stopped walking and bent over to whisper something in her ear.

"That of all those faces, you have the one that I covet the most—for it belongs to the soul that is the greatest of any I've known…"

Margaret pulled back from him for just an instant and studied him and the seriousness of what he had said. Then she laughed softly, blushed, and bumped him with her elbow, adding that his way with words had always melted her heart—and that if they weren't in the public eye and in the very middle of Market Cross she would find a way to say her love to him more earnestly.

It was a fine day. And when the boys were asleep, Ransom and Margaret embraced and reminded each other of their undying affection for each other. But the skies were about to change.

Two months later, in the dark, cold gloom of December, with the smell of snow and damp in the air, a messenger arrived at their door. The note was from Knox. It was simple, short, and straightforward:

> *I have been summoned to appear before the Queen's Privy Council on charges of high treason, as I had forethought. It reads that either my failure to appear, or my being convicted on the same, shall result in "my prompt and certain execution." There it is, my friend. Come quickly. You shall be of great use to me.*
>
> *Your true and eternal friend,*
>
> *In the name of Christ our Lord,*
>
> *John K.*

To Ransom, the letter seemed to bear a weight of finality. But he tried to dismiss any thoughts of that. He told Margaret he must go and help his friend, once again, to escape the fiery arrows of the enemy. Ransom had no desire to leave home and family. As he did, he prayed to God that their separation would be short, that justice would triumph, and that soon—very soon—he would return.

Chapter 67

John Knox was in his house, surrounded by several of the Protestant leaders. Methven had traveled to support him, as had the Earl of Glencairn. The trial was set for the evening of the following day. The Master of Maxwell was there also, but his advice to Knox was plain—and to Knox's ears, outrageous.

"Ye must," Maxwell urged him, "apologize to the queen, confess yer wrongs committed against her in this letter—admit that, though unintended, nevertheless the words of yer letter can be thought treasonous—and beg the mercy of the Privy Council. If fate and God above should smile on ye, ye may be spared death, and the reformed religion of this land shall be spared another war—"

"Confess to what?" Knox exclaimed like a cannon shot.

"The letter of yer own hand that summons Protestants everywhere to gather at the trial of Cranston and Armstrong and oppose the Queen."

"In *my* lifetime," Knox said ironically, "I've written stronger letters than that!"

"But not against *this* queen—mind ye, she has the love of many of Scotland's people and a great share of its nobles, sir."

But Knox would not be moved. The Master of Maxwell, before leaving, threw one final dart at his former friend and colleague.

"Well enough, ye are wise enough in yer own mind, it appears. But mark ye well," he said in a threatening tone, "ye will find that in the times to come men will not bear with ye, John Knox, as they have in times past."

After Maxwell left, Knox, Ransom, and the remaining group spent time in prayer together. And then all except Ransom departed. For several hours Knox and Ransom strategized. One of Knox's primary concerns was whether to respond to an invitation by none other than Sir James Stewart, now one of the queen's advisors, to meet with him and the Maitland of Lethington, the secretary of her cabinet, before the trial.

"For what purpose?" Ransom asked.

"They want to discuss my defenses—they say that they can be of great aid."

"I have never trusted James Stewart. He blows like a reed in the wind."

"Ye and he have never seen eye to eye. I have less concern for him."

"I speak now not with my heart, but my head," Ransom replied. "He is not in this for the good of John Knox, but for the good of James Stewart. And as for Maitland of Lethington, he is so close to the queen he is nearly sewed into the hem of her garments."

Knox chuckled at that, but confessed that he was never afraid of meeting with any man on any issue.

"I do not counsel against a meeting," Ransom said. "But I gravely counsel against your disclosing any of your defenses in advance of the trial. If you do, they will take that and make use of it in preparing the queen's case. Mark me well, my friend, they mean to convict you for treason and make an example of you."

Knox nodded his head, thinking Ransom's suggestion a good one. While he would make himself accessible to Lethington and Stewart, he would divulge nothing about his anticipated arguments for trial.

The next morning Knox went alone and met with both men. When he returned to his house, he was carrying a good-sized lamb shank he had picked up from the butcher and was wearing a smile. He told Ransom his advice had been well-founded.

"They did indeed try to pry out of me my defenses," he noted, "but only after they urged me to confess that I had wronged the queen in my letter. I advised them I feared my trial was already prejudged against me—and would be a fool to take them into my confidence."

Knox called in his mother-in-law and showed her the lamb. They both agreed it would make a delightful roast, and the pieces left over a fine stew, and then the bone, broth. Ransom smiled. He knew John Knox to always be a man who wasted few things—whether they were words for warring against heresy, or meat for a week's worth of meals.

The next three days Knox and Ransom divided their time between preparation for the trial, which they would do at the table in the main room of his house, and strolling up the royal mile for a break. Ransom was taken aback at first by Knox's boldness in walking in such open sight considering the assassination attempt. But he had always known him to be a man who spent more energy seeking God's approval than mulling over men's designs against him. It was a trait that had emboldened Ransom, and it did so again.

It was during those walks up the busy main thoroughfare of Edinburgh, past the hawkers, the craftsmen banging their hammers, and the yelling street urchins, that the two men had a chance to speak more intimately than they had in years. They talked about many things—occurrences of the past, hopes for the future. Ransom shared, in only the most general terms, his wife's comments about the Highlands and what to do if she was taken by God before him.

"Her sentiments did greatly puzzle me," Ransom confessed. "What should I do to comfort her?"

Knox smiled at that.

"I find it easier to divine the mysteries of God's Word than to explain the nature of His radiant creation, the woman." Then he added, "But I will advise ye to heed the advice of the apostle James—as to yer wife, then, be slow to speak but quick to listen on such matters..."

Ransom considered the advice itself to carry its own share of mystery—even deliberate ambiguity—yet at the same time it seemed to bear a measure of practical wisdom.

"I shall listen to her further on such matters before I speak my mind."

Back in the Knox house the two men labored over the anticipated case of the Crown for treason. Ransom described where he believed the core of the charges lay.

"The letter is the whole case against you," he said. "And in that regard I see two ploys of the Crown. First is the summoning of the Protestants from across the land to attend to the trial."

"Aye, I said it in the letter clear—but how is that treason, pray tell?"

"The Crown may argue," Ransom replied, "that you were trying to convene an illegal assembly to harass and interfere with the Crown's lawful trial of Cranston and Armstrong."

"Aye...I see..." Knox responded. "But there is nothin' in my letter itself that calls any man to do what is illegal or violent—but only to attend the trial and ensure that no new persecution of Protestant believers should begin."

"Of course. But still, the letter *implies* that force might be used by your supporters upon their arrival at the trial."

"But I did not call for force or violence—"

"Exactly," Ransom said with intensity in his voice. "Which is why you must emphasize two things—first, that you never called for a violent interference—that you summoned them for a *lawful assembly only,* and never an unlawful one."

"Good then," Knox replied. "And the second point?"

"That your letter was not a command such as a commander gives to an army—or a king gives to his country—for that would be treason. But it was—no more, no less—the call of a preacher to the Christian faithful to do as their consciences and the Holy Spirit and the Word of God might require."

"Which was my heart and mind on the matter—ye must know that!" Knox said with emphasis. "And ye put it well enough, Ransom. I was a mere preacher calling forth men to be Christians—not to be rebels..."

"Then that," Ransom said, "is what you must tell the Privy Council and the queen herself in your trial."

When the two had finished their last preparation for the trial on the eve of the proceeding, they prayed together at length and then retired for bed. While Ransom lay in bed he believed he had given as complete a defense to John Knox as he was able. They had committed the case to the Lord.

Yet Ransom also knew something else, and it kept him up late into the evening and into the next morning. That he feared that neither justice, equity, nor truth would necessarily rule the day. That this trial, in particular, would test the future of the commonwealth of Scotland—whether it would be a land of laws and freedom, or whether it would be a place where the great lever that turned everything would be in the grasp of a monarch's political and personal will.

Chapter 68

The trial was to be conducted in the evening of the following day. It would be held in the Council chambers of Holyrood Palace. Knox and Ransom walked the mile or so distance to the Palace in the cold night air of December. A large group of supporters accompanied him in show of good faith. But when they reached the guardhouse and the gate, only Knox—and Ransom as his counselor—were allowed to proceed.

They were escorted by two guards through the front gate and then into the massive courtyard that fronted the palace. For all of his visits to Edinburgh, this was Ransom's first to this mammoth building. He glanced around at the well-tended grass and flower beds, and over to the massive, cathedral-spired abbey adjacent. They walked behind the guards to the main door, which was set deep within arched and sculpted stone and flanked by three-story-high turrets.

Four guards escorted them inside. There was a rush of Court staff, advisors, ladies-in-waiting, and soldiers walking quickly through the corridors, chattering loudly. When their eyes told them who this robed, long-bearded fellow clutching his Bible really was, they lowered their voices, but grew much more animated in their whispered conversations.

Knox and Ransom were shown to a position just outside the Council chambers and told to wait. One courtier, who appeared not to be associated with the trial but who was an admirer of Knox, strolled over and engaged him in conversation. Ransom stepped away, collecting his thoughts. *Was there anything I missed in my counsel to John?*

He noticed an entourage of Council members sweeping down the halls toward him. In the lead was Master Henry Sinclair, Bishop of Ross, who was the President of the Court of Session. There was no love lost between Knox and Sinclair, and Knox had confided in Ransom that the queen was no doubt counting on him to lead the votes in favor of conviction. Accompanying him were the clerk of register and the comptroller—Sir John of Pittarrow, the justice clerk, and also Master Spens of Condie, the queen's advocate. Just behind Spens was his advocate assistant, a man only slightly older than Ransom but taller, and with a smug demeanor, holding papers and books in his left hand.

The advocate's assistant stayed back as the rest filed into the chambers. He stopped squarely in front of Ransom and stared him in the eye, but said nothing. After an uncomfortable moment, Ransom asked if he was known to the man or had some business with him.

"Business?" the man said with a look of arrogance. "Why, surely I do—I am the assistant to the queen's advocate. And I have business, as does my queen, with your leader, Mister Knox."

Ransom felt vaguely they had met before, but where or when he did not know.

"Young Ransom," the man continued. "Still old Knox's poodle, aren't you?"

Then Ransom recognized him. It was Harold the Terrible—his tormenter from their days together in the castle at St. Andrews.

"Harold?" Ransom said, searching the man's face. "Is that you?"

"Aye. It is—and I am here to help prosecute old Knox. It seems as if the student has finally become the master to the teacher at long last."

Ransom held out his hand reluctantly, attempting a gesture of goodwill before a trial that promised to have none of it. But Harold clasped his books and papers in both hands to avoid the gesture.

"And if Mister Knox is convicted—as I wager he will be—then I shall have further business with you too, young Ransom."

He gave a twisted smile and slipped into the chambers.

Ransom was still stunned by the encounter when someone grabbed him by the arm and started leading him down the corridor, away from the Council chambers, and away from Knox, who was still engaged in conversation.

"Hey," Ransom exclaimed, "what manner of affront is this? I am—"

"Of course—the counselor of Mister John Knox. I know that full well," the courtier said, leading him farther and then into a corner out of sight of the hallway.

"What do you want?" Ransom asked.

"To give you aid and comfort, Master Ransom."

"In what way?" Ransom shot back.

"In the only way that helps those who are walking up to the gallows and know not the way back down the steps."

"You talk in riddles."

"Perhaps," the man said. "But there is goodly truth if you will listen."

"My ears are open…"

"The queen's men have already designed to convict your master."

Ransom turned to walk away. "That is known to everyone, sir."

"But do you know this," the man added, quickly looking around to see if they were being watched, "that one of the queen's advisors has personal designs against you, Master Ransom—you."

"In what manner?"

"That if Knox is found guilty of treason this day, they will seek to go against his closest ally and confidant—just as the wolf who eats the duck will then go to the ducklings."

"More riddles—speak plainly, man!" Ransom whispered urgently.

"If Knox is convicted, they shall, the same day, swear out a warrant against you for the death of a French soldier in Edinburgh from these many years past."

"What proof of that do they have?"

"Enough to bring a parchment-thin case—but if Knox is convicted, the winds at Court will turn quickly, and any case from then on against an ally of Knox will be enough. One Court assistant has personally investigated the rumors and dedicated himself to it—"

"But what if Knox is acquitted of the treason charges?"

"My intelligence, well-founded I might add, is that they will abandon the case against you."

Ransom looked the man in the eye.

"Why should I believe you?"

The man smiled back with an odd look.

"I cannot say who is my superior—only that he is a friend of Elizabeth, the Queen of England. So dreaded a man is he that I dare not speak his name out loud. But his spies are everywhere…"

As the man turned to hurry away, he added one final word.

"And I, good sir, am one of them."

Chapter 69

In the Council chambers there were floor-to-ceiling draperies of purple and gold. Candlelight flooded the room with a golden glow from a hundred lamps and wall sconces around the room, and from the lighted golden bowls in several massive chandeliers hanging from the dizzyingly high ceilings.

There was a long mahogany table, almost the entire length of the room. At the head was a chair reserved for the queen. It was empty, awaiting the monarch. The seats on either side were empty, to be filled by the queen's closest advisors.

Closest to those chairs, and on either side, were seated the members of the Privy Council, whom Ransom had seen striding into the chambers shortly before. There were several more, including James Stewart, the Earl of Argyle, and the Duke of Chatelherault, who, like so many others, had traded sides again, now to be aligned with the power of Mary Queen of Scots.

Ransom was seated off to the side of the room, but close enough to bend forward and whisper to Knox if necessary. John Knox was seated at the far end of the table, closest to the door. Out of respect for the tribunal that would judge his case, he had removed his customary black cap.

Ransom hadn't had time to share with Knox his troubling conversation with the English spy. But he wondered what good it would have done in any event.

Better that John not know that his defense will not only determine his life, but mine as well, he concluded to himself.

A few moments of silence went by. And then two silk-coated heralds entered the room, blew their trumpets, and announced "Her Majesty Mary, the Queen of all Scotland and of all the Scots."

All of the men in the room quickly rose to their feet.

Mary entered the room slowly, and all that could be heard was the rustling of her great gown. It was scarlet red to match her fiery hair, which was pulled back and enclosed in a pearled headdress. Around her neck was a starched white ruff. Pearls and rubies and sapphires sewn into her dress glittered in the candlelight as she slowly moved to the throne at the head of the table.

When she was seated, Lethington sat next to her on one side. On the other was the Master of Maxwell, who had personally warned Knox that his support even among Protestants in Scotland might now be dissipating.

The queen's advocate reached over to Harold, who produced the indictment. The advocate read it out loud, charging Knox with treason against the queen and her lawful authority—punishable, he added solemnly, by death.

Before the proceedings could advance any further, the queen, who was staring at Knox and his bare head, began to smile, then titter, and then laugh out loud. When she had calmed down, the smile vanished from her lips and she spoke.

"That man," she said, pointing to Knox with her jeweled finger, "made me weep in our prior interviews—yet he never shed a tear himself. We shall see, before the night is out, whether we can make him weep!"

The Queen instructed her advocate to examine Knox on the handwriting of the letter.

"'Tis mine," Knox said without emotion. "I gladly acknowledge it."

"Did ye distribute the same by the means of many copies throughout the kingdom?" the advocate asked.

"Indeed I did. I gave this letter to trusted scribes to make true and accurate copies of the original and to thus send them around—"

Now Lethington jumped in.

"Ye trusted them to faithfully copy it, did ye?"

"Aye, 'tis true."

Lethington laughed scornfully at that. "Ye did more trustin' than I would have done!"

After a few chuckles died down Knox responded.

"Love," he said simply, "is not suspicious."

"Enough!" the queen said, interrupting. "Read the letter, Mister Knox, and we shall find the treason in it."

Knox proceeded to read the letter slowly and unashamedly. When he was done, the queen spread her arms dramatically to the assembly and spoke loudly.

"Heard ye, my Lords, ever, at any time, a more spiteful and treasonous letter?"

The table was silent, whether for fear of the queen, or fear of Knox, or confusion of mind, Ransom did not know. But their silence lasted almost a minute.

Now Lethington spoke again.

"Come, come, Mister Knox," he said. "Are ye not sorry, and do ye not repent, for the offense ye have caused against the queen?"

"Before I repent," Knox said, "I must know the offense I have committed."

"Offense!" Lethington shouted. "Look at this letter, man—in it you attempt to convene an illegal assembly of the Protestant citizens to come against the queen. This offense cannot be denied!"

Ransom was praying silently. Here was the very first point of his preparation of his friend and mentor. *Guide him, dear God,* Ransom said in his mind.

"I can deny it," Knox replied. "For there is…a difference," he said, continuing after only an instant of hesitation, "between a *lawful* assembly and an *unlawful* one. If convening believers in Christ together to ensure that several of their number are not unjustly treated is a crime, then I have been guilty of that crime ever since my foot set down once again on Scottish soil! But never was I charged with such a crime—"

"Then was then, and now is now!" Lethington argued back loudly.

"Yes, now is now," Knox countered. "And now the devil comes, it seems, to do by the twisting of justice that which God has not permitted by other means."

"Let us stop trifling with this man!" the queen said. She focused on Knox, eye to eye, and continued.

"By what authority do you convene the citizens of my kingdom in an assembly without my express command?"

Ransom now knew that the young queen had, in her cunning, focused on the essence of the treason charge against Knox. He also knew that the preacher's answer could well sink his defense if he were not careful.

"I answer, good Madam," Knox said, "that I have never—in this letter or otherwise—ordered any person, or group of persons, to convene in this land. I have no such authority. But I do issue statements, by the grace of God, and those that agree do respond of their own free will and assemble. I have usurped none of yer rightful authority in that regard."

The queen knew that the noose was still not tight around Knox's neck. So she went to the second element of the treason charge. In a sense, this was even the more incendiary.

"Your letter itself," she said in an explosion of emotion, "charges me with…'persecution of the few'—and by that you must mean Cranston and Armstrong—'that a door may be opened to execute cruelty upon the greater multitude.' Your words, Mister Knox—in your letter—are against me, your queen!"

Here was a troubling point, and Ransom knew it. Everyone in the room knew that it was treason for any subject of the realm to accuse, publicly, a monarch of perpetrating intentional cruelty or lawlessness. It was something that Ransom and Knox had discussed at length. But for a moment, Knox did not answer, and Ransom had a feeling of dread about that. After a few tense minutes, Knox asked if he were allowed to respond.

"Say what you can," she said, "but I think you have said enough against your own case already!"

So Knox began. He was neither agitated nor unsettled as he spoke.

"Yer Grace," he said, "whether ye know it or not, there are some papists in this land, remaining from the days of a queen regent, who have sworn themselves still to be the enemies of the Protestant evangel of Christ. They have sought—and still seek—the extermination of our Protestant cause, and of our followers, and of our doctrines. It is of those enemies I speak. We are an officially Protestant nation, and those who would rebel against our doctrines would rebel against Scotland—and against the laws of our Parliament."

"Your letter is against me," the queen insisted.

"Not against Your Grace," Knox responded, "but against those advisors who may cause you to be inflamed against the church. And anyone who counsels the destruction of the kirk of God is a son of the devil, and his father is therefore a liar and a murderer from the beginning, as God's Word tells us—"

But one of the lords at the table interrupted Knox with a shout.

"Silence, man!" he exclaimed. "Ye're not in yer pulpit now—ye're before the Crown of Scotland!"

"I am," Knox said, raising his voice, "in that very place where I am demanded to speak the truth—and speak it I will! I assure Your Grace," he said, turning to face the queen, "that ye have dangerous counselors, as did your late mother, Marie de Guise."

With that Lethington smirked a contorted half-smile, bent over, and whispered into the queen's ear. After a few minutes of hushed interaction between the two, the queen smiled and then addressed Knox.

And when she did, Ransom understood what Lethington had advised her. He had told her to bring up Knox's abusive verbal treatment of her previously, to show that his heart had harbored treason for some time.

"Do you not remember," the queen said quietly but as with the razor-sharp thrust of one skilled with the sword, "that in our last meeting your abuse of me caused me—your queen and the queen of your nation—to weep great salt tears—and yet you stubbornly witnessed it and pitied me not for it?"

"I said to ye then, and I will say again," Knox said with an uncommon gentleness in his voice, "that I find no pleasure in yer tears, Your Grace, any more than I find joy in the tears of my own children. The truth is," he continued in a soft tone, "that I am but a worm on God's earth. Nothing more. And I am also but a common citizen of this commonwealth, and a subject of yer lawful reign.

"But I am something else, though not by my doing. God for some reason has placed me in an office—and I dare not neglect it. I am a watchman both over this land and over the kirk of God such as is gathered in this land. Therefore I must blow the trumpet—and do so publicly—whenever I see the approach of danger—either to the land I love, or to the souls of its citizens."

After Knox had spoken, Lethington once again whispered in the queen's ear, and she whispered back. When they were finished, Lethington wore a look of smug satisfaction.

"Mister Knox," the secretary of the Council announced, "ye and yer counselor may return to yer house for the night. But do not stray from there."

And with that the proceedings were concluded. The queen and her entourage disappeared from the room, with Lethington sticking close to her. The lords and Court staff and advisors rose, but avoided Knox and Ransom as the two left. Then the doors to the chambers closed with an echoing bang as the Privy Council began deliberations. Ransom and Knox walked out of the palace and greeted well-wishers at the front gate, but begged them to go home and said they would be advised of the verdict on the morrow.

They trudged over to Knox's house and up the stairs into his rooms. His mother-in-law and the children were already asleep. The two men did not speak of the trial. Knox retired to bed, as did Ransom. But as he lay in bed, he could hear the clanging bells of the abbey, and then a few minutes later, at St. Giles Church up the royal mile. He knew then that a verdict had been reached. As he listened, he wondered about the imponderable mystery of the will of God. And whether the bells that were filling the night air were tolling *for* them—or *against* them.

Chapter 70

The news rippled through the palace. When it reached the queen's inner chamber, Lethington wanted to verify the vote, just to make sure, so he rushed down to the chambers to poll the members himself.

Meanwhile, a messenger and four palace guards made their way down the streets of Edinburgh. It was late, and the streets were quiet and empty. They stopped at Knox's house and quickly mounted to the second floor.

Ransom, who had heard the bells and believed that a verdict had been reached, had roused Knox, who was asleep. Both of the men were dressed and standing at the door when the heavy knock came.

Knox opened the door.

"John Knox?" the messenger asked, flanked by the guards.

"Aye, 'tis no other," he answered.

"The Privy Council has rendered a verdict upon the proceedings of this evening, wherein ye were charged with high treason, a capital crime—and punishable by death. And so they have made their decision…"

The messenger took a quick breath and finished his pronouncement.

"Their verdict, sir is 'not guilty.'"

"God be praised!" Ransom exclaimed. Knox praised God too, and the two men embraced each other. By then, the messenger and the guards had disappeared.

In the palace, Lethington was enraged and was yelling at every courtier he could find. He was screaming for someone to find Henry Sinclair, the Bishop of Ross, who had been counted on to bring about a guilty verdict. They located him as he was almost out of the palace. He was escorted to the rooms of Lethington, whose face was scarlet.

"How could ye have not convicted that old fool of a preacher, Knox?" he yelled.

But Sinclair was unusually calm, with the conviction of a man who had already faced the difficult task of bearing the burden that comes from doing the just thing—rather than the expedient thing.

"Tell Her Grace," he said without emotion, "that it was neither affection for that man, nor love of his profession, that moved the Council, and myself, to absolve him of guilt."

"Then what man—what?"

"'Twas the truth," Sinclair said plainly. "The simple truth."

Ransom gave his congratulations to Knox the next morning and then headed back to Perth on a fast horse, directly to his home. But when he arrived, the boys and Margaret were not there. The small cart and pony were missing. Though it was December, there had been a temporary thaw and some mild weather. The neighbor wife was washing laundry in a tub outside. Ransom asked if she had seen the rest of his family. She said no, she hadn't in the last day or so—though she had been busy attending to her own household and may have just overlooked them.

Then Ransom rode down the main street to the Market Cross section of town, but saw no signs of them there either. On a hunch, he then rode toward the outskirts of town, along the River Tay. He headed to a rolling hill he knew, that was in the quiet of the countryside, which rose up from the riverbank. It was a favorite of Margaret's. She, Ransom, and the boys had gone walking there on occasion.

He tied off his horse down by the river, which was splashing loudly over the mossy rocks, running fast from the snows that had melted during the thaw. He walked through a small grove of trees and then up toward the clearing at the top of the hill. Now he could see the figures of two small boys running after each other against the blue of the sky and the white billowing clouds.

He could see that it was Andrew and Philip. But he could not see Margaret. He started to jog. The boys saw him and in joyful recognition shouted, "Da! Da!" and came running down the path, almost tumbling down as they did. He scooped them both up, one in each arm.

"Where's your mum?"

Philip shook his head. But Andrew answered.

"Lying down…"

"Where?" Ransom said with a little urgency.

"On the hill," Andrew answered dutifully.

Ransom put the boys down and led them by the hand, quickly walking up to the top of the hill. Until, at last, he spied a figure lying in the grass on a blanket.

Margaret was on her back with her hands folded. Her eyes were bright, and there was a smile on her face.

"Hullo, townie lad," she said. "What news have ye for me?"

Ransom bent down next to her while the boys played and explained the not-guilty verdict.

She sat up quickly, wrapped her arms around him, and said, "Thank you, God, for John Knox's sake, and for the kirk of Christ, and for my Ransom…"

Ransom proceeded to describe his meeting with the English spy shortly before the trial, and how her instincts—that a conviction of Knox would bode poorly for Ransom as well—were proved to be quite correct.

He looked over the vista from the hilltop—the rolling landscape, stark with the black of the soil, dotted with small patches of snow here and there and gray, ancient rock outcroppings, and the dark green of scrubby, spongy moss.

"I know why you like it here," he said with a smile.

"And why is that?"

"Because from where we are sitting here," Ransom noted, pointing to the horizon in the north by northwest, "you can face toward the mountains and the great, deep glens of your Highland youth—the place where ye grew up, and played—and where yer mum and da are buried."

Margaret gave him a gentle look but did not answer.

"Dear," Ransom continued, "those things I just mentioned—I have figured something out. Those are the reasons you said what you did before I left for Knox's trial…about you wanting me to bury something for you in the glen of the Highlands, if you go before me, something from you."

"So then," she replied with a mischievous smile, "ye have it all figured out then—all by yerself—'tis so, then?"

Suddenly Ransom remembered Knox's advice.

"I'm sorry," he said meekly. "'Tis not true—I haven't got it all figured out. But it would be my pleasure to hear your mind on the matter. And I, as your loyal liege, shall listen close—as close as I am sitting with you now…"

Margaret kissed him gently and then sat back and looked out to the north and west.

"'Tis a simple thing with me, really," she said. "Nothin' more—but 'tis a powerful true thing to me, still."

And then she spoke to him plainly—not about mountains, or rivers, or cottage, or any place that could be merely seen or touched. She softly whispered about the geography of the heart—and that one place that had been kept, like a treasure map, within the secret memory of her soul.

Chapter 71

1601—Thirty-Nine Years Later

Ransom Mackenzie was leaning on his walking stick—the one made of hickory with a carved lion's head at the top, which his father had given him that day, decades ago, when he had to flee St. Andrews. He was feeling his advanced age and all the aches and pains that came with it.

It was early summer, and as he made his way down the vast hallways of Whitehall Palace outside of London, he wondered at the turn of events that had brought him there. Of course, on the surface, it was merely the fact that he had been delivering a talk in London to some officials of the Church of England who had extended him the invitation. But he knew that, in many ways, there was more to it than that.

He was glancing about the corridors of the busy Court of Elizabeth, looking for the faces of his son Andrew and his son Philip, who had his own son—Ransom's grandson, Peter—with him as well. But he could not find them.

As he thought ahead to the day's entertainments and festivities in the palace, he realized this would be the first time he had ever been in the same room with the Queen of England. It had been a long time since he had shared a chamber with any queen—the last time being with Mary Queen of Scots at the trial of John Knox.

How different are those two meetings—and those two queens! he thought to himself with some sense of irony.

Just then Andrew and Philip, both middle-aged, and Peter, who was in his early twenties, rounded the corner.

"I am sorry, father," Andrew said apologetically, "one of us should have escorted you through the palace while the others housed our coach—did you manage?" Andrew was a well-dressed, smooth-mannered man with dark hair and a cleanly trimmed beard and moustache.

"Managed well enough," Ransom replied. "Needn't worry about me..."

"Well, father, you've been here before, aye?...thought I heard Mum once say you had," Philip added. He was the same height as Andrew, but stocky and more muscular, and walked with a swagger. His red hair was long and slightly uncontrolled, his clothes well-tailored but more flamboyant than those of his brother.

"No, not here," Ransom said. "Not at Whitehall. I worked with John Knox in Hampton Court. I was very young...long time ago. We were all disputing about the issue of kneeling at Communion, as I recall..."

"Did you say 'kneeling'?" Philip said with a laugh.

"If you read more history books than adventurer's charts and maps," Andrew said to his brother a bit snidely, "you'd know why that was so important back then!"

"Father, you know I meant no offense," Philip added. Ransom smiled and assured him that none was taken.

As they neared the doors that led to the Great Hall, Andrew asked, "Father, have you ever met this William Shakespeare fellow?"

"No. But I knew his father, John."

"And we are to see one of his entertainments then?" Philip's son Peter asked. He was taller than his father—lean and athletic, with the same reddish hair, but with a slightly milder way about him.

"'Tis not exactly an *entertainment*," his uncle clarified. "'Tis a theatrical play—a tragedy to be exact."

"Wonder what your old Mister Knox would have thought about your attending such frivolities," Philip said with a smile.

"'Tis a good question," Ransom said, leaning on his stick as they arrived at the opening to the Great Hall, where palace guards with bronze-tipped spears stood at each side. "Though I know he was trying to write his own passion play at one time...I wonder..."

As they were shown in to the cavernous room, he could see that at the very front there was an improvised set with flickering candle lamps in a semicircle on the ground and the scenery of a castle constructed quite artfully inside the footlights.

The room was filled with red velvet chairs arranged in rows. In the front row was an empty throne for the queen. As they were seated, young aides hastened down the row and distributed printed bills that bore the title *Hamlet, Prince of Denmark*. And directly under that was the listing of the dramatis personae, with the names of the players and a sketch of the five acts of the play. The room quickly filled. Then, with the trumpets of heralds and the cry "God save the queen, Elizabeth of England!" she slowly entered with two ladies-in-waiting and two of her aides as the room stood to its feet.

Elizabeth was wearing a purple gown with a dark vest draped with long strings of pearls and billowing sleeves studded with various bows and gems. Her face, painted heavily, was a luminous white that did not well hide her old age. She had no trace of eyebrows, and her high hairline delineated a perfectly sculpted auburn-colored hairpiece that arched over her head like a halo.

She was helped to her seat and aided in sitting down. Then the players promptly swept onto the stage, bowed deeply and long to the queen, and scattered to their places.

Ransom found it a slightly morbid but artfully constructed tale. But as he watched it and searched the room for the author, he couldn't help but think back more than three decades past—to the year following the treason trial of Knox—and to his final connection with the playwright's father.

John Shakespeare had read of the trial in a London paper, and Ransom was mentioned in it—as was the fact he was a resident of Perth. Shakespeare later wrote to Ransom, congratulating him on his success, mentioning the deadly plague then sweeping England, and also noting the birth of his infant son, William, by his wife Mary Arden Shakespeare. Ransom felt pressed to send a letter back, and also a Bible, something he had long promised to his friend at Stratford.

He dated and inscribed the inside cover of the Bible, "To my good friend John Shakespeare, who aided me as a traveler, and was thus used as an instrument of the grace of God." He signed it. But under that, he added a short phrase he had often used and had even shared with John Shakespeare—a word of wisdom about the sovereignty of God that had often comforted Ransom. Then he sent his letter and the Bible by messenger. That was Ransom's last contact with the man.

As the play went on, Ransom was following the drama closely. But when the players spoke of the death of Ophelia, Hamlet's lover, Ransom's mind wandered off.

In the five years since the death of his beloved Margaret, he had felt the life slowly ebbing out of him. He remembered the words of John Knox—now dead for thirty years—shortly before his passing: "The world is weary of me," he said, "and I of it." Ransom's mentor had, toward the end, fixed increasingly on the brightness of God's kingdom to come, while the importance of the things of earth became ever dimmer for him. For Ransom too, the kingdom of heaven held much more than earthly life ever could.

Since Margaret's death and burial in Perth, Ransom had found it difficult to find passion in much of his work. He was offered a position at St. Andrew's University that he was inclined to accept, but only on the condition that his housekeeper, Jean Macleod, herself a widow, would move there with her sister to manage Ransom's house and personal affairs. His greatest joy now was occasionally preaching in the churches around Scotland, but he did less of that because of the rigors of travel—and, of course, his desire to see his children and grandchildren.

Yet those visits had become less frequent. Andrew was a busy and very able advisor to James, King of Scotland. James had succeeded his mother, Mary, Queen of Scots, when she was forced to abdicate. She was later arrested by Queen Elizabeth and, after long years of imprisonment, was finally executed for treason against England. But unlike his mother, James was a staunch Protestant and a warm supporter of the Reformation—though he would never allow the reformers' radical ideal of a popularly elected Scottish commonwealth to take root.

And then there was Ransom's son Philip. He was even more difficult to keep in one place. When he was in his twenties he sailed off on a ship manned by Sir Richard Grenville to a place in the New World called Roanoke Island. Upon his return, he had stayed in England and was now working with the newly formed Virginia Company and living with his son, Peter. Sadly, Philip's wife had died giving birth to their second child, who was stillborn.

A great thing has still been left undone, Ransom mused to himself, thinking back to Margaret and feeling overcome by a particular memory—though he must have muttered something out loud, for Andrew bent over to him and asked if he were all right. Ransom nodded, but could not let go of the thing that his mind was now fixed upon.

The only time he was able to focus back on the dialogue between the actors was toward the end of the play. In the last act, the actor who was playing Hamlet was speaking to a fellow named Horatio—his friend and confidant.

"Our indiscretion sometimes serves us well," Hamlet said, "when our deep plots do fail."

And then the character of Hamlet spoke something next that jolted Ransom with a sudden recognition.

"And that should teach us," Hamlet reasoned further, "there's a divinity that shapes our ends, rough-hew them how we will."

That last phrase, Ransom realized with a smile, was a near word-for-word recital of the inscription he had placed in John Shakespeare's Bible. Now Ransom was lost in thought. *How I have "rough-hewn" so many things in my life,* he mused, *yet God's sovereign hand was always there…to the very end.*

When the theater piece ended, and after the departing of the queen, members of the audience flocked up to Shakespeare, who Ransom could now see was also in the front row, decked out in a smart coat and tights, with a face that had the look of his father about him. But Ransom had little desire to wait to meet the playwright. He asked his sons and grandson to take him to the coach immediately.

"I am going back to Perth," he announced to Andrew and Philip, "and thereafter on a short journey to the northwest. Philip, may I have the assistance of your son, Peter, on that trip?"

Philip, taken by surprise at his father's urgency, glanced at his son, who nodded eagerly. "I will be glad to go with you, grandfather, if my da can spare me from the work in London…"

"Of course," Philip said. And so it was agreed.

Three weeks later, Ransom Mackenzie, his grandson, Peter, and a Highland guide had arrived at the destination. Peter helped his grandfather down from the covered cart. They were at the foot of the mountain in the deep glen. Ransom paused to search the valley for the Chisholm cottage as he remembered it, with its windows glowing at night by the hearth's light—but now, all traces of Margaret's childhood home were gone. Yet the mountain was still there, impregnable, looming over the glen.

"It is a long climb," Peter warned. "I wonder if you should try it, grandfather."

But Ransom would not be dissuaded. He used two walking sticks, one for each hand, and Peter walked slowly behind him, carrying a sack. It was a long and laborious walk for the old man, and they stopped numerous times to rest. When they had reached a particular pinnacle with a commanding view of the valley below, Ransom halted. He studied the scene. He smiled and nodded.

"'Tis the very spot," he said, breathless and with emotion in his voice. "I know it—oh, 'tis the place..."

Then he had Peter dig a hole in the earth at the spot and step back. Ransom slowly and carefully took something out of the bag. He lifted it so that the light shone through the crystal glass box, through the heather inside. Kneeling down with much difficulty, he placed the box and the heather crown within it down into the hole, and with his wrinkled hand he began to cover it with the loomy, mossy soil of the Highlands.

As he did, his mind was taken back to a hill in Perth, on the day when his beloved Margaret whispered to him the significance of this very place—and her desire to have some remembrance buried there after she was gone. For Ransom, standing on that high vista, it was as if the decades had vanished and she was there, in her fair beauty and with her raven hair blowing in the breeze, standing before him explaining it all.

Don't ye know, she said to Ransom with tears welling up in her eyes, *why that place in the Highlands on that high hill, is so important? And why ye must bury some memorial of me there? For 'twas on that hill I saw ye leavin' the valley on yer way to London, townie lad...and as I saw ye so small down there in the valley below, I didn't know whether I'd ever see ye agin. And so I prayed to God that He might bring us together again...and cried out to Him from my very soul...and He answered that prayer, Ransom—for here we are, ye and me—together...*

There on that mountain crest, as the wind picked up and the sun started heading to the horizon, sending crimson waves of color across the sky, Ransom placed a hand over his face and wept, overcome with all the journeys that had led him thence.

He had lived to see the crowning of powerful monarchs with the perishable wreaths of fleeting power, and he had lived to see their downfalls. He had also witnessed the awful and fiery deaths of the saints of Christ—martyred and crowned, imperishably, by the burning flames of persecution that had consumed their mortal bodies and sent their spirits to dwell in pavilions of God. But Ransom Mackenzie was weeping, too, because he knew that in his own right he had also been crowned in life—by the love of a woman—and that her love had been as tender as the heather in bloom, and as bright as a Highland fire.

About the Authors

Besides *Crown of Fire,* **Craig and Janet Parshall** have authored three books together, including *Traveling a Pilgrim's Path.*

Craig is a highly successful lawyer from the Washington, DC, area who specializes in cases involving civil liberties and religious freedom. He speaks nationally on legal and Christian worldview issues, is a magazine columnist, and has authored five novels in the Chambers of Justice legal suspense series.

Janet is the host of *Janet Parshall's America*—a nationally syndicated radio and television program originating in Washington, DC. An author and a cultural commentator in the national media, she is also a much sought-after speaker on biblical issues that impact the family and the church.

More Select Fiction from Harvest House Publishers

The Gate Seldom Found
Raymond Reid

The Gate Seldom Found dramatizes the true story of a little-known Christian fellowship that flowered late in nineteenth-century Canada. The saga opens in southern Ontario in January, 1898. Alistair Stanhope is shaken by the untimely death of his best friend, causing him to question his faith. Unable to find the depth of spirituality he is seeking within his church, he and his wife, Priscilla, begin to meet with a close circle of friends for support. From these intimate gatherings comes an awakening that touches many lives with the simplicity of following Jesus Christ. A novel that will touch your heart and refresh your soul.

The Edge of the World
Phil Callaway

In this tender coming-of-age story, a young boy discovers a hidden stash of money—and more trouble than he thought possible. As he unravels the mystery of its origin, he discovers an even greater mystery—the mystery of the grace of God as it is expressed through a small community of believers. With a cast of characters worthy of a Mark Twain novel, a mysterious illness, an astounding confession, and a lump-in-the-throat climax, this story is sure to bring laughter and tears as it entertains you and enriches your life.

THE OXFORD CHRONICLES

Inklings
Melanie Jeschke

American Kate Hughes is swept into her first year at prestigious Oxford University on the wings of adventure and romance. Lord Stuart Devereux, a fellow student, hopes to win Kate's affection with his charm and wealth. In stark contrast, her tutor, David MacKenzie—a handsome young Oxford don and leader of the Inklings Society—takes a different approach as he contends for Kate with convictions of propriety and old-fashioned chivalry.

This captivating tale of passion and purity under the dreaming spires of Oxford brings alive the university world of C.S. Lewis, J.R.R. Tolkien, and The Inklings.

Also by Craig Parshall
THE CHAMBERS OF JUSTICE SERIES

The Resurrection File

When Reverend Angus MacCameron asks attorney Will Chambers to defend him against accusations that could discredit the Gospels, Will's unbelieving heart says "run." But conspiracy and intrigue—and the presence of MacCameron's lovely and successful daughter, Fiona—draw him deep into the case...toward a destination he could never have imagined.

Custody of the State

Attorney Will Chambers reluctantly agrees to defend a young mother from Georgia and her farmer husband, suspected of committing the unthinkable against their own child. Encountering small-town secrets, big-time corruption, and a government system that's destroying the little family, Chambers himself is thrown into the custody of the state.

The Accused

Enjoying a Cancún honeymoon with his wife, Fiona, attorney Will Chambers is ambushed by two unexpected events: a terrorist kidnapping of a U.S. official...and the news that a link has been found to the previously unidentified murderer of Will's first wife. The kidnapping pulls him into the case of Marine colonel Caleb Marlowe. When treachery drags both Will and his client toward vengeance, they must ask—*Is forgiveness real?*

Missing Witness

A relaxing North Carolina vacation for attorney Will Chambers? Not likely. When Will investigates a local inheritance case, the long arm of the law reaches out of the distant past to cast a shadow over his client's life...and the life of his own family. As the attorney's legal battle uncovers corruption, piracy, the deadly grip of greed, and the haunting sins of a man's past, the true question must be faced—*Can a person ever really run away from God?*

The Last Judgment

A mysterious religious cult plans to spark an "Armageddon" in the Middle East. Suddenly, a huge explosion blasts the top of the Jerusalem Temple Mount into rubble, with hundreds of Muslim casualties. And attorney Will Chambers' client, Gilead Amahn, a convert to Christianity from Islam, becomes the prime suspect. In his harrowing pursuit of the truth, Will must face the greatest threat yet to his marriage, his family, and his faith, while cataclysmic events plunge the world closer to the Last Judgment.